REBECA

Author

David C Hanss

Published by the author

Inspired by true events.

Contents

Chapter One - The Beginning

Sarah managed to get herself pregnant at the age of fifteen, and by 1960 she had given birth to a little girl she called Rebeca. Sarah's parents at the time wanted her to have the baby adopted, but she could not even think of doing that. That upset her mother and especially her father who then turned against her. She was told by them that they would not allow the baby in their house. The nurses at the hospital did their best encouraging her to have the baby adopted, but she did have some form of support from the father who really wanted her to keep the baby, they were lucky in a way, as he was continuing his education, and his parents were only too happy to look after Sarah and their new granddaughter.

Sarah also had help from her brother, Peter who was three years older. Unfortunately for her he had just started a course at Nottingham University, so for the next three years, he was not going to be at home, apart from holidays. They lived in West Hampstead a part of northwest London. Of course, the first year after the birth was not easy for Sarah, being a new mother at her age she had to learn an awful lot about the needs of a baby, she often had help from Rebeca's father, he would look after Rebeca on Saturday mornings which gave her a chance of getting out and breathe again. If she ever had an emergency the father's mother never had a problem helping her out.

Sarah was an intelligent girl, she had topped her class on many subjects, but she had decided to give the first year of Rebeca's life, just for her. However, the year after she did not know how, but she was going to carry-on with her education. She liked people, and usually managed to get on with almost everybody, she was very upset about her own father, she felt that if it had been her mother's decision, she would still be at home. Financially she was alright, all she had to spend money for was Rebeca, her boyfriend's parents were so pleased to have her, and have the baby live with them. One thing Sara was good at, was helping James her boyfriend with some difficult homework and when close to an exam, she would help him revise, his parents loved it all. The baby was a little darling, by the time she had reached three months she was sleeping all night, there was an Alsatian dog in the house, and he loved the baby, it seems that he had taken charge. Rebeca was bought up with a lot of love, the baby's grandmother often called Sarah's mother to tell her how the baby was doing, she always told her that she would be most welcome to come and visit her granddaughter, she also would tell her how well Sarah was getting on, but she never came.

Sarah always looked forward to her brother coming home at holiday times, Peter could not often stay with Sarah, there was not enough room in the house, but he never looked forward to going home so he would spend as little time as he could with his parents, some days he would be with old school friends, and other days with his sister and his niece. As she became older, she always looked forward to his visits, even the Alsatian looked forward to Peter coming. One day was the last time Peter was making the trip back to West Hampstead, he had sat for his final exam and just had to wait for the results. He had already been recruited by a large design company in North London, Sarah and Peter had decided to share an apartment. She was doing well with her education, she was more than halfway through an online course she had taken with the Workers Education Association, it was a course which included writing and languages. Sarah and James had long ago decided to remain good friends, James himself decided to join the Airforce, and he was on track to become a pilot. Sarah and Rebeca visited their old home every Wednesday in time for lunch, every time they came it was a party day. All three made a fuss of them, yes there were three the third being the dog, who wanted to spend time just with Rebeca.

All James' leave times from the Airforce were always spent at home, where he looked forward to seeing his daughter visit him as often as possible. Both Peter and James got on well, the training for the flying sometimes was terrifying, so James had a lot to talk about, whilst Peter in turn had some close shaves in university with all the pranks he was involved in. James had joined a local Flying Club at Elstree Aerodrome, and he was able to rent a light aircraft, and sometimes Peter went with him. Once in a while, either Peter or James would suggest a meal out with Rebeca and Sarah, those were just wonderful days that everybody enjoyed. Even after almost four years since the birth of Rebeca, Sarah still had no contact whatsoever with her parents, it was always at the back of her mind, never to be forgotten. Although Sarah could have possibly worked part time because Rebeca had just started school, she instead concentrated on learning two more languages, she was a quick learner and language was right up her alley.

So far Sarah had managed with her government subsistence money, she even sometimes managed enough to buy clothes, she was well organised, she always had the future in mind, of course living with her brother made things much easier for her. Whilst Peter was in university and visited home, he always made a point of telling the parents about his niece Rebeca, he even showed them photographs of the little girl, they never commented not even once. His father especially was still upset about Sarah, he would use various reasons for his attitude towards his daughter: first he was most upset that Sarah had become pregnant, then he was upset that she did not want to part with the baby, and when he forbade her to bring the baby in the house, she had the nerve to disobey him, he was then upset about her moving in with the father's parents for over three years.

And now not only did Sarah bring up the baby more or less on her own and had done a good job of it, but Rebeca is also now at school and Sarah to top it all, is about to receive a degree all achieved on her own without any help from him. The other thing that upsets him and her mother, the more they hear on how well she is confronting the future, the more upset they are with themselves at having tried to run her life. They both know that she would love to be close to her mother and father, but she had been so hurt, she needs for them to make the approach.

Sarah could now write and speak in three languages, one is English of course the second one is French and the third German, she toyed with the idea of learning the old fashion German handwriting, but she thought it was going too far, this being the first year at school for Rebeca, Sarah had been looking for another interesting language to learn, especially one with a different handwriting. They lived in an apartment complex and their neighbours originated from Pakistan, they are a lovely family, and Aisha the young mother loves having discussions with Sarah, so one of those days when they were talking about languages Aisha suggested that she could perhaps give her help if she started learning one of the many tongues spoken in Pakistan, and that was now the next thing to organise for Sarah.

They say that the more languages one speaks, the easier it is to learn even more, Sarah decided to learn the national language of Pakistan, it is not an old language, it was adopted to replace English, for Sarah there is a plus because Urdu is written using Arabic Script, which in time will make it easier for her to learn Arabic. By the time her daughter had reached the age of six, Sarah used to visit Aisha next door and converse with her in Urdu, that surprised Aisha's husband, he could not get over it. With all the help Sarah was given next door, especially about customs, makeup and dress, she could almost pass as a proper native!

She had no problem getting Rebeca to school in the mornings because now she was working there as a language teacher, and for the first time in her life she was earning her own money, no more inquisition from government departments about why she could not work yet, somebody in that office must have been relieved, as well as that her father obviously found out, he never knew whether he was happy that his daughter had done so well, but then he was unhappy because she did it without his help. Her brother Peter enjoyed his work, and on top of that he was well paid, James also was climbing up the ranks in the RAF and now had a girlfriend, sometimes on a nice sunny day they would take Rebeca out for the day. Because she was now working it was not possible to visit on a Wednesday, so they changed the arrangement and both Sarah and Rebeca would have lunch with the grandmother and grandfather on Sundays, and the dog of course!

Chapter Two - At School

The school where Sarah worked had a population of almost 1,400 students, and it was well run, Rebeca was at the start of the middle school, she had moved up with most of the friends she had made and never minded going to school, there were over forty teachers in attendance every day. Sarah made some friends amongst the teachers, there were a couple of young women her age and the three happened to be the youngest teachers in the school, and they got on well together, at one lunch time they made a list of possible male teachers for a laugh. One man stood out over all the others, he was also young, he taught mathematics, his first name was Asif, he appeared to be extremely shy, or maybe it was a religious problem, his background was Pakistan, the three decided that by the end of the school year, they will have reformed him!

It was getting close to Xmas, and the school every year at that time would have the teachers get together and perform for the school, some years it would be a play, it could be an outing which included a game of football with the teachers against senior students, whatever it was it always made everybody happy. This year on the Friday of the breakup for the holiday, all the teachers in the school including the headmaster and the office staff, had to come in fancy dress costumes. Sarah had a brainwave; she never told her two friends what she was going to do.

She had spent a whole week practising speaking with a lower tone voice, with a Scottish accent, she also had help from her father-in-law, before the last war he had trained as a clown. Only Rebeca in the whole school knew that the clown was her mother, and she had promised not to tell. There was a prize for the teacher who was the last one to be recognised. It did not take Sarah long to sort out Asif, he was dressed much like a Berber in the Sahara Desert. She came close to him from his left side and before he had noticed her, she greeted him in perfect Urdu, when he turned his head, his first reaction was shock, of course he did not recognise Sarah; He had yet not said a single word, so much was going through his mind, he could not remember having noticed a Pakistan female teacher in the school, another little problem for him is that Urdu is not his native tongue, he can understand it, but he is not very good on speaking it, that's why it took him a long time to answer. 'Good morning miss--- oh I give up, whoever you are, I have not the slightest idea' Sarah realised right away that he did not know the language all that well, he spoke with an English accent, she told him how nice it was to have a party, as she could tell that everybody was enjoying themselves. Then she moved away leaving him to decide what it was, had just hit him.

After an hour it was the turn of the students, all the teachers had to parade one at a time on the stage and speak one sentence and the kids had to shout out loud the name of the teacher, that morning there were only three teachers left that had not been recognised, one of them being Sarah. It left her two friends thinking that she had not turned up that day, but they saw her daughter, so nothing made sense. Now the last three had to stand on their own in the front of the stage and slowly and clearly recite a poem, the other two were both men and recited two very expressive and loud poems, and they were both recognised, then it was Sarah's turn; she walked towards the front of the stage as if she had difficulty, and she needed to have had a walking stick to hold on to, she looked larger than her usual self, she was wearing a complicated clown outfit; one could only see her two hands and eyes. She recited a famous poem by the Persian poet Omar Khayyam, she was doing well with the lowered voice, but she did even better because she recited the poem in Arabic. Nobody in the assembly had the slightest idea who she was, the Head had started wondering if someone was playing a joke on them, Asif did not understand all the poem, he did some of the words, but he surely recognised the Arabic tongue as it flowed through the words. There was absolute silence, although no one understood the words, most felt the poem.

Now it was time for Sarah to reveal herself, the first thing that happened, was Rebeca running up to the stage to give her mother two towels, one was soaking wet and other one was dry. Sarah turned her back to the audience, at the same time she took off her all her extra cloths exposing her normal attire, gave her face a good going over with the wet towel, then as she started to speak in her normal voice she turned around to face them all with a broad smile, not even one person at any time had the feeling that it was her, five minutes later they were all still applauding, and the first person who came to speak to her was Asif, her two friends could not help but notice! He needed to speak to her and find out what she was all about, so after the holidays they were going to meet up in the staff room at lunch time.

The next morning Sarah returned the rented clown outfit, and they had some fun talking about what had happened. Sarah had to recite the poem again for Aisha who was most surprised, she told Sarah that she had captured the atmosphere of the poem, 'it was perfect!' That morning Sarah and Rebeca were invited next door for the evening meal the same day. Aisha and her husband wanted to have them there that Saturday night, they also had another guest coming, it was Aisha's brother-in-law, his name was Gohar, he also was a teacher, he was only one year older than his brother Aisha's husband. He was well spoken and a charming sort of guy.

Next door they had two boys, both nine years old, yes, they were twins! They often played with Rebeca, and they were looking forward to the evening, as they were going to be allowed to stay up late. For Sarah, Saturday afternoon was shopping and housework including doing the laundry, the good thing was that Rebeca always helped her, Sarah was well organised, that Saturday she had just that little bit less to do; no supper to get ready tonight!

Sarah at school taught both French and German, there was no call for Urdu. She now felt that she could venture into another language, the question was: which one. She thought of Latin and Italian followed by Spanish, then on other days she thought of Arabic, it had almost become an obsession for her, she had already had a go with Arabic for the poem. To give herself some breathing time one morning at the breakfast table she shouted out: 'Arabic!'

Aisha had cooked a complete Pakistan meal; starters was a red salad which was tasty and especially refreshing, and the main course was Chicken Biriyani, Sarah had often eaten that dish in Indian restaurants and now she could tell people that she had eaten the real thing, and it was superior to the restaurant version, she really loved it and she was going to cook it one day for her brother Peter and his girlfriend.

After the meal Sarah and Gohar sat next to each other in the living room, they spoke mainly about education and language, after a while they spoke in Urdu, he was most surprised that she could speak so well, him speaking English was no problem as it is still the official language with Urdu in Pakistan, however most people speak Punjabi, which explained why Asif had a problem. Aisha asked Sarah to recite the poem in Arabic so that both Gohar and her husband can hear it. It was no problem for her, Gohar had learned the poem at school and when he heard Sarah do such an excellent job of it, he could not hide the couple of tears that made their way down his cheeks. It had reminded him of the happy times he had at school, the good friends he will never see again.

The three children were playing a noisy game, shouting at each other, and it took quite a while for it to register, it was Aisha who spotted it, Rebeca all the time was speaking in Urdu as if it were the natural thing for her to do. It turns out that when Sarah was practising speaking in a new language, Rebeca would just copy her. They were careful not to pass any comments that the children might hear, but it really got Sarah thinking for the rest of the evening, and all night and then all-day Sunday. The evening had gone well, the food was great, the discussions gave everybody something to think about, it was reported later that Sarah enjoyed talking to Gohar and he in turn enjoyed talking with Sarah.

Peter was home that Sunday, and Sarah had a long discussion with him about Rebeca, this was after the long, amazing talk with her daughter. When Sarah found out that she could have a decent conversation with Rebeca in Urdu, and in French then not so good in German, as far as Rebeca was concerned it was just a game, she used to play by herself, just like her mother she had no problem ever learning a new language, she could not write it but that was to come. Just like her mother she was never near the top of the class in mathematics and geometry.

Christmas day had come and gone on the day itself, they were all at the grand parents' house, James and his new girlfriend were there, Peter's friend could not make it for Christmas, she had to be with her parents. James was almost shocked when he heard mother and daughter speak to each other in a foreign language which he could not understand, Sarah then told him that they were speaking in Urdu, and when he started to recover, they then spoke to each other again but this time in French. Oh boy that surprised not only James and his girlfriend but his parents as well. And now as everybody assembled at the table were congratulating Rebeca, the two started speaking in German. Everything just had to stop in the house, the turkey had to wait, the grandfather still had the carving knife in his hands, Rebeca took charge and announced that the German for her had been difficult, but the rest were easy, and best of all because it's Christmas that is the end, 'so you can all relax'.

Then she had another thing to add, 'I am so proud of my mother, I saw her last night reciting a poem, I did not understand one single word, but it was like music, and she bought a grown man to tears'. Sarah was a bit embarrassed; she now knew that the poem would have to be recited, but not until after lunch. The meal was great everybody ate too much, and afterwards it was time to open all the presents, excitement filled the room, when calm was restored, grandfather reminded Sarah about the poem. She told them first the name of the poet, only one other person in the room recognised the name, that was grandfather, then she told them what the poem was about; it was a mother giving her daughter advice for life, and it is written in Arabic around the eleventh century in Persia, the poet also happened to be an Alchemist who at one time was hired to make glass windows which now are very famous in a Cathedral in Chartres in France.

Then Sarah recited the poem, there was not another sound in the room, they were all mesmerised. Sarah could not wait until she was back at school, she had made up her mind to seek advice from the head about Rebeca, in the meanwhile she managed to research online. She found out that when she has conquered five languages, she can call herself a Polyglot, 43% of the world population is bilingual. That ability to learn many languages is due to a part of the brain called Broca's Area which in rare cases can expand as needed, some most unusual people can learn as many as thirty-two languages. This is one of the times Sarah would like to be able to discuss with her father and mother, she would like to ask him about the family, did anybody else was at least bilingual?

New year happened then it was time for school again, Sarah had not forgotten about Asif the young teacher, they met at lunch and had an enjoyable meeting over the food, she could not wait to tell him about Rebeca speaking Urdu, it turned out that Asif had two sisters, both older than him, he did not have a brother, which maybe was the reason for his shyness around women, she decided at that meeting to do something about it, first was to meet up with him, and then get her two teacher friends on the case. That first afternoon Sarah spoke to the head's secretary and told her that she wanted to have a talk with him about her daughter, to get advice. An appointment was made for the next day at three thirty when Sarah did not have a class. The problem for Rebeca being in the same school as her mother, who on the odd occasions had to stay late, then she had to wait for the lift home. Rebeca would end up waiting for her most times on her own, she did not waste that time, no she would start on her homework. Having the subject still fresh in her mind, and especially no interruption like television or playing games, it was one of the reasons why she was doing so well at school.

The next day at three thirty Sarah found herself sitting at the desk in the Head's office, she wanted to discuss Rebeca with him, but first he wanted to discuss Sarah and the Christmas Party. He told her that what she had done was completely unexpected, then he asked her when did she learn Urdu? And why did she learn it? She could not tell him why because she did not know herself, she mentioned that even Asif does not speak Urdu, but one thing that attracted her towards that language is that it is written with Arabic script, because that is the next language she is going to learn as she wants to become a Polyglot. That really surprised him, but he did not realise at that moment, that he was in for yet another surprise when Sarah recounted what she had discovered over the weekend about her daughter. He told her that she was right coming to him for help or maybe just suggestions, and they sat there for over an hour going through various scenarios for Rebeca, he had looked at her progress, and the reports for the first term in the school, she had the best record for handing in homework which on most subjects where close to the top of the class. One good suggestion he had was for Sarah to teach her languages and for him to organise extra lessons on Mathematics where she does not perform well. He also told her that she is the kind of student that will mostly make it to Oxford or Cambridge. In the car Rebeca asked: "what was it the Head wanted to see you for?" Her mother luckily was too busy driving in the heavy traffic, so she had a good excuse for remaining silent.

Chapter Three - Growing Up

Rebeca finished her year with flying colours, at first, she had not really enjoyed the extra maths she had to endure once a week, however she now enjoys the maths class, as she was no longer behind and at last, she had started to understand what it was all about. One thing she enjoyed twice a week is learning Arabic with her mother, sometimes she even was ahead of her, she caught on to the writing, she thought that it was very artistic and especially interesting. There was a rule at home, never to do schoolwork on Sundays, it was the day reserved for the grandparents, and playing with the twins next door.

Sarah always made sure that her mother and father were always made aware about Rebeca's progress through Peter who reported that, for the first time they were both beginning to ask about Sarah and their granddaughter, however Sarah did not want to change Rebeca's surroundings, for her to meet her other grandparents is not going to be easy for her, maybe it should happen during the summer holidays. Rebeca's life now was well balanced, and for her to find out that her grandfather refused to have her in his house, might just upset the balance.

There was a question now at the start of the summer holiday whether Rebeca needed to keep going with the extra maths lessons as she had now caught up and was keeping her head above water, Sarah let her decide for herself, the surprise was that no, she wanted to keep going until at least she was at the top of the class, in any case she now enjoyed the extra lesson.

It is not easy for a single mother to manage the finance of the small family, having a summer holiday at the beach was never possible. Peter's girlfriend's parents happened to own a small cottage near Falmouth in Cornwall and on the second week in July it was going to be occupied by Peter plus friend Juliet, Rebeca and her mother. That will be Sarah's very first holiday since she became a mother, and she intends to enjoy it.

There was a lot of excitement that first week of July, they were all getting ready for the holidays, to avoid the usual heavy holiday traffic, they were all leaving early on the next Tuesday morning, Peter had a reasonably large company car, and they managed to bring everything they needed for the holiday. Now Rebeca was thirteen years old, she was a proper little lady, she was never upset and always pleasant with strangers, when she travelled on the underground in London, she always looked out for Urdu or Arabic speakers, talking in their own language, she liked to hear the various tones that those people used when talking in their language, and on top of that she liked listening to their conversation, especially if it was about her, it gave her a good feeling.

It took Peter almost four hours to get to the little fishing town, then a half hour to find the cottage, it was tucked away at the end of a lane amongst a forested area. Nobody had been in the cottage for at least four weeks, in any case the neighbours would look in from time to time, and they even opened the windows on sunny days. The first thing for them to do was unload the food they had brought with them, then the clothes and the sheets and towels, Peter had with him a work laptop so that if he had any spare time, he could revise a new project. They needed to sort out fresh food, milk, butter and bacon etc, however tonight was going to be a treat, having taken advice they had already booked a table at a famous fish restaurant, they were all looking forward to it; although Peter had some work with him, he was looking forward to having the luxury of doing no work at all, for Juliet, Peter's girlfriend it was the first time she had been on holiday without her parents, for Sarah it was her first holiday in twelve years, for Rebeca she was just happy to be somewhere different to explore and learn about.

That first night was the first time that Rebeca had been exposed to total darkness, she could not help herself remarking about it, she could almost feel it on her face. The meal that first night was fish which none of them had ever eaten, when the waiter asked what they wanted, Peter told him that they had no idea and for the waiter to decide for them, but not too expensive, after the meal he had to ask what it was they had just eaten, and he made a note of it on his mobile phone.

Going back to the cottage was so different without streetlights, and another thing which surprised Rebeca when they were back in the cottage was the pure silence, there was no television, no radio, and no outside sound. That first night Rebeca could not get to sleep, she did not have a watch, and her mind was full of wonderment, she kept thinking on how nice the people were in the restaurant, all the staff were friendly and caring, it seemed that their happiness was based on your happiness, then she wanted to dream about the darkness and the silence, a thought which had never come before, she felt that she had to describe that atmosphere, and tomorrow she was going to write it down so that she will never forget it for the rest of her life, then she wondered in which language should she write it down with? At that moment she remembered her mother reciting that famous poem by Omar Khayyam and made up her mind, she was going to make it into a poem and write it in Arabic: then, she went to sleep at last!

Wednesday morning everybody got up at the crack of dawn, yesterday they had spotted the sandy beach, which was calling them all, so Juliet was the first one in the kitchen starting breakfast which was going to be the same every morning of this holiday, it was simply egg and bacon with a gigantic slice of fried bread, all unhealthy for a change, there was also a large container of marmalade. When Rebeca had opened her tired eyes, she had a lovely surprise, there was a little bird sitting on the window ledge looking at her, and it had been his singing that woke her. Little did anybody know this morning that Rebeca will be interviewed on nationwide Television by the end of the day!

A lot of nagging had gone on before Sarah bought a pair of running shoes for Rebeca, in her mind she wanted to be sure that she could wear them at least for a couple of years, her daughter at the moment was growing in a hurry, so when Rebeca tried the shoes on, her mother made sure that there was space for her feet to grow, those shoes were the cause of what became news.

Nobody really talked apart from thanking Juliet for the breakfast, they were in a hurry to take over the beach, and especially a parking spot within easy walking distance. After having packed some fruit, cold drinks and a few bars of chocolate, they all dived into the car and without losing his way Peter managed to park not too far from where they wanted to be, there was no problem for the food as there were many restaurants and takeaway cookeries. They made themselves comfortable and claimed ownership, for the day at least, of a good spot on the beach halfway between the shops and the water.

For Rebeca it was the very first time for her to swim in the sea, Peter went in with her to make sure that she was going to be alright. The water was only a foot deep for a long time before the sand started going rapidly downhill, Rebeca stopped when the water was up to her shoulders. The first mistake she made was to splash Peter who was behind her, because he splashed her back with a vengeance, then she did not realise that a big wave was coming her way, and she had no choice, it engulfed her, for a moment she could not breathe, when she eventually came out of the wave Peter was right there laughing his head off, that reassured her and she realised that she had enjoyed the moment, and now she wanted more, she had learnt to swim so now she was in water that was too deep for her to stand. Rebeca now enjoyed swimming into an incoming wave, and after the best part of an hour in the water Peter himself was getting tired so they came out then joined the other two who now were going to have their turn.

Whilst sitting on the sand watching her mother and Juliet playing about in the water, Rebeca helped herself to a small bar of chocolate, a thought came to her head, she had not written down last night's thoughts. 'Uncle Peter' she said, he turned towards her and without saying a single word he managed an expression on his face to let her know that he was listening to her, 'last night I could not get off to sleep for a long time, so I thought about many things, and I decided to write a poem about my thoughts, they were about the intense darkness and the total lack of any noise, not only that, I am going to write it in Arabic, you know Uncle Peter it's a beautiful language.' He could not find words for her at that very moment, but she understood that he was pleased for her, and just then the other two were coming back. Rebeca had noticed that now the water was not so far away, and she asked her uncle what it was all about. He had no problem telling her about the Sun and the Moon affecting the water, it was called the tide there was high tide and low tide, he then explained in more detail how it all works.

About a quarter of a mile towards their right whilst looking at the sea, there were some rocks that sometimes were submerged and other times in plain view, Rebeca was wishing she had some binoculars, and after looking, it seemed for ever, she decided that she wanted to go and see for herself. After a discussion between Sarah, her brother and Juliet, they decided that it was safe for her to go and look at the rocks, Juliet had been there many times when she was a girl, and it was a safe place. So, with a small bar of chocolate in one hand and her mobile phone in the other, Rebeca made her way there, she had discovered that she preferred to walk on the hard wet sand in her new running shoes, so she had them on. As the sea receded amongst the rocks it left pools of clear water, and Rebeca enjoyed exploring the life within the pools, she was amazed, she now wished they had not made her take the mobile telephone, now she only had one hand only to guide her around the rocks, which extended to the foot of a small cliff on her right, by now her running shoes were soaking wet, and they did not feel comfortable anymore.

When the sea was moving towards the shore, each time the pools of water were getting deeper, she happened to look back and immediately realised that she was going to be in trouble as the tide was coming up, so she looked for a way out. She found that it was possible from where she was to climb the cliff, so she changed direction and started climbing, the first thing that went wrong was that she lost her grip on the telephone, it went flying down and ended out of view, so she did not bother going back for it thinking that it was in the water, the next disaster, she caught her left shoe at the base of two rocks, her foot then was trapped, it was more her running shoe than her foot which would not budge. So, she did the only thing she could do, remove her left foot from the shoe, another ten minutes no more.

She had reached the top of the cliff, and then she found herself staring at a herd of cows, they almost surrounded her. Did they mean her harm? Or were they just inquisitive, she took the "bull by the horn" so to speak and patted the leading cow on the side of its neck, that did the trick, for the first time in her life she had to cross a field to get to a road that seemed to follow the coast. She stopped as she reached the road and had a good look at herself, she did not have a single scratch, however she was walking funny, she only had her right shoe on and on top of that it was wet. Whilst walking on the side of the road she wondered if she could move the shoe unto the other foot because it had begun to get sore and painful, she came across a bus stop that was equipped with a bench, it was pure luxury and she stayed there resting her left foot. When she got going again there were houses on the side of the road, she thought about knocking on a door and asking them to give her a lift, but she thought that she would look a bit silly, so she just kept walking.

Rebeca was making enjoyable time now, the walk became easier for her because there were Police cars, firefighters, and a big noisy helicopter, then a canon went off in the harbour somewhere, so there was a lot to see around her, which helped to forget her left foot. The road had started to go downhill, and she could see the beach where she had come from. Strange she was thinking the beach is now crowded, she kept going in the knowledge that now her suffering will not be for much longer. Two minutes later she was on the wet sand, oh what a relief for her left foot, she looked for her mother and uncle, and to her dismay they were not there, no, she could not see them, she deduced that they were all where she had just come from, so, as tired as she was, she started walking towards the crowds, it was heavens for her left foot! she walked in the water.

When she arrived near the crowds, she could not see her uncle who happened to be on the tall side, so she looked for her mother and Juliet. She did notice three people who it seems were setting up a large camera on a huge tripod, one of the three was a woman with a microphone in her hand, it seemed she was getting ready to talk in front of the camera, the way Rebeca was walking she was going right past them, so she started to slow down a bit with the intention of speaking to the woman. Rebeca pulled on her sleeve, the woman was not happy until she had a good look at Rebeca, and she realised that something was wrong with the girl. 'Miss can you tell me what is going on with all the police and other people over there, what are they doing?' the answer was prompt 'they are looking for a little girl just like you that is missing dear' Rebeca was good at putting two and two together, and was wondering if they could possibly be looking for her, her thought came to a stop when the woman with the microphone asked a question: 'What's your name dear?' the woman nearly lost her balance when she heard the word "Rebeca", who then explained what had just happened to her, when she told her that she had lost her left shoe, she showed her the bare left foot.

The TV person asked Rebeca to stay with her, and at the same time told one of the two men to rush over to the police at the site that they had found Rebeca. The good news spread faster than a grand prix car at full speed on the straight part of a track, and they all rushed to where the camera man was going back. When he arrived back at the camera spot, the other man was operating the camera filming the reporter interviewing miss Rebeca, who was loving it, especially when out of the corner of her eyes she spotted a policeman coming towards her with her left shoe in one hand and her telephone in the other hand. Yes, the shoes matched, just like Cinderella, Rebeca had been recounting her life so far, she was not halfway through when she had to stop. The police officer was ever so pleased to be the one giving back her shoe and telephone. It became difficult to do any meaningful filming whilst crowds started to push into their space. Rebeca now was trying to find her mother, Peter, and Juliet. She was not going to move until they had found her, eventually enough police officers where there with her and the camera crew to push the crowds back and give them space to breathe. Now she did not know why but Rebeca found herself in tears, so she did not see her very relieved mother come up to her, they were in each other's arms for a long time, with Sarah also crying. Peter and Juliet both had a problem getting to Rebeca, the police did not want to let them through, eventually of course they were there waiting for Sarah and Rebeca to resume a semblance of normality.

The reporter lady introduced herself as Debra, and she told Sarah that she had Rebeca on film already, she was telling her about her life so far, and Debra thought that she was well spoken and a good storyteller, she had enough for tonight's news, but she would love to do a program about her tomorrow, she is so interesting for a thirteen-year-old. Sarah looked at Peter then at Rebeca, who both nodded yes. Rebeca looking at her mother, thought that it would be a good idea for tonight's news program, if she was to tell what it was that had happened to her, that caused so much panic for which she was sorry. Debra was surprised and of course pleased, Sarah had no choice but to agree, so the scene was sort of reset, the camera got working again and Debra shared the microphone between her and Rebeca, and she told what happened, including her thoughts at the time and the encounter with the herd of Cows, she did not forget her aching left foot.

When they eventually arrived back at the cottage. Both Sarah and her daughter could not take their eyes of each other, Peter told his niece what happened earlier; when Sarah tried to call her there was no answer which became the first worry, Peter was the first one on the site and it was then worry number two, he was the one who called the authorities when he discovered her left shoe, and that was not too soon because he heard the telephone ringing, still dry lodged between two large rocks, and it seemed to him that within minutes the site was fully covered by teams of rescuers, from the beach, the air and the sea. The thought of having lost Rebeca kept coming back to the three adults, they all felt to be so lucky, and for now anyway she was never again let loose, it was a lesson well learnt for them, neither Peter nor Juliet had realised at the time, that this afternoon had brought them all a little closer!

Well last night had been a celebration getting their special meal, for having arrived, and tonight it was going to be a celebration for having Rebeca come back to them. Although they had not booked a table, the staff at the restaurant, went out of their way to accommodate them, they made a fuss of Rebeca and told her to order anything she wanted, and her meal was on the house. mothert, uncle, and friend were not comfortable with people looking at them, oh, but Rebeca had no problem and she often smiled at various people. There was a television which was on, and all eyes were on it when the news came on, and the moment little Rebeca was talking with Debra, one could hear a pin drop!

Sarah did not tell anyone, but at the time she was hoping her father was watching the news, it would serve him right she thought, then she would change her mind, and would have loved him just watching, tomorrow is going to be a big day, they will be meeting up with Debra and her crew in the hotel lounge, for Rebeca to tell her life so far. Sarah had made up her mind to find out when that interview will be broadcast, and she is going to ask Peter to call home and tell her mum and dad to watch their granddaughter on television, with Debra who happened to be a famous interviewer. Then, it was going to be Rebeca's turn to telephone 'her' grandparents, and after call James her father.

That night when they arrived back to the cottage, the three 'girls' only had one thing to worry about; what were they going to wear tomorrow? They had to be at the hotel by ten in the morning at least one hour before the filming, they had not realised but a makeup crew will be there to make them all look as good as possible. They all got up at sunrise, Juliet cooked a nice breakfast (she did not burn the fried bread this time!) and they all piled into the car at a quarter to ten. Rebeca's appearance on the news caused a lot of interest, her name was on the front page of most newspapers. When they arrived at the reception desk, the receptionist willingly escorted them to the television people, at the same time she managed to have a conversation with Rebeca, no doubt she will tell all her friends about it!

There must have been at least a dozen people with the television team, the first ones that they met were the makeup team, next they were all sitting down covered by a gown, having diverse types of makeup applied, then a hairdresser came along and sorted out all their hair. At last, someone of authority came to meet up with them, he introduced himself as the director, he was pleased to meet them all, he did not talk to Rebeca as he did not want to get her too excited or was it that he did not get on with children. Then Debra came to meet them, and she discussed how the interview will work. They were introduced to what really was a makeshift studio, there were lights everywhere, two cameras each with two men, then there was yet another smart business looking person, they never caught her name, but she was the producer.

The actual program was going to be at least a half hour long and it will be aired on Sunday morning, the setting was pretty good, both Rebeca and Debra were sitting on a long low settee, at each end looking at each other, in the background it was a view of the harbour through a large window. Sarah, Peter (including a pile of makeup) and Juliet were sat on a second settee which was facing the other one, one camera was looking at Rebeca and Debra, and the other one mostly focussed on the other three. Everybody had a clip-on microphone which the sound man assessed each time he clipped it on.

They were all sat in place, and Debra now was in charge, before they went 'live' she told Sarah, Peter, and Juliet that from time to time she will be asking them some questions, whatever she did or said she always managed to keep smiling at Rebeca, it was clever. There was at least only five minutes before they started, the director started speaking to the number two camera man, asking him to shoot the scene with the background of the harbour, there was a problem; the director was a Scottish man and the camera operator was of a Pakistan background, the problem was that he could not understand the man speaking with a broad Scottish accent. Sarah looked at Rebeca who got the message, she stood up directed her voice at the camera man and casually spoke to him in Urdu telling him what the director wanted. Talk about confusion, first the man with the camera thanked her also in Urdu, Rebeca translated, Sarah was smiling, and Debra could not believe what had just happened. She asked Rebeca what language she was speaking in, and she got a bit of education about all the Pakistan languages from Rebeca. She still could not believe that this very English rose of a girl with soft pink cheeks, could have learned that language at her age, she was beginning to think that there was more to little Rebeca than one could imagine.

The cameras were now rolling, and Debra introduced Rebeca to the viewers, Rebeca almost blushed when she heard the introduction, she never thought that she was that good! 'Rebeca, can you tell us about yourself?' without any hesitation the thirteen-year-old, turned towards the camera and started to recite about her life so far, then without stopping she started to talk about her expectations, she was not going to mention her mother's parents. She turned to look straight at Debra and spoke to her, 'I am so lucky when I was born my mother was only sixteen years old, so sometimes I feel that we both grew up together, my mother is very well organised, and even if I say so, she is so nice, she loves people and she is caring, and on top of that she is my best friend,' she stopped to drink a sip of water, she glanced towards Sarah who was visibly touched, and she was blushing. 'I must tell you all my mother is a teacher, and she is proud of being a Polyglot, last Christmas she recited a Persian poem in Arabic by Omar Khayyam, not one person in the audience of over twelve hundred could understand a single word, but at the end they were nearly all in tears, yes she can speak in Arabic, and Urdu, as well as I can, I love writing in Arabic it flows like a drawing, I was a bit behind in arithmetic, so my head teacher got me some help and now I have caught up, now I have more time to learn more languages'. She stopped because she felt that Debra was waiting to ask her some questions.

'Well young lady you seem to know who you are, there is no question about that, is this the first time you have been here?' Rebeca was well ready to tell more, 'Yes Debra, it is my very first holiday ever, I could not get over the absolute silence at night especially, and that total darkness, the first night I could not get off to sleep. It is also the first time my feet have touched the sea; I just love it all.' A quick brake for Rebeca and then she went on to explained what had happened yesterday when she climbed the cliff, as she reached the top, she was met by a herd of cows, at first she was worried, but then she talked to the leading cow, who seemed to have answered back, she walked by the side of Rebeca and lead her across the field to a gate, she kept looking back, the whole herd stayed there looking at her. Whilst Rebeca was talking, the Producer and the Director were in a huddle speaking to each other quietly, they were making up their mind to tell Debra who had a receiver in one ear, to ask Sarah to recite the poem, also told Debra that they had just looked up the word polyglot, which is a person that can speak five languages or more.

All this time the hotel had a huge reception room, used for weddings and various functions, the television team had arranged for a large screen to be installed so that some special people in the town could come and see it all happening, the Mayor and his wife of course were both in attendance and she wanted him to do something special for Rebeca, even the hotel were thinking the same, and the Commodore of the yacht club, who as it happens was also the commodore of the local national life boat institution wanted to take her out on a trip.

Rebeca went on to talk about her aching foot, and meeting Debra on the beach also how sorry she was having caused all this commotion, and especially upset for her mother her uncle and his friend who must have been very worried. Debra was almost pleased when Rebeca stopped for a moment, it gave her a chance of speaking with Sarah. 'You must all have been worried when Peter found one of her shoes and her telephone, can you describe how you felt at the time.' It was obvious for Sarah that the question was going to be asked so she was ready with an answer, 'That first moment when I heard that she was missing, and Peter had found her shoe, it was as if someone had punched me in the stomach, her shoes were so special to her that she would never let it go, then when I started to search with Peter and Juliet, my full attention was on the search, people arrived and I could see on their faces that they were as worried as I was, it helped me, the helicopter was also a big help for me, however the more people searching for my Rebeca meant, that it was going to get closer to the time we would have to decide that we have lost her,

I know that was wrong but I could sometimes feel that I would like to be the only one searching as it would extend the time when I could still have hope, and I was afraid that the chances of finding her were disappearing faster, and that was hurting me. The first day of her life was the best day of my life, yesterday is now the second-best day of my life, and I must thank all the people who have helped, it's so nice to know that so many people care.'

'Peter, how close are you to your niece?' He never expected that question, so he started at the beginning, 'When Rebeca was born her and her mother lived with Rebeca's father's parents, they are lovely people who enjoyed helping to bring up their granddaughter, I had just started a three year University degree in design at Nottingham University, when I came back to London during breaks I also stayed with Sarah and Rebeca, it was always nice to see how much she had grown each time. Then when I came back to live in London, I moved into a flat with my sister and her little girl. After a while Sarah had decided to carry on with her education and eventually managed a degree in languages, she now teaches French and German in the same school Rebeca goes to, we all get on well with James who is Rebeca's father.' Next was Juliet, who was able to express her delight when Sarah appeared, she never in her life so far felt so relieved, pleased and happy all at the same time, she decided to never take her eyes off Rebeca!

Then came the moment; Debra asked if Sarah could show the nation, how one could actually feel a poem, Sarah was not shy, but just a bit apprehensive, she stood up and Rebeca went and stood next to her, the camera focused mostly on Sarah and she took a deep breath so as to clear her mind, and off she went, it was so expressive, the words were almost musical, it was almost like an abstract painting, people listening to it were taken to another place, the Director was in tears, Debra was afraid that her eye shadow had started to run, in the hotel function room it was absolute silence. Then Sarah decided to explain the poem, 'The poet lived in Syria in the eleven hundreds he was very famous at the time and the poem was about a mother telling her daughter about life, thank you all!'

Debra now had to find a way to close the interview, and she did it by telling all that the mayor of the town was going to give Rebeca the key to the town, and that the twelfth of July every year from now on and for ever will be named "Rebeca day", The hotel are making a special meal for the family as guests, the lifeboat skipper will be taking Rebeca for a special cruise. And that was that.

Chapter Four - Still Growing Up

The meal that night in the hotel was magnificent to say the least, they had eaten well the previous nights in the fish restaurant, and a five-course meal cooked by the top chef, he even came to the table to make certain they were happy and to explain the next dish. Tomorrow the weather is going to be fine, and at twelve noon the mayor was going to make an official giving of the key, then the skipper of the lifeboat was going to give Rebeca three quarters of an hour tour of the sea near the town, after which the four Londoners were going to retire to the cottage for the rest of the day, Peter and Juliet were going to shop for food, as they might not be recognised, then Sarah was going to do the cooking. Of course, nobody had planned for the unexpected.

The whole crew were on the boat, they all stood to attention whilst they whistled Rebeca aboard, it was a lovely scene which was filmed, she was fitted with a proper size life belt, and the lifeboat was now at sea, the skipper let Rebeca push the throttles forward, she was so excited when she felt the actual power, the back of the seat was pushing her forward, then when the boat had slowed down she had the opportunity of steering, with help of the skipper of course, they were now almost ten miles away from shore, and apart for being able to see the town which one could only just make out, there was nothing to see apart from the odd ship in the horizon, Rebeca had already got used to hearing the ship's radio, and unexpectedly there was a call for the life boat; it was a mayday there was a sail boat in distress about seven miles from their present location, it was a sail boat with a family on board, the husband, the wife, one young son aged six and an older sister aged eleven, they had left Florida seven weeks ago, they were not in time to avoid an unexpected collision with a container that was floating just below the water by about two feet. The yacht was called "MAYBE" and the four had made it into their life raft, they had a portable radio with them, and they communicated with the Lifeboat. There was a problem because there was a slight mist which was caressing the surface of the sea. The crew of MAYBE were not able to send up any flares, so the skipper explained was he was about to do; he was going to send a flare and then another the skipper in the life raft can tell the crew of the Lifeboat which direction they should be looking for them, that is what happened. Just before they met up, Rebeca used her mobile telephone to call her mother and tell her that she was fine, Sarah was pleased for the call, but she had already knew.

The Skipper worked out that they would be with them in about ten minutes, he then told Rebeca that she now has to go below out of the way, the problem is that she pleaded with him to stay with them, because she wanted to photograph the rescue, it would be good for the RNLI, and at the same time she kept saying please repeatedly. He had no choice but to give up! When five minutes only had gone by, they could see the bright orange colour life raft aimlessly floating on the sea, as they arrived, they could only see one person who had to be the skipper of the boat, there was a canopy under which the other three must be. The life boat slowed right down, the engines went all quiet and there was some conversation going on between one man on deck and the man in the life raft, the sea luckily was not rough, so they managed to have the two boats meet, one of the lifeboat men threw a rope which ended being tied to the life raft. The first one handed to the crew was the young boy, second was the girl then the wife, after which the man disappeared under the canopy, a short while later he reappeared with a duffle bag in one hand, it contained some of their personal belongings, and one could see that whatever happens he will never let go of it. He managed to climb aboard without help and the first sentence he said, 'what do we do with the life raft?' He need not have asked the question, when he looked back two crew had pulled it up on board.

Then of course it was thanks over and over again, and then answering question after question; they had left Florida seven weeks ago, they made good time, they experience a mild storm, and up to today the whole trip was perfect, then they had to go below in the lifeboat where there is some accommodation for up to eight people, it's not too pleasant as one is closer to the engines and there are no windows, there is one crew who is in charge of the radar, this time Rebeca was only too pleased to go below with them, she had taken many photographs of the rescue, and she wanted to get as much information from them to use when she sells the photographs to the newspapers.

She sat next to the eleven-year-old girl, and they started talking, they were going to be there for at least an hour, so during that time she got to know the family quiet well. After a while the man asked Rebeca for her name, and he wanted to know how come she was onboard the lifeboat? She replied by suggesting that it would take over an hour to explain why! As a starter she told them that today she was given the key to the town, in a celebration where the whole town was there, she then told them that wherever they are on Sunday morning, they must watch a program at ten in the morning on BBC1. Well, I can tell you that I am famous over the whole country, they are going to name the twelfth of July "Rebeca day" and especially here there will be a celebration every year. She then added for good measure 'you would like to meet my mother?" Having Rebeca speaking with them, made them forget what had just happened, and although she wanted to ask them about their ordeal she decided not to bother them, and keep talking to them, passing little morceau's of interest about her life, she did mention that her mother is a polyglot, and that she herself can speak five languages, then she mention Urdu and Arabic, she already knows that she will be going to Oxford University when she is older, that was all she told them about herself, and she was right they were thirsty for more! The father who called himself Joe, asked Rebeca if her cell phone was working this far from land, it took a while for her to answer him, her memory had to do a bit of overtime, she eventually worked out that the "cell" phone in England was her mobile phone, and before eventually answering she looked to see if she had a signal, and she was able to confirm that it was alive so to speak. He then asked her if he could make a call with it, of course the reply was yes! Joe then dug into his duffle bag, brought out what seemed to be an address book, turned to a page, read the instructions and dialled a number, it was to call his cousin who is a professor of physics at Southampton University, he was expecting Joe and family to arrive tomorrow, and the cousin got a shock when he heard what had just happened, he asked for more details. Which Joe had to ask Rebeca for, such as the name of the town they were going to find themselves in shortly, he did happen to mention that he was speaking on a thirteen-year-old girl's cell phone who happened to be already in the lifeboat, apparently, she is well known. Yes, his cousin was surprised. And he told him that she has been in the news, and she is a smart little girl.

Someone Rebeca knew well was waiting at the dock to film her coming off the lifeboat, it was the same camera man who had volunteered to come with Debra, he never had a chance of having a talk with her about speaking in Urdu. Before leaving the boat Rebeca jumped up and gave the skipper a hug and a kiss, oh he has a beard! The dock had been cordoned off by the Authorities, there was Rebeca's family, television crew, one custom's man and two police officers. The Lifeboat crew stayed on board and now the custom man wanted to talk to Joe, Sarah stayed close to Rebeca but did not interfere with her talking with Debra and then in Urdu to the camera man who still could not get over it, especially that she could read and write in that language, when he asked why? She told him that it was a good introduction to Arabic, he shook his head in despair.

Debra wanted to talk to Julie, Joe's wife, who could not tell her too much about the sinking, it all happened so quickly, it was all happening in slow motion for her, she really woke up from that state whilst listening to a thirteen-year-old girl that kept talking, apparently, she is famous. Rebeca as a joke pulled on Debra's sleeve, she wanted her attention as she had something to tell her. 'Debra, I took a lot of pictures of the rescue on my mobile, can you please do me a favour and send them to some newspapers you think would appreciate them, they speak for themselves, if you give me your mobile number, I can send them all for you to use as you wish'. Debra gave her mobile number and told Rebeca that is what she is going to do, and on top of that she needs all her details including her home address because she will be receiving at least a couple of cheques from the newspapers.

For Joe and Julie, there very first requirement was getting some clothes to replace all that are now well under the sea in the English Channel, there was no immigration offices in town, so the Customs man made it his duty to collect details of the four Americans, who had just landed in town. The Americans where then escorted one by one to a world-famous store by a friendly Policeman, "Marks and Spencer" where they managed to purchase two days of cloths for the four of them, that included a large case. Joe had given the name of the hotel to his cousin, where they were going to be when he arrived to pick them up within four hours or so. The same Policeman stayed with them, and accompanied them to the hotel, the manager found them a good place in the lounge, where they could relax and even if they felt like it, have a snooze. Before leaving them there, the manager wanted to talk with them, to find out how they got on, no not with the disastrous sinking, with the thirteen-year-old little girl who kept them sane in the lifeboat!

Rebeca, Sarah, Peter, and Juliet suddenly felt some hunger, so, they made for a well-known fish and chips fast food restaurant, they were surprised when entering, as Debra and the camera man had just sat down, they immediately waved to Sarah and asked the family to sit with them. Whilst they were all enjoying the cod and chips, and the mushy peas, Rebeca started to talk about the rescue, where they were at the time, one could not see the land anymore, she told them how frighten she would have been in their place, they had been so lucky to be rescued in less than an hour after the boat had sunk. She then talked about being below, it was a horrible feeling for her, but then she was concerned about the family, they were hardly talking, so she went out of her way to keep talking, hoping that they could forget what had just happened, even though it was a short time ago. The mother Julie had realised what she was doing, and before they left the boat, she had thanked her, 'and I felt pleased for myself, yes, it was a nice feeling helping people in trouble which I will never forget.'

When they eventually arrived back in the cottage, first they opened all the windows and everybody slumped into four armchairs, all exhausted. Nobody could think about food, so nothing was prepared for that night, there was a frozen cheesecake in the fridge that by now must be defrosted, so they had that in mind as a snack for tonight. Peter remembered that they must make various telephone calls, to alert people that they were all going to be on television, the next morning which was Sunday on BBC1 at ten AM. The first call he made was to his mother and father, he told them both all the news, and one could not possibly miss it as it was the headline in most newspapers, so they already had read the other day about Rebeca's exploits, for the first time in almost thirteen years his father had actually said the word Rebeca, then Peter told him about today's exploit which will be in the newspapers tomorrow, including the photographs Rebeca had taken and sold to the papers. Then his mother came on the telephone, he had to repeat it all, she was excited, so much so that Peter was thinking that now they will want to see their granddaughter, he was sure.

The next call he made was to James, Rebeca's father; and yes he had read the press and felt so proud, but he does not tell anybody else about it, they would only start asking questions he does not want to answer, yes, he would love talking with Rebeca, Peter handed his phone to her, she had one hell of a long chat with her father, it was lovely for the others to hear her talk to him. The next person to make a call was Sarah she dialled Rebeca's grandmother and grandfather, the only ones she knew, and she let her speak as soon as they had answered the call, Rebeca told them all that had happened to her including todays happenings, they were so please to hear from her, they did not know if they were going to bother sleeping tonight, no, they want to make certain not to miss the BBC program in the morning, Rebeca told them not to be so silly and have a good night's sleep, make certain that they get up when the alarm goes off, and not have that extra lie in bed before getting up. Then Sarah called Aisha their neighbours and she told her all about what has been happening, and of course about tomorrow. For the moment in the cottage all the residents were still exhausted, Peter however started to look for the television to make certain that it was all in good order and BBC1 was working. It is usually kept out of site to discourage looking at it.

First thing on Sunday morning, again one could find Juliet in the kitchen, this time she was watching the bread fry in the pan, the heat was well down, and it definitely was not going to burn, there will be a big cheer. Next one in was Peter, then Rebeca and last but still not too late Sarah. As soon as Juliet finished her breakfast, she left the cottage and called on the neighbours who were friends of the family, and she told them to watch BBC1 in a couple of hours' time, of course she told them why as well. It was just as well she had called on next door, because she had completely forgotten her parents, she remedied that as soon as she had sat down, then of course she had to go through the search for Rebeca and the rescue in the English Channel, and yes, they are having a fabulous time but not exactly a holiday.

They never needed to invent a glue that one could use, to stick one's eyes to a television screen, that's what happened on Sunday morning at ten o'clock, as much as they had that proud feeling, looking at themselves was not particularly pleasant, everyone thought that next time they will be better, the exception was Sarah she thought that she had done a good job with the poem, and she was pleased having used a lower tone speaking in Arabic, they all wondered and discussed how many tears were they in the whole country. Rebeca thought that she appeared shorter that she really was, Debra is a tall person and that could be the reason, by lunch time they were all still in the cottage, all sat in armchairs in the lounge, nobody had uttered a single word for the last half hour or so, when all of a sudden out of the blues Rebeca asked a question, yes, the one nobody wanted to answer; 'Mum, why did you fall out with your father?' Sarah had discussed many times with her brother Peter when would it be at the right time to tell her the truth, and lately they were concluding that she was clever and strong enough to take it. 'Rebeca, come and sit with me here', she beckoned for her to come closer, and Rebeca came and sat on her lap, then Sarah started again; ' Rebeca my dear I must tell you that my father is an old fashion person, and on top of that, from his point of view he can never be wrong, and on the odd occasion when he has no choice, and his own error is pointed out to him, what he does, is retreat and hopefully never speak to the person who he believes had offended him by pointing out his error, my mother never argues with him, yes absolutely never, so she appears to be supporting him, she has no choice.'

So far so good, Peter and Juliet were listening as best they could, never saying a single word. Rebeca was definitely interested, and Sarah was thinking that she had done well so far, so she went on, 'at the time you were born Rebeca, things were very different in England, most adults had seen the war, and people did not feel free to live as we do these days, and there was one thing that must never happen, that was for a schoolgirl to become pregnant, you have to believe me, all kinds of things would kick in. What it seems was important was one's relationship with the neighbours, everybody had to behave, and if your unmarried daughter became pregnant, the neighbours must not find out at all costs, all over the country there were homes for expecting unmarried mothers to spend almost the whole nine months, and the baby was born there, then it was all very well organised after the birth, the baby was taken away from the mother as soon as possible, then given to a family to be adopted, the mother had no choice, a week later she was back at home, the neighbours were always told that the girl had gone to stay with a relative somewhere far away. Now with me it was a little different, I never had a big bump in front of me, so nobody had any idea that I was expecting you, your birth was a last minute rush to the hospital, and the moment I saw you, nothing on this earth could make me give you up, the nurses tried I guess doing their best, they never had a chance, so they gave up, the last problem was your grandfather, he thought that he had the answer, he marched into the hospital, found me, again marched up to my bed and attempted to give me an order, at the time you were sleeping and there was a light cover over you, so he never looked at you, and the order, well it was more a choice that I never really had, I can tell you now it took me a couple of years to recover.' Remembering the occasion that she had tried to forget all these years Sarah was now in tears finding it hard to actually speak, Rebeca who was looking away from her mother because of the way she was sat on her lap had not realised that her mother was in tears, but as Sarah was finishing that last sentence her voice was hesitating and trembling,' Rebeca was drawn to her mother realising that she was crying, so she turned around and now there were two wiping their tears.

Peter and Juliet also became emotional, that last difficult sentence that Sarah only just managed to utter, was what her father had come to the hospital to tell her, it was: come home whenever you are ready but be advised, that I will not allow this baby in my house ever! There was a silence in the lounge, everybody needed a break, the first person who spoke was Rebeca; 'mum, I am so pleased that you have told me, now I understand why we lived with my dad's parents all this time, oh yes now it all makes sense, I am so pleased, oh mum it must have been so hard for you, I am sorry, and I am so happy, I feel lucky to have a mother like you.

It took over an hour before everybody had recovered, Peter was pleased that at last the subject was no longer taboo, and now they can all talk about it, for him at least he understood that Rebeca has not been hurt about her grandfather, Juliet also felt the same. Sarah was so busy trying to forget her father, that it had not got to her mind, about Rebeca not being upset. Rebeca herself was feeling for what her mother had to go through thirteen years back, and as well was so pleased that she had such a determined mother. She was going to ask about her own father, and his parents but for now she did not want to upset her mother some more.

That night was yet another celebration and Peter opened a bottle of white wine to drink with now the well defrosted cheesecake, he poured about a quarter of an inch of wine into a glass for Rebeca, she loved it, after that "wonderful" meal, Rebeca rushed to the kitchen to do the washing up, it had not taken her long to work out that the washing up was going to be easy, only four small plates and forks. They then waited until the sun had set and it was dark, and all went for a walk down the lane to reach the sea, they had a good look at the waves that appeared to be luminescent, and by the time they arrived back at the cottage, it was straight to bed for everybody.

Chapter Five - London

On Monday morning the weather was fine, and a search started to look for any Sunday Paper, there was a local paper shop and Rebeca asked them if they had any of yesterday's papers left, the lady behind the counter recognised Rebeca, and she was pleased to give her four Sunday papers, and on top of that the lady wished her luck, Rebeca left the shop with a beautiful feeling. They were all in the car and they decided not to look at the papers until they get back to the cottage. First, they drove to a little harbour only 1 mile away which had a little beach of its own, and that is where they went, so hopefully they might get away with it and not be recognised.

The water was warm and there were hardly any waves, so all four enjoyed a splash fight, Rebeca got the worst of it, her being so small, they had brought their own food and drinks, Juliet had been there before and was well aware that they were no shops, Peter started to feel the sun on his back, so he came out of the water and quickly put his shirt back on, Juliet then joined him, which left Rebeca and her mother swimming side by side along the beach, every time there eyes met Rebeca had a big healthy smile for her mother, no words were needed, they were both very happy! They had all caught the Sun and by four they decided to go food shopping for tonight's diner. They arrived back at the cottage by five thirty in time to have a big cup of tea and have moisturising cream rubbed on all their backs.

Supper was now on, they were again all sat in the four armchairs and Rebeca handed everyone a Sunday newspaper, between the four papers they counted eleven photographs which Rebeca had taken on the lifeboat, one of them was particular good, it was the one as Joe appeared from inside the life raft holding the duffle bag for dear life, the lighting was just right and one could see the absolute determination on his face, no way whatsoever was it going to fall in the water! That night they went for another walk, not quite as far as the night before, but far enough to be tired when they got back.

Two more days which followed what had happened the day before, no they did not go to the little harbour again, they all missed fish and chips and cold fizzy drinks, one of the policemen caught up with them and he wanted to know if they were enjoying themselves, the answer was unanimous from the four it was a big yes, they had decided not to call this week a holiday, no they have named it the happenings week.

Of course, eventually they had to return to London, on their last full day, they went to the fish restaurant and the hotel to thank them personally for their kindness. The drive back to London was not difficult, but the first thing which they all noticed was that the air did not feel clean as it had done by the sea. Aisha made a real fuss of them, especially Rebeca, there had been several reporters wanting to talk with them, today was the first day nobody had turned up so far. Nobody had mentioned grandfather, and especially Sarah, who was hoping not to have to go down that path again.

They all had a laugh when Juliet started to unpack the leftover food, she had just one egg in her hand exclaiming 'I should have left it behind, what the hell can we do with that one egg?' Sarah was also busy packing the washing machine, Peter was cleaning out the car and Rebeca had a big smile on her face and would not tell anyone why! It had been a very special week for her, and she needed time to get back to normal, that is if it is ever going to be possible. What the other three had not realised was that she had a plan.

The next day Rebeca was gone all morning visiting, one of her school friends that does not live too far away, she could not wait to tell her all that had happened to her, on this so called holiday, they had a lovely time, and as it happened her friend had seen her on the television on Sunday morning, and she screamed the house down, to show them all at her home that her friend was on TV! She told her friend that she was going to receive money from all the newspapers, and her mum was going to help her open a bank account. 'Oh, just think I'll be able to spend my own money!'

Before leaving her friend, Rebeca phoned her mother and told her a liar. She was getting the OK from her to stay until three, her mother did not refuse, and Rebeca was on her way to visit somebody. Peter once had showed her his parents' house, and that is where she was going.

She was walking with a defiant step, she did mean to get there, there could not be is a single though that could dissuade her on what she wanted to do, and now change her mind and abort her mission, never! That is why she had a smile all this time, she had planned what she was going to say to both her grandmother and father, she could not wait to be knocking at their door. It did take her over an hour to reach that door, now she is pushing the button which made the bell in the house "ring the changes," for the life of the occupants within.

Rebeca could hear some mechanical noises on the other side of the door which started to move inwards, there was a man there, he said nothing but stared at the little girl, then he recognised her, and he said enquiringly 'are you Rebeca dear?' The answer came right back, 'and you are my grandad,' he picked her up, and whilst holding her in his arms he shouted as loud as he could 'Mary', Rebeca now found out the name of her grandma for the first time ever.

The second question he had for her, was she on her own, she quickly replied yes of course, and by that time Mary had arrived, she could see her husband holding Rebeca and immediately worked out that it really was her granddaughter in her house, at last! Mary shut the door and they moved into the front room, which as it happens was spotless. Then she was transferred to Mary. Both her grandparents found it difficult to speak to Rebeca, they were both feeling so guilty, how could they have rejected this lovely little girl? Well, that little girl could feel their problem, it almost reminded her of the family in the lifeboat, so, off she went about her life so far. She let them know about her life with her father's parents, they had been so pleased for her to be there, even after all this time they make her and her mother most welcome every Sunday for lunch. 'You know my mother takes after you grandad, she is just as pig headed as you are, you have both lost out, I know there were many times when my mother was trying to decide about something, she would say, oh I wish my dad was here he would have the answer.'

That gave him a little bit of hope, he told her that she had done well, they had seen her on Sunday morning, and they have a copy of all the newspapers which had articles about her. 'Did you know grandad, my headmaster at school told me that I will be at Oxford in five years' time I am doing so well at school, oh yes all those photographs of the rescue which have been printed are going to earn me almost three thousand pounds, this week mum is going to help me open a bank account, that's posh you know.' There was a pause and Mary suggested that they should have a cup of tea with a Victoria Sponge she had made. Rebeca told him that she will show them all the photographs that are in her telephone, he was pleased, he could not wait but he did because he could hear that the tea was going to be with them, in no more than a moment. They were surprised when Rebeca told Mary that she drinks her tea without milk or sugar. She then carried on about the tea and gave them both a quick lot of facts: most of the rest of the world drink tea without milk, that way you can taste it without having to make a strong tea which is not good for you, I bet you both don't know why it is the custom in England to add milk, and to add it first in the cup, well it was because England at the time had sufficient rich people who could afford to have China cups that were so thin that one can almost see through them, and the milk was to stop the cup from cracking. Then she took her phone out of a pocket, messed about with it and handed it to Grandma who was sitting next to him on the sofa, and they both started looking at over one hundred and fifty pictures, of course they recognised Sarah but at different times they asked her who it was in the picture, and of course she was always able to tell them.

Between the lovely tea and looking at the past a whole hour had gone by, and now Rebeca took charge; 'Grandad, can you drive me back please it's a long walk and I am supposed to be there in a half an hours' time.' He had no problem with taking her back home, he already knew where she lived, they had driven past it many times. They were now all three in the car and Rebeca was sitting on the back seat, and whilst talking she texted her mother, telling her that she had twisted her right ankle, now it was hurting her and it was difficult for her to walk, so her friend's mother was going to drive her back, she should be there in a quarter of an hour.

When they arrived Sarah and Peter were waiting for her, they did not notice the car because the sun was in their eyes, Sarah got a real shock when she saw her father get out of the car, her mind had been preoccupied with Rebeca's injury, just as he had completely got out of the car, his daughter on her way to Rebeca almost knocked him down, out of the corner of her eyes she noticed the little girl smiling away pleased with herself, all this time she was holding her father to steady him, that hold ended up being one long hug, they only broke it off when Mary had reached them, so it then became her turn, Peter was more than pleased, at last!

Next Sarah made sure that there was nothing wrong with Rebeca, and all five ended up in the apartment. Before any of them were sitting down, somebody called for silence for a special announcement; it was Rebeca being authoritative using a loud commending voice, she asked them all to repeat at the count of three what she is about to tell them, and they have to be loud with it, 'one two three ''I Bear No Blame'' all five shouted it as loud as they could, and it was just like a miracle had happened, everybody were all at ease!

Sarah was happy to be telling all she could about Rebeca, and there was an awful lot to tell, they already knew a lot from Peter, and also Mary had often talked to James's mother in the past about Rebeca, they stayed until seven, then went home, Rebeca saw her grandparents every day, with the exception of Sunday when the two of them had their usual Sunday lunch with the other grandparents. Every day Sarah when lying in bed trying to get to sleep, had the same thoughts, they were always about her daughter, she could never get over it; the way she played everybody, she very much had surprised Mary and her husband, just arriving at their door, then she tricked them to drive her home and be confronted with Sarah, then Sarah herself was well fooled about the injury to her foot, but what had intrigued her the most, coming from a thirteen year old girl making them all shouting out a statement of peace, that one she will never in her life forget, and she will never understand her daughter, she is not only clever but she seems to have control over people, where it had all come from, she had no idea.

Now they have been back home for almost two weeks, and two significant things had happened, that is apart from the reunion. The first cheque arrived, it was for three hundred pounds which was used to open a restricted bank account, she was too young for the bank to give her a cheque book. Then even more exciting for all, Debra came to visit Rebeca and Sarah, she had a very smart looking young man with her, Debra was genuinely pleased to meet up with Rebeca, first she introduced the young man, his name was George and he happened to be one of the many television producers. Like a grownup she shook his hand, and right of way she had the nerve of asking him what it was he did in the television business. Poor guy he almost stepped back he was taken by surprise by Rebeca being so adult, Debra enjoyed that moment, she had told him that she was a "one off", and now he believes her.

Well, George came to see Rebeca, because he wanted her to appear from time to time, on a television children's program called CSM which stands for Children's Saturday Morning The idea was going to be for the viewers to follow her life for the next ten years, once every six weeks. She will be picked up by car, driven to the studio, entertained, and fed then brought back home in the same car, she can have one person with her if she wants to. There will also be photo shoots and the odd appearance. She will of course be paid. George was waiting for Sarah to have questions, but Rebeca was the one with all the questions, 'if I am waiting about on the set, is it possible for me to have a teacher most likely either for maths or perhaps English.' That was a question which he had never been asked, he had no choice but to answer in the positive, yes of course was the answer. Then another question, which was even more adult; 'If I have to take some time off school, can you speak with my head master and advise him, that I will have a teacher at the studio, who will be in contact with the school, and then know what I should study for that day, I think that way, my head master will approve I am sure'. Then she turned to her mother: 'Mum I think it's a good idea, you think so?', the way she was looking at her mother who had realised before she was asked, that it was a "Done Deal". George was more than pleased, as he was looking forward to working with Rebeca.

There were a few things to iron out, a contract to be signed at a later date, a call for George to make to the school, and next to tell Sarah that he is going to arrange for one of the directors to meet up with Rebeca two or three times at least before her first appearance on the program, he was going to try his best to arrange those meetings before schools reopen for the Autumn term.

Chapter Six - Back to School

All this had brought a bit more pressure for Sarah, there was the problem now of having new clothes for her, after all Sarah was not abundant with money, the problem however was easily solved, her father offered to pay for a whole new wardrobe! Rebeca herself did not think that there was a problem, now that she is earning money, as well the pictures of hers that were published. Rebeca had three meetings with a charming lady, who was the director for the program. The meetings all took place in the director's home in Hampstead, only a short bus ride from Rebeca's home, however the director came to pick her up and of course bring her back. Rebeca was much impressed with the home, it was full of large photographs of well-known actors, and there were many sculptors, a couple of them were abstract, and Rebeca could not take her eyes of them, she was completely mesmerised. The director realised and asked Rebeca what she thought they represented, she was concentrating on one, she replied by describing what it could have been the artists intention, showing an uprooted tree laying horizontal on the ground which she called: ''life having a rest,'' at that moment the director realised how interesting it was going to be working with that little girl! After that first meeting when the director arrived back home, she first called Debra to tell her she was absolutely right, then called George the producer, and they had a long pleasant positive discussion about how they could use Rebeca for the very best, they were going to start by not making her learn things to say, at first anyway because she herself is full of knowledge, she told him about the sculptor incident, which was something that does not usually come out of the mouth of babes!

Somethings now had changed on Sundays, and the Sunday meal alternated between grandparents, the meals had to be as early as they could have it, because the afternoon was for studying for Rebeca's own subjects which at this time was languages, but of course that could change if she decided on another non-school subject, Saturday morning was only for catching up if she had got behind with her homework in the week. In the afternoon it was time with her friend with whom she played games, sometimes chess or they would go to the park, or even just watch television. She had started watching CSM, so that when she meets them all next month, she will know who they all are, the two girls decided to find out more about the program she is going to be on, obviously it was well known, it had been running for many years, all children had watched it at one time. The two girls then researched everything about it, including the name of the originator who had long ago retired.

The first week back at school was unusual both for Sarah and Rebeca, they were both sometimes congratulated and other times asked an awful lot of questions, so far Rebeca did not want to tell anybody about the CSM business, however the head was going to know shortly so she thought, but as it happened, he had already been contacted by George, the good thing was that he approved of it all. So that was what could have been a problem put to one side and forget about. One of Sarah's teacher friends noticed that Rebeca had grown in the last three months, and she remarked about it to Sarah, who had not noticed, she was pleased to hear that, as Rebeca had hardy grown an inch in the last twelve months. Now she remembered during that shopping spree for the new wardrobe, that a lot of the clothes that fitted her last year were a bit too tight on Rebeca, and although the ones they bought were all that same size, they must have been all slightly larger than the ones they had tried that did not fit. Rebeca did not find out, but her mother now was hoping to have a bit less to worry about.

During the day the head wanted to speak to Sarah and Rebeca, and he wanted to see them at the end of the school day, he was pleased to be able to tell them both that he had approved for Rebeca to work from time to time for the television program, he told Sarah that he was pleased for her for not giving up on her education, he was then surprised to hear that it was one of Rebeca's conditions that they furnish her with a teacher, so that she does not waste any time in the studio, and she had surprised the producer when she told him herself that it was her condition. Her mother sitting next to her affirmed that indeed it was her, she never got a word in!

The next day Debra called Sarah to tell her that her first appearance will be in approximately in six weeks' time, she will do her best to be there at the same time, Rebeca thought that it was nice of her, and from now on it is going to be homework before anything else, now she has to decide whether to more or less finish learning Arabic, or go back to clean up the German first, she could not learn both languages at the same time, and stay up to date with her homework. She told her mother that she would sleep on it, then she asked her if we knew any Arabic speakers, the answer was no, so now Rebeca is going to do a bit of research to find somebody somewhere who she could converse with in Arabic, and that will speed the learning!

October is when Rebeca was born, on the very same day as her birthday the Arabic solution solved itself; what had happened was unexpected, it was a Wednesday the fourteenth of October, her birthday, Sarah had to attend school with all the teachers, for a special early meeting before school started, so Rebeca arrived at school earlier than usual, she had to hang out in the playground for almost half an hour, there were already children messing about in the playground, they formed various groups, so Rebeca looked around to see if she knew anybody in any of the groups, she spotted four or five girls huddled together. She realised after a while, that there was a girl in the middle of the group who was being abused by the others, so she started to walk towards them, as she got closer to the group, she could see what was happening; the girl was obviously frightened, the others were all shouting at her and pushing her about.

Rebeca could understand right of way what it was all about, they were all first-year students, and the poor girl was wearing a head scarf, she must be a Moslem and that was the reason for the abuse.

Rebeca shouted to the girl in Arabic, asking her to just walk away from them, and come towards her. The shock of hearing this ''English Rose'' speaking in Arabic with an authoritative tone brought the other four girls to a complete standstill, then they moved away. It turned out that Fara who had just turned twelve, with her parents was a refugee from Iran, they lived quite close to Rebeca, her father was an architect and her mother who as it happens did not speak much English stayed at home. Rebeca had solved her problem, Fara was relieved about the abuse for the moment at least, and she was still in a bit of a daze, she could not work out who Rebeca was, she never heard an English person speak so well in her language. Rebeca walked into the school building with her, and at the same time gave her some good advice; she told her not to come to school that early, and she asked her if it was possible not to wear a head scarf, because that on its own, it gave her a label, which is why she was attacked. Then before each going their own way. Rebeca asked Fara if she could visit their house so that she could speak to both her mother and father, the answer was yes, and Fara was going to tell her parents when she arrives home, and they will arrange it for tomorrow.

Sarah was not happy to think that some pupils could be so awful, but she was pleased that her daughter managed the situation well, and now if Rebeca can play her cards' right, learning Arabic is going to go well. The next day after school Sarah and Rebeca gave a lift to Farah, who had invited Rebeca to her house to meet her parents. They were nice people, the father was working in the local council planning department, he was well spoken, and he appeared to be a kind person, the visit was mostly all in Arabic except when Rebeca came across a word she did not know. They were well pleased that Rebeca had helped their daughter, and they appreciated the advice given to Fara, going to school a bit later made sense to both of them, but not wearing a head scarf was not going to be easy for them, Rebeca argued just a bit with them, she told them that if she went to their country she would be forced to have a scarf, but in England it is up to you as far as the law is concerned, but if Fara was to always wear one eventually she would become a second class citizen, that is the problem, it is a matter of perception by others, you might just have realised that religious people are very much in the minority in England, and that is one of the problems, then she asked Faras' mother if she had learned English yet? The answer was no, she started to tell them about herself, and she explained that she is a busy person, did you see me on the news in July? The answer was no, so she told them a very shortened version of what had gone on, plus that she was going to be regularly on television, starting in six weeks' time, but I have put aside two hours a week to learn more Arabic especially reading and writing, then she addressed herself to the mother, telling that if they were to spend two hours together every week, it would be beneficial for both of them. The father, mother, and daughter all smiled at that idea, so Rebeca told them that before Saturday she will have worked out a time, and she will be happy to walk over to their house. The father asked her how old she was, she told him that yesterday was her fourteenth birthday, at the same time she told that she is fluent in Urdu and French but not too good in German, poor guy, she left him shaking his head from side to side having a hard time believing what he had just heard, Five or six minutes later she was home telling her mother what she had proposed, and they were both happy. 'Mum, what was that special meeting about yesterday morning?' The answer was useless, 'nothing dear.'

Nine in the morning on Saturdays for two hours, is when Rebeca was available for at least the next three months, for the double lesson with Farah's mother. After a while they both developed a system, Rebeca would say a short meaningful phrase in English, get the other one to repeat it at least ten times, then write it down and read it aloud, then after a short discussion, it was then Rebeca's turn to repeat it at least ten times and write it down and read it aloud. That system worked very well for both, and progress was made. Rebeca had become a special friend to the family, she always arrived back at home with a bag of delicious homemade sweets. One day she proposed an idea which she had thought about, 'Right I sort of understand why women feel that they have to follow a custom, the main reason is because they don't want to appear different to all the other women, so I have an idea for Fara' she paused for effect which was a good idea, as it gave them all time to ruminate on the subject. 'I have in my bag one of my collection of scarves, if Fara could wear it around her neck, it will look absolutely normal, she will get used to it and that will be a problem solved for ever!' Fara's parents were both looking interested, Fara herself was smiling a broad smile, her mother was looking at her wishing that it were herself now not wearing a head scarf! Then the father did not want to hurt Rebeca, and surprisingly told them all that it was a clever idea, and Rebeca made a gift of her scarf to Fara. As she left for home, Rebeca could not miss the father moving his head from side to side again as he had done on her first visit, she was ever so pleased.

Rebeca's first taste of a television studio was on the second Tuesday in November, the first shock for her is the time she was going to be picked up, seven in the morning! To make matters worse her mother could not get the time off work, she had too much on that week. The driver was ever so nice, he reminded her of her grandfather, he gave her the choice to sit next to him, or at the back, she chooses to sit in front and keep talking to the friendly driver. The studio was not that far away, it was at Ealing Studios about twenty-five minutes away in Ealing she remembered once watching a film in black and white that had been made there, that made her feel good. When they arrived, first the driver stopped at a gate and spoke to someone, then he stopped again in the car park, and escorted her to a reception area, also made certain that somebody else was taking charge of her. A lady gave Rebeca information; advice and rules for the whole building, the first rule was that one's mobile telephone must be on silence, which is when the studio area is entered then it must at all costs be switched off. The lady told her that they are going to meet with the director who will decide if they want to change her clothes, with the director there will be an advisor for what she should wear, they had not decided if they wanted her to look even younger or older, that will decide her attire, is she going to wear the same every time? Then there was going to be the question about makeup. Rebeca half expected that it would be like that. Then the same lady told her after an hour or two she will meet the cast for today and the crew, and she can ask any question to anyone at any time.

Rebeca heard a voice behind her, it was Debra, oh! Where they both ever so pleased to meet up again, it was never ending hugs and Debra told the lady who so far had been looking after Rebeca that she will take over now and proceed to the director's office. Rebeca was looking forward to meeting the director again, she was wondering what it was they were planning for her to do. When they entered the director's office, there must have been a dozen people there, they were all going to have a say on what they wanted Rebeca to do, and to wear, it was not the first time that the team had worked with young people. They had all studied Rebeca and although they much appreciated her skills, they all had the feeling that this fourteen-year-old little girl, can surprise others by them finding themselves wrong footed. She would not do that to be mean or gain points, it was always for the best reason, with a touch of common sense.

The director had already decided to let Rebeca have her own way, for the first and second appearance and then attempt to give her a scrip for her to follow. Now they had to decide on her attire, which was not an easy decision to make, most wanted her to look younger, as that will be more impressive and work well because of her height, no, her lack of height! Then it was a matter of makeup and hair style;

good, the makeup was just a suspicion of pink on her cheeks, her hair was not going to be cut at least for now, it was combed into a tail at the back with an elastic-coloured band holding it in. Then there was the question of the dress, they choose pink to match her cheeks, then it was the turn of the presenter, who asked Rebeca if she had a new story she wanted to tell, and if so, what is it about? At last, they are asking her for something, the last hour had been a bunch of people deciding, what they were going to do with her, never once asking her opinion. And yes, she had a story she could tell, it was about her new friend Fara, she did not mention names of course, and she told the whole story as it happened, about teaching English at the same time learning Arabic, then the suggestion for Fara to wear a scarf around her neck. That started a heated discussion because a couple of people thought it might offend some Muslim parents. Rebeca took control and told them all in no uncertain term that girls that age do not have to wear a head scarf, it is not part of the Muslim religion, she has that knowledge on good authority. It seems that one of them did not to believe her and was sticking to his own view. Rebeca took a liberty and was now in control of the situation, she started to speak fluently in Arabic, of course that was not going to be enough for the young man, she asked him if he had ever read the Koran, he nodded in the negative 'well if you wish I will attempt to remember a passage about hair cover for women'. Poor guy he gave up! So that is what she is going to talk about, after she has been introduced by the presenter, who thought it was going to be a good show today.

A lady came around with a trolley covered in drinks and biscuits, of course there was coffee and tea and to Rebeca's delight a choice of two milk shakes, she picked the banana one, but no biscuits, not even one. Then she was taken to the wardrobe department to try on a pink dress, when she tried the first one, yes it was the right colour, the right fit but it did not look right, so the lady asked her to take it off and Rebeca just refused, why? The lady asked, and Rebeca answered. 'What it needs is a black wide belt, that's all.' The lady had a young assistant who did not wait to be asked and darted into another room and came out with the belt Rebeca had described, and before the lady in charge had uttered a single word it looked fantastic on the pink dress Rebeca was wearing, there really was a little problem because it made her look a tiny bit older! But it made her look both pretty and intelligent, so that had now been decided. The lady could not wait to tell all the others what to expect! She enjoyed having her hair brushed repeatedly, they sprayed something on her hair she had no idea what it was, but the result was really nice, it was the turn of the makeup people, and it did not take more than ten minutes to accentuate her pink cheeks. The last thing now was back in the wardrobe department for shoes, Oh heavens! How stupid can they be to expect me to wear those ugly shoes; that was Rebeca's first thought when she looked at a pair of plain black shinny girls' shoes, they were the ones with a single strap and buckle, there was absolutely nothing smart looking about them, and in any case, she would not feel comfortable in them, so that was that.

It was eleven in the morning, and Rebeca sat with the presenter and discussed in detail what she was going to talk about today, then she met some of the regulars, there was a comedian and three more children all a tad older than her, she got on well with everybody else in the crew, they were going to start filming at two this afternoon, and Rebeca was looking forward to it. The director understood Rebeca was going to be a difficult child, however because of her knowledge and being driven by common sense, they might from time to time learn different things, she had come over as a diplomat who does not want to upset anybody, but at the same time she has no problem getting her way, all for the right reasons.

Lunch was nice they were all well looked after, they all ate in the same large sort of canteen come restaurant, even the producer and director were there, and they had no problems it seems circulating amongst the crew, for Rebeca it felt like a large family. At two there were all in the studio, the director asked Rebeca to take a chair and sit directly behind her and learn by watching. Then suddenly there was complete silence except for a lonely voice, counting two minutes down. The first thing Rebeca noticed was how important the lighting arrangement was, it seems that they all wanted to be in the light, the presenter was the first one that started talking, she introduced today's program, which included a special guest who they had been looking to appear, and today is her first appearance. Of course, that was Rebeca, and after the usual programs had been delt with it was Rebeca's turn, somebody had quietly disturbed her sitting behind the director, she followed the person to the side of the "stage."

Whilst in front of the camera, Rebeca could not see the absolute concentration everybody had watching the little girl about to speak and tell her story of the day; she was almost like a long distance runner, she took her time carefully explaining as she went along, her punctuation was close to perfect, she had no problem building up to a subject of interest, eventually when she came to the end of the story about Fara and the scarf, she made a joke saying that they should call that scarf: Rebeca's scarf! That had been unexpected but welcomed. The director and others were already thinking that she was going to be good, and they were going to make sure that Rebeca was not going to be showered with admiration, it is not good for a child. That went all wrong, people had become emotional and could not help themselves congratulating Rebeca, who thought what she had done was normal. That first day Debra took her home, she wanted to talk to Sarah, who eventually managed to have the afternoon off, she was home when Rebeca arrived with Debra.

The first question Sarah asked: 'How did it go?' she really had not have needed to ask, she could see looking at both, that they had a big smile, yes, a big smile. First it was Rebeca who told her mother that all the people there were all so nice, she told her about the pink dress, and how she complimented it with a wide black belt, she felt special in it, 'yes mum they took an awful lot of photographs of me,

I loved it all'. Then as she was still talking, she went into her bedroom to call her friend. Now Debra had the chance of speaking with Sarah, she told her about not looking too excited when Rebeca finished her speech, but all those good intentions were completely forgotten, she was that great!

By next Monday everybody in the school had watched the whole program, the headmaster was really intrigued with the scarf story, he had already been told, that Fara had changed the way she wears her scarf, and he had never realised that the instrumental person, was Rebeca herself! Yes, he agreed, it should be called the Rebeca scarf. Monday also was a difficult day for Rebeca, all kind of remarks were floating around her, and she wanted to get on with learning, it appears as if that is going to happen again, so she did not try to draw attention to herself. By her third television appearance, it was no longer a big deal at school and in any case Christmas left its mark, so now whatever Rebeca was up to, did not matter anymore, every Saturday morning it was always the same, a double Arabic and English lesson, Fara's mum was doing well, she was surprising herself, she had attempted to learn English with the help of her husband, he was not a patient man, and from time to time the lesson would transform itself into an argument, but with Rebeca it was always fun, and she loved teaching the little girl her own language.

It is now April and they are thinking of a holiday, obviously the cottage in Cornwall was still available and they were tempted, Peter and Juliet were still together, and one night when the four were all in the apartment, Juliet surprised the other three, apparently her mother and father both, would absolutely love to meet with Rebeca and her mother, they are invited to have lunch with them one Saturday, they live just south of the town of Oxford, in an area called Little London, it is by a lock on the Thames called Stanford Lock, a very picturesque part of Great Britain, after lunch they will be given a ride in a beautiful motor boat. Of course, they had no problem accepting the invitation, and they were already looking forward to it.

Rebeca was not worried about missing the Arabic lesson, as it happens she had not caught up with her mother, no, she has gone right past her, she would almost be able to pass as an Arab girl if she was to hide her face, her reading and writing were now on par with Fara, and the best of all, Fara's mother is beginning to think of getting a job, and that is really good news, that family is so happy, and yes Fara is still wearing the Rebeca scarf, not only that she has convinced a few more girls to do the same, Oh yes the television people, were never approached by anyone about the scarf in that first episode, so after all Rebeca was right.

The weather was improving every day, and one of them when the forecast was planned to be a sunny day, was the time that Peter drove them in his car to Little London, it took two hours to get there, and they were met by Juliet, who then introduced her mother and her father. They all entered the house and were directed to the lounge, where they were offered a cup of tea, it was a weak tea without milk made just to be refreshed before lunch which was beginning to appear on the dining room table, Juliet's father Robert stayed with the guests and for something to talk about, he started to describe some parts of the house which they will see later, then he asked if anybody had ever been on a motorboat, that question was really for Sarah and her daughter, Peter had often been on their motor boat on the Thames. A sole voice answered that last question, 'yes I have had a whole hour on a lifeboat helping the crew of a sailboat that had sunk in the English Channel.' Robert realised that he had forgotten, yes, he did see some of the photographs in the press. The very first thing Rebeca has said to Robert put him at a slight disadvantage, and he must correct that soon!

Robert spent his adult life as a diplomat for the British Government, he was educated at Oxford and for at least twenty years after they were married, they lived in various British Embassies in the Middle East, they spent the longest time in Egypt which they both loved. There is some French spoken in Egypt, then of course the people there mostly speak Arabic, and Robert can speak both. Lunch was a complete surprise for Sarah and Rebeca, it was a typical Arabic meal; Couscous with Lamb and so many vegetables, the Couscous was as light as a feather and the vegetables were in a huge dish covered in a tasty clear sauce, Sarah and Rebeca had never eaten such a tasty dish, they will never forget it, with the meal they all had mint tea, there was no desert only a few biscuits that were covered in what looked like honey and they were to die for! In the house on the ground floor, Robert had a huge study which itself accommodated a library of books, that much Rebeca had never ever seen in a house. She mentioned it, and he was pleased; 'Rebeca would you like to go and see all the books?' Of course, the answer was yes, and off they both went to the study where Robert was going to do his best to recover from his first Faux Pa. Rebeca attempted to memorise as many book titles as she could, some of them interested her more than others. Unusual thoughts went through her mind, if Peter marries Juliet, Robert will become a relative, yes then I can borrow some of his books that would be good. Robert could almost feel that she loved his books, no he did not have the same thoughts, she did pull one book out, placed it on a desk and carefully flipped all the pages to get the feel of the book.

Another surprise for Rebeca when Robert started to talk to her in Arabic, he spoke well but he still had an English accent, he had been smart in using a couple of words that really did not belong in that sentence, he was hoping that it would catch her out. She had a bit of a nerve, she was sat at a desk and he was still standing, so before she replied to his question, in Arabic she more or less ordered him to sit, and much to his surprise he did what he was told, there was a clear notepad and a pencil on the desk, and she took the liberty of using them both, and wrote her answer to him in Arabic, she handed it to him and whilst he was reading it she corrected his use of those two words, at the time speaking in Arabic without the slightest trace of an accent! This fifty-eight-year-old man had no chance! He was now beginning to feel comfortable with Rebeca, especially after he heard her speaking first in French with a Parisian accent, then change to a Provence accent. He realised that he had met his match, and he was pleased, at last with Rebeca's cooperation he can exercise speaking in those two languages, even more strange, he was thinking of Juliet and Peter! They sat for an hour at least, talking about languages, about the Television show she is on, he had never watched a children's program, he told Rebeca what a good idea about the head scarf, when she told him that Saturday mornings she teaches English to an Iranian lady, who in turn teaches her Arabic, that's how come she can pronounce the words correctly.

'Now, this is the time you must hear my mother recite the poem by Omar Khayyam about the mother talking to her daughter.' He had completely forgotten that Sarah also was a linguist, and in any case, it was time to re-join the rest, they are supposed to be boating that afternoon. The rest were all in the lounge waiting for them to come back, and when they both walked in there was a round of applause. Robert told how he was impressed with Rebeca, he said 'my god, she knows more than me!', she turned around oh, that's only because now I get an awful lot of practises. He thought how can a girl that age be so considerate? Then he asked Sarah if she could be so kind, he was told that she knows a lovely poem by Omar Khayyam, he would be so happy to hear it. Of course, Sarah had no problem, Rebeca asked him if he had a handkerchief? And said no more. It all went quiet; Juliet's mother and father were all ready for it. Sarah started and by the time she had finished, both Juliet's parents had wet eyes, it was a lovely scene, Robert turned to Rebeca and quietly told her that she was right.

They all piled into Roberts big car, and in less than five minutes found themselves by the bank of the Thames, next to a beautiful well looked after motorboat, Rebeca could not wait to get on it, it was almost the same size as the Lifeboat last summer. They had brought some food for tea, and after a tour of the boat, it was time to cast off. Rebeca did not dare ask if she could "drive" the boat, out at sea was easy as one is not liable to crush into another boat, but on the river, it is a different story, but she stood next to Robert all the time watching his reaction with other boats, he could sense that she was absorbing everything around her. They had travelled at least five miles going towards London when Robert asked her if she wanted to steer the boat, the answer of course was yes, and that little girl started to steer. She had sat on the seat, and without having been asked, Rebeca said out loud what manoeuvre she was doing whenever another boat was coming toward them, and Robert did not help her at all, he seemed to be more pleased than she appeared to be. Peter and Juliet already knew where they were going and were now getting ready with rope in hand to dock at a favourite place which is a little deserted island in the middle of the river.

The sun was shining, it felt warm there were no mosquitoes, and the setting was so perfect. It was now time for tea which they all had on the rear deck, Rebeca was interested and asked Robert if she could go below to look at the engine, he went with her. She had not realised that there were two engines, and that they were so big, she had a good look around them, and she kept pointing to various things on the engine, each time asking Robert for the name, he was so pleased to tell her everything she wanted to know. Then she noticed a third engine, which was minor compared to the other two, he had to explain that the engine she is looking at, is only for making electricity to charge some big batteries which he pointed to. He asked her to touch the side of one of the engines, it was pure white in colour and exceptionally clean. When she did touch it, she was surprised because it was still hot. They went back on deck Rebeca pleased having had a look at what drives this boat, and Robert also pleased that somebody was interested with the engines and even more so because it was so unexpected.

They all returned having had a wonderful afternoon, Rebeca could have stayed there all weekend, she would have been ever so quiet, parked in the study reading as much as she could, Robert wished that Rebeca could have stayed also. But now that he knows her and what she can do, he is going to help with her education, to make sure that she will be going to Oxford as he had done himself.

Chapter Seven - Holiday Time Again

'Mum, what does an ambassador do?' Rebeca three months later, for no apparent reason remembered Robert that sometimes he would be (Acting Ambassador). Sarah had to do a bit of quick thinking, and she told her daughter that he represents his own country and conveys information to the country he happens to be in. 'So, mum it's a good job then,' of course the answer was yes. There was going to be a brake for Rebeca, the television crew were all on holiday for two months. Fara's mother did get a job working in the hospital nearby, and they both decided to give their Saturday morning a rest for the summer, but in the meanwhile if neither one of them needed any help, they could always speak on the telephone. As the end of the school year was coming closer, all the subjects that were taught needed to have exams for the students, it changed the atmosphere in the school, everybody were revising.

Rebeca was pleased with her French which had been easy for her, she realised how lucky she had been with maths, and ended up fifth in the class, which was alright but not her best, all the other subjects, she was tops with straight A's. Now she had started to leave Arabic for a while, and she wanted when she is back at school, to make a real push and at last conquer the German language, the problem with her is that some while back she had taken a dim view of all the unnecessary long words, they tend to ad words to other words to make a new one. She was going to learn enough so that she can call herself a Polyglot like her mother. After the German she was going to learn about government and ships engines, those two engines in Robert's boat have stayed in her mind all that time. But during the summer brake she is not going to study too much, she has not yet told her mother that she would love to be able to recite her poem, and others from the same Poet. Her and her friend have been looking at boys, telling each other, which one at school they would not mind going out with, strange when she is not with her friend, she would not give a boy a second look.

It was decided that they will spend two weeks in the cottage at the end of July, but before that time had arrived there was some very good news, Peter and Juliet had decided to get married, and now they are officially engaged, that has made two other people very happy. It also means that there is going to be a change for Sarah and her daughter, when the marriage takes place Peter and Juliet are going to buy a house for themselves, and Sarah will have to move somewhere else because the apartment they are in is too big for them, but that will be next year. Rebeca cannot wait to be fifteen, she does not know why, it is just a feeling. She is lucky her bank account keeps going up, she has never spent any money from her account, but she already has plans for it, one Sunday Robert came to visit with Sarah and Rebeca, he came on his own just to have a chat with the "little girl". He brought three books from his library, he thought she would like to read. One was about ancient Greece, another one was a technical book on ships engines, then there was a book about Egypt in the twentieth century. Sarah thought it strange that her daughter would be interested in ships engines, it just does not make any sense.

Robert will know if she did read the Egypt book, because he has a mention in it! He stayed about an hour and a half; he had been on his way to London to meet old colleagues. He left Rebeca with a dilemma, which one is she going to read first? It was in the end easier not to select the first one, no she selected the last one which she was going to read, and that was the one about marine engines, she was going to read it at the cottage, it felt right for her, so, she started with Egypt. Before supper Rebeca had finished the second chapter, not a single sound had left her bedroom, she found it fascinating that was not surprising, she just loved learning about her surroundings and life. Rebeca, it turns out had two great advantages, the first one was the ability to read fast, and the other one was a photographic memory, her uncle Peter also had a good memory, not so much for words but for shapes.

Rebeca had some revision for school the next day, so she addressed that on Sunday evening, but still managed an hour or so on Egypt before going to sleep. Two weekends later, there was a big party, everybody who were acquainted with the newly engaged couple were invited to Juliet's parents' house, and planning had started, of course Sarah and Rebeca were first on the list, and Peter's mother and father were invited, but they both found an excuse to not go. Something had happened the last three months the little girl was not so little anymore, it was as if someone had wound her up, at last she was growing, and she had to have new clothes, one dress she had not worn yet, she now was saving for the party.

It took her a whole week, to read about Egypt the first time. There were many times in the book when old Egypt was mentioned, Rebeca had never learned about the old Egypt a long time before Christ ever appeared, the other thing she only realised towards the end, when she had seen the name "Robert" before a surname it dawned on her that it was her friend Robert who had lent her the book, now she knew Juliet's' Surname, and she will surprise her the next time she meets her.

From now on there was not too much pressure at school, it was close to holiday times. Rebeca was trying to be officially evaluated in Arabic, then this summer she wanted to clean up German finally. The two weeks soon came, Rebeca started to look a bit more mature wearing the new dress that she had chosen for herself, her mother at the time was not excited about it, but now seeing her in it, she looked adorable, she even had a new pair of shoes, she had learned at the television studio how to use make up, how to walk when wanting to be noticed, how to brush her hair; it had been almost an acting class. A week after the party, they were off on holiday to the cottage the four of them.

Rebeca did not return either of the three books yet, so far, she had read the Egypt book twice, she wants to refer to it when she was struck by something new. She had read the one about Greece once, but she thinks it deserves another quick look over, the engine one she is taking on holiday with her. Driving to Oxford took a bit longer than last time, Sarah had no problems there seemed to be more traffic this Saturday afternoon. Rebeca never lost the way there; they did not have to stop to look at a map or double back on themselves to change roads. Again, it was a warm sunny day a tad warmer than last time, oh! There were a lot more cars than last time, and when they arrived at the door they were greeted by Juliet's parents, Sarah was surprised when she heard her daughter greet both the parents at the same time, 'good afternoon Mr and Mrs Collin' she could not understand what it was all about, However Robert understood right of way and he winked at her, she just quietly said 'yes' they were developing their own code, these were exciting times.

Sarah and Rebeca did a tour of introduction around four or five groups of people, many of which recognised Rebeca from the television program, she never minded answering questions, always surprising people with the answer, that did not last too long, because the first chance she had was in the study, on her own attempting to learn all the titles by heart, after a while she realised that she was making a mistake, because there were just much too many books, so, she took her mobile telephone out of one of the two pockets in her dress and she managed to photograph the lot! Some snacks were being served and she felt a little hungry, not for food no, for treats, there was nobody else her age there, so she had to make do teasing the odd person including Juliet who was helping with the snacks, Rebeca went up to her and told her that she is not going to be Miss Collin much longer, they both enjoyed the joke. Rebeca told her how she found out what her surname was and that she thought that he had planned it, to see if she had read the book, they both had a smile, later there was three cheers for the couple with everybody holding a glass of Champagne, including Rebeca with less liquid in her glass.

There was a lot of talking and laughing, and of course a fair amount of alcohol consumption. Rebeca had settled herself in the study, reading what looked like an old book which was covered in leather, the book was published in 1820 the pages had become yellow from old age, and the paper was thick compared to todays, but best of all it was about mathematics as it was then, she was enjoying reading about the past, how people were able to discover almost anything, these days Rebeca came to the conclusion that we take too much for granted. She was disturbed by two young women who needed her attention, she knew one of them already, she was the bride to be Juliet, she had a friend with her, called Janet, they had both been close friends at university, they were known as the twins, because their names were so similar. Janet gained a psychology degree and now works in a hospital taking care of people who have mental problems. She had heard a lot about Rebeca, and she would love to have the opportunity of evaluating an idea, which she had about Rebeca. Janet had earlier asked Robert if they had a pack of playing cards in the house, and yes, it is in the top left-hand draw of the desk in the study.

Juliet introduced her friend Janet, telling Rebeca at the same time, if they could play a sort of a game with her, no problem, Janet pulled the pack of cards out of the draw, she gave them to Juliet, and asked her to take five cards out of the pack, place them face up in her left hand, then carefully place them face down in a random fashion on top of the desk, then spin right round just once and see how many cards she can identify before turning them over. She managed four out of the five, Juliet was congratulated, then it was the same thing for Rebeca, and when it came to the last bit, she had no problem naming the five cards, and they cheered, Janet was the clever one, she did not have to do it. Then it was Juliet's turn again with ten cards, oh a disaster this time she only managed three cards. Then it was Rebeca's turn with ten cards, to make it harder for herself she spun three times which surprised Janet, she managed the ten cards almost without thinking, and she herself asked to do it again, but with twenty cards, just then Robert walked in to see what they wanted the cards for, when he realised what was about to happen he had to stop and watch, he saw Rebeca place the twenty cards randomly on the desk, go out of the room and speak to her mother, then come back, surprised that there were now almost ten people watching, waiting to see if she can make it work for her.

'There were three Aces' she said as she picked them up one by one, 'Ace of spades, Ace of Clubs, Ace of Diamond', there was complete silence, then 'would you prefer I picked them all with a story one by one for the excitement, or shall I do it all at once?' There was not a single sound, so Rebeca decided to take her time and make little comments with each card, then there was a big cheer at the end, and people in the garden started to come in, they were all too late for that grand finale, and eventually there was the "Twins" and Robert left with Rebeca still in the study. She now was going to come clean with Janet, too late she had gone, but there was still a good audience, she then explained what she was going to do next. She asked a chap there to shuffle the cards, she then placed the 52 cards face down on top of the desk, asked someone to keep track of the time and tell her when 5 minutes had gone by, she started talking to herself more or less addressing Janet, 'that was not a game you wanted to play, no you wanted to find out if I have a good memory, well, I can tell you that a couple of months ago, I did the same with 60 cards, and that is the first time I knew that I could manage more than 52, my goal is to manage 100, I spend ten minutes every day in my room, you are the first witnesses to my memory, I know that it is one of the reasons I have no difficulty learning anything I want to learn, it's like a girl wanting to be a champion swimmer, she would have to practice every day, she would need a coach and I don't'. She knows now how to stun an audience, and she had realised that she was playing well. One now could smell the coffee, it was going to be dark in a few minutes time, and before leaving Rebeca gave Juliet, Janet, Robert and Peter a big hug telling each one that she is hoping to see them soon, and mother and daughter were off with Rebeca again on the front seat.

It is now the last week at school, and holidays will be here before next week, so there is not too much time spent learning, but a lot of planning is going on, the same time next week they will be on the road that will take them to the cottage. Rebeca kept going back to the party, although she enjoyed being there, she does not know why she did that showing off with the cards now she wishes that she had not done that, she is still obsessed with growing faster, she well understands that she is going to go to one of the Universities in Oxford, she does not want to take languages at University, no she wants something a bit more practical, she has no interest in Medicine, Architecture or the arts, she does not want to become an accountant, Rebeca does not do well, when she finds herself not able to decide what she wants to do, for her this is the time to point towards her goal in life, she is just hoping that by the time she reaches fifteen she will be able to see the road ahead, so for now she just had to keep going with her eyes well opened.

Well, that's what she did right up to when she was sitting in the back of her uncle's car, with her mother next to her. Juliet who was sitting in front, kept referring to what Janet had told her about her memory; first it was most unusual, then there are a lot of jobs that she would be well suited for. In fact, with her memory, she could learn anything she wanted. Janet did not realise, but that was Rebeca's constant thought these days. One thing she knows, is that she will have polished the German language before her next birthday, then she has to decide what next? Nobody ever enjoyed being driven on motorways, it really gets dead boring that constant noise the tyres make on the road surface, sometimes always for a short time, the road surface is so smooth that there is no noise, then it's like waiting for the other shoe to drop, and the noise is back. The car begun to slow down as Peter was approaching the Services after Bristol, and they all needed to get out.

Peter laughed to himself, the three girls had to make a dash to the lady's room, it is always the same! He just had to wait to lean against the wall, watching all the lady's coming out hoping its somebody he knows! The three were all smiling looking at him with the appearance of a Zombie. Next was the busy cafeteria, yes, there was a queue then they were searching the place for at least a couple of trays. 'Mom, can you get me a ham sandwich or salad, a cake and a Coke, and I'll go get a table' the order had been given and approved so Rebeca started the search for an empty table, it would have been easier if she was at least six feet tall, but eventually she noticed people just getting up from a table, and she went straight for it, before she actually sat down and made sure that her mother knew where she was. She had no problem moving all the used dishes to one side, and she had sat so that she could see the three moving slowly, then a strange thing happened; on the neighbouring table there were four people sat having almost finished their meal. Rebeca could not help noticing that they suddenly had stopped talking, one of them in particular who must have been the mother, had twisted her body to the left as much as could, on top of that she was doing the same with her neck. There were two children at the table, and Rebeca could hear her name, it had been the very first time Rebeca had been noticed.

It had been the girl who had noticed her first, she whispered the information to her younger brother, and he agreed with her, the father had no idea what the fuss was about, and the mother had to make sure that her daughter was right. Well, what an affair it turned out to be! The daughter spoke to Rebeca and asked her if she was right, the answer of course was that it really was her. They had a conversation, and they were told that she was on her way with her mother, and uncle, his fiancé to a cottage for a couple of weeks' holiday. The girl and her brother kept asking her questions: does she enjoy being on the television? Is she stopped often? What is she going to do when she grows up? That one was not an easy question, and she answered it without having a single thought about it, she just replied, 'sail around the world on my own!' then she was saved when her sandwich arrived. For the rest of the day, she tried her best to forget that reply, no of course she was not going to sail around the world, she was still making up her mind when she told them, only because it was a quick sharp answer they would accept, and then get on finishing their meal.

It took another four and a half hours more to reach the cottage. Sarah and Juliet stayed in the cottage organising whilst Peter and his niece, took a drive to the Fish restaurant to book a table for tonight, it was not yet open, but the door was not locked, and there were people inside getting ready for tonight's meal. The chef was sorting out some details about tonight's menu, he had his back to the door and the moment it opened; he turned around to tell the person who had walked in that they were not yet serving, what a shock when he noticed Rebeca, he lunged at her, picked her up and gave her a big hug, he was so pleased to see her. He called out to his partner at the back, she thought the place was on fire, then it was her turn, Peter was so pleased to see those two happy people, and of course they had just one free table for tonight, and yes, they will cook the same fish again, and they are most welcome.

What Peter and Rebeca did not know, was that the mayor was also eating in the same restaurant, and the chef called him the moment they left for the cottage, and the two of them organised an unusual surprise for tonight's meal. In the cottage everything had been aired, tea was now on the table, and slowly they all sat to have at least a cup of tea, and a completely dried croissant which should have been eaten in the car, but they had all forgotten about it. After they intended to relax until evening, Peter and Juliet were sat in the garden, no doubt talking about the forthcoming wedding, Sarah finished the washing up, then made the beds, and Rebeca found a good spot in the lounge, and she started to read the huge reference book on marine engines. She was learning something on every page, she did spend a lot of time understanding how a diesel motor operates, it took her a while to work out how the diesel engine fires at each stroke, no, it does not have a spark plug! When the piston is coming up it sucks the fuel into the cylinder, and before going back down the same fuel which has become a gas is compressed to such an amount that it explodes which eventually forces the fuel back in.

She thought that now at least she can understand how it works, and the rest of the afternoon, was a series of discoveries, and every so often one could hear the odd, pleasant exclamation. Rebeca at one time just could not believe what she was looking at, first a little pleasure boat engine with one cylinder only the size of a small washing machine, then a ships engine three floors up the size of three houses side by side, one could see some of the nuts in a picture that were every bit as big as a car tyre, she could not imagine one person who would do a technical drawing that big, and then had the nerve to start making the thing.

By the time seven arrived, they had all changed to go to the restaurant, Peter wondered why change? They were in a small fishing town, big enough to have a Town Hall, which was only a few steps away from the restaurant. They found it difficult to find somewhere to park the car, but eventually there was a spot exactly right for them. There were a lot of people sort of milling around with nothing to do, the restaurant looked to be ever so busy, and after at least ten minutes of window shopping, Peter held the door handle, then opened the door with it. The place was absolutely packed with people standing about it seems they were all waiting for Rebeca to arrive, she was cheered many times, the mayor asked for silence and then he gave a speech in honour of Rebeca who did not blush, no not like her mother!, they were all surprised and pleased, then the "patron" showed them to a particular well-dressed table situated by the window, all the people who had stood in the restaurant now were outside, and out of nowhere, musical instruments appeared and music started. Many musicians joined them, and they started with Spanish music and dancing, it was a concert which had been planned and well-rehearsed for that Saturday, but when they discovered that Rebeca was going to be there the mayor reorganised it.

Again, they had a lovely meal which the four enjoyed, and best of all they all seem to care for Rebeca, which was nice for her, she completely forgot about her future for the whole evening, and she really did not want it to stop, Peter thought better of driving back, he had drunk too much to be legal on the road, so it was up to Juliet to do the driving and they got back to the cottage with no difficulty. In a way Sunday was a disaster because it rained all day, but for Rebeca it turned out for the best, she managed to get to the halfway place in the marine engine book. She managed to learn the names of all the manufacturers of engines, the smallest ones all the way to the largest ones, that was in the morning, after lunch she learned about all the auxiliary components that were fitted to the engines, such as starter motors low-pressure fuel pumps and high-pressure fuel pumps and many other things. By about seven in the evening, she had hardly talked to anybody, and she had decided that she had done enough learning for one day. Now it was the time to play games, it was not possible as supper was on the table, oh boy, that Juliet happens to be a good cook.

There was a chess game in the cottage, and after supper they had a competition to see who the best player was, no, it was not Rebeca and she was pleased about that, her uncle Peter was the winner, however Juliet was an excellent player, but Peter had the edge over her. Sarah had a couple of quiet moments, she had been realising that her whole life the last fourteen years had been shaped by her daughter, and it is not going to be too far away when she will find herself completely alone. From time to time, she had been attracted up to a point by a couple of very nice guys, but it seemed that Rebeca always got in the way, and maybe now is the time to start looking especially as her brother will soon be gone with Juliet, and then in four- or five-years' time Rebeca could also be gone to Oxford. 'What's up mum? The answer was always the same:

'nothing darling' Sarah always had her dad to fall back on, these days they got on together very well, they often had long philosophical discussions which were always interesting, but it was not enough for her. So, that Sunday night when they all went to bed, there were two happy people who could not wait to fall asleep into each other's arms, there was one person who was beginning to feel all alone in this word, then there was yet another one who spent much too much time thinking of her own future. Well, they all got off to sleep!

The weather brightened up Monday, and they became proper holiday people, a spot on the sandy beach, in and out of the water at least three times, the odd ice cream, sausage and onions, chips on their own, a couple of Mars bars, coca cola. If all that was not enough, they had the nerve of ending the afternoon with a beef pie and a portion of mash potatoes each, that ended up being the last meal of the day. Tomorrow Tuesday the supermarket will be open, and they will do a whole week's shopping, they had an enjoyable time, with lots of laughter and fun teasing each other. But, by eight o'clock they all agreed that this was the last time they were going to have such a feed, they were all feeling full and uncomfortable around the midriff. That night all four found it difficult to get off to sleep. When somebody had said 'well tomorrow is another day' what they really meant was; tomorrow will be a better day we hope!

Again Tuesday was a sunny day, and after breakfast there was only one thing which had to be done, that was food shopping, so they did not waste any time and right after the washing up had been all finished, they piled into Peter's car, and before they had time to talk about anything they were in the parking lot of the Supermarket, there was no arguing, both Sarah and Juliet took charge of the shopping, and not before too long they were all back in the cottage. Not a single person dare mention the beach, no, instead Juliet mentioned the lawn, it was in a serious state of needing a cut, so she organised for Peter to help her, and for Sarah and Rebeca to have a nice walk into town, that made everybody happy, and next it was mother and daughter happily walking side by side all the way to the harbour, they both enjoyed being on their own for a couple of hours at least. It took them over a half hour to reach the harbour where all the fishing boats were. Rebeca had spotted something; 'oh mum look', she was pointing towards a little group of workmen, that were hauling a huge engine out of a fishing boat, Sarah did not dare ask what it was about, so she just answered, 'I see Rebeca, shall we go and take a closer look?' That is what was going to happen in any case, Sarah was being pulled with some force towards the scene. At the same time, she was trying her best to work out what it was Rebeca could see.

As they approached closer, Rebeca had a big smile, she recognised one of the men helping to set the engine down on a pallet, so that it can be transported, yes, she was sure it was him, he had not noticed her getting closer, she waited until he had finished his task, and called him 'Hi skipper!' All this time Sarah was still wondering what was going to happen next, she was pleasantly surprised when the man had not even looked back to see who it was, but exclaimed as loud as he could 'it's my Rebeca!' And of course, when he turned around, she was there and her feet had left the ground, he had completely forgot that he was wearing dirty greasy overalls, but that did not matter, he was so pleased to see her. Sarah stayed back a bit, and managed to listen to their conversation, first he had to tell her that he had something for her, it is at home, he will go and get it for her, then he asked her if she could remember the articles that were printed about the rescue of the American family, 'Rebeca did you ever see their names in any of the articles'. Rebeca could not really answer that question because at that moment she could not remember taking any notice of the names, she could remember the name of their daughter, because she did speak to her, it was Rose.

Then he told her that the father is a famous politician in America, and he has been in touch with the Royal National Lifeboat Institution to obtain your address, he is planning something special for her, the skipper had no idea what it was. Then it was her turn, and she told him that she would love to spend an hour or so if it was at all possible studying a marine engine, because she now knows all about them. It took him a while to digest that information, it confused him a bit, but then he thought; well, its Rebeca! It turns out that they were not going to move the engine until tomorrow, so the skipper thought this would be the right time for him to find out why she was so interested. He was going home to change and clean up and come right back with something special just for her, before leaving he sorted out a clean rag for her to use when she starts looking at the engine. He had a quick pleasant word with Sarah, then left.

Sarah had a bit of an idea, because she had a look at the book that had taken all Rebeca's attention this last week, and she stood by whilst the engine was being almost dissected by her daughter. Sometimes she could hear the odd comment coming from her: 'oh, that makes sense now, now I know what a starter motor looks like, that big round thing on top must be the air turbine', there were many mentions of motor parts. She discovered who was the company that had built that engine, she also worked out that the gear box was still attached to the engine, where the injectors were, and which one was the alternator. By that time the Skipper had returned, for a while he just stood behind her listening to her talking to herself, all the time being amazed that a fourteen-year-old little sweet girl would know all the names of every part of a marine engine and be able to identify all the parts. He gave her a bit of a shock when he spoke to her, she had not realised that he had been there all the time, and then he asked her if she knew how the engine worked; the immediate answer was, 'of course', and then because he has said nothing in reply as if he was expecting more, she carried on telling him that the diesel engine was invented in France by the son of a German couple who had emigrated there and had another son who was also born in France. The problem with using a reciprocal engine for a boat, is that there is a speed limit for the propeller, if it turns too fast the propeller will destroy itself. So the first consideration on the design of a marine engine is that the pistons must travel up and down as far as possible, it is called a long stroke, and if it is still too fast for the propeller they use a gear box to reduce the speed, at the very top of the stroke the piston has compressed the air which has been charged with fine drops of the diesel fuel and it becomes so hot that it explodes pushing the piston back down which in turn rotates a big shaft called the crankshaft and that is all there is to it!

The Skipper almost needed to sit down, he dare not ask her anymore questions, he needed a rest, so he started to talk to Sarah, and he explained to her that the Royal National Lifeboat Institution had given Rebeca a Certificate which tells that she attended the rescue of Yacht "Maybe" which had sailed all the way from the USA with a family on board, Rebeca had used her own camera to photograph the whole rescue, and attended to the family who were still in shock when she was only twelve.

There was still time for all to attend the local fisherman's snack bar for a tea or coffee, the Skipper lead the way and introduced Rebeca and her mother to all the fishermen there, they had all heard about Rebeca, some of them had even seen her on television, when it all quietened down and the three had a chance to start talking, The skipper could not help but to try and understand why, yes why marine engines? So, Rebeca had no choice but to tell, and now her mother was going to find out what she had not dared to ask. It was not going to be easy for her, she started by recounting that Saturday when they visited Juliet's parents, how she had been impressed by Robert's motorboat, she had gone below to look at the two engines, they impressed her, she steered the boat going down the Thames, she had to move over so as not meet head on other boats coming up river, she docked it on an island all without any problems Robert was amazed, and before they left to go back home, Robert had made up his mind which books he was going to give her, one of which was about marine engines. The last few weeks at School, she found herself under pressure, especially learning German, and her way of dissipating the pressure she was feeling, was to learn about something completely unrelated with her normal studies, that's all there was to it, as it happens, she found it all fascinating, and now she is ever so pleased having that knowledge. Sarah also was pleased that now she understands her daughter just that much more, and the Skipper was even more surprised how smart she really is, he is going to tell that story to everybody he knows.

Peter and Juliet had cut the grass and sorted most of the garden, they had a rest whilst waiting for them to come back, now something had gone wrong they thought, it was almost past lunchtime and they had not yet returned, what happened? They were both feeling hungry, so eventually they gave up waiting, and started to lay the table for lunch. It was typical, just as they started eating, mother and daughter walked through the door. They could not help noticing Rebeca holding a large envelope; oh, they have been shopping, Rebeca had a big smile, now they could not wait to find out what had happened. Sarah took over and told Peter and Juliet all that had gone on between the Skipper of the lifeboat and Rebeca. First, they wanted to have a look at the RNLI Certificate, they were more than impressed, Rebeca is going to show it on television. Then they found out about the marine engine business, including the reason. Then lastly about the American family that was rescued, when Rebeca was already on board the lifeboat. They are going to be in touch with her with a surprise! It turned out to be a perfect sunny day, however nobody was interested in going swimming, but they knew that they should get out and Rebeca had what she thought was the best solution for this afternoon; the other three were all not that keen but since neither of them could come up with an idea, they adopted Rebeca's plan for the afternoon, it was a long walk down to the beach, then walk along the sands to the rocks and now climb the now famous cliff, across the field with the cows, then walk back home, they should then all be tired and hungry, a perfect day!

First it was the application of sun cream for all, then four bottles of water and 4 hats, and they started maybe a little hesitantly walking towards the beach, the adults kept a conversation going, so as not have to think of the distance they are going to cover. Rebeca was simply putting one foot in front of the other, it worked for her. When they reached the beach, they all took their shoes off, and walked mostly in the water towards the rocks. Of course shoes came back on after they had sat on rocks to dry their feet and they started climbing, Rebeca in the lead, she was hoping to meet the friendly Cow at the top, and she was not disappointed, especially Juliet was not happy going to the top, the herd worried her, but then she could not go back, especially when Rebeca had started to talk to the head Cow who seemed to understand her, Peter grabbed Juliet's hand and more or less pulled her up to the top. After a while they all enjoyed the company, they were all friendly and curious, when they arrived at the gate even Juliet turned back and said goodbye to the Cows, from there on it was all downhill, and as predicted they were all exhausted, the good thing nobody got sunburn, they had been away for two and a half hours, and now they are occupying all the armchairs, and none of them intend to get up, not for a while at least. Sarah, Peter, and Juliet all thanked Rebeca for what turned out to be a brilliant idea.

The rest of the holiday went well, they ate out once more in the fish restaurant, and one night in the hotel where they were made very special people, there were some holiday makers who were trying their best to work out who they were, nobody told them, and most likely they never found out, Rebeca had taken Peter to see the engine on the dock side, and explain to him what everything was, she even took him for a coffee at the fishermen's snack bar, she was recognised , and a couple of the customers asked her if she was having a good time, he enjoyed himself talking to the fishermen.

Chapter Eight - Scotland Yard

The journey home this time was without any problems with the traffic, they stopped at the Bristol services again, which was not busy like last time. It made for a relaxing brake from the driving, a while later as they were approaching London, Juliet suddenly remembered a question she had been wanting to ask Rebeca for over a week, it was a bit awkward for her because she had to turn her head right back to see Rebeca. 'I have been meaning to ask you if you thought the Cow understood you when you spoke to her, that day on the cliff. The answer came without delay, 'that first time when I had reached the top of the cliff, it worried me a bit when I saw them all, then I noticed the cow that must be the leader, so I went straight up to her and caressed her neck whilst speaking in a friendly tone, that had seemed to do the trick, but then I realised that the cow was smart, I thought it best to go the shortest way to the road, but she pushed me towards the right, which eventually led me to the gate I had not previously seen, whether she understood me, we shall never know, but, yes she understood where I needed to go, so now it is difficult to decide and just for the sake of it, I would say yes.' Peter who was driving said that he agreed with Rebeca and that she had given a satisfactory answer.

They had left the cottage all nice and clean, the garden trimmed up, they had a nice chat with the neighbours, and they are all certain to return soon at least for a brake. Juliet's parents use to spend a lot of time there, but now they both are not keen on the drive, in any case where they have their home now, is almost a cottage in the country by the river instead of the sea, and that is where they will all be on Saturday next week, and of course Rebeca is looking to bringing back three more books, she had the image in her head, but every so often she would look at the photographs she had taken, to try and decide which ones were the best. It was a strange few weeks, no school for mother and daughter, that first week back home Rebeca had nothing to read, she met up with her friend, and the two went down the West End on the underground, they never told their parents which made it even more exiting for them, they walked the whole length of Oxford Street and looked at all the dresses in the shop windows. They did not stay long, although it was exciting for them, they were beginning to feel guilty, so as soon as they had reached Tottenham Court Road Underground station, they could not wait to say goodbye to the West End, and they kept smiling all the way home. They never told anyone about that outing, that was a secret between them, there was some good that came out of that trip for Rebeca, if she needed to, she could describe nearly all the big stores windows, some of the stores had so many windows that she counted them, and one day she will be surprising somebody for sure.

About twenty minutes away walking, the two girls could reach a famous shopping centre called "Brent Cross" and they often went there for the afternoon, they never bought anything but always had a cake and a soft drink at different snack bars. One of those days when the two girls were visiting the shopping centre, something happened that was going to change both their lives. They had decided to have a pot of tea for two, accompanied by two lovely big chocolate eclairs, that was always their special treat, and it was even more special because it was not a snack bar, no, it was a proper posh restaurant, which happened not to be too busy for a change. Waiting for the eclairs to arrive made the treat even better. On the table next to them there was a mother with a baby in a pram and a little girl sitting in front of her mother, the three made a constant noise which did not bother anybody else. The table next to the mother was occupied with two men, they were of maybe Pakistan appearance, both well dressed in smart looking very black beards, Rebeca noticed that they were talking sometimes in Urdu but other times in Arabic, and often they would mix both languages in the same sentence. Before they had both finished the chocolate eclairs, the mother with her two children moved away, now Rebeca could hear every word the two men were speaking, and when she understood what they were speaking about she realised that they could be in danger: the men were deciding which day they were going to drive a huge truck full of explosives at the gate that leads to 10 Downing street, the official home of the Prime Minister. Rebeca could not tell her friend whilst they were still there, and she had not solved the problem of what to do next, at that moment the waitress had come by to remove dishes from the table. Rebeca had it! She asked the waitress if she could take a picture of the two of them, the waitress obliged, and Rebeca made a lot of noise on how happy they were, one of the two men had a quick look and reassured himself that even if the girls could hear what they were saying, at least none of them could possibly understand, so they were still safe in the knowledge that it was impossible for the authorities to have planted a microphone. Rebeca excused herself, left her friend there telling her that she had to rush to the ladies, she was gone no longer then ten minutes, when she got back, she was out of breath. Whilst away from the table, she had managed to dial 999, and reported what was going on and where, she already had a photograph of the two men. She told them that she is a little white girl who happens to be fluent in Urdu and Arabic, they might have seen her on the television, she is going right back to the table to record the conversation until they leave, please don't send anybody in uniform, they could well be armed.

First the woman at the other end of the telephone, had started to doubt Rebeca's story but thought that she had recognised the name, so then she decided to do something about it. She called the most senior person on duty where she was. That started a real action two men and one woman all three in plain clothes and fully armed, were propelled to the Brent Cross shopping complex, they knew whereabouts was the restaurant, and made their way to the table where Rebeca and her friend where sitting, the woman in the group went straight to Rebeca and greeted her by apologising for being late. Rebeca understood right of way, but her friend was well perplexed, but because Rebeca appeared to be alright, she just went along. The two men were still there and did not seem to be ready to move. The three sat down with the two girls, and when the waitress came by, they ordered a pot of tea for three, but before she moved away Rebeca asked the waitress again to take a picture of the five of them, this time she had to take about three pictures to get them all in, and one of the shots included two good photographs of the two men with the beards. Again, the woman spoke and not knowing Rebeca's friend's name, she clearly addressed her as Janine and she told her that her mother was busy at the reception of the restaurant, why does she not go and surprise her? The poor girl had no idea what was going on, and only because her friend was using sign language and much approved for her to go, so, she left them.

At the entrance to the restaurant there were two policewomen in uniform, they grabbed her and without having said a single word, they took her to an office not far away where they were able to sit with her and tell her what exactly was happening, they reassured her that Rebeca was going to be alright, and by now half of the people nearby were all undercover police. One of the police officers sat with Rebeca had a much better recording system, so now the conversation of the two possible terrorists was being well recorded. The police were not going to arrest them at this time, but they wanted to find out what they were up to, and detain them at the right time, one of the policemen had handed a note to Rebeca's friend which she had handed to one the policewomen, it was telling his superiors that it seems that Rebeca was right, so it has now become a major operation, and they have to find the truck which is loaded with explosives.

The first action they took was to tell Rebeca to send the pictures to Scotland Yard, they did that by scribbling a note that included the Telephone number, it did not take her long to send all the pictures, and the recording so far. It took less than five minutes for one of the policemen at the table to receive a text from his office, telling him that the two men had been recognised, and that they are very dangerous, they are already under surveillance, and they meet in a public place where they cannot usually be listened to. They would have arrived either in one car or perhaps in two cars, they already know the cars both the men drive, so they are now searching for the cars to place under them a GPS tacking device, which will tell them where they are at any time. Rebeca all this time was well exited, she kept thinking to herself, (oh boy, this is better than a holiday!) She had a clever idea on what was going to happen next, and she was looking forward to it. All the London police force was now on special duties. Rebeca had not yet had the opportunity to tell them all that she had heard, and the time was going to come soon when they find out the details of the plan, these two terrorists were about to execute. They all had to leave, as the two terrorists had left the table and made their way to the huge multi-floor car park. A signal went to the crew that was identifying the cars that they were on the move; they had come in one car only and the police had dealt with it. Now at last they can relax again, the first question from one of the policemen was; 'you can really speak Urdu and Arabic?' he asked her, the answer he did not expect, 'and German and French as well, with English, that makes me a Polyglot' they had no idea what that was, but it sounded ever so complicated, one of them thought it would be a good question for a pub quiz.

Rebeca joined her friend in the office, and now she can tell the man who it appears to her was in charge, what she had heard before she started to record. His name was Paul, and he was most attentive wondering what it was that triggered this young girl into action. 'Paul, I must tell you what it was I heard that got me going, I had started to listen to their conversation, because they were both talking using two languages, Urdu and Arabic, I thought it so strange, then I realised that they were talking in a sort of code that would be most difficult to follow. So, I must have tuned my ear for the fun of it to try and see if I can make any sense of the conversation. And when I understood what they were planning, I was shocked!' Paul happened to be a patient person, but today he was beginning to lose it a bit, he needed the facts not the story, well he did not have to wait much longer. 'What I heard was this: they have a big truck somewhere which is loaded up with five tons of explosives, and they decided right in front of me, that both of them were going to drive it Tuesday the seventh of September at ten in the morning, they are going to crash the truck against the security gate at 10 Downing Street and blow the whole place up, and the two friends will meet again in heaven!' she had to have a rest, Paul then had only one thing to say to her, 'Rebeca you are a real Angel, so many people owe their lives to you'.

Paul used the office telephone and called his superiors, to tell them exactly what he had just heard this little girl tell him, there seemed to be a long silence at the other end, but eventually Paul received some instructions: they were already following the car, and they were hoping that the two might just drive to where the truck is parked, but in the meanwhile, could they take the two girls to their parents, and bring back Rebeca if possible with her mother, it turns out that they already had a file on Rebeca, something to do with the rescue of the crew last year. Paul thanked the restaurant for helping them, he told them that they will eventually find out what happened. Then first, they dropped off Rebeca's friend, who had become most excited now that she had found what had happened, she also realised that had they started whispering, they might have been in danger. Her parents were not only surprised but pleased that she had Rebeca as a friend. Next it was the turn of Sarah to be not so much surprised but shocked, and of course she wanted to go to Scotland Yard with her daughter.

The two police officers sat in front of the car, had to hear the whole episode of today's happenings, from the point of view of a young girl, whilst she was giving her mother all the details. When they arrived a lot of police officers and women wanted to look at Rebeca, it was not easy for them as they were immediately ushered into a conference room, where they were met by various officials, one of which happened to be of Pakistan descent, obviously to test Rebeca's knowledge of the language. After the introductions Rebeca was tested before anything else, the man who is going to do the testing, started to greet her in Urdu by asking her how she was, interestingly, there are two separate dialects, and Rebeca asked him which one he wanted her to use, and because she well understands both. He said nothing to her and just waited for her to answer his first question, but she wanted to play a game with him, Sarah realised what she was doing, and especially that she had been offended by the questioning of her ability, which had not been questioned many times in the past. Eventually she told him, that he is a nice man who happened to be doing something he had been ordered to do, then she changed the dialect, which made him react a bit as if he had received a shock, others in the room could not help but notice. Then before he had a chance of replying to her, she kept going telling him that she also speaks Arabic, German and French, she went even further by reciting a poem that sounded as if it had been written by Omar Khayyam all in Arabic, then finally she asked him if he had ever heard the Poem. At last, it was his turn and he answered yes, and before he could manage another word, she replied, this time in English that he was mistaken, as she had written that poem a week ago. All assembled there except for Sarah had not a single clue of what had just happened. 'Well, I must tell you that this little cunning girl here, was playing tricks on me, and I must admit her knowledge of my language, is far superior to mine, and she even recited a beautiful poem in perfect Arabic which she had composed herself just a week ago. So, you can all be certain that Rebeca is competent in many languages', and he was happy to be leaving the room.

The superior person who had taken charge was a very smart looking man, he was well dressed, and well spoken, he was well disposed, and he sat next to Rebeca, he asked her to repeat all that had happened so far, including especially the conversations she had heard between the two possible terrorists. She did not only tell what she had heard, but she also told them about her own thoughts as she went along, which was most informative for the team to hear. One of the officers suggested that she has a good memory, she told the man that he was right, but he did not know just how right he was. She then started to describe both men in full detail, including one with a scar on the back of his left hand, the other one who must have had an operation on the right side of his nose. They all had the photographs in a folder, and sure enough she was right. She then told her "Audience" why she can learn so much is because she has a photographic memory. Eventually they all realised that she was not a shy person, she was sure of herself and full of knowledge. They all had the information they required, and yet there was another unrelated question they would like an answer to, if possible.

This time Paul was the one asking why would the state department at the White House in Washington DC want your details and record? This time Sarah answered that, only a few weeks ago they had learned that a certain person who happens to be a personal friend of the President wants to surprise Rebeca, they don't know how but they do know why, two years ago Rebeca was a guest of the RNLI, on one of their boats, they had already travelled at least 15miles, when a sail boat called a mayday because they were sinking, it was this man with his wife and two children, they were more than 20 miles away and Rebeca stayed in the cabin with the skipper and when they reached the family floating around in a life raft, first Rebeca took as many photographs as she could, but then the four had to go below, to Rebeca it was obvious that they were all traumatised. So, she went down with them and just kept talking about her life, which made them forget about the last couple of hours, when they left, the man especially could not thank her enough. One of the police officers now remembered, because it was in all the Sunday papers, she was now aware that Rebeca was also a television personality.

Rebeca now had things for them to take care of, she did not want her name to appear anywhere in the media, it was alright for them to mention that it was a fourteen-year-old schoolgirl who helped them, but no more, however if she decides that she wanted publicity, would it be alright for them to confirm the facts. The other question she would love to be there when they discover the truck which is loaded with explosives, so that she could take some photographs, she realises that it will not be possible, but could they at least tell her that they had found the truck, and how they dealt with it.

She wonders now what she would do in their situation; her first idea was to disable the engine, no, because they could always tow it there, they could water down all of the explosives and make them ineffective, of course it depends on the location, if it is in the middle of a field they could just blow it up, the other thing is about the two terrorists, and for certain they will have no choice but to shoot them both dead. Paul asked her if she had got all that from the movies? No, she said 'it's just common sense!' Well, unexpectedly Paul drove mother and daughter home, he wanted to stay with Rebeca just that bit longer, in case he learns even just a little bit more, he was totally fascinated, he could not wait to tell both his wife and his daughter about the last four hours.

Next week was the last free week before having to go to school, the first thing Sarah said to Rebeca, was that she had not asked her permission for the two to go to Brent Cross shopping centre, it is one her mother could not win ever! The answer was typical Rebeca. 'Mum, just think how many people would have died if I had not followed my instinct!' Not another word was ever said about that subject, but of course when Peter came back, he had no choice but to sit and listen, in the back of his mind sometimes he would think that Rebeca learning all those languages is not going to result in anything useful in the future for his Niece. But now he can see how useful it can be. Then they drove to Grandfather and Sarah's mother, they spent two hours with them, they were both so excited but not too happy not being able to tell their friends. Then they drove to Grand Parents No.1, and they also had the same reaction, they in turn called their son James, and ordered him and his girlfriend to come over right of way. They turned up all worried thinking that one of them had taken ill. Before they arrived, James's father started to realise that James had not yet shared the knowledge of Rebeca with his new girlfriend, he was sort putting it off until he thought the time was right. The father thought it best to warn Sarah and Rebeca. Before James opened the front door, he was already aware that at least Sarah was there, but he got a big shock when Rebeca run up to him and put her arms around his neck, at the same time shouting out as loud as she could that she was pleased to see her dad! He just froze, and then she looked at his girlfriend whose name was Lara, and Rebeca told her that her father was somebody special, and he is the nicest man I have ever known. Then looking at Lara she said that she hopes that Lara loves him very much. And there was an answer, 'I do love him very much' and now they were already for today's happenings. James was so proud of his daughter, all these years he had never talked about her, he was always shy of introducing her in a conversation, nobody else had any idea that his daughter at the age of fourteen was a television personality and could speak five languages, no, he did not know what a Polyglot was!

After everybody knew what had happened, Sarah decided to tell them all about Rebeca and the man who was checking to see if she could speak Urdu and Arabic, she should not have done that, because now, she remembered about Rebeca's new poem. And of course, she wanted her to recite it again, but now there were conditions which she had not expected, well one condition at least; 'mum I think that my poem will sound even better if it is after yours! And in any case Lara has not heard yours yet, what do you think Grandad? And of course, the answer was yes with a smile, and at the same time he checked that he had a hanky in his pocket. James who sat next to Lara was heard telling her that she will not understand a single word because it is all in Arabic, but she will understand the poem, it is sad. And now Sarah had got up, and her personality completely change, sure enough Grandad pulled out his hanky, James was so silent, and Lara was seen wiping her eyes a couple of time, she could not get over the experience, she grabbed Sarah's hand and said, 'thank you Sarah'. James's mother rushed into the kitchen to make everybody a cup of tea, and after they all had tea, it was Rebeca's turn. She stood up, walked to the end of the room, and recited her new poem, in the same tone and delivery that her mother had just used. There were no tears but so much adoration from all, her mother thought that it was beautiful and absolutely in the style of Omar Khayyam, and it complemented the great poet's work.

Whilst they were away from home, Peter had called Juliet to tell her about it all, she in turn told Robert her father, who now was halfway to London to hear it all from Rebeca herself. He had come on his own and made certain he had at least half a dozen books for her. The two managed to arrive back home, just after seven, and as soon as they entered the apartment the door telephone started to ring, it was Robert, so they let him in and he came up the stairs with three books under his arm, it would have been too heavy to carry the whole lot. Sarah was surprised but Rebeca thought it normal. Robert had not expected the apartment to be so clean and tidy, he was a tad out of breath, and he sat down right of way. Sarah asked him if he needed a drink, and for him to tell her which one, she gave him a huge choice starting at Rhum finishing with cold water. He asked simply for a black coffee, then he asked Rebeca to tell him everything that had happened today. She now could tell the story making it more interesting, because she included all her thoughts, and her punctuation now helped to build up tension, and of course she included her new poem, and especially the comments from the Urdu speaking officer. He was absolutely thrilled for her, and he told her that she should be proud of herself. And that whatever happens she deserves a medal at least. Peter was there and he had been thinking of starting the supper, he had been feeling hungry the last hour or so, Robert realised that he was holding up their supper, and he, himself also was beginning to feel hungry, so he suggested that they all go and eat out. They all had a lovely meal which was followed with the absolutely luxury of the kitchen sink staying dry!

Robert went back up to the apartment with them to bring up the rest of the books, he just could not get over it, he needed another coffee before driving back home, so they were all sat there, now saying goodbye to Robert, when the door telephone started ringing, Rebeca jumped up to make sure she was going to be the one to answer it, she was right it was someone for her, yes, it was Paul who was keeping his promise. He came up to tell her that the man with the scar on his left hand, first went to an address in the Eastend of London, which must have been to drop the other man to his home, and then he went to the outskirt of the Eastend where there are a lot of commercial buildings and many various Yards where mostly old used trucks go to be stripped for parts. They waited for all the staff to leave, and with the help of a police dog who can smell explosives, they were able to identify the actual truck. For now, they installed a GPS tracker device in the truck just in case it is moved before the two men were arrested, and they had not yet doctored the truck or the explosives. Rebeca thanked him very much, Robert identified himself, he explained that in a few weeks' time he will officially become Rebeca's Uncle Father-in-law, they all had a laugh on how complicated it all sounded. Before leaving, Paul wished for Peter to have a wonderful wedding, he left accompanied by Robert who now wanted to be on his way home. The three who were left, decided to stay up late watching a film, because all three already knew that they would not be able to get off to sleep, they all had much too much on their minds.

By lunch time the next day, they were beginning to recover, Peter had not gone to work, he managed to take the whole day off, Sarah was now into schoolwork, she was supposed to work out some new lessons, although she had advertised that she can teach Arabic, she never managed to get enough pupils to make up a class, so that was going to be another year where it did not happen. Today was Thursday and school officially starts next Tuesday, for the pupils, but one day earlier for all the teachers, so Monday Sarah will be going to school on her own for the first day. This Saturday they were having tea at Roberts and especially Rebeca was looking forward to being there. So today is a recovery day, and tomorrow it is all about school, so far that leaves Sunday free, but with Rebeca one cannot be sure of anything, a long time ago Sarah had learned to never take Rebeca for granted.

Rebeca had a nice rest, she had spent the best part of the day looking at the latest news, just in case! By teatime, the telephone had not rung, and nobody came to the door. By the evening Rebeca had sorted her books etc for school. Robert never told anyone, but he had been in touch with the present Dean of the College he had attended when he was at Oxford, and he requested an interview with him, which was granted, after all they have been friends for years, and they both had some free time on Saturday morning, so Robert planned to drive to the college in Oxford. The next day, which was Friday, Rebeca sorted her schoolbooks and pens and pencils and a large pad for note taking. And now she felt like reading, it was annoying that she had too much choice, so eventually she picked one for its cover, not even knowing what it was about, but since Robert had picked it for her, she was going to be happy reading it.

The book was about the life of Winston Churchill, first the mistakes he had made when he was much younger and then how his life changed when Hitler went to war against us. She had never realised that he was such a good painter, he had done many paintings in Marrakech in Morocco, when she read about it, she could not yet understand how light can help an artist. It turns out that is why he was there it must be the reflection from the sands because it is well known to be a good light. She came across his famous speech at the start of the war, 'We will fight them on the beaches!' She could not put the book down, because not only was it about a great man, but it was also about the second world war, all that time she was realising that both her grandfathers must have been in the war. Sometimes Rebeca would conclude that she still has an awful lot to learn. Only six weeks to go and she will be fifteen, she is counting the minutes! Next week it will be September and that first week there are so many things for Rebeca to do, to think about, and to plan, plus the first television show about her life she is attending, it seems to all be happening at the same time. She had to formulate a plan: stop reading after Friday night, be prepared to have to answer many questions on Saturday afternoon, help her mother to start looking for a new slightly smaller apartment, revise all of last year's subjects especially maths, perhaps seek help from Peter, decide once and for all not to attempt another language, until it becomes necessary, keep an ear to the news to see how the police have dealt with the two terrorists. And now of course she was curious, about what part her two grandfathers, oh yes and Robert had played in the war. Robert could be the first one, and she will be seeing him this very Saturday, so that was now set in her mind.

She had a telephone call from Paul, he wanted to come over, and would it be all right for him to bring his wife with him, she would be pleased to meet her, in abouts an hour's time. Rebeca told him that it was OK with her, she did not consider her mother who was well used for her daughter deciding anything she wanted to decide, Sarah was warned that Paul was coming shortly, and he will have his wife with him. It turns out that Paul's wife happens to be a practicing child psychologist, and after hearing of her achievements, she just had to meet her, her name is Rosemary, Paul had told Rebeca. The usual quick tidy up happened long before the couple arrived. Both Paul and his wife had a shock when Rebeca opened the door, and she was the first one to speak: 'good afternoon you two, Rosemary, it's so nice to meet you, although perhaps it is not quite fair,' they both started to look not quite embarrassed but perhaps on their back foot, then she continued, 'well I guess he has told you all about me, and he has told me absolutely nothing about you, so please sit on the settee and tell me what you would like to drink' then she gave them an exaggerated list of almost everything one can drink from water to Rhum. Sarah just came in to rescue the two drowning guests, and it they decided that it would be tea all round. Rosemary found it much easier to talk to Sarah, all the time understanding Rebeca was not going to open up to her until she had put her cards on the table. But at this moment Rebeca wanted Paul to tell her what they had achieved with the case so far. It was quite a lot, first thing they worked all night to substitute the five tons of explosives with the equivalent size of a neutral substance, then they changed the charge of the detonator to have as much power as a firecracker, they installed a camera with microphone in the cab, so that they can monitor them at all times, if they were wearing a suicide vest, and it had gone wrong, they were going to blow themselves up before the truck had moved from the parking lot, Rebeca remarked that the hole it would make in the ground, will be their personal gate to hell, then she followed that with a sentence in Arabic which was no more than a calling them a pair of dogs which for Arabs is the ultimate insult. She apologised for that sentence, but she meant it. The other thing they had done was to install cameras all over the place, just in case they find out that the man who runs the yard was himself involved.

Rosemary had been with them for almost an hour, and so far, she had not managed to ask Rebeca a single question, Paul was aware of that and so was Sarah, but now that the business was over, Rebeca turned round to Rosemary, and asked her: 'how shall we do that? Shall I give you a resume of my life so far, which might take at least a couple of hours, or shall I sit still whilst you ask me a whole list of questions, or maybe it would be more civilised for you and me to have a conversation about our lives?' Rosemary noticed the "s" at the end of Lives, she was not happy about that, but she had no option but to pay the price. Paul was ever so pleased he had never seen his wife who is always the one in control in so much trouble, he thought to himself that it will do his Rosemary good, a new experience for her. After having to adopt a completely novel approach, eventually they both got on well, Rosemary discovered that she had a lot in common with this little girl, in a way they approached problems the same way. Without ever saying a single word both Paul and Sarah managed to communicate with each other, they were both having a problem not laughing! As it happened Rosemary was a nice person, and eventually they became good friends, Rosemary tried on a couple of occasions for Rebeca to go into medicine, but that was never going to happen, because a plan for her whole life was being decided by others!

Saturday was terrific, Peter drove them to visit Robert and his wife, there was another couple already there, the man was a personal old friend, again from university days, like Robert he had been able to retire early, he looked to be a friendly type of person who showed a lot of interest in what Rebeca was up to, Rebeca had gone straight into Robert's study, and he followed her there. He introduced himself just as plain Harry, Rebeca told him who she was and what she was doing in Robert's study, then completely out of the blues, she turned to him and in a matter-of-fact way asked him what it was he had done in the war. He did get a shock, it was the last thing he ever expected from this girl, and the question worried him, so for now he just told her that he was in the Army mostly working in an office, he never saw any action, which he would have loved to be in. Rebeca some months back had decided that Robert had not been honest with her when one day she had asked him what it was that he used to do before he retired, he tried his best to avoid telling her, but after a lot of asking he just said that he used to work in the Army behind a desk, the way he told her did not sound sincere, and now she felt the same with Harry. She was thinking, no, it is too much of a coincidence.

There were many photographs in the study, and Rebeca was now going to study each one, that is after Harry had stopped asking questions, then she had what she though was a brilliant idea. She pulled out the old pack of cards from the desk draw, and she sorted out ten cards, looking at each one, she then handed them to Harry who was only too pleased to have the ten cards in one hand, even though he did not know what was coming next, then he followed her instruction, he had no problem with that, and he placed the ten cards face down on the desk, thereafter she did nothing with the cards, she talked to him about school, and then she asked him to identify the ten cards. It was a total disaster for him, he managed only two of them and he had surprised himself, he did not know how bad his memory had got to. Then he asked her how many for you? She answered no problem for ten, he told her to give him the whole pack of cards so that he can shuffle them then he asked her to place the top ten face down, she started but then did not stop until the fifty-two cards were all face down, he though, that now she is going to do a trick. And he nearly fell off his chair when she correctly named all the cards before turning them over. 'is it or is not smart Harry' 'I have seen that done it is some memory you must have Rebeca' she was happy to answer him, 'you know Harry I always have a problem when I do that with two packs, because I can never lay my hands on a second pack, so because of that I have invented a new scenario, and just watch', she now had the whole pack in both her hands, and then she deposited the pack face down on the desk. 'Now Harry I will count to fifty-two backwards' that is what she did and then she called out correctly all the cards as she turned them over. He was absolutely stunned, him and his two cards so far nothing made sense, he was almost wishing that he had never met this girl, then he though how selfish that would be, and now he can see what Robert was telling him. Her talent must be nurtured at all costs, it must not go to waist.

At last! She was now on her own in the study, and she started looking at all the photographs that were displayed, strange she thought, there was not a single picture of Robert in uniform. Suddenly, she felt so pleased with herself, she noticed that what she had thought were two thick books, which were high up on the top shelf, were two photograph albums. And now she was going to find out for the last time! Down came the two albums, but not before Rebeca had found a chair to stand on; she had started to grow but not fast enough for her to reach so high. She was now going to start real research, she was feeling so happy, and she was hoping not to be disturbed. She buried herself into a large old fashion leather armchair, and she started at the beginning of the first book, there were many pictures of their wedding, followed by Juliet when first born right up to about now. Most of the pictures were taken outside the cottage, then she came to an end. So now there was just the second album left and she started again; this time most of all the photographs were taken during the last war, the camera was not so good as the quality of the black and white photographs never seemed to be in focus, but still acceptable, and now she had hit the jackpot! She never discovered a picture of Robert in uniform, he often had been photographed with others who often were in uniform, it looked as if they were always officers, she even discovered at least four pictures with Robert and Harry, both without uniform, and some time there was a third man again without an uniform, the conclusion she came to, was that they were all in the forces, but at least Robert and Harry had what one might call an unusual job that kept them out of the reach of usual military rules. Was she ever pleased with herself, and now she was going to have some fun!

Rebeca was careful to replace both albums back on the top shelf, then she replaced the chair, and she took from one of the shelves, yet another book on diesel engines, she left it open on the desk as if she had been reading it. Off she went and rudely interrupted a conversation the adults were having she told Robert that it was urgent for him and Harry to follow her to the study, they both looked at each other and followed. She had already moved two chairs for them, and she directed them both to the chairs, then she did not sit, no, she kept standing slightly looking down on both, they both so far had not said a single word. Now the attack started with Rebeca telling both of them that they had deliberately lied to her, and she did not appreciate that; 'Robert you lent me a very nice book about

Churchill, which I read then in turn it made me wonder if my two grandfathers were in the war, which as it happens they both were, now, when I asked you the same question, you told me that you had a desk job in the Army, so you never saw the war, at the time I was not convinced that what you had told me was the truth, but for now I would just wait until I know you better, but today, I also asked Harry and what struck me was he more or less had the same answer. So, I put two and two together and I have concluded that there is a reason you two here do not want me to know the truth, so, Robert and Harry what is the truth?' They looked at each other, of course she was right and neither one of them really wanted to tell her, but then they both had the same feeling that Rebeca is going to find out sooner than later, they really needed to have a sort of a conference on their own, before deciding on what action to take, so Robert asked Rebeca to give them two minutes on their own. That was quickly achieved when she walked out of the study and joined the others, who asked her what was going on, and with a broad smile she answered, 'I gave them both a dilemma they are not able to resolve, its good fun'.

They invited Rebeca back to the study, and now Robert became very serious, and he told Rebeca, that in about one month time, she will definitely learn what it was him and Harry did during the war, he promised her, and Harry also nodded yes to her that she will know then, but please Rebeca keep what you have discovered to yourself, do not tell anyone not even your mother or even Juliet, that is very important, by the way you will never be able to tell anyone ever, so remember that. She realised that she had come across something she is not supposed to know yet." Well of course I believe you and you can be sure, that I will never tell another person, but just now you two failed completely, solving my puzzle, its shame on you both". They both got the message and agreed, they left smiling, but before joining the others, they had a couple of words, and in a way, they were pleased because Rebeca for them was even more the right person.

On the way back Sarah attempted to find out what had gone on with Robert and Harry, she had not believed the story about a quiz, she knew there was much more that was going on, but in no way was she going to find out. Sunday morning she had forgotten all about it, by lunch time which they were having at home, the telephone had rung, not for her but for her daughter, it was the television Director, who wanted to tell Rebeca that the next filming was next Saturday morning at the usual time, she made the mistake asking Rebeca if she had a good holiday; one thing for certain she was to bring with her the RNLI certificate and now they were all primed to receive the next eventful happenings for Rebeca. Monday, Rebeca as planned was spending the day at home on her own, she managed at least three hours of reading about Churchill. She did watch the news on the Television and then literally she put her feet up, and a while later, both Peter and Sarah were treated to a lovely meal cooked by the only person at home, she did them proud! Tomorrow was another day and mother, and daughter made their way to school. Rebeca was so pleased to meet up with some of her friends, the girl she had rescued from the bullies came up to her as soon as she could, she told Rebeca that during the summer holiday she managed to tell at least another dozen girls that the schools now want a head scarf to be worn around the neck, and so far it is working, she wanted her to know, and her parents wish her well.

At lunch time Rebeca attempted to see the head, without even asking her mother, and lucky for her he was just finishing a sandwich, she asked if he could take five minutes or so, because she wanted to warn him in advance, that she might be all over the front pages again, with a horrific story she had been involved in only two weeks ago. When Rebeca wants something, she always knows how to present the question. He really did not have too much choice, and he told her to get on with it: it took her over ten minutes to tell him everything that had happened at Brent Cross shopping centre, and then at Scotland Yard followed by the two visits from Paul and at the moment they are waiting for the seventh of the month or if things happen before it could even be today, Please sir it is important that you do not tell this to anybody else, you can understand why I am sure, and thank you sir. Then she left before he had a chance of asking her anything, so he did the next best thing and found out where Sarah was, and he called her to his office. When she came in she had no idea that Rebeca had come to forewarn him, as soon as he mentioned that she had just been to see him, she replied 'yes it is all absolutely true, I was in Scotland Yard with her, and to this day I cannot get to terms with what had happened, did she tell you about the officer who attempted to test her on the knowledge of Arabic and Urdu?' He replied in the negative, 'then I better tell you, I think that she was offended by being tested, so she was almost rude to him by asking him which particular dialect he would like her to use, then for him she recited a poem in Arabic which was written in the same way that Omar Khayyam wrote, after she finished it, she asked him if he knew that poem, he answered yes, then she informed him this time speaking in English, so that everybody else could hear, that it was not at all possible, because she had written it only last week, I can tell you that was not a happy man, and he left soon after.' That was the end of the meeting, and as Sarah was leaving, the head felt proud of being Rebeca's head teacher and of course he was not going to tell anybody else.

One day Rebeca saw her mother getting friendly with one of the teachers, they were both having fun teasing each other, he was the geography teacher, and he doubled up as the religion teacher, that's when she discovered what an Atheist was! He was a decent person, a bit younger than her mother, not married and best of all Rebeca approved of him, she never told her mother thinking that if they get together, at least she would have had nothing to do with it. That is the way she wanted it. This Friday is the seventh and attentive for Rebeca, she could not tell anybody until the arrests had been made. Well, what happened at the truck park, was for both parties' own plans not to work out the way they wanted it. The two terrorists arrived as planned, they did speak to what seemed to be the man in charge, who told them in Arabic "may god be with you" which meant of course that he had knowledge of their plan, the police had a problem and arrived late, the terrorists also were having a problem starting the truck, all this time there was a police helicopter three thousand feet above the ground, who would not be noticed from below. All the time telling the police force to hurry up because the two had already climbed into the cab, and they thought that they were about to leave, to make matters worse the Heathrow air traffic people were going mad because they had to divert some aircraft because the helicopter was one thousand feet to high. The police had listen in to all the cameras they had planted, and they had enough evidence to arrest all the workers in that business, both the men in the truck talked to their mother and father who were very much in the know on what was happening, then last they both talked to an Iman who happened to be the one who gave them the idea and the encouragement, so before the news was going to get out, the police were arranging arrests all over the place, and once that mission had been successfully accomplished at least a dozen cars and vans arrived in the parking lot, at first they kept out of the way of the truck, then they arrested everybody else. The two in the truck realised that it had all gone wrong, so they pull on the trigger and instead of being in heaven, all that happened was the sound of a couple of firecrackers. The police rushed the truck and brought the two down and a third police van was filled with the last two. After having filmed it all they left three police officers there.

Paul's wife asked him if she could be the one to call Rebeca, at the time Rebeca was in a classroom concentrating on a math's lesson being taught by her number one teacher, she had organised her mobile phone not to ring, when she felt the vibrations, she looked and it was Paul's telephone, she put her hand up and told the teacher that it was most urgent for her to leave the class, nobody ever tried to argue with Rebeca, all he did was to nod yes. As soon as she was in the corridor, she accepted the call, and was pleased to hear Rosemary's voice telling her all the good news, and that there is going to be a news conference at three in the afternoon at Scotland Yard, and they are sending a car at this moment to pick her up from school, will she tell her mother who if it is possible for her to come to. Because she was only just outside the classroom, she went back in, and instead of walking back to her desk, she went straight up to the teacher and more or less whispered: 'Sir, I have to leave the class, but please make sure that you watch the amazing news tonight coming from Scotland Yard, you will see me on the tele!' then she quietly walked to her desk, picked up her schoolwork and left the class, the teacher never said single word but was very excited wondering what she had been up to. Then it was a visit straight to the head, she told him about the press conference that afternoon, and that they were sending a car for her and if possible, have her mother as well.

'Rebeca, have they managed to arrest the two men' she replied to the head 'that is yes and no, I mean yes the two men were definitely arrested, but with nine more people, nobody got hurt, the two never went to hell, and it's a great day for a celebration, now sir you can tell anybody about it, and you will see me on the news tonight I am sure. It would be nice to have my mother with me.' He then sent the secretary to Sarah's class to ask her to come to the office. In the meanwhile, Rebeca remembered something she had forgotten to tell the head, and off she went again: Sir I have just realised I had forgotten to tell you about tomorrow, the Dean of a famous Oxford College, wants to spend a couple of hours with me, and so far, I do not know why. I am told that he will soon be in touch with you, and again I do not know why, but I am sure that I will find out tomorrow, so we better keep our fingers crossed'. She was smiling all that time; all he said after all that is that it will be interesting to find out.

It was Robert who had told her about Oxford, and he planned to take her there, however Rebeca with her fabulous memory managed to completely forget about appearing at the television studio sometime in the morning, so when she was in the car with her mother on the way to Scotland Yard, she called the director lady and told her. 'She has to be in Oxford in the morning, and most likely will not get to the studio until the afternoon, and by the way she will be on the news tonight, and you can use most of the details I was involved with, we can do that tonight or tomorrow in the morning when I am on the way to Oxford'. That was agreed for tomorrow morning. Sarah was so pleased to have been able to go with her, just like her daughter she also had a permanent smile, what had happened in the morning had already leaked out, when they arrived at Scotland Yard, there were already a crowd of reporters and photographers, they let the car pass without really looking inside, they just spotted a woman with a girl, all they knew was about the arrest, After the driver parked the car 6 policemen came out and surrounded mother and daughter. They were made most welcome by the Chief Constable, who could not wait to set his eyes on the little girl. Well, it used to be little, but the last six months she seemed to have caught up with the growing, and now she will eventually be a tall good-looking person, her fifteenth birthday is next month, and she will look her age.

The press conference was set for three this afternoon, and it was only twelve thirty, and a lunch was being served for a dozen people which included Sarah and Rebeca who had the place of honour at the head of the table, she almost looked funny! They asked on how much she wanted to talk to the press, the answer was straight to the point, 'as much as you let me, of course I cannot talk about the arrest, but I don't mind talking about the discovery, and there I have a choice, and it will be for you here to decide, I can add my thoughts as I go along, or not add my thoughts, gentlemen the choice is yours!'. The Chief had thought that people around him must have exaggerated the skills of this girl and now he had given up looking for negatives. The only thing in his mind was that he thought to himself that when she becomes an adult, she will be a formidable person. He was the next one to speak, 'Please Rebeca, I would love to hear your thoughts, what a good idea that is, so do it!' Paul's wife

Rosemary had also been invited, just in case a problem develops with the girl, she has stayed in the background, and when Rebeca spotted her she was pleased that she was there, and after the meal she went over to her, and the two had a friendly chat, during which time Rebeca just in a matter of fact way, told her what a good idea for her to be here to possibly give support, Rosemary had been unsure that perhaps Rebeca will rebel like she did with the translator, but now it was a big relief for her. One of the policemen asked Rebeca if she wanted to see the film of the arrest, they just have time as it is at least one hour long, she decided not to watch it at the moment, she would like to see it all on her own with plenty of time, then as an exercise she would like to write a report on it, because it seems that a lot of unexpected things happened, and she would find it interesting.

The press conference started with the expectation that it was something very special, all the press were there, including many television commentators, including somebody special, it was Debra who could not miss seeing Rebeca, because she was sat next to the Chief Constable, they connected, and Rebeca pointed to her watch hoping that Debra understood that they will meet in a short while or soon anyway. There was a big screen on one wall, and somebody called the meeting to order, and then it was silence and the Chief started to address the audience. A couple of the reporters now had put two and two together and realised that the girl they had noticed in the car must be somebody of great interest. The Chief must have talked for a quarter of an hour about the actual arrest, he gave them all the details possible, then he pointed to Rebeca and told everybody to listen to her carefully whilst she tells them her personal story. So far questions had not been allowed, definitely not whilst Rebeca was talking, but when she has finished, they will all get to ask anybody questions.

Rebeca by now had perfected the art of telling that story, and she started; all the time when she though it to be right, she mentioned her thinking behind her actions. She happens to have a clear voice, and there was not a sound in that room whilst she was speaking, at the end she just had to mention the translator, which gave her an opportunity of reciting both the poems, and there were a few giggles when she recounted the story when she asked him if he knew the poem, and he replied yes, and she told him that she had written it only a week ago to compliment the original one. She did not stop there, no Rebeca gave a little speech in Arabic mentioning her idea that the terrorists, missed their chance of getting through the door to hell when there was no explosion, after she repeated it in English, and then she was done. For at least one whole minute nobody spoke, it was taking a while for all her information to be digested. The first question was for her: Do you realise young lady, that if it had not been for you, we might have just lost the government?'

Rebeca had not been ready for that to come up as a question, and she answered by telling the person, that at the onset of what happened she decided not to delve on it, and eventually completely forget about it, because with her study and life one needs a clear head, and that would always remain as a cloud, so it is alright to talk about it, but only clinically as part of a study. Some of the reporters started to queasily look at each other. It was hard for them to believe what this girl was telling them. Debra was feeling tearful, she loves Rebeca, and she still could not get over it. Then it was the turn of the helicopter pilot, speaking about his problem with air traffic control, then the woman who answered the 999 call, and finally there was a famous prosecutor who gave them an idea of what the charges are going to be for all the people involved, especially the Iman who started it all, as well the four parents were included. Sarah all this time, had kept out of the way, but now people had begun to leave, and a few groups discussing something or other had begun to form, and one such group had four people; they were Rebeca, Sarah, Rosemary and Debra who had been introduced by Rebeca herself. Debra said that she cannot wait until she grows up and starts in her career, Rosemary suggested that now she should concentrate on her education, and although she was aware not to flatter her, if possible, she just had to tell her how clever her answer about her having saved the government was. Before leaving the room, the Chief Constable came to shake her hand and at the same time telling her that if she needs to know anything, she should always call him first, so that whatever it is she needs, he will arrange it, then speaking so as not to be overheard he mentioned that it is possible that she will be hearing from the Prime Minister, then he left. Debra then told Rebeca that she will most likely see her tomorrow morning at the studio, she was surprised when Rebeca said no, because she has been invited for a discussion with the Dean of a famous college in Oxford, and at this moment she is not allowed to tell anyone what it is about, not even her mother knows, and she will not be with her either.

They had organised a driver for her and her mother, but it was not to be, because Paul and Rosemary had decided to be the ones to drive them home. Before Debra left, Rebeca gave her a big hug, they are going to be friends for life. Rebeca sat in the back of the car with Rosemary who enjoyed the conversation with her friend, when they arrived although having been asked up for a cup of tea they declined Sarah's invitation, and now they were on their own absolutely exhausted, and the first thing they did when they walked in, was to take the telephone off the hook, they most definitely did not want to be bothered with the press. But they had luck because they already had a main meal at lunch time, so it was not too difficult to heat two bowls of tomato soup with two chunks of bread, that was not only just what they could eat, it was also all that they could manage to cook! Next Rebeca received a call on her own telephone from Robert, no, he had not seen her on the news yet, but his television is already on for recording the news, why he had called is to tell her that he was picking her up at eight sharp, they have to be in Oxford near nine, no, she does not need to bring anything, and afterwards he will bring her back, So it was going to be an early night.

Chapter Nine - The Wedding

Rebeca was ready in good time, Robert called on the door telephone, he did not bother going upstairs, and two minutes, they were on their way to Oxford, the talk in the car was of course all about the press conference, Robert thought but did not tell her how clever she was, he told her instead that it had been a most enlightening press conference, everybody must have understood what really had happened, and last night he wondered if any of the ministers had realised that today, they are lucky to be alive. Then after a while Robert got serious and started to talk about Oxford. One thing he impressed upon her, is that what was going to happen to her at Oxford is most unusual, because today her future is being planned, and she will be let into real secrets which she must never reveal, not even to her mother, and if ever one day she marries a man, he also will never be told, and for all that, you will have special powers to use for the good of mankind and this country of course. You will be fifteen next month, and that is when you will be involved.

They had arrived at the college, a most beautiful building with a lawn to die for, various ornate looking Towers, and she noticed that Robert had to bend his head down a few times to get through doorways and eventually they reached the Deans' quarters, when he opened the door, before anyone uttered a single word, she cried out, 'oh its Samuel!' It was as if they had both been shot, they froze all the time asking themselves how did she know who he was? She already expected for them to be shocked, she wanted to make an impression, and it worked! 'Samuel I must apologise, because it is the only name, I know you by, and you do not have to worry, there is a simple explanation for my knowledge of your first name. No, it is not written on your door, and I never attempted to research it, which I could have easily done, it was because I had worked out that

Robert and Harry were both avoiding telling me the truth, so, unknowing to both of them I looked into Roberts two photo albums and I discovered that there were only two pictures of Robert, Harry and yourself in uniform, one of the pictures had the names handwritten below each person, so you see it was not sorcery or magic, just a good memory that's all, one more thing, next month when my Uncle marries Robert's daughter I will feel more comfortable calling Robert, Uncle Robert!' Now they were both smiling!

'Well young lady you certainly live up to your reputation. Yesterday I recorded the press conference, and I must tell you, I know that you were playing the audience, and you did it well, it was a pleasure to watch, I only wish that I had been there, and I am happy to welcome you to my quarters.' With that greeting, the kind old man held out his hand, and she shook it, the three sat down on three chairs and Rebeca started a new life. It begun by her listening to the longest explanation she had ever heard in her short life, but she was ready for it. 'First Rebeca, I must tell you who we are, a group of us all learned people, we all work for a government department which has never been named, we are just known as "Them", you had already met two of them, that is Robert and Harry, and now me. We have offices within MI6 because it is a secure place. You can imagine that we do not recruit many people, and when we do it is always somebody like you, so eventually you will be in good company, with people very much like yourself, and you will enjoy a fruitful life, where you are free to consider all kinds of possibilities that will come to you. In the meanwhile we will help you with your education, first example: I will have a meeting with your headmaster, most likely here, where I will offer to accept his best student every year, to be accepted in one of the colleges, right up to the time when you have obtained your degree, for him to pay special attention to your education in his school, I think he does that already I am sure. Right after your birthday next month you will officially be an employee of the government, and you will receive a salary, from time to time you will receive various reports on a computer that we will supply you, all those reports will be hidden within the machine and only you will be able to open them, at least four times a year there is a meeting at MI6, and until you are old enough to make your way there, Robert will take you, from time to time, we might suggest for you to take a look at a subject which would be interesting for you to learn, now we prefer that you learn as much as you can, by the way that it why Robert lent you the book on marine engines, and you did ever so well.' Never mind Rebeca, but Sam had to have a rest before he continued, so he called for a pot of tea and buns then he waited for Rebeca to ask questions.

'Can I still continue with the television program?' the answer was yes, 'what happens if I am too busy revising for an exam?' the answer was not forthcoming until they had finished the tea and buns! There were questions going through her head, the questions were mostly addressed to herself, it was a whole series of "what ifs" that kept coming up, she could not wait for them two to finish the buns, but within herself she was happy, and then he started again. 'Yes Rebeca your education is going to change, first there will no longer need for you to sit exams, instead of revising you will be learning even more, and when you are eighteen, I will be welcoming you right where you are sitting, I hope you approve, but it still leaves a problem we yet have to address, it is what others will think when it looks as if you cannot be bothered to take exams, but am sure there is a solution, that could be a good one for you to work out, what do you think! Next month when you have officially joined, you will be given a gold bar, it is thirty millimetres long, fifteen wide and four thick, it will have your name on it plus a long number and a crown, you must never show it to any of your friends or relatives, not even your uncle or mother. The eight top men in Scotland Yard have one each, and it is used to show any police person in the country that they have to follow your instructions whatever it might be, look Robert has his, and I bet that if he is stopped for speeding he will show it to the policeman and tell him it is urgent, you will also need it when you visit MI6, it will get you anywhere, not a single door will ever be closed to you, even in the forces, what people do with them, they stitch them in a little safe pocket in their cloths and keep it there'. And now he was getting tired and hoping that he had done well, and Robert was going to give her even more information on the way back. But before they left, she had to fill in a couple of forms which included details of her bank account, at that point she asked if at least she can explain to her mother a story she has not yet worked out, about her doing some writing for a government department, because her mother has access to her Bank account, which is up to date because of the Television Program she is in. The reaction was exactly the sort of thinking they were expecting from her.

It was now eleven thirty and, on the way, back Rebeca called the director and asked her if it was worth her coming to the studio, and it was, so Robert drove her to Ealing, and she asked if he wanted to hang about as her guest and see how it all works, and he was extremely pleased. The man at the gate remembered her and let the car through no doubt thinking that Robert was the chauffer! Sarah was pleased that it all went well for her, and that she had time to make it to the studio. They had nearly finished all the filming for the day, and when Rebeca arrived, they just had enough time to do her presentation, this time with Debra which was unusual, because it was all about yesterday's news, Debra herself was hoping to learn a few more details, and she was hoping to be able to spend a bit more time with her, Rebeca introduced Debra to Robert and the two got on very well, they seemed to have something in common and they were going to meet again, that intrigued Rebeca, and she is going to find out sooner or later. That is going to be her first report, that's if it's alright with both of course. Rebeca had rushed in, but she did not rush out and everybody there wanted their turn to have a word with her, they were all so happy!

It turned out that the Director needed to see Rebeca before she left, Debra already knew and suggested that Robert went, what had happened to Rebeca got the BBC people thinking ahead. Rebeca was no longer a child, she has turned out to be very watchable, she always has good ideas and now they would like her to start thinking of doing a ten-minute talk on Sunday mornings, of course she was only too pleased to accept, they were going to talk about a new contract and the increase money. Eventually Robert dropped her off, this time he went up and he had a word with Sarah, telling her what the Dean had suggested about not taking exams, and the Dean has sorted her a little job on the side for a government education department, from time to time, they will ask her opinion on various subjects, the other thing which is important is that she already has a place in four years' time at Oxford, the head of the school has been asked to attend a meeting in the College with the Dean. 'Sarah you might have already realised, but it is important you do not tell anyone about it, especially at school. Rebeca was there at the time Robert was telling her mother, and she agreed with everything he told her.

Robert left and now there were just the two in the apartment, Peter was not coming back as he is staying with Juliet tonight. They had a visitor, it was the couple from next door who wanted to congratulate Rebeca, they had seen her on the news the night before, and they were so pleased for her, they realised now how useful it had been for her to learn their language, there was another thing, some of his friends who are leaders in their community, would like to throw a big party for Rebeca, would she like to attend, it would be wonderful, Sarah did not have a chance of answering that question, no, it was Rebeca who told them that she would love to go but she will have to take advice from some people who now are more or less in charge of her life. That did not surprise them, but it really surprised her mother, she was left thinking 'what's going on!' And of course, Rebeca was going to put it past Robert because she is extremely aware, that she could possibly become a target. Sunday, she went to play with her friend, and they had a lot to talk about, they stayed out of busy places, she did not want to be recognised,

Peter came back and when she returned Rebeca visited her two sets of grandparents, they all made a fuss about her as usual, and they could not get over the press.... No, they now call it: Her press conference.

The three that Sunday evening ate out in a local Mexican Restaurant, the good thing about the restaurant is that it was close to them, the not too good thing was that the food was not the best, she was recognised by one couple who did not approach them, so that was good, whilst they were eating they decided that when they get back home, the first thing they are going to do, is to reconnect the telephone and hope that it does not ring. The talk in the car the next morning, is whether the head is going to ask them both in the office, Sarah was hoping not, and Rebeca really wanted to talk to him on her own.

They have a break at eleven, and the head called her teacher five minutes before, asking him to tell Rebeca to go straight to his office at the brake. She knew what to expect, but he had no idea about what she was going to tell him. Oh, when she walked in, he just had to congratulate her, he also had watched the press conference, he told her that he felt so proud overseeing her education. He did not know what was coming next, and she told him that he was going to get an invitation to Oxford to discuss her education, she told him that they are going to be good to him, she also told him that she is going there as soon as she reaches the age of eighteen, she does not need to have passed an exam, in fact they do not want her to take any exams, no instead learn more, of course we realise that it might complicate matters, but as long as we keep it a secret it should all go well, 'So please sir until you have been to Oxford, we need to be totally silent on that matter.' Then she asked him what he thought of her big reply of the question she was asked at the press conference. 'Rebeca, I could not have done better, that was a master stroke.' The bells were ringing, and she left for the next class. One thing that was different in school which had never occurred before was that the pupils in the six forms, all wanted to talk to her, she had become popular amongst them, the teachers had well noticed it, and it was nice for all.

On the way home Sarah asked her if she had heard from the head, and of course the reply was yes, she had spent a quarter of an hour being congratulated, but she still had the opportunity of telling him about his forthcoming meeting in Oxford, and her never having to take another exam.

After a couple of days, things went back to normal at school, which was good for Rebeca, she really wanted to get on with learning, and now all thoughts and planning were about the wedding next month, her birthday which was two days before the wedding was never mentioned, lucky for both Rebeca and Sarah it was not a Church affair with bridesmaids etc. so there were no preparations on their part. Rebeca had a good idea about the apartment they were in; when Peter leaves there is going to be a spare room, and with what she knows now, she will need to have a study, a place for a new computer, a place for a big bookcase and a fair size desk with lots of draws and last a filling cabinet. So, they should not move, and because she is going to be paid wages, she can contribute towards the rent. And she can do that without having to worry about how much money is in her account. Sarah was bothered about her daughter paying her some money towards the rent, when she made that feeling known to Rebeca. The answer was so simple; 'Well you better get used to it Mum!' and that is exactly what Sarah managed to do over the next few years, she did peep into her accounts from time to time and was always surprised to see her bank account going up and up, she once had a funny thought; 'If ever I get married at least my daughter can pay for the wedding!'

His secretary would not tell anybody else where the head was on Friday, she did tell Sarah that apparently, she thought he had gone to Oxford, because he had asked her to book a train ticket for Oxford, so during the weekend mother and daughter thought that either one or both will be visiting the head on Monday. On the Saturday Sarah drove Rebeca to the studio, who had told her about the meeting between Robert and Debra, and she was dead nosy! Debra was there and she had a long talk with Sarah, Debra and Robert think that they are both related. And Robert was going to do his best to find out during the week. Rebeca learned that day that she is almost the top in the television ratings, the press conference was part of the reason they thought.

At five to eleven, the telephone rung in two classrooms, to inform Sarah and Rebeca's teacher that they have a meeting at eleven with the head. They both met on the way there, and neither wanted to be the one to knock on the door, so it was resolved by both, knocking at the same time, there was a count, one, two, three knock! Sarah did not notice but Rebeca sure did, there were two chairs at the front of his desk, and he greeted them both with a 'Please sit' whilst pointing to both chairs, usually a visitor only has one unspoken choice which is simply to stand. He told them that he had never in his life met such a nice man as the Dean he was with on Saturday. Rebeca told him that he was nice and considerate when she met him, she calls him "Sam" which surprised both her mother and the head, she did not tell them the reason for that. The head agreed with the plans, yes people here must not realise about the exams. And at that moment he had the answer, he told them that it is so simple, she officially will be taking all her exams at the College on Saturdays, why? Because they themselves want to track her progress without any influence by a teacher, that's all there is to it. He told Sarah how nice the College is, they are going to take one of his best students every year with a bursary. He told Sarah there is something special about Rebeca, and whatever happens she must have no barriers to having the best education. Near disaster the school bell had gone off over a half hour ago, when they all realised, so it was a quick goodbye and a run to the two classrooms, Sarah was sure that her room had been turned into a foreign Jungle, and Rebeca was attempting to find a plausible excuse, however neither of them needed to have been worried, the secretary had it all sorted, and she also had noticed the two chairs!

Not much happened until Rebeca's birthday, she received a letter from "Them" telling her all kinds of details, about her income which is going to start at two hundred pounds a month for the first year, and will double every year thereafter, she will receive the proper documentation every year in time for her to declare her total income for that year to the tax people. A man called Bart Soul will be in touch with her from time to time, to perhaps give her some instructions and to see what is interesting her at the time, and he will meet her when Robert brings her to the next meeting, which is a time he is looking forward to, at the same time he is wishing her a happy birthday. Sarah had a cake for her, and her present was a modern copying machine to use at home. They were many more presents for her from so many other people all over the country. The telephone never stopped ringing from well-wishers. Peter and Juliet had already rented a house and he was slowly moving everything out of his room, Rebeca kept an eye on it hoping he was leaving the desk, she found out the next morning that she was out of luck, so she managed to get her mother to come with her to IKEA and buy a desk which they will have to assemble themselves. Then it was Saturday, the wedding day.

Sarah drove the two of them to Robert's house where the wedding was taking place, it had been well organised, there was a small orchestra, the whole house was decorated with a multitude of fresh flowers, the food was to die for, the bride was radiating beauty and sheer happiness, there was a surprise for Rebeca, no it was two surprises; the first one was Debra who introduced Sarah and Rebeca to her husband, the second surprise was especially nice for Rebeca, she made the old man smile, when she introduced him just as my Sam, he told Sarah that he happened to be the Dean of the college she is going to in four years' time, and how proud she must be to be Rebeca's mother. Rebeca wanted a quick chat with the Dean, he agreed, and she paused the question she had about the invitation with the neighbours she told him that she had thought that it was not wise having too much exposure amongst their society, he absolutely agreed with her, tell them that the television contract will not let you do it, unless they are involved and you would rather not do it, they will manage to spoil it all.

The after effect of the wedding was strange for mother and daughter, they had got so used to having Peter around, and now, there was just the two of them, and they were going to redesign the apartment, Sarah's bedroom was large enough for her to have a small settee and her own fair size television, Rebeca now had two rooms, her bedroom was on the small side, but her new study was even larger than her mother's bedroom, and she was going to add the large book case and the desk complete with a computer and copying machine, she asked her mother for some sewing implements, she might even buy a second hand sewing machine, now her mother was getting confused, she had never heard her daughter talk about sewing, so why now? 'Because I feel like it mum!' In a few weeks' time Robert was taking her to her first meeting, and with a small ceremony she will be given the gold bar which she will have to hide in her clothing, so she needed a means to do that, of course her mother must never find out. Now she was happy at school in the knowledge that she never has to sit for an exam, she only wished that she could tell the whole world about it, but it is not to be, and that is something now that will be with her for the rest of her life. She is looking forward to that first meeting hoping that she will meet nice people who can be her friends.

Chapter Ten - The Prime Minister

Weeks have passed since the wedding and Rebeca's birthday, and one Tuesday when both mother and daughter arrived home, from having spent a day learning and teaching at school, they discovered an unusual letter addressed to Miss Rebeca, the envelope was thick and had the Crown impressed on it.

There was only one thing to do, of course it was to open it, Sarah was just like a kid, she could not wait to see what was in it, she did her best to put her head in front Rebeca's, she wanted to be the first one to read it, there was almost a fight, they were having fun, then to be fair, Rebeca held the page so that her mother could read it at the same time. It was an Invitation to spend a whole day with the Prime Minister with his wife and the whole Cabinet at Checkers, the Prime Minister's country residence. Rebeca could bring two guests with her. She had to answer of course to accept and then give the full details of the guests including a copy of either a passport or driving license. Sarah of course let Rebeca have the choice, which turned out to be a surprise for her mother. Number one was Sarah, there was never any doubt about that, the other one was her father James which surprised Sarah. Rebeca was going to answer the invitation tomorrow, first she had to call James, who had sent her an amazing birthday gift which was a Saxophone which she had started to play. Would it not be a good idea when a woman is invited to a do, one should include a parcel of fashionable cloths for her to wear, it would save so much agony, but yes, definitely, but it was no problem for both mother and daughter, because they had only a short while back bought new clothes for the wedding, so, they were well fixed up on that subject.

It was easy for Rebeca to contact her father, she sent him a text, and she got a reply almost immediately, of course he wanted to be there with her, the only problem at the moment was that he was in a RAF base somewhere in the Middle East, can she send him a copy of the invite and he will do his best to get there, he gave her the email she needed to use, and that is what she will be doing at school tomorrow, she will get help from the head's secretary, who will be only too pleased to be of assistance, they now are almost friends which is very nice for both of them. That night she was on the telephone for ages, to Robert and both her grandparents, she also spoke to Paul and his wife Rosemary, and after all that she spoke to Debra, all this time her mother cooked a lovely meal for the two of them. By lunch time the next morning there was not a single person who did not know that Rebeca was going to spend a day with the Prime Minister and the whole Cabinet.

Rebeca did not have to call her Sam, because he called first to give her some advice, he told her just to be herself and not try to get one over them, before you go try and read up on the state of the economy, so that you can ask the Chancellor some interesting questions about the decisions which are now in front him that he has to make shortly, talk to the minister of transport about the state of the roads, especially in Wales, yes study as much as you can, try and get a view on the problem and make sure you speak to all the ministers, I know it is a lot to ask, but then you are going to be there all day, when you are asked what your plans are for the future, mention Oxford when you reach eighteen and after you want to work in the Government, where important decisions are made. She absolutely agreed with him, and she is starting that first evening, she really loves researching facts about anything. About a week later, there was a special delivery from Number 10 Downing Street, it included three passes for the entrance to Checkers, a map and information about the day which is going to start at ten thirty in the morning, both Rebeca and Sarah read it all and now realised that it was going to be a long day, then she found out that her father was going to arrive in England early in the same morning, he is going to be flown to an undisclosed RAF Air Field and then he will be transported to

Checkers by Helicopter, and he is coming in his best uniform, Rebeca was ever so excited about that, she had to tell his mother and father as soon as possible.

The week before was the first quarterly meeting that Rebeca is going to attend, Robert is going to call on her at seven in the morning, and she is going to be there all day meeting at least thirty people, she is definitely looking forward and absolutely loves the idea of walking into the MI6 Building, one small problem, she cannot share that with anybody else, and she is doing her very best to not think about it and perhaps in time just like with Robert, it will be second nature. She often wonders these days, if in her lifetime, will the occasion ever arrive that she must show the" gold bar". She well realises that the little gold bar is immensely powerful. The Prime Minister, the Chancellor of the Exchequer, the Minister of Defence the Minister in charge of the home office and the Minister for the Police. All are briefed on the role of "Them" including the Gold Bar. So, she is going to be in good company, in a position of influencing events, in the future. It turned out that she will have become the only "Them" person who ever had the opportunity of meeting the whole cabinet at the same time!

No school today, up extra early waiting for Robert to call at the door, then very excited being driven to the south side of the Thames in the centre of London, parking was no problem whatsoever for Robert, and they both walked through the front door which leads to a huge reception hall that looked to be well guarded by police officers, all brandishing machine guns. Robert had a card with his photograph on it for the security person at the barriers, Rebeca did not have one yet, so Robert handed her his gold bar. And when they went through, he was first showing his card followed by Rebeca, opening her palm to show the person who she was, and that is all there was to it, it had all happened so fast that Rebeca did not have the chance of enjoying it. After at least ten minutes of rides in two lifts and half a mile of walking it seemed, they arrived at a large ornate steel door which opened as they walked towards it. Now Rebeca has a better idea what a group of thirty or so people look like, she immediately recognised her Sam (that was the way she had started to refer to the Dean, and best of all he did not mind, and whenever he heard her using the expression, he always had a smile.)

The next person who spoke to her was Bart Soul who had already contacted her, he was pleased now to have met her, and told her so, he explained to her that when she leaves today, she will be taking her own computer back home. There will be a sealed envelope stuck to the bottom of the machine, which she will have to retrieve and open to read all the instructions. Under no circumstances should any other person read the contents of the envelope, she should learn it all by heart, and then when she is certain that she can remember it all, it is to be destroyed. Rebeca now is going to be introduced to all members, she now knows four of them, that is including Bart. Who stayed with her and did all the introductions. Everybody were all pleased to meet her, they all had a copy of the film the police made of the arrest and Rebeca's press conference, she was congratulated almost thirty times, every single person in that room wanted to have a word with her, and they all offered to give her as much help as she wanted, it was also mentioned that she will find in her new computer the details of every member, that is the address, telephone number email and their own particular skills.

The meeting was called to order, for Sam to give a little speech about Rebeca and to present her with her own gold bar, at which time she was cheered by all in the room, then drinks were served, and Rebeca was toasted. And now she was one of them and her secret life had truly started! 'So, you two have you had an enjoyable time in the science museum?' Sarah was asking, although it was obvious that they were both happy. That was the reason for the day away. 'Mum, look at what Uncle Robert has bought me?' It was the computer of course, and that was only another lie, no doubt one of many more! Robert wished them both well at the Prime Minister's party, and he left happy that it had all worked out, the computer was in a box well sealed, so Rebeca decided to go next door and tell them about their invitation. It was nice they perfectly understood, and best of all they agreed with her, she did not tell them about the Prime Minister's party, she was going to wait if it is a good idea to tell the media or anybody else, she was beginning to think about circumstances of any of her actions, and now she was no longer that little girl, she was focussed very much on her future, and strangely it now gave her mother more freedom.

The head at school was only too aware that Rebeca was going to meet the Prime Minister shortly, but he had no reason to have a talk with her, he had already told her teachers that she is not going to sit for exams, she already has a place at Oxford, and any test that she should have to take, will be taken at the college on a Saturday morning, he also told the whole school that every year Oxford will be happy to accept one of the best students that will be nominated from the school, and they will have to thank Rebeca for it.

It is now Thursday, Saturday is the day of the Prime Minister's Party, so that evening Sarah thought that it would be a good idea, to look at what they were both going to wear. Sarah was first and her dress did not even need ironing, she tried it on to see that it was still a good fit, and there was not a single stain on it, she could not stop looking at herself in the mirror, Rebeca agreed with her and fetched the shoes that go with the dress, and now it was perfect. Then Rebeca slipped into her dress, but the slipping did not go well, oh there is a problem; the little girl is no longer a little girl, she had thought during the wedding that the dress was a bit tight but did not worry about it, but now it has gone too far, it was bound to happen but nobody ever thought that it could change that fast, so there was only one thing to do; tomorrow after school Sarah is going to drive straight to the Brent Cross Shopping Centre and they will do their very best to find the ideal dress for Rebeca. After a one-hour fruitless search, there was only one store at the end of the centre that could have the perfect dress. As it happens it was the store where Rebeca heard the infamous conversation, and although she had not told her mother what was on her mind, because she wanted first and foremost to find a dress, which as it happened was the first one she laid her eyes on, when they first walked into the dress department, she tried it on and just looking at her mother she could tell that it was right for her, now she started to look like a young lady, they bought it and Rebeca grabbed her mother's hand and lead the way to the restaurant, they sat at the very same table, the girl who had served her that fateful day was still there and best of all she recognised her, and they had a happy chat. Sarah was pleased to see the place that her daughter had described to her all those month's back. Rebeca would have liked to also buy a pair of shoes, with a slight heal, but thought about it and realised that her feet also are growing, and she might only be able to wear them once, so she said nothing. Both had been tempted to eat out, but because it was Friday, they are going to pick up two good portions of fish and chips with mushy peas to eat as soon as they get past the door of the apartment.

One good thing about having fish and chips, there is no washing up, which gave them more time to plan the next morning, first should they eat well, (egg and Bacon) or should they only snack, eventually they chose one boiled egg and one slice of toasted bread each, they did add fruit juice and a cup of tea, after all the planning they went to bed early, and then after a good night's sleep they were up very early, they took turns in the bathroom, Sarah applied her makeup, and then made sure that Rebeca's cheeks were rosy enough, they had the breakfast on the move and by eight they were in the car on their way to the party, Sarah could never follow a map and finding the place was difficult, she had to make a U-turn twice before arriving at a most beautiful set off gates. She then had to show the three passes telling the guard that the third one was going to arrive in a RAF helicopter, he already knew about it, and he is due to arrive in the next half an hour, she was told where to park, and off she went. There was yet another guard who made sure where Sarah was parking, and then he showed her the entrance, and now for the first time in her young life Rebeca was entering this world of politics, little did she know that day, how much it is going to be part of her life.

They were both made most welcome, asked if they wanted a tea or coffee, they were thirsty having eaten their breakfast in the car on the way there, they did make a mistake, they forgot to bring a bottle of water at least, they both asked for a milky coffee, and that is what both were drinking when the Prime Minister came over to have a word with Rebeca, she surprised him by giving him a firm handshake, first they had to be very English and talk about the weather followed by the traffic, then he started to ask her serious questions.

The first one was why did she learn Urdu and Arabic? She had no problem giving him an explanation, it took her about ten minutes, and he was all ears, he really wanted to know, she felt that, so she told him all. She used to listen to her mother who is a polyglot learn various languages, and she would try and repeat what she was pronouncing in another language, sometimes it was French, or German, when her mother started to speak in Urdu, she used to play with the neighbours two sons who were a bit younger than her, and after a while she begun to understand the boys who also spoke in Urdu, because years back both their parents had come from Pakistan, so one day when they were playing she just spoke to the boys in Urdu which shocked her mother and the boy's father. Now she had a choice and she decided to learn the writing which happens to very much like Arabic writing, so she added Arabic and became fluent in two languages for the price of one. Rebeca went on and on telling him about her education up to now, he was almost mesmerised, he had never met such a young person who was so well organised, she even told him that she realised how difficult it was for him to decide on various aspects of national problems, she even had the nerve to suggest one way he should go with a well thought out argument. He could not believe that it was coming from a fifteen-year-old girl.

In the meanwhile Sarah was incamped with the Education minister, they agreed on a lot of subjects and he was pleased to hear from an actual teacher, that made a change for him, and he found it to be a refreshing person to talk with, there was no pretention, and she was definitely a non-political person, Sarah looked around from time to time for her daughter, but she was not to be seen anywhere, her and the Prime Minister had moved to a small private lounge, he thought that he might learn something from her, and he did. Rebeca had asked and she was told that the Prime Minister was allowed to know that she was one of "Them" so shortly after making herself comfortable, she pulled out the gold bar and showed it to him, Now he was beginning to realise what a special person it was he was talking to, and he had never felt the way he is feeling right now, of course he knew about "Them", but now he realises how powerful they are, and they should be listened to, if Rebeca is a typical example. He was realising that he was sitting with a fifteen-year-old person that understood an awful lot about the world around her who when she grows up and becomes Prime Minister herself, he has that feeling that she would be better than him, then on top of that he is grateful that she actually saved his life, and he never wants to lose track of her ever.

There was a commotion when the noise from a helicopter drowned everybody speaking, Rebeca stood up, grabbed his hand and cried out, 'come on sir it's my father just arriving' it looked so strange this girl pulling the willing Prime Minister outside to reach the Helicopter in time to greet her father James, he was looking so smart in his uniform, he had to step on the ground even though the rotating blades never stopped. Rebeca, still holding the Prime Minister's hand introduced him to her father, who stood to attention and saluted the Prime Minister, then the three walked back together, now no longer holding hands and having almost twenty people looking at them, the helicopter was gone, and it was a relief to have normality again, no more noise. One of the guests she knew already, it was the Chief Constable, she really wanted to have a chat with him in private, and off they went to that same small private lounge, he was surprised that she even knew that it existed, and on top of that its location, he was the only other person that she could confide in about the gold bar, and when he saw it, it took him for ever it seemed at the time to pass a comment, he was so pleased for her, he was also pleased that just like himself other people had believed in her, and she deserves it. She then told him how difficult it is going to be for her 'I guess your wife and most of your relatives know you have the same, but for me even my mother has no idea, and on top of all my schoolwork I am employed by the government.' Yes of course he realised that it is not easy for her, but she now has some very powerful friends who she can count on, he told her that he knew about five of them, and they are all nice well educated people, again he was so pleased for her, he reminded her, to call on him anytime she thinks he could be helpful, I would love you to visit me from time to time just to see how life is treating you'. She promised to do that, and then she joined her mother for a while, and managed to have a chat with her dad, he would not have been happy to miss this occasion with his daughter, and he was having an enjoyable time.

It is now one o'clock and it was Rebeca's turn to be surprised, twenty six people walked in to the Dining room, what a room! The table was so large, there was a place for everybody, usually the Prime Minister sits at the top of the table on his own, but today it was different because Rebeca had been placed next to him, it was a place of honour, and she looked great there, many photographs were taken, and before they started the meal, there was a toast for Rebeca, when the cheer went up it almost brought down the beautiful ceiling, every member of the cabinet were cheering her because they were all still alive! Her father could not stop the tears, he had never been so proud in his life, Sarah who was sitting next to him held his hand. The meal was, one could say complicated, it had six courses, each one in turn appeared to be the main course, the adults finished off a multitude of wine bottles. When eventually the meal was finished, everybody moved to the great room, and Rebeca started to have a chat with every Minister in the room. Without exception they were all more than surprised with her up to date knowledge of all their subjects, with three or four of them, she actually gave them advice which they were going to use, one thing that was certain, she made friends with all of them, and each one told her that she can call them anytime for information and advice, and they will always be pleased to help her.

There was one nice thing at the end, Sarah was going to drive James to his parents as he is staying there the night and maybe two, Rebeca and Sarah eventually walked into the apartment at six thirty, and all they could do, was to make a huge pot of tea and attempt to relax without falling asleep. It had been a long day, especially for Rebeca, talking to more than twenty people was a bit too much for her, and now she is paying for it. Sunday is going to be the day she plugs in the new computer and finds out about her job; she is looking forward to it. And now she is also looking forward to a simpler life, the television work is not difficult, it is recorded which makes it much easier for her, and it is now just a ten minute slot where she talks about her life and her thoughts, so sometimes she records two or three episodes at the same time, and that takes the pressure of her, she also once a week calls Robert for a quick chat about anything on her mind, of course she gave him all the details about the party in Chequers, and he was pleased for her. James was going back on Sunday evening, and his father drove him to the RAF airfield he was flying from, there was a real good photograph of him being greeted by the Prime Minister who at the time was still holding Rebeca's hand, he could not wait to show all his buddies. Before leaving London, his father decided to drop by Sarah's apartment so that James could say goodbye to his daughter. She thought it was nice of him, and she showed him her new computer, he was really impressed 'it must have cost a fortune Rebeca', she explained to him that she has a part time job in the government, it is only about two hours a week and she gets £200.00 a month and next year it will double and again the year after, and on and on. He was amazed when she told him she already has a place at Oxford when she turns 18, then she told him about the exam situation, and he could not believe it, he did ask her about the two terrorists affair, and she was only too pleased, to tell him all about it. Before James left he had a long talk with her mother, before he went out of the door, he gave Sarah a big hug, at the same time telling her that she had been a wonderful mother, that hug ignited something in her, he could have hugged her longer, and when she went to bed that night she stayed awake for a long time thinking about her life, up to now it was always about Rebeca

She now knows that her daughter is beginning her own life, and in any case when she is eighteen, she will be living somewhere in Oxford, and this apartment will feel to be a lonely place, so she better start her new life sooner than later. She did think every so often to write a book about Rebeca, but that felt to be a lonely time, she is wondering about joining a group, one where there are more men than women, she is still looking. The same young teacher she often passes some time with, now they always have their lunch together, there is nothing going on, but it is always a nice feeling being with him, yes, he is a nice man, but unfortunately not her nice man, in the meanwhile a routine has set in, and nothing more has happened to Rebeca!

Chapter Eleven - It's Nearly Time for Oxford

The last four years seemed to have flown by, Sarah learned another language, it was Swedish, well there was a reason for that, it was Johan. She did not have to go look for him, no, he arrived at her school as a maths teacher, he is one year older than she is, they now have known each other for three years, and it appears to all that they are much in love, and the best part is that Rebeca really likes him, and of course he could not help liking her, they often have serious discussions at which time he can never understand Rebeca's powerful knowledge. As it happens, she has done very well at school, the students around her, think that she must have learnt the twenty great books of the Encyclopaedia, she always knows the answer to a question, sometimes a teacher will rely on her for information.

There is a reason for Rebeca to have so much knowledge. She had stopped appearing on the children's television program. But now she appears on her own short program on Sunday mornings, she always has her point of view on various subjects that are always interesting and mostly reflect on what is happening at the time. The BBC producers cannot understand how she knows so much and have a personal view about the subject she speaks about, but many people around the country would never miss watching her.

The explanation for Rebeca's ability is a secret to most, only thirty plus people know what is happening, and they will never tell. That Sunday four years ago after Rebeca had said goodbye to her father, she dashed into her study and carefully unpacked the new computer, read all the secret instructions and switched the machine on, there were two passwords for her to use, one was for general computing, but the second one was most special, because it opened the organisation "Them". It took her almost a whole week to discover the power she now had at her hands. Every member like her, would spend an hour or two a day maybe a week or even months, researching an idea they had produced, and when they thought it complete, they published it on the secret system. It could be thirty or 60,000 words long, but whatever it was that somebody had published it was always relevant and interesting. That is how she was able to produce so many ideas, some of which even got adopted by the government, it was almost required for all security cleared ministers to view. That group had been doing this since the second world war, but they had never been able to directly influence the government, but now for the first time ever they were able to talk to the whole country, they were all glad that Rebeca was one of "Them."

It is the last week for Rebeca in school, and she is making the rounds of all her friends which included the head, and especially his secretary, she gave her math teacher a hug and yes she gave him a big kiss, he had been able to teach her well, and if she were to sit for an exam she would get an A or even A+, she now took maths in her stride, she never did bother to learn another language, no she concentrated mostly on politics, later that week she visited the mother of the girl she had helped with the scarf, who was ever so pleased to welcome her, Rebeca had been responsible for having changed her life completely, she now has a good job and her daughter is never going to forget Rebeca, she still wears her scarf around her neck, and if ever any relative of the family pass negative remarks about the scarf, she tells them to get lost, she has never been bullied since. Then she sorted out the nineteen-year-old boy who was now going to Oxford, to make sure that they meet up from time to time, he was another who was ever so pleased with her, she is the reason for him going to Oxford. Rebeca is leaving a trail of people who are all well disposed towards her. Sarah is going to find it a bit strange driving to school on her own, still, it might not be for much longer, as they say, 'Watch this space!'

There is one man on this planet who has no problem thanking his God for sending him Rebeca! It is Robert who loves boating, he has had a problem because nobody else in the family also loved boating. He finds himself with a powerful sea going boat which is stuck in the Upper Thames region never doing more than idling both engines, but an angel was sent to him, after the very last school day that angel called him on the telephone and suggested that she will accompany him on a trip in his boat from where he lives all the way to the cottage and back.

Was he ever excited, he seemed to be jumping around the house, his wife had never seen him so happy, he had started planning, he wondered if they could make Ramsgate in one day, it all depended on the weather, oh he has so many things to do, he will need to be up to date with his charts, tell the insurance company, should they invite another person, will they sail at night, which would be ever so exciting, is his life-raft up to date does the radio still work, he had not used it for years, there was so much to do to prepare for what will be a magnificent trip, will Rebeca get sea sick? Then he realised that really, he should at least attempt to recruit another person, and if possible, a couple, he remembered talking to Debra, her father had a boat, and she used to go on trips with him. So, he invited her and her husband to join them, he knew that she would love to spend a couple of weeks with Rebeca. Debra had no problem accepting the invitation, but unfortunately her husband was not able to take the time off, the good thing however is that she was owed a lot of time, and she was excited about the trip. So now there will be three on board, one of which is planning to find out Rebeca's secret.

It was Sunday morning, and Rebeca had not had the time to prerecord her ten minutes, so for a change she was going to be live on the screen, and immediately before her there had been a party-political broadcast, where a member of the opposition talked about something that was ridiculous. He must have lost his senses; it was like telling the entire world that the earth was a plateau and one can fall off it. Everybody who had watched it must now be telephoning the leader of the opposition, to make sure that he never appears again. Only a few people had watched that broadcast, it appeared to have been the saving grace for the stupid man, but that is not what happened, because when Rebeca mentioned it, now the whole world could not wait to watch a recording of it, it did upset the leader of the opposition, he could not blame Rebeca, who was not taking a political side, just making the point of the man's stupidity, that Sunday evening Rebeca received a telephone call from the Prime Minister congratulating her about it, then he started asking her about her life these days, she told him that she is starting in Oxford University after the holidays. But before it is going to be a boat trip with her Uncle Robert on his boat, she told him where the boat was now, and where they are taking it to. He asked her to call him when she knows the date they are leaving, there is a special reason for that. It is so strange they were talking as if they were old friends, but then that is the way Rebeca talks to everybody.

Her mother has never worked out why her daughter spends so much time on the computer obviously typing away some times for one or two hours nonstop and when she gets the chance she has a look into "words" and cannot find any new writing, she does not want her to know that she is attempting to keep track, so she cannot ask her, but it is making her a little suspicious, especially when she comes up with an idea for a subject she has never talked about and even read about. Sarah now is excited about the boat trip, it will be the first time that she will be separated from her daughter, and she is beginning to feel apprehensive about it, but then when Rebeca comes back from the boat trip, she herself will be off almost for good. These days Sarah is not completely alone, she has a new friend, his name is Joe, and he is also a teacher, he is not in the same school, they met at a teacher's conference, and just like her he is a single parent, as his wife died in childbirth, it was a boy, now just turned seventeen, so they have a lot in common and they meet up once or twice a week. Rebeca has met him, and she thinks he is a nice guy, the problem is that so far, he has not fully recovered from his wife's death all those years ago, but since knowing Sarah he is beginning to improve, he is well aware of his problem, and sometimes they discuss his situation. Sarah has invited him for a meal one day, best part is that they are both looking forward to it.

The pressure is now on for the trip, Robert picked up Rebeca, she is staying overnight at his house, and the idea is for her to help him give both engines a full service, then check the date on the life raft, which was one year too old, but Robert decided that it was good enough because he also has a large size dingy with a powerful motor, and they do not intend to be out at sea when the weather is on the rough side, in any case it is too late to get it serviced. Rebeca for the first time in her life managed to get her hands covered in an awful dirty black grease, she enjoyed doing all the work she was given, and she did a decent job, she would be happy to do it all again. Sarah was waiting for her the next day still not understanding what was going on with Rebeca and her computer, she had spent a lot of time looking at all the files and found nothing, she also looked at the emails and she appeared to have never sent any, so now she was even more confused than before, so she made up her mind and do what she should have done before, simply ask her.

Rebeca arrived back with Robert with a big smile, they were leaving next Tuesday at six in the morning, the three of them were going to sleep on the boat Monday night, Debra will be picked up from Rebeca's home Monday afternoon. As soon as Robert left, Sarah asked directly why it is there was no evidence of the many hours of typing she had done, 'oh mum. It's quiet simple I always destroy anything I have typed because it is always ideas I have and they do not need to mess up my computer, so I bin them all, and after a week they disappear from the recycle bin, that is the way the computer has been programmed, maybe it is because it's a government machine, I'll ask someone one of these days, and I will tell you.' Sarah bought it! Rebeca had already asked Robert about having a photographer on board to keep a record of the trip, he said it was a clever idea, then Rebeca called Debra and put the idea past her, and the reply was yes of course, she had just the right person for the job. It was a young lady called Joan, who happened to be an excellent photographer, and she will make a movie of the whole trip. First, she had to take the time off, and the BBC almost wanted to send a director along, but that was not on for the crew.

The planning started in earnest, and now there are four on board, Roberts' wife was enjoying herself teasing him about one man and three girls, she kept on saying that he had been planning it for a long time, after a while he stopped defending himself as it was a waste of time. His wife did help him with the shopping and gave him advice which he did not really need but accepted, he was going to miss her, but for her, she was looking forward to being on her own, to do as she pleases. And before they had realised, it was Monday night, they all sat in the saloon going over the basic rules of seamanship.

Robert had planned it all and they all went over it, it was still early in the evening and the first meal had to be cooked, Debra offered and four ready meals came out of the freezer and in turn spent four minutes in the microwave, bread was now on the table, a bottle of rose wine and four glasses were also occupying space on the table, and within twenty minutes all were busy eating and drinking, Rebeca did the washing up, after which time Robert spent over an hour explaining to Rebeca how to read a map. Rebeca had to bite her tongue; she had been about to tell him that they do not have maps on a boat they are called Charts. They then sorted the cabins, at the very back of the boat, called" Aft" is the master cabin which is ensuite and that is Robert's cabin, then there are two more cabins, each with two berths they are for Debra and Joan, at the very front of the boat called "forward" are two berths formed in a V, when two people sleep there their feet almost meet. And of course, there is the main Toilet called the "head" which is situated opposite the kitchen which is called the "galley." The disadvantage of sleeping in the V berths is that the bow of the boat cuts through the water when under way and it is not too easy to fall asleep because of horrendous noise, but some people love it, so everybody parked all their effects, they all sat on deck before turning in for an early five o'clock call.

Robert was up first, and he organised the breakfast, he made as much noise as he could to wake up the crew, and it worked, the girls decided amongst themselves the order in the morning for the use of the head (shower room) and Joan was first, so that she can film the other two before and after the makeup session, which on board has to be kept short if at all. It was wonderful Robert thought, he had never seen three women get ready so fast, by half five they were all sat eating a healthy breakfast, at six Debra was casting off, not forgetting to jump back on! The sound of the two engines was very reassuring, there was a mist hanging just above the water, and the scene was to die for, Joan started some background photography to use later, she just could not resist it.

Robert was hoping that most of the eighteen locks they have to manage will be maned, which will go faster for them, however the lock keepers don't start work until at the earliest nine o'clock, and they stop for their lunch, so they will have to organise themselves. He is hoping to make Walton on Thames before night fall, that will be a total of seventeen locks. They hope to pass at least four locks before eight thirty. They will have to be organised for it to happen, the speed limit is supposed to be five knots, but where there is nothing near the banks Robert moved up to ten knots, Rebeca was a little surprised that he would break the law, but soon forgot about it. They did manage to get to Walton on Thames, and they managed to dock for the night. Joan had a great time when there was a lot of shouting, each time when entering and leaving a lock, both Rebeca and Debra had to jump ashore each time holding a rope in one hand, tying it down and then open a sluice, and when the water was no longer running in then move the gate, and that always took the two of them to push like mad. When the lock was maned, they did not have to get off the boat, it was just a matter of throwing the same ropes to the nice man who would tie the boat, they always gave him a big smile! They had seen a lot of scenery on that first day, and they all want to be there when the film is edited, they felt a bit guilty with some of the replies they gave Robert, of course he did not mind, it's par for the course with a new crew, it's just a good job that they were not in a sailboat! They were hungry but mostly tired, and they had to be up early again in the morning. Debra had cooked some vegetables, and now she was frying twelve sausages in a big frying pan, she asked if anyone wanted a drink of wine, and there were no answers, the others were too tired to think about it, before turning in Robert told Rebeca to follow him, they went down to the engine room, and he showed her what to look for, which included of course looking at both dipsticks to make certain that we had not lost any oil. Whilst they were in the engine room, he explained why he went faster from time to time, the two engines are very powerful, but they do not like being at low revolutions for too long, so, the practice is to rev up whenever possible, now that she understood she will never worry about it again. They are now beginning to get excited at being in London tomorrow, so it was a quick supper and now Robert started listening to the shipping forecast as often as he could, because after London: it is the sea!

It took them just four hours to reach St Katherine Docks Marina, the whole crew were looking at everything they had known all their lives, all the bridges they had all gone over never even wondering what was below, they went past HMS Belfast shortly after they went under Tower bridge and immediately after, straight into the marina where Robert had booked a place for the night. They had arrived early enough in time to book a restaurant which was next door to the marina. There is a well-known yacht chandler, only a quarter of an hour walk from the marina, so the four went there, Robert bought an Admiralty Tide atlas for the English Channel, before making their way to the restaurant the crew took the opportunity of having a proper shower in the marina facilities. Robert did not bother, however whilst they were all gone he decided to fill up the water tanks, he was amazed on how much water three women can use, next stop tomorrow is Ramsgate, and at last he is going to do some real sailing, as the waters between the Thames estuary and Ramsgate are treacherous because of the many sand banks which are never exposed, so as tempting as it is to aim in a straight line one has to navigate around the sand banks, they do not want to come aground! Oh, they all looked pretty now, they are going out tonight, so the three just must look their best. The meal lasted over two hours and it was well enjoyed by all, especially the two bottles of wine, no, Rebeca only had one glass... They did not have to leave too early the next day, the tide was coming in until ten in the morning, after which they will have a strong tide taking them to the sea. That is exactly what happened, by two in the afternoon they were just one little boat floating around this huge sea, with nothing to look at. For Rebeca it was thrilling, especially as she was at the wheel sailing by the compass only.

The excitement increased as the sun was disappearing in the horizon, and now one could not see anything at all except the light on the compass, the other constant was the sound of the engines which seemed to change for Rebeca every time she swallowed, eventually she got used to it, she had regular visits from Robert who was making sure that she was on the right track, and of course asking her if she was alright, does she need a rest, he was amazed how resolute she was, she had made up her mind that it was exactly what she wanted to do, and she is doing it! What she did not know was that all this time he was in the saloon looking at a portable GPS which told him exactly where the ship was, and he showed the others how straight the lines were, she must have worked hard to keep steering without deviating at all.

Joan took some pictures of Rebeca concentrating at the wheel, she looked so determined, it will take a good photograph, Robert returned to give Rebeca a new direction, as well he told her to keep looking on her right and shortly, she will see some lights, which will be the town of Ramsgate, and he told her that they should be in the harbour within an hour and a half. He went back to the saloon and before he had a chance to make himself comfortable at the table, there was a loud call for him from Rebeca. 'Robert look! I can see all those lights in front of us,' she was ever so excited, and he explained to her where they were, first there were two coloured lights the green one was on our left and the red one on our right. 'Well Rebeca that means that the ship is heading straight for us, now you can also see two white lights, one almost on top of the other, we are on a collision course, so now we will turn 10 degrees to the right and you will see the two white lights move away from each other, the closer to each other, so now you were heading on 256 degrees, so tun right and head to 270 degrees and within three or four minutes, you will notice the lower light appear to the left of the upper light, and we will be safe, on top of that depending on the speed of both ships you will see less and less of the green light. Rebeca just had her first navigation lesson, and soon enough the lower light appeared to have moved to the left, Robert was right, she was the one person who avoided a collision just by making a small turn to the right, she felt good. Half an hour later, she did not scream but she made sure that they all heard her say, 'I can see Ramsgate now'.

Now both Robert and Debra came to the bridge, to see for themselves and she was right of course and in a short while they will arrive at Ramsgate harbour, Debra went back down to have a chat with Joan, they were deciding what supper was going to be tonight, first they wondered if they were in time for some fish and chips which would solve the supper problem, now they could see the harbour, and it is a good thing as the start of a fog was upon them. Robert was hoping that it will be gone in the morning, their next stop was Brighton marina which should take no more than seven daylight hours and there was only a light wind forecast for the next few days, so after Brighton it's going to be a long trip to Plymouth where the boat must be fuelled. Robert followed the directions and turned towards the right when they entered the harbour, then immediately on their left were pontoons for visitors, it was all well-lit and Joan noticed a fish and chip shop which was still open, so as soon as the boat was secure it was a big dash from them all, it was four portions of cod and chips with a couple of large gherkins and to top it all, four tubs of warm mushy peas. Whether they did or not, they all looked as if they were loving it, and they were not supposed to waste any time getting through it all. They all four had a good night's sleep, Robert had to get up once because he could hear a regular banging on the hull, all he had to do was tie a rope to avoid the contact, then he went back to sleep in his king size bed, oh what luxury!

In the morning, they could not use the marina facilities because they had not yet registered their arrival last night, which meant that they did not have a key to the club. They decided just to get with it, there was no wind, so they left even before having a cup of tea, breakfast was going to be on the go, so they left, made a right turn and sailed close to the coast on their right, four miles on their left is where the Goodwin sands are, and the water is not deep enough for boats. When Robert called the port of Dover, asking for safe passage past the two entrances to the harbour in fifteen minutes. They could already see one of the big ferries coming across from France, it looked as if it will arrive before them, which is a good thing, they were told that they had one leaving in less than ten minutes. Robert was asked to give them another call just before arriving at the first entrance. The radio had become quite busy and when they were passing Beachy Head at Eastbourne, they could hear all the communication to and from Brighton marina. Debra was at the controls, she could see the marina, but something caught her ear, it was some Frigate calling the marina asking them if they had yacht Happy girl there, Robert came right up, he was a little worried because they had left Ramsgate without ever having made contact with the harbour people, surely they would not send a warship for such an offense, in any case there was no body there to speak to, the ship had to repeat the question at least three times, and then the marina now understood what the question was, and the answer was negative. Robert decided to take them all out of their misery and he called the ship itself, giving them their position, and asking them how can he help? One thing for certain Robert understood that it was a Frigate with a series of numbers, there did not seem to have a name, if they do have one, they do not intend to use it.

They replied by asking him to switch to channel 82, which he did of course, the man on the radio told Robert to wait a short while because the captain wanted to speak to him. Now things were getting complicated, Debra thought that something good must come out of that call, Robert was not at all sure, however Rebeca who had joined them on the bridge knew what it was all about, for the second time she quietly pulled on Debra's sleeve and when she turned around, she could not miss the big smile she had, and realised it was something Rebeca had organised, or at least knew about, and it reminded her of the first time she had pulled her sleeve to get her attention, in any case they were all pleasant thoughts. The Captain had a good commanding voice, and he told Robert that they are on duty in the English Channel and he has been ordered to make sure that nothing unduly ever happens to Rebeca, he presumes that she is on board, Robert answered yes and told him that they are staying the night in Brighton and tomorrow they will be making their way to Plymouth to refuel, The Captain told him that the day after they arrive at their destination, they will send a tender to bring the four of them back to the ship for a 24 hour trip, please bring a change of clothes and especially a camera, you will be seeing what it is we do, and we are looking forward to your visit.

Debra was looking at Rebeca who was trying her best not to look at Robert, who made her look at him and said only two words, 'It's you.' She was not going to deny it, and then she told him that she had had a call from the Prime Minister, and when she told him about this trip that is what he planned for her, Robert was realising more and more that Rebeca had a lot of power, and she knows how to use it. One thing; the man who had answered the call at the marina, heard the start of the communication, he could not understand why a warship wanted to see if a yacht had arrived, so when they turned to channel 82 he did the same and heard all of the conversations, and now they did not know who, but they knew that it was somebody very special, a VIP and he told the whole office, so now when Happy girl (the boat) comes in, two men are going to help the crew with mooring the boat, and it is going to be a camera day!

They did not have much time to get their act together at the marina, all they had was one quarter of an hour, they sounded the fog horn to tell people that something special was on the cards, they also just had time to make an announcement on the public address system which is hardly ever used, the crew on board Happy girl heard the announcement itself, and they did not know if they were pleased about it, it's going to be photo shouts, interview and tonight they will end up even more tired than the night before, the photography started as they came close to the wall of the harbour entrance. Robert had no problem finding a spare birth for Happy girl because he was directed to the closest one near the entrance, and no one had to jump unto the pontoon, all they had to do is hand someone the rope.

The manager of the marina asked permission to come aboard which was granted, he explained to Robert that they were aware of Rebeca being on board, and they wanted to make her welcome, whilst he was talking to Robert, he had not realised that she was now right behind him, ready to surprise him, Robert realised what she was up to, and played along with her. He told the manager that he will call her, but please be careful, she moves just like lightning, he could see her smiling at him, and he called her as loud as possible just as if she had been in the engine room, and as the last sound died away, the manager had a shock when he heard right behind him her voice 'Yes uncle Robert' he jumped, he was definitely taken back, then when he turned around he was facing, this beautiful eighteen year old who had just played a trick on him, he recognised her from four years ago, he had thought at the time that she was very self-assured and maybe a bit mischievous, and about that he was right, at the end he was pleased to have met her, and they both got on well.

Debra came out, the good thing is that she has been on the television for years, and is always recognised, so now there were two personalities with their own photographer, who never stopped filming. The manager addressed Rebeca and Debra and asked both what they would like to do, for Debra it was to have a cup of tea, but Rebeca had what she thought was a good idea for her, before they close she would love to visit a mechanical workshop to have a talk with an engineer who works on marine engines, it did not surprise Robert of course, but it astonished everybody else, the workshop was almost half a mile from where they were, and the manager drove Rebeca in his car to the workshop, he did not have to explain to the engineer who she was, but he could tell him what she was after, so the man made her welcome and then showed her an engine that was all in bits on the bench, to his amazement she could name every item on the bench, she even noticed a broken ring on one of the pistons, she pointed to it saying that it must the cause of the problem, as that cylinder would not be able to compress fuel enough for it to explode at the top of the stroke. 'Would it not be nice if when a cylinder has that problem, the piston was able to disconnect itself, both the engineer and the manager were taken aback, she must know a lot about engines, again the manager was looking at this tall well dressed and beautiful eighteen-year-old who has such knowledge, especially about greasy and dirty mechanical things, the two did not seem to go together. On the drive back the manager did not say much, he was too busy thinking of his daughter who happens to be one year older than Rebeca, and only cares about clothes, boyfriends and on rare occasions cooking, what did he do wrong!

That night they were invited by the Mayor of Brighton to a special meal, which went well, and they were back on the boat before it was late, so now Robert had to plan for the long trip to Plymouth, there is a 24 hour Supermarket at the marina, tomorrow early in the morning Robert and Debra are going shopping with a list they are making this evening, they will check the engines in the morning then after everybody had a shower in Brighton marina's wonderful facilities and then it is 21 hours nonstop to Plymouth, so it is all day and all night cruise, when Robert is sleeping Debra will be in charge, and that is what it is! In the morning, they were all refreshed, they had a good breakfast, and the shopping was dealt with, then it was goodbye to the nice people they had met, even the engineer she was with yesterday came to see them off. The only person who mentioned the warship was the mayor last night, he did ask Robert about it, who could not really tell him anything, apparently it had been arranged by Rebeca herself, he was not there to see them off. Debra and Rebeca pulled the ropes in soon after the engines had started, and they departed.

In less than an hour they were abreast the Isle of White, they had made good time, well the tide was pushing them along but after another hour the tide will turn for the next six hours, and they will be fighting it all that time, so one has to develop patience , they worked out a sort of rotor, there will always be two on the bridge; first it will be Robert and Joan, then Debra and Rebeca they will do a three hour turn, at night the two that are not on the bridge will turn in and sleep, any coffee or tea which is required at night will be made by one of the two on the bridge. But in the daytime, they can all be on the bridge, when underway never on the deck. Robert was following a chart which was laid out on the chart table, he would make marks on it as they went along, the radar was always on so was the GPS map, so they had three separate way of knowing their position at all times, Robert had drawn a line with a soft pencil to indicate where they should be, and if the boat moved away from that line the person steering would have to alter course slightly to be back on track.

At one time in the afternoon Rebeca and Joan were sat together in the salon, Joan was in her thirties, a friendly person, she told Rebeca that she was looking forward to spending time on the Frigate, 'just think Rebeca, all those sailors there, I love them all already', Rebeca could not understand what she was all about, it did not make sense to her, how can somebody love a person they have never met, she did not reply to Joan's idea of love, but then she thought to herself, yes there might just be a nice decent young man in the ship's crew, yes that could be interesting! At six that evening Robert and Joan had just relieved the other two, so it became Rebeca and Debra's turn to cook the supper, and they had the choice for the menu.

There was a bit of a breeze and it was on the cold side, to start with they opened two tins of Heinz vegetable soup, that was the starter, then from the freezer they placed in the oven four chicken kieve, they found a large tin of cooked boiled potatoes which they emptied into a large saucepan and placed on a low heat, they found a fresh cauliflower which they placed into another large saucepan after having cut it in half twice with enough water, and that went on the hob as well, on a low heat, between the two of them they worked out how to lock the three pans so that they cannot move, there was a bit of a swell outside and the boat was going from side to side, all this took an hour. Rebeca for a while could not stop watching the potatoes sliding from side to side in the water.

On the bridge bowls of soup were placed on the other table, there was also a couple of slices of bread, and they were both asked to call down when they had finished the soup, after which they each had a plate which was looking really good with the chicken and vegetable all dressed up and hot, for desert it was a banana followed by a strong sweet coffee, they did the washing up as soon as possible, and Rebeca and Debra played two games of chess, nobody really won because Rebeca was teaching her adversary how to play the game. It was a good thing that the chess pieces were all magnetic and did not move once on the board, otherwise they would all have ended on the floor, and an hour later they turned in just for one hour, when it will be time for them to be on the bridge.

Debra gave her the choice, to steer the first hour, and that is what she wanted, so that is how they started the night, Debra now had one thing she wanted to do, and that was to find out how this Rebeca can be so up to date with everything around her, she even knew things that had never yet been published! How was she going to get it out of her? Well, she never did, Rebeca answered most questions by asking why Debra wanted to know, she soon had realised what Debra was up to and she played around with the answers, eventually Debra could not help but realise that she will never find out, and that made matters worse for her, it is going to stay in the back of her mind until one day she eventually finds out. When looking to their left (port side) they could observe at least eight ships going the other way towards Dover, or going to Rotterdam, they could always see the red light and the two white lights, sometimes the ship's radio would come alive, not always in English, it would normally be one ship calling another.

The three hours passed without any problems, the next thing they were aware of, was the relief crew coming up for their turn. They were tired enough to fall asleep as soon as they had stretched on the bunk. Rebeca and Debra woke up before their turn when the sound of both engines had changed, Happy girl had just entered the outer Plymouth harbour, and in less of a quarter of an hour Robert and Joan had managed to dock the boat. It was just before four in the morning, still dark and Robert and Joan then had a chance of another sleep, all got up at eight. That night they had made good time arriving at Plymouth two hours before Robert's expectation, the next leg of the trip will be the last one and they will arrive in the fishing port in another three or four hours, so, the idea is to take it easy. The yacht club like Brighton has very good facilities, and they are all going to have a shower, the other good thing is that there are two restaurants on site, and they are both serving breakfast, on top of that nobody was offering to cook the breakfast!

It took over two hours before they were back on the boat, and the orders were to clean up, Happy girl must look her best arriving, so the decks were cleaned, all the bedding was aired on deck, then folded to perfection for Robert to inspect, just like the army, and they all enjoyed the joke, they had to move the boat to the fuel barge, and carefully Robert filled both tanks, then he made his way to the office to pay for the fuel and the stay for one night, then he much surprised Rebeca when he gave her the job of leaving. It was her who started both the engines and gave the order to cast off, she had no problem navigating her way out of the harbour, and when well out to sea she turned right to her starboard side and followed the course that Robert had plotted, all that time she had been completely on her own on the bridge.

It had been a test that Robert wanted to see, he was pleased and now they could all go to the bridge. In an hour and a half, they were halfway there, it shook everybody when the radio came alive with a call from the Frigate which was about twenty miles away, they were making sure for tomorrow morning. They are going to pick them up from the harbour at around eleven, this time Rebeca answered and told them that they are looking forward to being on board. One good thing which is going to make entering the harbour a bit easier for Rebeca, is that it will be high tide, so the harbour will appear to be larger, which will give Rebeca more room to manoeuvre. She now was excited, and she was going to do her best, especially as a lot of people had assembled to see Happy girl arrive and dock, the onlookers will be surprised when they realise that she was in command of the boat, her old friend the skipper of the lifeboat also is going to have a surprise, he already knew that tomorrow she will be on the Frigate, and he very much wished that he was going to. Rebeca used both engines to turn Happy girl around, then reversed into a space which had been reserved, every move she did was right and at no time did she have to correct where she was placing the boat, it almost looked professional, her crew where all on deck each with a rope waiting to tie up, and now happy girl is in her new home!

The first person to greet the crew was of course the skipper, who had no problem recognising Rebeca, she was now a tad taller than him, they greeted each other with a big hug that had almost become eternal, they were both so pleased to be together again, it had been four years and he told her that he thought about her almost every day, Debra happened to walk by the two of them as the skipper was asking her, how the hell Rebeca do you get all those interesting things on your weekly programs? Rebeca did not answer him, but Debra is going to have a chat with him a bit later. Robert's neighbours at the cottage organised for them to have the use of a car, and he was there to greet them, it was not a new car, Mr rust had started working on it, and so far, he must surely be pleased with his handy work! But as the second-hand car salespeople would say, it is a runner. Joan had an enjoyable time with the photography, all the people that had come along got to see Rebeca docking the boat, it all made for good photography. Next, they arrived at the cottage, and they managed to get themselves organised, they were going to limit the use of the kitchen to making Tea and Coffee, that's all, Breakfast, lunch and Supper were all going to be made by others, Robert telephoned their special restaurant, first he found out that it was still the same people who were only too pleased to see them again. And yes, they will expect them at around seven.

Robert was beginning to realise again that the other three were getting ''pleasantly'' worried about what to wear tomorrow, he kept his mouth shut! Eventually they all four arrived at the restaurant, and again they were made most welcome, one good thing happened, the meal was chosen for them, the only choice they had to make was the wine, and they had a laugh talking about last night's meal, with the potatoes gliding on the plate on the same direction of the swell, as the boat was going from side to side, the potatoes on the plates were doing the same, and Rebeca and Debra laughed every time they remind themselves about it. They were going to stay for a week at least, Robert was leaving Happy girl there, so that he could drive down with his wife, and go out on the boat on nice days, he always felt at home there. There was a problem that so far had not been solved, it is an important problem to which there are various solutions, it was getting back! The skipper offered to take them to the railway station, or Peter and Juliet can drive down and have six in the car on the way back, they could get a chauffeured Limousine at least to Plymouth to catch a mainline train to Paddington in London, whatever happens Robert must come back to sort out the boat.

In the morning, they were already in good time, Robert drove "the car" down to the harbour, where the fishermen's coffee shop was open for good, homely breakfasts, where they were sat, Robert could see the entrance of the harbour, and when he saw the navy tender arrive, they all got up and made their way to meet the navy. There were four sailors on board, looking very smart in their Sunday best, Joan was excited just by the uniform, but she kept filming. They were helped on board by two of them, then they were off at speed, it was a little rough which made the trip to the Frigate exciting. It took three quarters of an hour to reach the warship. Some reception! the captain did his very best to make them feel most welcome, he especially spent a lot of time greeting Rebeca, then he explained what today's excitement is going to be, they are in luck. The authorities have been tracking a sixty-foot sailboat which left Brazil two months ago, todays orders is for the Frigate to intercept the sail boat as it enters the English channel, the crew of that boat is carrying almost a ton of Cocaine, and they have to be arrested, at the moment they are approximately 50 miles from the Frigate, so it will take two and a half hours to reach their position. The captain introduced a young officer as their guide whilst on board, and the first place they were visiting, was their accommodation. So that is where they went, Rebeca was the last one to see her cabin which was well fitted out, the young officer waited outside for Rebeca to reappear, and when she did, the two of them collected the other three, Rebeca realised that he is going to be with her almost all the time, so she asked him 'what do I call you' he replied by return, 'miss just call me Norman', well she replied, 'then call me Rebeca' and that became an introduction for Rebeca to the nice young man she thought about a couple of nights ago. Before going to the bridge Norman gave them all a tour of the ship. Joan was surprised when she found out that they were women sailors in the British Navy, why did she not know that before? That was her question to herself. It is going to be an early lunch today because, they are going to be busy when they reach the sailboat.

It looks as if talking on the bridge is not the thing to do, either the captain or first officer do all of the talking, and it is usually orders, Norman had explained all that before they had stepped onto the bridge, however it was a lovely view, from there one realised how fast they were moving, that is what Rebeca was thinking, she asked Norman if she could go to the engine room, he was surprised by her request. He told her that it was no problem, but if the others want to stay on the bridge, he will have to get someone else to cover for him.

That is what happened, and Rebeca now was on her way to visit the engine room, whilst they were traveling as fast as possible. Norman had never been there whilst the ship was underway, and on the way down he asked her why she wanted to see the engines, she just replied that she had studied marine engines, and she wanted to talk to the chief engineer; as it happened, he would never be willing to let a woman in the engine room, he was a little bit old fashion, so when he saw the young officer with a girl enter his domain, the hairs at the back of his neck went up! He was not a happy man, at this moment he was very apprehensive whilst his engines were close to full revs, but after all, Norman was an officer, so he asked him the reason for this girl. Norman did not know what to say, 'well she would like to talk to you about your engines' That was a new one on him, so he managed to find two pairs of ear defenders, and after they had been placed correctly, he invited Rebeca to the noisy engine room itself, as soon as his office door opened the noise it itself, she thought could kill you. She stood there for a while, then turned to the chief and asked him what the stroke of the pistons was, she suspected it must be at least one meter, that was his first surprise, because it was one point two meters, then she spotted some oil dripping from the left engine only, yes he knew about it, and before he had time to say anything else she told him that a seal was about to pack up altogether shortly, she asked him why it had not been changed at the last stop, for that one he had no answer, then she told him that he will be glad when they catch up with the sail boat, because he will be able slow the engines and be certain that they can get back home with two engines. She told him that before leaving she would like to have a chat with him about his work, Norman now was the one who was surprised when the chief told her that she is welcome to visit at any time, on the way back to the bridge, he asked her where she studied marine engines, she told him that she had read three books on the subject, that's all there was to it. He could not wait to tell others, the chief could not keep that revelation to himself, he was taught a lesson by an eighteen-year-old good-looking girl, he still does not believe it!

Joan had gone off on her own filming as much as she could, and sometimes she would come across a woman sailor, then spend time with her, finding out how life was on board for her, and every time she received a positive reply, they all were happy to be on board, they were treated just as if they were men, and no to the last question they are not allowed to fraternise with the men. That was the one thing that put her off thinking anymore about joining the navy! They had their lunch in the officers mess, that is where they found out what was going to happen, Norman had sat next to Rebeca and the two of them became oblivious of everybody else, they both could not stop talking, it was a getting to know you chat, which they were both enjoying, both Robert and Debra were well aware and also a little surprised to see Rebeca talking to a "Boy".

The ship now had the sailboat on their Radar and planning had begun in earnest, they do not want the sailboat crew to be aware of them, because if the Frigate is spotted too soon it gives the crew of the sailboat time to throw all the drugs overboard. So, the plan is for them to make a large circle and eventually position themselves behind the sail boat by three in the afternoon the sun will be behind them on the sail boat, which means that the crew on that boat might eventually see that they have another boat behind them, but because of the sun they will not find out that it is a warship, then it will be too late for them to do anything about their illicit cargo, after the arrest of the crew, four sailors will then continue the journey in the sailboat to the nearest large harbour in England.

The Captain had a break which he spent with Robert and Debra, mostly talking about Rebeca and himself, yes he enjoyed his work, sometimes he could find himself homesick, but that would not last too long, a Frigate being a smaller ship, there was only a short chain of command, and the ship run more like a family than a British navy Warship, they sometimes had to fire their guns, but normally it was all peaceful, today made a nice change for them, and they will be the talk of the base in Portsmouth. Robert told him that he had been an officer in intelligence during the second world war. It was pleasant on the bridge, the view was great, now using a code they had declared radio silence, so there were not expecting any new orders, now the sailboat was close and still out of site and within three quarters of an hour they will be directly behind their target, and the Frigate will be on action readiness.

Norman and Rebeca had made a couple tours of the ship, stopping sometimes because she wanted to know more about what she was looking at, she stopped almost for a half hour to learn about the submarine detection system, (sonar) which was always working, she asked many questions, and got all the answers she wanted.

Norman did manage to tell her that she was an interesting person, she had heard that often, but this time she managed to blush! He had been in the Navy since leaving school, he had three years in the officers' college and this was his very first posting, she told him of course that in few weeks' times, she will be in a college in Oxford, but she will still do her weekly television show on Sundays, she told him to watch it Sunday after next as he will most likely be mentioned. Now the Frigate is right behind the sailboat, and all they must do, is to catch up with them, that is after they had launched two fast gun boats, each with a well-armed crew. It all worked just like clockwork, the two fast boats caught the villains by surprise, they had no choice but to give up, not ten minutes had past, and the Frigate was in sight of the sailboat. The attack crew had four men arrested, and one of the attack crew, with a pistol in his right hand went searching below where he found a fifth man who had just undone a through hull fitting which now was letting in tons of water. He called out for help with a spanner to close the valve. There was almost a foot of water in the cabin, which they will be able to pump out, they then returned to the Frigate with the five prisoners, and the crew who are going to sail this boat back to England was transferred to the sailboat for them to examine it and make sure that it is in a seaworthy condition for them to sail back, also did it have sufficient drinking water and food?

It turned out that it was well equipped' and they left the area before the Frigate. The skipper of the sailboat was English but the other four were foreign, nobody could make out which country they came from. All five were now in prison cells which all had both a microphone and camera well hidden, the English man was on his own, it looked as if the other four were not pleased with him. The Captain called for Norman to call him back on the bridge, and when he did he was asked if Rebeca was with him, and she was, so next he was told to take her to the radio room, then she was asked if she knew the language they were speaking, yes it was Arabic, so there she was for quite a long time listening to their conversation, after a while she thought that she had recognised the name of the man in England who had organised it all. They always thought that they would get away with it, and they still had no idea that the authorities had been watching them ever since they had left Brazil, they were blaming the skipper, and they were not looking forward to spending time in prison. Apart from that they talked about their lives in the past and the future, all four had been seasick during the voyage which not even one of them had enjoyed. The evening meal was a special occasion especially for the guests, there was going to be fireworks on the deck and the meal for all the crew on board is going to be served by the officers, whilst a four men band is going to play some music. Of course Norman was one of the officers serving the meal, there was a good chance that he is going to be on duty all night and part of the morning, which means he might never see her again, so, when he had the opportunity to serve Rebeca, he had placed a note for her under the plate, and as he was depositing the plate in front of her, at the same time he whispered telling her that he had written her a note, and where it was. That was some excitement for her, she wondered what he had written, and the moment she had finished what was on the plate, she moved it around and at the same time dropping the note on her lap, she waited until they accidently were looking at each other and she smiled. That was the last time she had seen him.

Sometime in the night the Frigate was going to dock in Plymouth to discharge the five prisoners, then it is going to turn back to meet up with the sailboat and when passing close to the fishing harbour, the tender will take the crew of Happy girl back to their harbour, in the morning as they were leaving a wonderful ship, all four felt sad, they had such a good time, now it's almost back to normal, Robert made sure that his boat was in good shape and had some long discussions with the harbour master who is Rebeca's friend the skipper. The harbour is too small to have permanent visitors, so they made a deal between the two of them, they are saying that Happy girl is there in case the lifeboat has a mechanical problem, and that the lifeboat crew can use it in an emergency, which means that it will be well looked after which pleases Robert. The sailboat with three million pounds worth of drugs on board is going to arrive at Plymouth the next day, they will be met by the police who will take charge of the evidence, in time the Admiralty Marshalls will place the boat in an auction, the funds after the sale will mostly go to a navy charity. The crew are staying in the cottage for another three days of swimming of the beach, then it is the job of packing everything they can into a bag small and light enough to be carried on a train where, at the end of their journey they will be met by Sarah and Debra's husband at Paddington station.

Rebeca needed a rest, she had a fabulous time; she will never forget, she still has the note from Norman who wrote telling her what a lovely person she is, and he felt that they had a lot more to tell each other, he gave her his mobile number so that perhaps, they can text each other, that is what she is going to do as soon as she can. Nobody talked on the train, they all had different thoughts about their last experience, first the trip down the Thames was exiting mostly because of the unknown ahead of them, finding out about the Frigate especially for Robert was very exciting, how did she manage it, yes she did a good job saying nothing, boy, the girl can keep a secret! These were his recurring thoughts. Joan was amongst all those sailors, she never even got the chance of talking to one of them, what is wrong with her! Debra her thoughts were about the film she is going to make with all the photography she is going to edit, then it turned to Rebeca, how did she manage to get the Prime Minister to arrange the Frigate? The other thing was the old problem that Rebeca will not resolve for her, yes and why not! Then of course Rebeca had many thoughts, she was impressed with the two engines in the Frigate, she loved talking to Norman, then she would remember that she will call the Prime Minister to thank him for his kind gesture, then there was Oxford and now she was worried, she kept giving herself a question which so far, she has not been able to resolve, should she get help?

What had become such an important question for her was; should she still address the Dean as "Sam", "her Sam" or simply "Sir"? She knows that Robert would say "Sir." Then she started to think about Norman, why does she miss him? That has never happened to her, how can she be missing someone, having known them for only 24 hours? She did something that helps her when there are too many questions passing through her head, it usually works; she picks a foreign language, one she is good at, and poses all the questions to herself in that particular language, luckily the train was arriving at Paddington station, and within a few minutes she is going to be reunited with the person she has lived with all her life, she loves her mother! They had arranged to drive Robert home first and then come back to the apartment. Debra was met by her husband, and they drove Joan home.

Sarah wanted to know about the trip, by the looks of her it was obvious that Rebeca must have had a good time, she told her mother that the whole trip was exciting, she had not realised that the Thames was so long, she loved navigating the boat especially at night time, she stood by the side of a huge marine engine that was driving the Frigate at a high speed, she got on well with the chief engineer with whom she had a great discussion, she more or less mentioned everything that happened, however she never mentioned Norman! She now had two days until she makes a recording for Sunday's program, but first she wants to discuss it with Debra before the film is edited to make sure that they do not contradict themselves. Her mother surprised her; the head had at school asked her if she knew how her daughter had so much knowledge, she must be in touch with some profoundly serious people in government. It was not the first time Sarah had asked her and this time she is not going to be happy until her question has been answered. 'Well mum it is so strange, even Debra was asking me the very same question, and even her was not pleased that I could not give her an answer, what I do is read as much news as I can, workout the consequences of what I have learned and usually I get it right, however sometimes I have a feeling that I am wrong so I throw that out, I cannot explain that to myself, so how can I ever explain that to anybody else?' now Sarah was confused, and had no idea what so ever how to add anything more to her question.

Some of the executives at the BBC had been wondering the very same thing, at least one of them had asked Debra, in any event they did not want to make a big deal about it and then upset Rebeca, the next day was spent all day with her father's parents who wanted to hear all about her trip, especially the role of the Prime Minister, the day after it was the same but with her mother's parents, they could not take their eyes of her, they were finding it hard to take it all in, sometimes when there was just the two of them they would feel upset having missed the early part of her life, they were both jealous but pleased that James's parents took charge at the time. One evening she found the time to draft an article for "Them" it was about the arrest of the sailboat that had come all the way from Brazil.

Just three weeks and she will be at the Oxford College. She now must be careful with her own telephone, so far Norman and Rebeca have exchanged four sets of texts. She seemed to have made a good impression with the captain, he had seen her on the television, he is up to date with her exploits, but he had never realised how smart she was, even telling the chief engineer that he had a problem with one of his engines which should be fixed as soon as possible. Oh, yes she did remember to call the Prime Minister, she thanked him as it was such an exciting trip, she also told him that the crew thought that it was something she had arranged, but again thank you it was such a lovely surprise I will never forget, when she called him, he was in a cabinet meeting, and he took the time to speak to her, she felt that he was sincere when he told her that he enjoyed hearing from her. Eventually she did speak to Robert, she asked him about the Sam business, of course he had the right answer: which was: when it is only the two, Sam is ok and when other people are there it's Sir. It was a Tuesday the first day in Oxford, and Robert took her there, her accommodation was going to be in the college itself for the whole three years, unlike the other students they had prepared a small one room apartment which is usually occupied by lecturers, this way her very important computer will be secure, and she will be safe, if she buys a car, she will also have a parking place. Robert wanted to have a word with the Dean, so they both knocked at his door, his face completely changed when he realised that Rebeca was there, he was so pleased to see her, especially to tell her what a great job she was doing in the secret department, although Robert wanted to have a chat, first the Dean wanted to personally show Rebeca her quarters, he told her that other students will want to know why she has that accommodation, it is because she is involved in the University, he then told her who to visit next and the Dean and Robert both wished her luck, and for the first time in her life, she was truly on her own, that was exciting. There was so much to find out in the university and in Oxford, she will have to meet all the other students, including the chap from her school, she is going to wait until her mother should be back home, and she will call her to tell her how she is doing so far.

She made her way to the registration office, where there was a crowd of students all waiting to register, so Rebeca had no choice but wait with the others, which turned out all right, because the girl in front of her was only too happy to be talking to Rebeca, they both felt the same, that feeling of being lonely. The girl when she turned around and was able to look at Rebeca, recognised her from the Sunday morning program, her father always watched her every Sunday, her name was Paula and she was on an English Literature course so they were never going to meet in class, as Rebeca was learning all about political science, they had already arranged to meet at meal times, until they know their times, after registration, it was accommodation, Rebeca still had to be there to obtain the details of her accommodation which included the keys and the rules. The man she had to speak to, made a fuss about giving her the key, he could not believe that a student had the right of a lecturers flat, and he was preparing to do something about it, everybody in the room could not have missed the goings on, and now they were all listening. He had already picked up the telephone, and about to start dialling a number, when Rebeca told him that he better be careful, because the Dean himself had taken the time, only a half hour ago to show her the apartment. So, he begrudgery handed her the key, Paula who had seen it all happen in front of her was speechless, and now was looking forward to lunching tomorrow. Rebeca had to meet up with Robert again, before he left to go back home, all her effects were still in his car, between the two of them and a couple of trips, her apartment was all setup, Robert stayed long enough to make certain that her computer was in working order. There was a commissioner who was at the main door all day long, he was there to help the residents and direct visitors, he took to Rebeca right of way, and over the three years they were to become good friends.

Chapter Twelve - More Learning

It did not take long for Rebeca to make friends in Oxford, everybody had realised that she was a protégé of the Dean. There was an online discussion every other week with "Them", they discussed mostly affairs related to "Them". It was the first time any of them had direct contact with the media, they all wanted to have a say in the direction they wanted to go with this new power, so there were always things to discuss with Rebeca to make sure that she does not put a foot wrong, a couple of times she had come too close to the line.

Now she does her best not to expose herself by seeming to be knowing too much, on her Sunday morning talks. At Oxford she attended all the lectures, and best still she studied each subject before the lectures, each time she managed to ask at least one awkward but serious question, which sometimes the lecturer could not answer. They were usually pleased for her to be in the class, but always apprehensive of not being able to give her an answer, it would sometimes use up the rest of the time discussing her question. She had taken to cook all her own meals, the College was not far from a wonderful covered market, she always managed to do shopping there twice a week, sometimes she would invite her friend Paula at the weekend for a meal, she would discuss politics with her, and in turn Paula would attempt to give her friend the latest she had learnt about English Literature. That exchange of subjects did well for both, at the end of a session they both felt that they had learnt something interesting, some days Rebeca would tell her friend a question she should ask about Literature to the lecturer, it was always an awkward question, the next time they would both have a laugh about the lecturer's reaction. Rebeca never invited one of the boys back to her apartment, her and Norman kept correspondence going, they were in touch at least once a month, at which time they were getting to know each other well. She had three regular visitors, her mother, Debra and Robert, the other student who was in her school was doing well, she went out with him a few times to the market to help him select various foods for him to cook for himself, they would often have coffee where they would talk about the old school and especially the head, whom they both liked. There was not even one person in the College who begrudged her the position she had. She was known for partaking in practical jokes, they were always good fun, even the Dean had fallen for one of them, his reaction was simply a big smile!

The first year just flew by, the few times she had gone home for a holiday, she never stayed long, except during the summer holidays, which was always with her mother, down to the cottage, if Robert was there they would attempt to go out in Happy girl, she would always meet up with the skipper, both mother and daughter would sometimes be invited to his house for a meal, during those couple of weeks it was lovely for both as they were recognised wherever they went, they were always greeted with a smile. The cottage these days was well used, Peter and Juliet would come for a long weekend, Robert would always have his wife with him, it all made for "Happy families" During the second year, the Prime Minister was re-elected for the second time, and Rebeca sent him a nice letter congratulating him. He replied by return and at the same time he invited her to attend a party he was giving, about that she was pleased and looking forward to it. Rebeca called Joan the photographer and asked her if she would like to attend the same party, to take photos, of course she wanted to go, so Rebeca wrote to the PM and asked if it was possible, and the answer was yes of course. What Rebeca had forgotten was that Debra all this time had been making a documentary movie about her, and that invite to the PM's party was going to be very much part of that movie. The Prime Minister was one of the few people who knew about "Them". He was never surprised to hear about Rebeca's ideas on Sunday mornings, he did not know how it was achieved, but understood they were her source of information. Both his wife and secretary got to know Rebeca well, he often talked about her and of course his secretary read all their correspondence. The party was on a Saturday afternoon, again at Chequers, Joan did the driving in her car and Rebeca did the navigating, that was a mistake they managed to get lost. At one time when Joan was making a uturn on a narrow road, she had to stop for a moment, 'oh Joan look at this field, how beautiful it is'. It was wheat just like the sea but gold in colour with waves made by the light wind, that was the first time she had seen such a beautiful site. There was one of the Royals in attendance who particularly wanted to have a chat with Rebeca, as soon as it was possible, Rebeca showed him the way to that little lounge where she had been last time, he was surprised that she walked around the place just as if she was living there, there was no guess work for her selecting the correct door.

He was much impressed to find himself sitting with Rebeca, in a quiet room where he could attempt to learn about her. He started with general chit chat, then he wanted to know as much as he could about her education. She did tell him about never sitting for exams at school, she told him that her main interest, is learning and finding solutions that make sense when a problem presents itself. He had never met a person who had a photographic memory, she mentioned her two pack card trick, he kept shaking his head in utter disbelief, she recounted the time she had spent on the Frigate when she walked into the Chief Engineer's domain, 'it was like taming a Lion' she said to him, but we parted good friends, he had not realised that I have studied marine engines and we were talking on the same level. ' Yes when I was leaving the Frigate, he came all the way up to the deck to wish me good luck, when I was fourteen the skipper of the life boat allowed me to steer the boat which at the time was on its way to rescue a family who had just crossed the Atlantic and have their sail boat sink about twenty miles from Penzance, you might have seen the photographs I took at the time in the Sunday papers, after they had been picked up from their life raft, they were installed below and I stayed with them, they were all four in shock, and I just talked to them about my life right up to the time we had entered the harbour, both the husband and his wife gave me a big hug and thanked me when they were leaving, apparently he is some big politician in the States. I remember the Chief Constable in Scotland Yard, telling me that the FBI were asking about me, he had never found out what it was all about, so I told him about the rescue, and I am aware that one day I am going to visit them. In a few months I have to decide, if I want to continue at University or go out to work, I know that he BBC would like me to become a television personality, but that would not suite me, you are the first person to know, but I am thinking of visiting the Chief Constable and ask him to organise for me to do the training, so that I can get into the mind of a Policeman, he has told me to ask him for anything and he will always do his best for me'.

The man himself was lost listening to Rebeca, he was beginning to realise that she was a special person, the other thing she had was her own mind! He could not wait to find out her secret so, he thought that this was the best time to ask her. 'Rebeca, there is something I would love to know about you?' He had started using a firm voice, but when he looked at her, he could see that no, this was not the right time, and before he had a chance of saying another word, she gave him some education. 'You are about to ask me the question everybody I know has already asked including my mother and all my relatives. To start with I have many friends in important places, I treat them all equally I have never ever called a man "Sir", to me we are all equal, there are many subjects that a person becomes expert in, I speak to most of my friends on a regular basis, they are then all waiting for me to ask them the latest news on their particular subject, which they have ready for me to digest, usually with some discussion. So, you see, it is not difficult when you know how, of course some people chose not to believe a single word, but for that I care not!

He had realised that playing the Royal Card, after hearing her little speech was going to be a waste of time, no, he did not believe a single word about her story, but he well understood that she was never going to tell. It must have been the first time in his life that this Royal Person had not got what he asked for, he was almost pleased, life had always been too easy for him, he appreciated Rebeca's candour, he never wanted to miss out and he gave her his private telephone number, he also told her that he would be only too pleased for her to call him, and if she needs any help, he is here for her. They were seen walking back to the reception together after a long absence, both with a broad smile.

The Prime Minister was the first one to reach her, he asked her if she had a good talk with his Highness, there was no one close to them, and she replied 'I don't know about his Highness, I just know a nice man, I did tell him I have never even called a man with the word "Sir" in front of the name, he knows now that I don't recognise titles, and he wants to meet up with me one day, he really wanted to butter me up so that I would tell him where I get all my information from, and as you know I am not allowed to divulge that part of my life, he agreed with her and together they had a secret which for both was a nice thing. Joan had managed to capture, "the man" walking with Rebeca, it turned out to be a winner which was published in every newspaper and most magazines, they both looked happy and at the same time a little guilty. The Prime Minister's wife asked Rebeca if when she has finished her education, she could entertain the idea of joining a group of women who are always trying to improve lives for young mothers, Rebeca surprised her by being positive to take part when she leaves University, in the meanwhile she would like to observe at least one meeting with the group.

There were two High Court Judges, both had that serious look, almost as if they were both on duty, so Rebeca went out of her way to befriend them, the first one was pleased to be talking to her, he never asked her how! She was especially pleased about that, she thought to herself that if ever she had done something so wrong that she was to find herself in front of a Judge, there is no doubt that he would be a fair person. Then she approached the second Judge, who gave her a nice welcoming smile, he did not shake hands with her, but he was holding something in his right hand, and when he was certain that nobody could see him, he opened his hand and revealed that same little gold bar, it really took her by surprise, and when she recovered, he suggested they find a quiet corner so as to have a nice chat, it looked so strange to others seeing her taking the Judge away to the same small room. Just the same reaction as the Royal, 'how does she know her way around Chequers?' She had never met up with him at the quarterly meetings of "Them".

'You have not realised I guess but I have written to you at least four times, it was always about the Law, and twice you have used my comments to make an important point that got the legal fraternity to react, you have become our most powerful voice,' He was so pleased to have had the chance of telling her, and of course she replied: 'I have been well aware that I speak for you all, sometimes I succeed in adding my point of view, always to make certain that the whole idea comes from me so to stop people looking too much, even then, I am often asked where do I get my ideas from? My mother has given up, so has the producer of the Sunday program, the nice man they call the Royal had planned to ask me the same, and before he did, I managed to Fob him off, at the same time I told him that I never use titles, so far in my life I have never called a man sir, however a military rank is completely different, by the way, the Royal man asked me to call him on his private number if ever I need his help, or just a bit of conversation. I must be the first person he knows that does not recognise his Title! He was well surprised about my audacity, he told me that for once in his life, for a short time only the so-called Royal had become something he could never be, that is a normal human being, and for that he thanked me, and I could tell that he meant it.'

The Prime Minister had not yet managed to have a talk with Rebeca, he also needed to have a chat with the Judge, he excused himself and visited the two that had almost stopped talking in the little lounge, and when he walked in unannounced on the two of them, they were pleased to see him, the Prime Minister was well aware that both the Judge and Rebeca both carried a gold bar. First he wanted to discuss Rebeca's future after the University, he already had something in mind for her, to do with the House of Commons, an awful lot of people wanted to direct her towards an interesting career, always for the best of course, the problem would have been that she is too independent, when she told about her plan, spending six months learning to think like a policeman in the police college. It surprised both, but then they could not work out her reasoning, it might just be the first training she gets up to.

When the Judge asked a second time, she told him that to be a success you must at least understand how people think, she looked at the Judge and told him that six months later she will be asking him for help to work for another six months in a Barrister's office. There was some more, one for certain becoming a crew aboard a large warship to study how the crew work as one! She told them that after that she might be ready to enter politics, that put a smile on the Prime Minister's face, now he was happy. The Prime Minister's party had been a great success, it was enjoyed by all, Rebeca did not manage to speak to every person there, but she had managed to get tired, and she enjoyed sitting in Joan's car and just relax, of course the driver could not stop talking, she was full of all the important people she had spoken to and photographed, she told Rebeca that she had a real treasure of photographs, it is very rare for her to have been allowed to photograph the party, she could name every person who was there. 'You know Rebeca I could not have done all that, without you having been there, everyone saw me take the picture of you and the Royal, thereafter no one dare refuse me, your just bloody amazing! How do you do it?'

Norman ended up in hospital having twisted his left foot going down a sharp set of stairs on the ship, after some tests in Hospital he was diagnosed with a bone problem, which was not too serious but meant that he could not go back on duty on board a ship, now he was still recovering in the Naval Hospital. The first Saturday Rebeca managed to talk her mother into driving her to Portsmouth, she was going to surprise Norman with a visit. They arrived at the gate which was the only entrance into the Royal Navy part of the harbour, it was not at all what she expected, to gain entrance one needs a pass, which takes a few days to organise, Rebeca and her mother had come unstuck, the guard who was not letting them in had not recognised Rebeca, so that did not help.

The guard was asked to call a superior officer so that Rebeca can have a talk with him, reluctantly he obliged and called a young officer, who right of way recognised her, he had seen the photograph of Rebeca and the Royal, and in any case, he remembered her trip on board the Frigate. He asked who it was she wanted to see, she told him, and he jumped in the car and directed her mother to drive, when they reached the Hospital, he accompanied them all the way to Norman. Sarah did not go all the way with Rebeca, but stayed back with the young officer who was only too pleased to be talking to Rebeca's mother. A nurse now was leading her towards Norman, she saw him first, he was sleeping at the time, she quietly sat on the side of the bed, and she whispered his name in his ear, he must have thought that he was dreaming and eventually he woke up. That scene should have been filmed as he automatically sat up, pushed his arms out in a welcoming gesture, and she fell into them. Not a word was said as he was holding her, they were both surprised at each other, and she could not miss seeing her photograph on the hospital bed side table. It all made the trip worthwhile, and at last they started to talk. First it was finding out what had happened to him, then he wanted her to tell him what she had been up to, yes, he did see the photograph with the Royal, he told her that she looked good. He asked and she told him how she got here, and that the guard at the gate would not let them in, apparently it is not visiting time, but it was not difficult mostly because he is an officer. All that time they were holding hands, he thought that he was going to be discharged within a week, at which time he will finish his recuperation at home. They stopped talking for a while and just unbelievably stared at each other, he could not believe that she was there, and in turn she could not believe that she fell into his arms, and on top of that it felt good, they were both beginning to feel guilty having Sarah waiting for Rebeca who then suggested fetching her, and that is what she did. Before today her mother had no idea that her daughter had met a young man, so for her it has all come at once.

Eventually the same guard saluted Rebeca when they were driving out, he must have found out more about her! The plan was to wait for Norman to be sent home and Rebeca will visit him for a day at a time, his parents already were aware of Rebeca, she was now on the last few months of her course and could well take Wednesdays off to visit him at home and now in her own car she never had difficulties following a map and finding her way in towns. His father never had to pick her up at the railway station, and now that Norman was back in action, that is learning about military intelligence, he was home every weekend. Rebeca had less involvement with the students on her course which now was giving her a bit more time to do all the important things in her life, she had already asked her friend the Chief Constable about joining an intake of recruits as soon as she has finished her degree, it was now all arranged, it was for her to say when. Sometimes she would spend all of Sunday with Norman helping him study his course. One day he could not help himself, telling her about the time he had realised that he had automatically thought that they would be together for the rest of their lives, he had been worried about her reaction. Well he need not be worried, she said 'I think of that sometimes, I guess one day when we are both settled, people might be expecting us to get married, but Norman it is important for me that it is our own decision, there is another thing in the background of my life that you know nothing about, even my mother does not know, she does realise that I know many influential people, I can pick up a telephone and call let's say a Royal person, a Prime Minister, a High Court Judge, a chief Constable, a BBC producer and many more well-known and influential people, when we do get married, you will have to understand, that mostly the conversations I have with some of those people have to stay with me, if you ever wondered how I am able to have so much information in my head, that is why, and please keep all that to yourself', she was almost certain that she had got away with it, and he forgets about it and does not start asking question then we will get married. The last term at college, seemed to drag for Rebeca, everybody else were all revising, which she did not need to do, so she started reading books on the British Police force, how it started and how it compares with other nations, then she read the books all police officers must read and know well. When she will be on the course, she wants to spend less time learning and more time observing, she will have to give the Chief Constable a report and perhaps some changes he should make, so she wants to be ready, at the moment she has a bee in her bonnet, she is actually thinking of learning a sixth language, but first she want to make certain that it will be useful for her.

Eventually she did sit for the exam, and she was the first one out in the knowledge that she will get top marks. The first Monday after the exam she had tea with the Dean and his wife who really enjoyed her company, when the Dean's wife had left and there was only Rebeca and the Dean in the room, she told him about her plans including a possible marriage, she explained to the Dean how she hopes she had pulled the wool over Norman's eyes. He agreed with her that at first it is going to be difficult for her, but in time they will both get used to the situation, he is sure of that, she is going to vacate the small apartment in about a weeks' time, she thanked him for his kindness and gave him an enormous hug, however it is not all that bad because they will meet every three months and no doubt they will exchange emails from time to time.

Chapter Thirteen - The Police Force and the Law

The latest training course started at eight in the morning of the first Monday of the month, she could have walked there from home, but it would have meant leaving too early, so Rebeca drove herself to the Police college, it was two months before Christmas, and for her everything had been well sorted, she was ready for anything. She told herself to enjoy every moment of the coming experience. The course usually starts with twenty cadets, but this time an extra one had been added, the officer in charge was not too pleased, he did not appreciate having one extra person added at the last minute. He was just told a couple of days before by his superior who could not tell him why, but told him that it was a special person, a woman at that, he had worked out all the various teams and now he was stuck with an extra one, his wife told him to stop complaining, and that there must be a reason for it all.

The week before Rebeca had her hair styled with a short cut, yes, she did look different, which is exactly what she wanted. She was the third person to arrive, she then found herself in a fair size room where form filling started, that did not take long, and one then had time to get to know all the others who joined that first day. Rebeca talked to everyone, they were all exited, and she started her own work that first hour by asking each one why they joined the Police Force, that night she wrote what the answers were, from wanting to help people, liking the idea of more power, better than being unemployed, and one last odd one, it was a bet he lost! She was pleased because she understood that she got the real reasons, not always the ones which had been written in answer to a question on a form! She was going to keep track of the rest of the others to see how they get on. By lunch time the form filling was over, and they were shown their quarters, that was another problem for the officer in charge, she was the only recruit who made her way home every night, on that point he argued with his superior who could do nothing about it, it all came from above, nobody could do anything about it. Rebeca was aware that it could possibly cause trouble, so she had decided on a plan to remedy the problem. The problem is that every time she thought of a plan, it never seemed to be right, so she looked for an opportunity to present itself, she really did not want him to know what she was up to, so at first, she is going to be a perfect student and make him feel appreciated. She is worried about the physical exercises she will have to do, that is going to be something new for her, she has started at home in an attempt of getting fit, her mother now can hardly keep up with her, one day its books the next day its push ups. Sarah has begun to ignore her daughter, it is easier for her, in any case she has herself to look after as now for the first time in her life she has fallen for a widower who happens to also be a teacher in the same school. The head asked Rebeca if she could come and give a talk to a group of the older students about her university experience, of course she was only too pleased, and they enjoyed her taking time for them. That was another annoyance for the officer in charge, she was allowed to take time off from time to time, so she kept it to the minimum.

A month had gone by, the man's attitude towards her was even worse than she had thought possible, but one day it all changed through an accident. That morning, they all had a go at the parallel bars, it was a difficult exercise for everybody, one must hold on whilst upside down, most could not achieve that task, especially Rebeca who was hopeless, when she was doing her best which was nowhere good enough, the gold bar dislodged itself and fell on the mat, disaster! He spotted it as it fell right by his feet, next he picked it up and he was speechless for a time, he looked at it, read her name and noticed the crown, he knew what it meant but could not believe his eyes. She realised what had happened, so before he had the chance of saying a single word, she asked for it back and suggested that they go where his mobile telephone was and she will call the Chief Constable on his private line, and he can listen to her conversation with him about this new problem. He really had no choice in the matter, at first, he did not believe that she could call him directly, so they left all the others to practice by themselves whilst they went to the changing rooms for her to make the call. He was even more astonished when he heard the Chief answering the call which was on loud speaker, asking Rebeca if she was alright, she explained who was with her and what had just happened, the Chief told the officer to first-hand the bar back to her, under any circumstance tell nobody else about it including his own wife, and visit him in Scotland Yard tomorrow morning at eleven sharp, it is a national security problem so I remind you again of the importance, then using a more fatherly voice he said goodbye to Rebeca. Luckily nobody else had noticed what had just happened, they had all more or less thought that she was going to be told off, but when they both came back they seemed to have become good friends, he had realised that he had stumbled unto some intrigue, and he started to think that he never treated Rebeca as a total stranger, as if he had known her in a different life, and then at last the penny dropped and yes it was her! Oh boy was he ever a happy man, a private meeting with the Chief Constable, a Television star, international intrigue, possible promotion and after all she is a lovely person who can't get on with the parallel bars!

He did go to Scotland Yard the next morning, somewhat apprehensive, was it all a joke? No to his surprise he was expected, there was no time wasted and he was sitting on the other side of the desk with the Chief Constable, taking the time from his busy schedule to talk with him! Some complicated explanations were given to him, which now did not make too much sense, he left the office with the certain knowledge that he had accidently come across some strange undercover goings on, and that lives matter should it become public. He is to never ever mention what he now knows, in the next few months he is going to get calls from people who work in the background of the Police force, and he will most likely be recruited to a much better position, when he discovers what it is all about, he will realise the importance of his silence. All the people involved are all bound by the same secrecy that he now also must be bound by. He started to put two and two together and he was beginning to get a picture; what was Rebeca doing on a Royal Navy warship? What was she doing with the Royal? Why does she attend the Prime Minister's parties? There is something going on, isn't there? Those were his thoughts driving back to work at the Police College. It was going to be difficult for him not to speak even a single word to Rebeca, but that was a definite order. In any event this secrecy made him special, and he liked that, so he went back to work a happy man. The other twenty in the class did not take long to discover that he was no longer upset about Rebeca. One of them Samantha had become friendly towards Rebeca, and they would often talk at lunch time, she had the same problem doing physical exercises, which made for two people in the group who would attempt to use their intelligence rather than muscles, but they both knew that they must persist.

At lunch time Samantha asked Rebeca if she had noticed that he had arrived late and so far, he had not screamed at her, she did not reply, just acted as if she had not understood the question, and of course she did a better job of attaching the gold bar! Yes, there was no more orders shouted at Rebeca, they all realised that things had changed, and the Sargent Major attitude had disappeared, he was now approachable, the course progressed at a better rate. Before the six months had passed, they all discovered who Rebeca was, she had managed to think like a police woman, she was pleased about that, before actually leaving she had a long chat with the man in charge, before she had the chance of saying anything, he thanked her for showing him the way, he had realised that after he had changed his approach towards discipline, everybody worked better and he managed to get them all through the course which was unusual, he thanked her for it, he did mention that it was taking a long time but they intend to move him to Intelligence, she was pleased for him, and after congratulating him for a job well done, she said goodbye to him, they parted just like two ships passing in the night! She was now officially a Police woman, and it was time for a change, the Chief Constable called her on the telephone to tell her that her report was excellent, the other thing was that this intake all did well, it must have been her being there, she told him that in due course she will send him her own report, he had not expected that from her, and he was looking forward to it, she was going to mention the course on this Sunday's broadcast. Now she was going to dig into the Law, but first she gave herself just five months to get up to speed on the law, she managed to visit ten lectures on different aspects of the Law in England, she did not need to sit for the exam, but she had no problem to be taking the exam in five months' time, of course her good friend the Judge organised all that for her, including a place in a very influential Law Firm in Fleet Street who were really looking forward to her joining them.

Norman was always busy studying how the Navy use intelligence as part of their weapons, he had never realised before how useful it is against an adversary, he enjoyed every day, he is on an actual course with three more officers, they all get on well and always help each other, all four feel privilege to be on the course, almost every day, Norman speaking to himself, would thank Rebeca for her guidance. By now he is getting to find out what an interesting person she is, on top of that he still could not understand how it is that she knows that many important people, she seems to be free to go almost anywhere she wants to go, he was pleased for her that she did so well in the Police Academy, but he still cannot understand why she did it. And now she has decided to have a look at the Law, and again why? In the end it is only Rebeca who knows why! The BBC would like to know some more about Rebeca, but they already know that it is not likely to happen. They themselves cannot complain, she is always on time for recording but sometimes live, it is always her choice, and she has never let them down. She now has a contract and earns a large sum, which has now given her enough money to buy a decent house, and she keeps looking out just in case she comes across something that pleases her. Sarah is now well settled with her Widower, whose name is George Teller, he has two grown up boys who have already met Rebeca, the good thing is that they all get on together, and best of all he has a nice house near Uxbridge which is not too far from the school. Rebeca and Norman, these days are discussing marriage, so it appears as if everything is working out. Or is it! One of these days at the time that Rebeca was studying Law, the four young Naval Officers were given a tour, no, not exactly a tour more an appreciation of the work MI6 perform, they are intelligence driven and often work with naval intelligence, so it makes sense for both parties to be in the knowledge of each other, that morning the four naval officers accompanied by a superior were entering the prime building of MI6. Their first reaction having just walked through the great door was to admire the marbled entrance, then they were pointed towards what looked like a secure reception area, where they will have to be identified and cleared to enter.

Norman almost fainted when he realised that he was looking at Rebeca who had not seen him, walking into the building obviously just after having been cleared. He said nothing and nobody noticed that he had a problem, he wanted to run after her but it would not have been possible for two reasons, the first one was that he had not yet been cleared he had realised that right of way, but the second reason, talking to the operator who was checking him, he had asked him where that door led to, the answer was strange: 'I am not allowed to tell you sir, in fact I could not even tell you for the simple reason that I have never found out, why do you ask?' The senior officer who was with them heard the conversation, later he asked Norman why he was interested in that doorway: 'well it's like that, I must have made a mistake, but I thought that I had recognised the woman who went through, but I guess I will never find out.' Now the group was walking up the curved grand stair case, the senior officer who was right behind Norman suggested to him, that he had always wondered about that entrance to somewhere, and today he was going to find out by asking a friend that they are going to meet, Norman was pleased that the man cared, and that might just give him a clue, perhaps it is something to do with the Law that Rebeca was involved in, then he stopped thinking about it and got on with learning. It was not until at least two hours had past that his superior called him over, he was talking with someone he obviously knew, and introduced him to Norman, 'I can tell you what I know after working here for fifteen years about that doorway on the ground floor, we are supposed to be spies, intelligence experts, and not a single person that I know has ever found out for sure, very few people are seen going in or out of that area, I have been told in the past that they are all very special people, and it is better we do not know who they are, and what it is that they do, we also know that they are all ranked well above us, on top of that they seem to have very special privileges, I have asked a few of the operators who check you in and out, all they can tell me is that they have never seen their identification, so, for me I decided a long time ago to forget all about it, that is one worry less for me. There was another four days before he was going to be with Rebeca, so now he was getting worked up with a myriad of thoughts running through his head.

The four days went past of course, Rebeca was at the door, they embraced then sat for a while talking general stuff, he asked her what she talked about on her program earlier, and she told him, then he told her that a small group of them had visited MI6 earlier this week, he looked for a reaction, there was none, then he told her that he had seen her there, he described the doorway she went through, fully expecting her to tell him that he must have made a mistake. But her answer was not what he expected at all: 'Well Norman, I must tell you something; I love you very much, you are a wonderful person, and I will be proud of taking your name and being your wife for the rest of my life. I can promise that I will never but never tell you a lie, it would be too easy to do that, but not honest. I will tell you; Yes, it was me you had seen that morning and if you do not want me to tell you a lie, please darling do not ask, it is most important that you also keep that secret, when I say nobody. I mean nobody must ever hear that from your lips, not even your mother or father. On the job you are learning you well understand that you are not allowed to tell anybody about it, not even me, and that is the way it has to be, I know curiosity can be good but it will not reward you if you were to find out, I have learnt to say nothing when I could have scored points on somebody, but I am pleased with myself that I can hold my head high, and I know that in time you will be the same I will never ask you a single question that you are not allowed to tell, thank you Norman and there is something else I can tell you, I think that I have found a house we can buy not too far from here. It did not take him long to realise, that she had taken the bull by his horns so to speak, he felt proud of her, now he realised that she was involved into something which was bigger than the two of them, he very much appreciated her honesty, she could have told him what it was all about, but he now realises that it would not have helped him, he would have attempted to hear everything, which maybe could have turned out to be dangerous for her.

And now; what about this house Rebeca! She actually was glad that it was over, she had told him enough for him to realise that she was honest with him, and now they are both secure with each other, next they both jumped into her car, and she drove to the house she had seen earlier, they parked outside, got out and then imagined what the interior would be like, they could see the two gardens, especially the one in the back was huge, they wrote down the agents telephone number and that was going to be her first call Monday morning. Back home she told him that these days she has become a high income tax person, one income was the BBC that paid her rather well, then she told him that she was also well paid by people she cannot talk about, 'yes for your information it is all very legitimate and on top of that I have accumulated almost half a million pounds, I know it's a lot, but I have been earning good money since I was fifteen and I don't spend much on myself, so do we get married first or buy the house first? Norman, there is another thing we should consider, should we wait to get married and perhaps buy a house before you have finished the course, that one Darling is for you to decide.' His father had overheard some of the conversation, he apologised to them both, he was pleased that they are going to marry but thinks that they should wait to have a bit more money for the deposit, it will make it easier for them to get a mortgage, and he is sure to be able to help them both. Rebeca was ever so pleased to hear about Norman's father kindness, she told him so then added that she has been careful all these years and saved enough money to buy a small house (that was not exactly true, but she did not want him to be hurt). Norman was pleased with her he had noticed the way she handled the situation. That Sunday they still had not decided both about the house and the marriage, both had never thought about the wedding itself, little did they know or realise but it was going to be very big affair!

Monday morning Rebeca had a lot to do. First the house, then it was a matter of reading and digesting the last law book she was going to read, she had managed to attend a few lectures and it was getting close to the final exam time, she was ready for it, and from now on all she wanted to think about was the Law. Twice she had a call from her friend the Judge who was concerned for her, each time she gave him a quick resume of how far she had got, each time he remembered himself before law exams, and he was never as confident as Rebeca appears to be these days. The exam came and went, she was a little disappointed, she did not get an A+ oh no it was only a straight A, which of course was good enough to join a firm of Barristers. They had heard a lot about her, especially from the senior Judge who used to be in the same firm, and they all made her most welcome, at the time none of them had any idea about what they should do with her, they knew that she was only going to be there for at the most six months, so after a lot of planning they decided to treat her as if she was fully qualified and see what happens. When Rebeca found out she was ever so pleased, on the very first day she appeared in a Court as the leading Barrister's number two assistant. That firm did all their work for the government prosecuting, Rebeca did not get involved in the case itself, but on that first day she caught on, and became aware about the running of the Court. After returning to the office after each case she would have a list of questions which usually started with "Why," as time went on the questions became less and less. Sundays there were no problems for Rebeca to talk to Norman about her experience with the law, she really loved it, he was getting close to having finished the course he was on, he did get a lot of help from Rebeca which really made a difference for him, if his grade is good enough he had the possibility of working in Whitehall which would please them both, that house they had looked at all those months ago, was still on the market and they were looking forward to making an offer on it.

The last three months the media all had a field day, it was sad, a Policeman with a Policewoman called on a house in Liverpool to arrest the man in the house. The man who was due to be arrested was in his fifties, thirty years ago when he was fifteen years old he was discovered to have a revolver which he was looking after for one of his mates, someone reported him, his room was searched and the revolver which had no ammunition with it was discovered under his mattress, it turned out that the revolver could have never fire a shot, so when he appeared in Juvenile Court, because of his age and the revolver was not dangerous, he had to spend three Saturdays all day learning discipline which was mostly physical exercises, they started at nine and finished at three in the afternoon, and the whole affair had been forgotten. The man in question had violated the driving code by driving four miles an hour too fast past a speed camera, the problem is that he was contacted twice about the offence, just by the authorities and the Court sending him a letter in the post, unfortunately he never received any correspondence at all. The man Geoffrey about ten years before had moved and duly changed his address, both for his license and for the car he had at the time, the authorities had changed both, the car was correct but the person who typed the address for his license made an error, instead of typing 37 they typed 97. Geoffrey had a good job he also had three children and was happily married, it was his wife who answered the door that morning, she let the two police officers into the house, and from the bottom of the stairs, she called out as loud as she could that there were two police officers' downstairs who wanted a word with him, he was just getting dressed and came down whilst pulling up his braces.

The Policeman mistook his arm movement for Geoffrey about to take a shot at him, so very unfortunately the policeman as quick as he could pulled out his own service revolver and shot Geoffrey straight into his chest, as soon as he realised that he had made a terrible mistake he dashed to the car retrieved and old pistol which had the number machined off, and a couple of live rounds, he managed to get back to the scene just before the man's wife came back in from the back garden where she had been hanging her latest wash, she did not see the Policeman wipe the gun and squeeze Geoffrey's hand around it. The Policewoman saw it all, did not move and worst still never said a single word, she obviously realised why he planted the pistol, it was going to make it easy for him to overcome his mistake. What had happened earlier, before they left the station, he looked up Geoffrey's criminal record, and his brain did not let him read any more than, he was once prosecuted for having a revolver, as far as he was concerned Geoffrey was a dangerous criminal, he was ready for the worse, if he was to tell what had happened he would most likely be prosecuted or at least he was going to lose his job, but then why did he keep the other gun, once the Police woman had said nothing she thought that all she could do was to stay with his story!

Within a quarter of an hour the place was invaded by senior Police people, medics and experts who photographed the scene. That evening, one of the seven Deputy Constables from Scotland Yard presided at a press conference, telling the media that so far all they know is that one of their Policemen had fired a gun in self-defence and killed a fifty-four-year-old man. They have started an enquiry and when they have more news they will publish the result, both officers involved have been placed on leave for the time being, there will be an autopsy and further along an inquest will take place. They will not stop until they have a full picture of what had just happened. The dead man's wife was interviewed by one of the television companies the next day, she was emphatic that her husband never had a revolver in the house, he was not that type of person, no, she had no idea where the revolver had come from, it had never been in the house, she had never seen it.

The same Deputy Constable was put in charge of the enquiry, his name is Tom Saunders, he is a well-educated and a fair person, the next day he wanted to interview the Police woman who was there, it turned out not to be an easy task, he had the feeling that she was doing her best to avoid him, so instead he went to the Police station involved and talked to their superior to find out what the arrest was all about, where they arresting a known dangerous criminal? He discovered that it was not the case, that really upset him, and he started digging into the facts, with the help of their commander they discovered that in reality Geoffrey was no criminal, they looked at his record which showed him having stored an unusable pistol when he was fifteen only, officially he was prosecuted, but that was a minor offence which should have been deleted at the time. If his wife is correct about the revolver not having ever been in the house, it does not bare thinking about the Policeman involved, on top of that he is getting fobbed off from his partner the Policewoman, Tom now had some direction, he now has a better idea of what could be possible, so back at the yard he had somebody find the four possible telephone numbers, two house phones and two mobile telephones, his communication department at the yard were asked to see if at any time since the incident, have any combination of those four telephones had been connected together. It did not take long for him to have the answer which was "yes", they had talked with each other the first time for at least one-half hour, the second time over an hour. The problem for both was that they had been ordered not to communicate with each other, they were told that verbally and in writing.

It is now the second day after the event, the Policewoman eventually called Tom Saunders returning his call, she apologised for yesterday explaining that she was still distraught and could not face talking with anyone, he used her own words to ask her if she had talked to anyone about the case, she replied that she had not talked to anybody about the incident and definitely not to her partner, she suggested that the man's wife was there at the time he was shot, that, he did not believe, so by the end of the second day he was making up his mind that they are both lying, he went to see the Chief Constable to tell him the latest. So now it was going to take time before everything has been done, including the inquest. In the meanwhile, the media were having a wonderful time berating the Government, the Police, and the Courts, they brought up all the mistakes which had been made but mostly forgotten, sometimes it was upsetting, but it sold a lot of papers and the nine o'clock news on television had more viewers than normal. The inquest was not much help, they would not call it an accident, but then they would not call it a crime either, so it was left in the end for the Police to decide to call it a crime. The firm Rebeca now works for was contacted by the Prosecuting arm of the Court and after a long-detailed meeting, it was decided to go ahead and prosecute the Policeman who fired the gun, that was good news for the Media who started saying that they had thought that he was not a nice man! His defence relied on her testimony only, and so far, she had been interviewed many times and never changed her story not even a little change, it seemed that her testimony was well implanted in her brain, she was the one to crack, so the prosecution was keeping their fingers crossed so to speak.

The Court in due time was set to hear the case which started on a Monday at the old Bailey The prosecuting team led by Rebeca's boss arrived first in the Court, there was three of them, the third one being Rebeca. The Chief Constable was there as an onlooker, so was her friend the Judge who of course was well known by all the other Judges. Then the Defence team arrived and took their allotted place, the Policeman, not in Uniform was escorted in and sat in the box, then last of all the Judge was announced and he walked in through a little door at the back of his seat. The case started, first it was for the Jury to make themselves comfortable, they had been recruited the day before. The Judge declared the Court in session, after which the prosecution gave a reason or two why they were prosecuting the Policeman, followed by the defence, saying the opposite. Then it was lunch time. Rebeca did not leave her place and all of a sudden she had two men wanting to talk to her about the case, they were the Chief Constable and her friend the Judge, she told them both something which was most interesting for them; her team had decided that if they think that they are not going to be successful at the end, they will eventually recall the Policewoman to the stand, and let Rebeca deal with her.

What a surprise for the two, the Judge especially had never heard of something like that to have ever been attempted, they both wanted to know what her approach was going to be, she would not tell them, the Judge that evening was going to call some of his legal friends to come and witness Rebeca doing her best, that is of course if she is going to be doing it. He would have loved to tell the media, but that was not possible "Yet", just like a world cup football game the whole of the British Isles were watching the news minute by minute, the Pubs were tuned to the news channel and every time someone reported the latest in the Court, all talk stopped, by Thursday, the prosecution had done a good job, asking the Jury to believe the widow, the defence however did a much better job and it felt as if the Jury were disbelieving the widow, it was hard to have them believe that two police officers could come to Court and lie so eloquently, no, it did not make sense, so, before closing the prosecution, Rebeca's leader asked for the Policewoman to come back on the stand, that was going to be tomorrow as it was gone four in the afternoon, the defence Barrister objected strongly, the problem he had was that the Judge himself had discovered the plan, he was only too keen to see the famous Rebeca take over, the Defence at that point had no idea that she will be the one to cross examine the witness.

Rebeca was well ready the next morning, the court was absolutely packed, her appearance had leaked during the night, that itself had become news, which did not help the witness. The defence Barrister could not make up his mind on what he should do about it, he was not aware that Rebeca had a law degree, it had never been made public, so perhaps he can stop her doing a second cross examination, but whatever, he was now on the defensive. The Policewoman herself was not looking forward to going through it again, she was aware that Rebeca seemed to succeed with everything she has ever been involved with, she could not prepare again because she had no idea whatsoever what Rebeca was going to ask her. In good time the Court filled up with every possible person except for the Judge. Rebeca had a hard time deciding what to wear, no, she was not going to wear the normal black robe and wig, she wore a well-fitting grey suit which gave her an air of authority.

The Court now was silent waiting for the Judge to walk through his little door. He almost had a smile, he was obviously in good form also like everybody else wondering what Rebeca had up her sleeve, whatever it was he intended to enjoy the day. He gave a short speech before starting, addressing the unusual circumstance of recalling a witness just before the case had ended in the Court, he also explained that the person who was going to cross examine the witness, was well qualified and within her right to do so, all this was for the defence team who would no doubt have complained about Rebeca, as far as they were concerned had never even studied law let alone have a Law degree! 'Call the witness' the Judge said, and the woman arrived this time dressed in her Police uniform, she also was playing the same game as Rebeca. Her name strangely had never been mentioned, only her rank, but that was going to change shortly, she was reminded that she was on the stand with the original swearing in still active, and she agreed, then Rebeca got up and slowly walked towards the witness.

Rebeca started by asking the Judge for his permission to show the witness on the stand Mrs Pearson, the Police Badge that is hers, that surprised all in the Court, well not quite all as the Chief Constable was only too aware that Rebeca officially was a Policewoman in London. The Judge gave her the permission and Rebeca handed it to Mrs Pearson who had a good look at it, but at the same time started to get worried, why, she did not know. 'You see Mrs Pearson, just like you I am a Policewoman, oh I must also inform you that I also have a Law degree', her defence team hearing that, now realised that Mrs Pearson was on her own, and not only that but the witness was now visibly shaken, she had already lost the self-assuredness' she had when first entered the Court. Then Mrs Pearson got what seemed to be a lecture from Rebeca, although it was many questions. First Rebeca told her that she realised only too well the position she was in that fateful day, her partner had become the expert and was always explaining new things to her and why she lied for him. 'Mrs Pearson, do you realise that if the Jury found the accused guilty, your chance of seeing Peter your husband and two young sons tonight will be diminished to the point where you will be arrested this afternoon, don't they deserve the truth?' then she addressed the Judge, 'your Honour may I ask you a question?' his answer was quick, 'You may'. And then her question although addressed to the Judge was for Mrs Pearson to hear. 'Your Honour at this stage of this trial, should Mrs Pearson decide to change her testimony, would she suffer any negative action by the Court?' He answered definitely no. Now Mrs Pearson was exhausted, she had nothing left to fight with, and when Rebeca went through the whole affair with her one step at a time and bought her back to reality, she agreed with Rebeca that when it happened for a while she was traumatised and did not say anything or even move, she later felt guilty that she had not rushed up the stairs to see if she could save the man, later that evening she had a telephone call from her partner, and she did not want to speak to him, he did all of the talking, he was shaken, he eventually hang up, she had started to write a report on the incident but she could not even think of what exactly happened, then later he called her again and this time he was insistent on his version of what happened and I began to feel sorry for him, so I went along with his scenario. At that moment something happened to Mrs Pearson, she burst into uncontrollable tears, the Clerk of the Court rushed around to the witness with a box of tissues. The Judge was really good realising that they were arriving at the truth at last, he patiently waited for Mrs Pearson to regain her composure, when it happened Rebeca was the next person to speak, she came close to Mrs Pearson, using a calm understanding voice she spoke to the witness asking her if now she wanted to change her testimony, she did not answer Rebeca with words, just a lot of nodding in the affirmative, the Judge then asked her one question, did her partner go to the car to pick up the old revolver? 'It is what he did your honour, I apologise for my deception before, I cannot explain why I did it.'

Rebeca went back to her team where she was congratulated, at the same time one of the Jurors beckoned to the Clerk of the Court because he had a message for the Judge, it was on a piece of paper addressed to his Honour, we have decided unanimously that the accused is guilty as charged, so if you wish the case can be terminated right of way. The Judge read the note out loud to the Court, and immediately the Defence team started to object, then to complicate matters even more the accused asked the Judge if he could make a statement, it was granted, he stood up and changed his plea to guilty, so that was the end of the Court case for now anyway.

After the Judge had left the Court, the witness came to speak to Rebeca to thank her, now she can sleep again, the supreme court Judge Rebeca's friend came to fetch her, and they made their way to the Judges' chambers, he wanted to thank her and tell her that she would do well to practice law, also that he would never forget this case, then it was time for the usual press conference on the steps of the court, one problem there are no steps in front of the Old Bailey. The press had a field day, so-called experts on the news program were taking her cross examination apart proving absolutely nothing, when asked Rebeca would only say that it was common sense after all.

The Chief Constable was more than pleased about the result, eventually the Policeman's sentence was fourteen years, Mrs Pearson did however lose her job. The next two weeks Rebeca did the tour of all her great friends. She still could not decide which language? She managed a couple of interviews which were fun, she visited her old friend the Dean when they arranged for her to give a lecture to the students, then she had a bit of a break and she spent a whole week with Robert and his family, they both loved the discussion they had every day. Something important was going to happen soon, she had not been looking forward to it, but in reality, it was good news for her mother as she is going to marry her teacher partner, but first move into his house, well for a while Rebeca was going to be on her own not for too long because in good time, she is going to marry Norman and move into the house they have decided to purchase. She did put her next six month trip on the battle ship on the back burner for a while, there was too much going on in her life at the moment, Norman was very busy on his course, so she did not see too much of him, she did go visit her old head teacher who was only too pleased to see her, he also had followed the court case and again felt so proud of her.

Chapter Fourteen - Disaster Struck

Rebeca and Norman were so close to making an offer on the house they both liked, then working out a date for the wedding. Now Sarah felt that she could wait no longer to move in with her partner so one night she asked Rebeca if she minded being on her own in the apartment, she will soon be gone when they purchase the house, they have their yes on. No way was Rebeca going to stand in the way of her mother's happiness, of course the answer was for her mother to leave as soon as possible, Rebeca had already been cooking for herself, because her mother would spend most evenings with George at his house, the main difference now was that when she gets up in the morning, she will be on her own. She realised a few weeks later that if she does not tidy up from time to time the place would always be in a mess when she returned, so, one day she made a list of things to do, and slowly it became a habit for her to keep the apartment in tip top shape, then she would never avoid inviting someone in because she had left it all in a big mess.

One good thing happened, she decided to learn Russian, and that was that; she even went out of her way to not give herself a reason for the Russian. Now she visited the neighbours more often, and sometimes they invited her for the evening meal which she appreciated, she never liked cooking just for herself. Next Sunday is when her and Norman were going to have the last visit of their dream house, and officially make the vendor an offer which they hope will be accepted, Rebeca was starting to get excited. Norman was finishing his training with the Navy, a few weeks more and Rebeca will officially be a "Navy Wife" and her life is for sure going to change. One evening they were speaking on the telephone about the visit to the house, he had already made an appointment for the next Sunday at three in the afternoon and for a change he is coming at lunch time Sunday to pick her up, if that morning she was going to be in the studio he will pick her up there. In her opinion she did not think that it was a good idea, but then, she did not want to upset him, so, she went along with it, all the time having the thought in her head that it was a bit strange, but that is what it was! That Sunday arrived of course, and she had managed to do the recording on Saturday morning, so she waited for him to arrive all excited. Rebeca had made too much pasta the night before and there was a lot of pasta without any sauce but cold in the fridge, she peeled a large onion, sliced it then fried it with butter and crushed garlic in a large frying pan, then mixed all the cold pasta in the pan and as it reached the right temperature and almost perfection, Norman was at the door. He could not help noticing the lovely smell. She asked him to sit at the table, they started to eat the pasta, at the time Rebeca thought that he must have an upset stomach as he was eating ever so slowly, she did ask him, he replied no without lifting his head to look for her reaction. They finished the lunch with chocolate ice cream, and she then made some coffee, she was now beginning to worry as they did not have too much time to spare, so she talked about it, he was not too responsive, and after he had finished his coffee, he had something to tell Rebeca.

She developed a very odd feeling, there was something wrong, she tried to guess but never came close. He eventually told her something that was going to change her life, he had come to the conclusion as he told her, that he absolutely loved being with her, but he was not in love with her and making the decision of buying a house and marrying was too much for him, when he saw what she had done in the trial, and how she received all the adulation of everybody, he could never keep up with her and he would just be hanging to her coat tails, not a comfortable place to be and by the way he had never made that appointment to view the house a second time, then he was gone. There she was in the middle of her apartment sitting on the floor crying her eyes out. She cried on and off for the rest of the day, the used dishes were still on the table, on top of that she never slept, she had been injured and it was going to take her more time, not to get over it but get used to it. She blamed herself being too clever, not being able to tell him about "Them". He was the first man she ever loved, the next day that thought gave her a tiny glimpse within her darkness, her thoughts about it were that if it was the first then there must somewhere be a second! Eventually she managed to do the washing up and clear up the place, she did not fancy eating until the late afternoon, she did no work but watch a program on the television about Russian folk songs, they were all inspiring which gave her hope and of course it reminded her about learning that language.

She had a snack before going to bed, she was so tired that she slept right through the night and woke up full of enthusiasm. After a good breakfast she walked all the way to her favourite grandparents, they had not seen her for a long time, they were more than pleased to see her, and of course she stayed for lunch, the grandmother had a feeling that there was something wrong, she asked her and got an immediate answer, 'Norman has left me'. The Grandmother was a clever person, she did not tell her that she felt sorry for her, no she told her that it was part of life, and now she has learned something, which will question her the next time she meets a possible partner. 'Think how it would have been if ten years on, you with two children and he had decided that it was no longer what he wanted, my dear Rebeca you have had a lucky escape this time, so it is time to put your chin up!' Later in the afternoon she walked back home with a positive step, she did stop by a supermarket and bought herself a small chicken which she cooked for tonight's supper, planning to eat only half of it and the other half tomorrow night cold with a healthy salad. Her next quarterly meeting was in two weeks' time, so tonight she is going to start planning for that next meeting. After supper she just had to talk to someone, she did not want to tell her mother what had just happened, she did not want her to feel guilty leaving her on her own, but she called Debra and told her about Norman. Just like the grandmother, she did not feel sorry for her, but she did tell her that for a man she is going to be a difficult person to marry, but she is sure that one day she will come across a nice understanding man who has a lot of his own interests, 'that's the way it is going to work Rebeca, mark my word!' They talked for an hour then after a tidy up it was time for bed.

Usually Rebeca can plan the Sunday talk in a half hour but this week, it took her longer she kept wondering if Norman was going to watch it, should she mention it, if no other reason but to convey that she is not upset about it, she decided a firm "No" That Sunday morning program was all about present politics, within an hour of the broadcast Rebeca received a telephone call from the Prime Minister to thank her and remind her again on what a fantastic job she had done in Court, they are still talking about it, he had a visit from the US ambassador. She interrupted him at that point, 'I bet it was about me?', she had been waiting a long time, in fact the last ten years to hear from the people she helped to rescue, first they asked the skipper of the Lifeboat for her details, then the FBI were in touch with Scotland Yard to make certain that she had never been convicted of any crime, that was almost five years ago and now the Prime Minister, am I right?' He answered yes, 'Rebeca they have been following you all that time, first they did not want to disturb your education, because they are going to ask you to stay with them as their guests for a period of three months, did you know that some months back your man became the Vice President?

And now he is in a good position to make you very welcome, he did ask if you had a passport, so may I suggest Rebeca that you get with it and get yourself a passport ASAP' then he added, if it all works out you will no doubt visit the White House, so I suggest that before you go you come here and have a meeting with the Cabinet so that you are well informed and you have some proper questions to ask their Politicians'. She agreed with that, she went online to see how easy it was going to be for her to obtain a passport, all that came at the right time, it gave her a perfect chance to forget about

Norman. She was now expecting either a call or a letter, she got it wrong it was an email from the American Ambassador, he was asking her to visit the Embassy at a time to suit her, she is to call his assistant to arrange the visit, the subject was about a three-month trip to the United States, the other thing was that they will arrange for her to be picked up. Rebeca called the assistant; it was arranged as a lunch meeting at the Embassy next Wednesday. She had just started her course on Russian, but now she had to put it to one side. The first thing she did was to call Robert, and discuss all the possibilities of the trip, all she knows so far is that it is for three months, she was pleased about that, she will have enough time to absorb America, she might even like the place, she already was making a list of the places she would like to visit. She could not help mentioning America in her ten minutes on Sunday morning, of course she told Debra and remembered on Sunday morning to tell the BBC producer that she will have to change the Sunday morning show, yes, she might even do it from America!

Wednesday had arrived, so had the Chauffer who was at the door waiting for her to come down, next she found herself entering the Embassy, she was treated as if she was a special VIP. The building was very impressive there was a lot of marble, a huge spiral staircase, ornate doors, and uniformed armed security people at every corner, she was led into a beautiful room where the Ambassador was waiting for her, as it happened his wife was there to, they all shook hands and thereafter sat down on silk covered armchairs.

'Well young lady you must have made some impression on the Vice President, I know that it was as long as ten years ago, but a lot happened during that time, first he did not want to mess about with your education, because he wanted to make the trip really worthwhile for you, that family have a few pictures of yourself spread around their house, they think of you every day, I personally think that they have completely forgotten the role of the Lifeboat, no, they think it was you who had saved them, especially his wife and his daughter, they are lovely people and they have planned a trip of a life time for you.' He stopped for a moment and looked at his wife who was smiling away, it was a matter of her availability with the dates they were planning for her. The other consideration, they wanted her to give a few lectures about her life in some Universities, there was also an idea from their son that he would love for her to be able to fly a light aircraft, she could learn, it's not difficult if she is interested. Then it was lunch time, and that is when they were going to fire a volley of questions, the first one was about the Court, how did she know that she was going to be able to change the Policewoman's testimony. 'A year before I had done the training to become a member of the London Police force, I realised the association of two people put together, in time they will trust each other, then it will be difficult for either of them to contradict the other, in the job they are almost as one, she was so certain of the result that it never entered her mind that if they lose the case she will end up being prosecuted and locked up.

There were no other witnesses which is the reason why she would be safe to lie. I played on her emotions, something Rebeca's lead Barrister was not able to do, the Judge would have stopped him. The Judge himself wanted to find out whether I was any good, so he let me go on, I have a friend who is a High Court well respected Judge, who I guess had a chat with him the night before, that also helped, but the best thing from this case is that the woman although having lost her job, now is a better person, did you know she thanked me! She also told me that she had not been able to sleep since that fateful day.' She gave them time to absorb all that information, nobody had touched the food yet, so it was decided for them to start eating and then perhaps ask Rebeca another important question. It did not take them long to be asking the old question which she was used to answer, of course she did not tell them where she was getting the information from for the Sunday morning BBC program, she had no problem going past go on that one.

After the meal the Ambassador said goodbye to his wife and then got down to business with Rebeca, first it was a question of transport, both the Vice president and the President himself were coming to England in three weeks' time to talk with the Prime Minister, they were also having a Royal meal at Buckingham Palace, she could perhaps join them, and go back with them on Airforce One, he did not have to go further, she really liked that idea, so that was settled, they will work out something exciting for the trip back. She had only one requirement whilst there, once a week she will need a half hour in a television studio to do her Sunday morning talk, the BBC will be ever so pleased. And of course, she will be extremely happy to give the odd lecture here and there about her exciting life, then she explained her famous card trick with the two packs of cards and her memory, she can always add that to a lecture. When he understood the card trick, he could not get over it, he now wishes that he was going to be home whilst she is there.

She can bring as much luggage as she wants and then he asked her a lot of questions about food she can eat, does she swim? Can she dance? Has she got a partner? That one question almost gave her a problem and she hoped that her little delay in answering was not noticed, he then told her that she does not need to apply for a visa, but to be sure that she holds a valid passport, she will need it coming back, in six months. Rebecca managed a doubletake, 'I thought I was going for three months? He just told her that he had been told himself that it was for six months She was driven back home with that lovely feeling that she was wanted, and now she felt back on track. Later in the week she had a long discussion with the producer, who was going to do everything possible for her to do the program from the States, it was going to make it even more interesting. She called the Prime Minister to tell him about the trip, especially going on the President's aircraft, she will no doubt meet him, Next she was able to talk to her mother about it, Rebeca could hear the excitement in her voice, she called Robert who wished he was going with her, he loved the idea of flying a light aircraft, he suggested that she should write an article for "Them" explaining what was going to happen, and perhaps she will receive some good ideas, just then the telephone was ringing, it was Norman who wanted to apologise about the other Sunday, but he could not find a single idea that would have made the shock any easier, he wanted to remain friends with her, she told him that at the moment that idea was not welcomed, but in time she hopes to remain a friend. She did feel that he really meant it, it was not just his guilt.

Chapter Fifteen – America

Getting her passport was easy for Rebeca, the Chief Constable signed for her, the passport office was alerted and within one week her passport was delivered by hand, the meeting of the President and the Prime Minister was scheduled for three weeks' time, shortly thereafter Rebeca will find herself in America. She is so excited about the trip, broadcasting from New York City was going to be so different, flying in Airforce One, meeting the President, flying a small aircraft and meeting with the people she had helped rescue all those years back. Debra went with her to do all of the clothes shopping, Debra enjoyed watching Rebeca methodically choose cloths, she was fascinating to watch, it was easy for her because she had a perfect figure for the couturiers, they all made their first attempt at a new dress, exactly her size, even her shoes were easy to find, they would stop for elevenses, for lunch, for tea, it always ended a nice day and Rebeca's wardrobe never had any room for more, but she always managed.

Debra a couple of times asked her if she still misses Norman. She thought about him sometimes, but it longer upsets her, and after all, if the man did not want to live with her, there is nothing she could ever do to change his mind, yes, as a friend she will now be happy to meet him occasionally. Sometimes she would think something she had heard a few times which goes something like this "it's better to have loved than to have never loved", for now that was good enough and perhaps maybe one never knows she might just love again! Some days she wonders what it would be like if she loved one of "Them", at least they would understand each other. She decided to tell her mother about Norman, she would not want her mother to hear it from anybody else, her mother might start to worry for her, she also wanted to have other people at that time so that her mother could not ask her any awkward questions. So, she invited her mother with her partner also with his two sons to come over for lunch next Sunday, her partner and his two sons were ever so pleased to be spending some time with Rebeca, all three thought a lot of her. She wanted to cook the meal so that her mother could see that she was doing alright, so it had to be prepared, that took her all of Saturday afternoon plus all the morning Sunday. Her talk at the BBC was recorded and it was about single people living on their own, and how the law could possibly be changed to make their lives a bit more pleasant. When they arrived, Rebeca was happy to show them her passport, when her mother asked why, then Rebeca told them about her trip in a couple of weeks' time, they could not believe it at all, no, it's' all true, then she had to show them her new clothes, now her mother was wishing that she had been with her, but she was pleased that Debra helped her. She started the meal with a Greek salad, after the main course was a whole leg of Lamb with roast vegetables, desert looked simple enough, but tasted almost out of this world, it was an apple pie which had been laced with a cup of brandy and cooked with dark brown sugar, it was wonderful and had a taste to compliment the perfume. Whilst they were enjoying the apple pie, Rebeca speaking as if it was a nonimportant after thought, mentioned that Norman is no longer part of her life, she made it sound as if it had been a mutual decision, so her mother expressed a mild sorrow, and no more was said about it. Sarah also could not help but notice that Rebeca kept the apartment spotless, which pleased her.

This next week was going to be a hard one for Rebeca, during the week she was going to record twenty ten-minute segments for the Sunday morning program, that will give her time to organise herself, she was not taking the gold bar with her on the trip, but she was taking her special computer. It was never mentioned in the media that she was going away for three months, oh no! it's now six months! She thought that she already had much too much coverage and did not seek anymore. She was hoping that she was not invited to the Palace for the big meal, she did not want to meet the Queen, for her that would be a step too much, if ever she was to meet up with her Majesty, it would have to be arranged out of view with the public and be a most informal meeting, that would be alright.

A week before leaving, the Prime Minister asked her to Ten Downing Street for a meeting about America, there were some people with the PM, one was the Foreign Minister who spent a lot of time with her talking about American Politics, she had the distinct feeling that he was treating her as if she was an ambassador, he did not seem to realise that she was going for fun, it was just a holiday. However, she did take note, the problem for the PM and his Foreign Minister was that she was for six months going to be at the centre of American Politics, they were hoping to learn from Rebeca having spent all this time with them. She told her neighbours that she was going to be away for six months, they were pleased for her, and when she told them where she was going and with whom she was going, she also made a joke about the airline she had chosen, before she left them, they found out that it was true, they were amazed, they really were. That last week before the trip Rebeca visited everybody she knew, including the Dean, they were all, without exception pleased to see her, it made her feel even better. Now she never thought about Norman, she was surprised how quickly she forgot about him, she came to the conclusion that Love is ever so strange, it does not make sense; she made up her mind to study Love when she comes back, she must remember to take her Russian book with her, so far she had made a good start in the Language, she was not too happy with the writing, it felt odd, some of the letters were the same or almost the same, she wondered if her hosts knew any Russian people, no she realised that she should keep all that to herself, she could remember the restaurant in Brent Cross shopping centre, those two had no idea that I spoke their language and at the time that was a plus, so if one never knows it might be the Russian just come in handy one day. The night before she was already feeling a bit homesick when she emptied the fridge, unplugged it and left the door open, she ended up with three large suitcases, her computer was in one of them. She had a pile of documents that referred to "Them", she had arranged for Robert to pick up a spare key in case the apartment was broken into. It is not common knowledge that she is going away for six whole months, she did give Robert a spare key to the apartment, he is ready for action if he is needed. That was her last night, she did not sleep well on the contrary for the first time in her life she experienced a nightmare, she woke herself up screaming, it was all about her grandfather not wanting her in his house, he was shouting at her to move away from the front door. She looked at the clock, it was only five thirty, Rebeca sat on the bed for ten minutes trying to understand what had just happened. Now she was up early and ready for the pickup, the chauffer was on time, he helped her get the cases downstairs and, in the car, she locked the door, and as the car was driving away, she managed a quick look back, she was now on her way to Northolt, a military airfield where the President's aircraft had landed, the Chauffer drove her straight to the plane (Airforce One). Her host opened the door, she immediately recognised him from that far back, yes, he was a tad older that's all, before saying or doing anything else he gave her a big hug, and she felt already at home.

There were men and women in uniform saluting them as they went up the stairs, and entered the aircraft, she had seen the inside of commercial aeroplanes in films and television programs, all the rows of seats and not having much room to oneself. Oh, nothing like this in this aircraft, no it was just like being in a building, with offices above and proper accommodation below, she shared a cabin with the President's daughter, who happened to know all about Rebeca and was ever so pleased to be sharing with her, of course they were not going to stay in the cabin as it was only a seven hour flight to Washington, in the daytime, there were also two lounges and they were going to stay there for the whole trip, they both had a lot to talk about, which kept them busy, they were both served breakfast, and later lunch, in between it was a matter of which drink you wanted.

The Vice president was always called by his first name which was Ronald, she had no choice, it felt strange at first but that is what she will call him in the next six months, never sir, never Mr Vice President, and never his surname, the President's daughter also had a name, it was Alison, they were going to meet often during her trip, it was just as well that they got on so well, Alison now has a sort of a plus over the girls in their group, she was the first one to have a long conversation with Rebeca, during the second part of the flight Ronald joined them, so now the talk changed, it was no longer about dresses, shoes, and boyfriends. Ronald wanted to talk Education and Vocation, not sailing! Then about an hour and a half before landing, the President joined them he already knew a lot about Rebeca, he just wanted to have met her. He was mostly interested on what career she was going to pursue, there she could not help him, she was of the opinion that the career will pursue her, in the meanwhile she is enjoying the wait, she did make a small mistake saying that she has two incomes, she immediately realised, hoping he did not ask her what the second income was, she was saved by the Bell, he had just been called away to answer a telephone call. The only hiccup was possibly from Alison, who might have put two and two together. It felt strange for Rebeca, they left England at ten in the morning, her watch was showing almost five in the afternoon and the clocks on board were just coming up to twelve. It took her a while to realise the reason for that, had they flown much faster they could have even arrived before they had left, that is the advantage of flying in the same direction of the sun, going in the opposite direction the clocks go forward and you will lose time. She was going to research all that whenever she can find a book on the subject.

They have landed, more uniformed personnel saluting almost anybody going past them, they took no prisoners! Everybody just had to be saluted, Rebeca thought it stupid. She said goodbye to Alison and the President, three people were waiting for them, it was Laurie his wife, Jim his son and Rosella his daughter who from the time she was born has been called just Rose, she recognised Laurie but not the other two, it was just like old friends meeting again. Ronald and Jim had no problem handling her three suitcases plus one of his own. Normally he would never touch a suitcase, it was always looked after by the Air Force, but he wanted it to be coming from him, it was just a feeling he had, and that is how her whole trip was going to go, they were so nice. The Chauffer is driving, and five people are in this large limousine, behind them there were two more cars, with secret service men, they always follow the President and the Vice President, they were on their way to Number one Observatory Drive, his official residence in the Northwest of Washington. The house was built in the 1860 and it is worth a look at. Laurie took her to her room at the same time showing her around so that she can start to get her bearings.

Although it was almost one o'clock there was no lunch, only a huge mug of coffee or cold drink and a decent piece of chocolate cake, after all they had a full lunch on the flight, this afternoon for Rebeca was her evening, and not having really slept the night before, as much as she wanted to get to know them, she was feeling tired but for certain did not want to appear rude, so she stayed up as long as she could, talking to Jim and his sister. It was so strange for her; they could still remember every word she had spoken on the Lifeboat. Maybe they could see that she was tired, after all their father almost went straight to bed, so Jim suggested to her that perhaps she should go and have a decent sleep, Rose took her back to the bedroom, placed a bottle of fizzy water by the bed side, also offered to help her hang her clothes, Rebeca told her she was too tired to bother with that, if she wakes up early that is what she will do, she set her watch to the local time, Rose left, Rebeca before starting anything laid on the bed for a moment and just fell asleep for at least ten hours, she surprised herself and woke up at around two in the morning, the good thing was that she was still feeling tired. She drank water, which was very refreshing, she switched the television on, Oh disaster! The sound had been turned all the way up, in a panic she did manage to find how to turn the thing down again. She could hardly understand a single word they were speaking of course; she should have taken up Spanish! This time she changed into her pyjamas and carefully slid into the lovely bed, even the pillow was just right, and she started her second sleep in America. Waking up the second time was a bit of a shock for her, she looked at her watch and realised that she had slept a further six hours! There was no sound whatsoever in the house, she had not realised that all the walls were thick built with stones and the doors also were thick, it was what they called a proper house.

After having had a shower and dressed, she had a go at unpacking the first case which mostly contained her dresses, she hung them all, not in a wardrobe, in a room which had no windows, but three cloths rails, shelves for shoes and draws for sweaters and underwear, there was also a basket for the wash. Then there was yet another room, which was well lite with a dressing table and mirrors, she had no problem adapting to this new set up. And now she had a strange feeling, for the first time in America she felt hungry! It did not take her much time to brush her hair and make herself look as good as she could. Before leaving the room to go exploring she opened a second case and managed to set up her computer, yes, there was WIFY in the room and now she really felt at home. On her way down the stairs, she heard voices and went towards them, the family were all sitting at the dining table obviously eating breakfast together, Ronald got up first to greet Rebeca and show her place, they were all hoping that she had had a good sleep, she told them that in fact she had two sleeps, she had not realised how tired she had been. Now difficulty started, they asked her what she would like for breakfast? Rebeca tried her best to guess what she should ask for, it was obvious that they were not going to get up and cook it for her, she had realised already that they have a chef in the kitchen at their disposal, so in the end she asked for something she had been looking forward to; 'could I have a couple of pancakes with maple sirup and some Canadian bacon please' Strange all four seemed to be happy on her choice of breakfast. Rose asked her what she thought about

America, it was a bit early in the trip for anyone to form an opinion, but Rebeca answered of course, she said that she did not yet know America but so far, she felt like a queen. They told her to use the telephone anytime she wanted, at the same time reminded her that because Ronald is the Vice president all conversations on the house telephones are recorded. Jim and Rose took no notice of that. Rebeca told them that she is supposed to call a television Producer who is going to work with her to arrange her weekly ten-minute slots, apart from that she is completely at their disposal. It appears that Rose and Jim oversee Rebeca's wellbeing, they are the ones who will mostly arrange her days. Laurie is the one arranging her lectures and Ronald the official visits etc. Rebeca asked them what should she do if Alison calls her wanting to take her out? The answer was nice it was to accept as she would have already planned it with them. After all that, Rebeca told them that if any of them want to be with her at a studio when she records her ten minutes, they are most definitely welcome. The other nice thing is that there is no transport to worry about there is always a limousine with a chauffeur available, and the usual escort! so for certain they were staying home this morning, Rose was planning to take her out this afternoon, so in the morning they might walk around the wonderful garden. At lunch time there was only Rose and Rebeca in the house, all the others had gone, walking around from room to room was strange for Rebeca, so far, she had seen three photographs of herself.

Lunch was not the main meal of the day, Rose and Rebeca sat down at around twelve thirty, the chef came in and asked what they would like, Rebeca let Rose make the choice, it was corn on the cob with lashings of butter followed by a piece of apple pie with a big chunk of cheddar cheese on top and of course the never-ending pints of coffee. Before the trip Rebeca had made up her mind to try all the food that was offered to her, so for a moment she was happy to try the apple pie with the cheddar and to her surprise she loved it, what a good idea she thought at the time. Before Rose and Rebeca went out, the call was made to the producer, he was pleased to hear from

Rebeca but even more pleased when he found out where she was staying, he gave some details on who to call in Washington to be able to record each week her program. It is in the NBC news studios who are only too pleased to oblige, at the same time they want to discuss with her the possibility of arranging a similar talk for the States on the cable network called MSNBC, so now she had another call to make to yet another producer, who luckily knew a lot about Rebeca, and even him was surprised to hear where she was living for the next six months, they left it for now until Rebeca discusses timing with the Vice President, she did not know about any arrangements that had already been made. Eventually they did not really go out, Rebeca decided that yes, it would be a good idea to go for a walk in the beautiful garden that surrounds the house, then go back in the lounge and get to know each other, Rebeca wanted to know everything about Rose, has she finished her education? Is she going further to college, in which case for learning what? Has she got a boyfriend? Does she get on well with her brother? What does she remember about the trip and then the rescue?

The first question was easy for her to answer, now she is taking a year off but then she is going to college to get a Law degree, then she added that perhaps they could go to a court one day and watch a trial. Rebeca thought that it was an excellent idea, at the same time informing Rose that she also has a Law degree. Rose was a bit sad telling Rebeca that no, she does not have a boyfriend now, Rebeca then told her about her boyfriend who became her fiancé and then turned into her ex-fiancé, that had been his idea, and she was devastated at the time. What was nice was that Rose gets on ever so well with her brother, they are best friends. She had found the trip across the Ocean dead boring, nothing to see day after day, when the boat sunk, she had no fear whatsoever, she knew that they would be rescued, her number one worry was for her father, she felt his disappointment at his failure and at having let his family down, even though it was never his fault. Seeing this girl in the Lifeboat was so reassuring and it bought her one step closer to normality. 'Rebeca seeing you that day, I remember that scene every day of my life!' she turned to her guest and gave her a big hug. Rebeca was touched, she had never realised the effect she had that day on at least one of the crew of that fateful yacht! She is beginning to understand why her photographs are displayed around the house, to one of them at least she represented the light of life, she understood her visit was not just for fun, it was almost like a pilgrimage that they did not have to go on, no, the pilgrimage came to them!

In a way this afternoon was a bit difficult for Rebeca, she had not fully realised what she meant to that family, it was something she will have to bear for the rest of her life, Rose seemed to have unloaded something on Rebeca which will make them special friends for the rest of all their life's. They spent the rest of the afternoon, with Rebeca telling the story about having heard the plot in the restaurant that day, Rose seemed to have heard something about it, but never had any details on how Rebeca had saved the whole government, and how she became good friends with both; the Prime Minister and the London Chief Constable, who both will do anything for her, oh yes! Even one of the Royals! Rebeca now decided not to tell Rose anymore about her life, she is going to wait until the whole family has heard that story, before telling them about the court case she managed to influence.

When she gives a lecture, it will always be about her life, from as early as she can remember, then at the end with question time she will answer questions about our society in the present time, she happens to be an excellent storyteller, which makes recounting serious happenings fun for her, she has a feel for how the audience is taking it. Jim was the first one home, his sister started to tell him about the court case, but Rebeca interceded telling her that they should wait until they are all in a room, where she will recount it with all the exciting details. Jim could not wait to hear the rest. He had not realised that Rebeca had a law degree, also that she is now learning her sixth language which is Russian. She has also obtained a degree in politics at Oxford, he then told her that he obtained a degree in commercial design, he now works for a famous design company. It was interesting as Rebeca's Uncle is also in commercial design, she could talk a bit about it, they both felt comfortable with each other which was nice, then Laurie arrived back from some social good works she attends to once a week, she has a lot of friends there, they actually do good work, she wanted to know what them two had been up to all day, Rebeca was not shy in telling her exactly what they had been up to, at the same time setting the scene for tonight's revelation about her stint in a famous court in London, where a policeman was being tried for murder and the only witness was his policewoman partner, the case was almost finished and the Crown who were realising that they had not been able to show with certainty that he was guilty, as a last resort asked the Judge if Rebeca who had a law degree could possibly cross examine the only witness a second time, of course the defence were all against it, but the Judge who had been briefed by another Judge who is the head of the Supreme Court, decided to let her try her skills.

Rose was extremely pleased for the rest of the family to hear how Rebeca managed to win. The problem now was going to be Ronald, will he come home early for a change, he always has a busy day and usually has to plan well in advance an early evening at home, they were all surprised when they heard his car arriving, he told them all that nobody could have stopped him coming home to Rebeca, they were not surprised but Rebeca herself although a little embarrassed, felt so good. Ronald had been talking to the President who told him that tomorrow, Alison his daughter had arranged a tour of the White house for Rebeca and Rose, so tomorrow morning they are going to ride with her father who will get them into the White House.

Supper was at six, it was steaks in a wonderful sauce, the starters were a dish from Brittany in France called "Coquille St Jack", desert was a never ending chocolate cake with ice cream, after the table was cleared it was Rebeca standing up facing her audience telling in detail including her own thoughts, how she turned the table in the court case against the Policeman, she did not forget when the "false" witness the Policewoman came to see her at the end of the case to thank her, 'now I can sleep at night thank you Rebeca'. That had been a great moment for her which she will never forget, of course at the same time they found out that she was also a qualified Policewoman, which completely surprised them. Not like last night Rebeca was not at all tired, so they all sat in the lounge discussing politics in America especially the two-party system, which is hard for everybody and makes it most difficult to change laws. Rebeca thought to herself that she has a wonderful opportunity to study the politics in America, after all she is now living with the Vice President, what more can one ask for! And Ronald also was thinking, how does that girl know so much about politics, and she has some very good opinions, where has it all come from, then he remembered talking to the Ambassador in London who had asked him to find out where she gets all her information, he was beginning to find out why.

The house woke up at seven and by eight there was Ronald, Rose Jim and Rebeca sitting at the table having breakfast Laurie was going nowhere today so she stayed home and stayed in bed a bit longer, they all went back to their room for ten minutes and the car took them to the White House, a quarter of an hour later they were flagged through the gates. Rebeca had only ever seen movies of the interior of the White House, that is how it really was, Alison was there to greet them, Ronald went straight into his office and the three girls walked along a never-ending hallway to the accommodation wing. On the way they were passed by many people, there was one group obviously discussing something at least important to themselves, one of them was the President himself, as soon as he looked at Rebeca, his attention was directed towards her, he grabbed her hand and asked her how she was, this her first trip here, she answered 'Just amazing!', he then told her that he would love having a discussion with her one day, arrange it with Alison, the group he was engage with at that moment were all influential politicians, all wondered who this Rebeca person was, they could not help but ask him, his answer was short but correct. 'You will all find out soon!'. The girls ended up in the accommodation wing. Next door was the communication department, Rebeca wanted to have a peak if it was at all possible, two minutes later there she was discussing some of the latest technology, she did make a faut pas, after finding out that there was a direct telephone line to London and she asked the man who seemed to be in charge if she could make a call on it, the answer was simply 'why not' the man had not thought much about it when he handed her the telephone, she picked it up and it started ringing right of way, she could not help recognise the voice at the other end, it was the Prime Minister, who fully expected to hear the President at the other end, instead all he could hear was a very apologist Rebeca, she told him that they had let her lose in the White House, she had asked if she could use the telephone to call home, but as soon as she picked it up it started calling Number Ten.

He realised the state she was in, he told her that it did not matter one bit, as well as that he was ever so happy to be talking to her. All that reminded her again that she should at least send her mother a text, so tonight she will be staying in her room working on her computer, she did find a proper telephone and found the time to call the MSNBC studio to arrange a visit for her first recording, also she wanted to meet with the producer, when she did speak to him, there was a small question he did not have the answer to, so he told her that he would call her right back, she then told him that perhaps that is not possible because at this moment I am hanging around in the White House, he nearly fell of his chair! The poor guy. What he would give to have the chance of hanging around the White House, He knew that she really was a powerful woman, he was beginning to find out just how powerful. Her matter-of-fact way she had told him, stayed ringing in his ears for the rest of the day, he had to call their news desk to tell them, that was the first time her name had been mentioned in the media, yes Rebeca is in Washington DC!

They all had a wonderful day in the White House, they said goodbye to Alison who was now in charge with arranging an informal meeting for her father to have a chat with Rebeca, he had heard the mistake about Rebeca calling the Prime Minister, he had a good laugh about it, The next day is Saturday, it will be Jim's turn to show Rebeca around, if the weather is alright he might just take her up in his Cessna, the airfield is not too far away, she is actually looking forward to it.. Ronald also thought it amusing, Rebeca's call to the prime Minister, all the time thinking that it was a war like emergency, he was so pleased that it was only Rebeca. Best of all it was in the news in England, so Sarah now will be reassured that her daughter is alive and kicking! That Friday evening Rebeca wanted to turn in on the early side, she wanted to do some more writing, read all the information from "Them", and attempt to have a good night's sleep, earlier that evening she had asked Jim if it was possible to visit an active warship, he was going to arrange it with his father. Bright sunshine, a cool shower, a nice breakfast, just the right clothes on for flying, that was Rebeca and Jim sorted, he flew from a small airfield which was in the country, well a long way from the main airport and the military airfield. On the way there she could not help thinking about her own father, him being a pilot if only he could see her now.

The airfield had the semblance of being a club, everybody knew everybody, there was even a bar there, now Jim was going to give her an unofficial lesson to see how she manages at the controls. Her first thought was how noisy the engine is, on the ground the windows were open, but just before being airborne when there are no more openings to outside, it was slightly quieter, now the noise was coming from the undercarriage, not like a car it was not sprung and made an absolute racket as they went along the taxi ways, they stopped for a couple of minutes at the beginning of the runway; the engine went full power, they moved along faster and faster until the wheels were no longer touching the ground and voila' they were in the air. It did not bother Rebeca one bit; she was enjoying it. After a while he pointed to the altimeter, which was showing two thousand feet, when it was obvious that she could refer to it, he gave her control of the machine, she grabbed the column with dear life, he explained that it was not at all necessary, it just needs a light touch, he asked her to pull back an inch, when she did that, the aircraft started to climb and within a couple of minutes they had reached two thousand and three hundred feet, next he asked her to go back down far enough to stay at two thousand and three hundred feet, but before attempting it for her to take note of the speed, the needle was at one hundred and twenty miles per hour, then as she climbed the needle started to move back to one hundred and five miles per hour. She did not have to ask him why? She had worked it out already. 'Well Jim I guess that if I descend now the speed will be over the original to about one hundred and forty, am I right?' Of course, she was right and that surprised him, the other thing which made him wonder a bit was when she asked him what the stall speed of the aircraft was. Coming back to the field he explained what the attitude of the plane should be, what speed she should aim for, and what they call the rollout once over and close to the runway, no, she did not land it that time, but it was going to happen soon enough.

Back in the flying club she met some of his flying friends who were all interested in talking with her, first they loved her accent, then they realised that she had an abundance of knowledge, especially about foreign lands, the Police and the Law, one of his friends was studying the Law and was more than keen to converse with her about it, has she ever practiced the Law?, the answer was yes just once when she broke a Policewoman's testimony, she had to tell the whole story, she made it sound even more exciting than it actually was. It was when she talked about that case that they realised that she also was a Policewoman, that now were more questions, why? She then explained how she managed to talk her way into the Police College for a six-month course which she passed with flying colours, she also told them why; she wanted to find out that when two Policemen are coupled together, first they want to be able to protect the other, sometimes that protection goes too far and they will lie for each other, that is the weakness in the Police service. It was beginning for the time to leave, so she left them with a thought, whilst looking at Jim, she told them that she happens to have a photographic memory, so she has no problem what so ever learning almost anything, she asked them if there was a pack of cards in the club, and yes there were two packs of cards, again looking at Jim she told them that they were bound to come back to flying again, but before she does come back could you amongst yourselves find a winner who can know which card is which after having looked at them and placed them randomly face down on a table, some people can only go as far as five cards others at fifty cards and others even more, once you have a winner, next time I am here I will show you my version of this little game. 'By the way Guys, I think you have a lovely sport here, I guess the number one idea for all of you is to stay alive, so Happy flying everybody!'

Jim was a pretty good driver, nobody seems to drive fast in America which surprised Rebeca, it was all about moving from one express way to another then a local turn off, that is almost every drive for Rebeca the next six months. That night she made a point of telephoning her mother even though she might be in bed! They had a lovely talk and especially a good laugh about her accidental call to the Prime Minister, she already knew that next Friday evening she was to give a lecture about herself to some well-known University in Washington, she was not going to prepared for it, apart for possibly bringing two packs of cards with her, she will go along with the people, she will attempt to make them all laugh as much as she can, her mother was ever so pleased to have heard directly from her daughter. Tomorrow is a second Sunday that the BBC are using one of her twenty recordings, but the Sunday after Rebeca wants to make certain that the BBC have an up-to-date story from her, which she will record in Washington during the week, it will be the first time that it will also be broadcast in another country, so this one is a little more difficult than usual. That evening she was told about Sunday mornings, it was always a visit to Church for the whole family, so of course she was included, must be up early, dressed as best as one can and by ten in the morning be entering the Church, always greeted by the vicar himself at the door. This will be the second time ever for Rebeca to go to Church, she did not mind of course, it gave her a chance to reflect on her own life, but better still attempt to understand religion, after Church.

Sunday became a day of celebration for the family, a big meal at lunchtime with all the family who can make it that day, she met cousins, uncles, grandparents and one other guest, a retired elderly man who used to be Ronald's partner in their law firm, he is now a widower and lives on his own, Rebeca took to him and they had two very long conversations, at first he could not understand why she did all the work to obtain a Law degree with never having the intention of making use of it, after some reflection and a second discourse with Rebeca he started to understand what she was about, he did ask her much to her surprise if she was at all religious, he smiled when she answered 'I prefer for you to thinks of me an atheist, he had never all his life met anybody so sure of themselves, of course she told him how her friend the high court Judge managed to twist things a bit so that the judge on the only case she was ever involved in, would let her cross examine a vital witness the second time round, and then get the witness to change her testimony, at the end of the trial she came over to thank her. Obviously, she had told him the whole trial, and he found out that she was also a Policewoman, just as he was leaving, he had a word with his ex-partner Ronald, he told him that she ought to be a Judge. That day spending a whole hour in the Church, she learnt quite a lot about architecture, she did spend a long time observing all the beams which were holding up the ceilings, she admired some of the stained glass windows with scenes that repeated themselves, Rebeca attempted to listen to the main sermon for today, she would have loved to be seating in a way that she could observe all the people looking either foolish or fast asleep, it was so boring, the nerve of it is that nearly all parish members shook the minister's hand on the way out, most telling him that it was a beautiful sermon, she wondered how bad the sermon would have to be before anybody said anything about it to the minister on the way out. That evening they all turned in early which was a good thing for Rebeca, she wanted to read all the various articles from "Them", she also wanted to reply to an email from Robert. It took her over two hours to digest all the various ideas from Them, she managed to send Robert an email, more or less telling him what has happened so far, she also gave him her mothers' telephone number so that perhaps he could give her a call and tell her some of what she is up to, maybe it was still on her mind, she told him her thoughts about going to Church, she hopped that he will understand. Before turning in for a good sleep she made a point of contacting the producer fellow to make an appointment, possibly next week, she slept like a baby right through the night.

First thing on Monday morning Rebeca called the producer guy and arranged to meet with him at eleven in the morning at their studios, she was bringing a friend with her, Rose including an escort. So right after breakfast Rose and Rebeca got ready to be driven to the studio, who by then had researched all they could about Rebeca, they made a fuss of the two, at first they had no idea who Rose was, but when she came with the secret service as an escort, they were ready for anything, as it happened almost everybody liked the Vice President, when they found out that he was her father, they felt a little honoured at least. For Rebeca it became not unlike an interview for a job which she had not expected, so she changed her attitude towards them, she was going to play games, she wanted to leave them wondering what had hit them. She was in charge, and told them what type of lighting she wanted, what the background must be, she even told them what she wanted to hear for their introduction. Then, after it was finished, she wanted to record a second ten minutes just for the American networks which they will be free for them to use, so that they can evaluate her usefulness. The staff there were looking at each other wondering what else she is going to order. They agreed and it took them almost an hour to set up the studio the way she wanted it, she stood in front of the camera and started talking, mostly about local English matters, she did mention that so far everybody in America have been so nice. What she discussed mostly was a problem which had just showed its ugly head, she gave them all her point of view on the solution. Now the producer was beginning to wonder how on earth can she have the knowledge of something which had only just come to light over in England, there was too much distance and certainly not enough time, it did not make any sense. So now he was able to transmit the talk to London, Rose who had witnessed the whole thing so far, just like the producer was having a hard time attempting to work it all out. Now there was time for the test talk she is going to do for America, they left the same background, they were expecting something like 'Oh, I love your country', it turns out that last night she read a small article by one of Them about the President having decided to donate a huge sum to one of the small Caribbean countries which had just been totally devastated by a gigantic storm, only a very few people were aware of it, at that moment the government were deciding how they were going to tell people.

The news department were told about it at that same time, they decided to take a chance on it, and broadcast her talk within the hour, boy oh boy; the telephones started ringing almost everywhere, for a while the studio worried in case they had made a mistake, but no, all the rest of the media were on to them to find more about it, and who was that person, they had never seen her before. At that moment Ronald was in the President's office, when they were told that some young lady called Rebeca had just given a talk and at the same time released that information, they looked at each other and both bust out laughing, there was a third man in the office, it was the one who had questioned the President in the corridor asking him about Rebeca, 'you asked me about Rebeca and I told you will soon learn about her, remember?' Then it was headache time for them, 'how the hell did she get the info? The words from the Ambassador in London started to ring in his ears, he had told the President that in England every week she is completely up to date with the news, many so called experts have had a go at finding how she does it, and so far, nobody knows. Then he explained to them about the first time they had seen her ten years ago, she was there a fourteen year old little girl appearing on the deck of the life boat, she had no business being there, she was almost like an aberration, she did not belong on the life boat, we all four were traumatised at the time, and seeing her was like a mirage, then she stayed with us below for around two hours and never once stopped talking mostly about herself, that is why we have pictures of her everywhere in the house, we still feel that it is her who saved our soul that day.

That same night the President called his daughter Alison and asked her to bring Rebeca in the white house as soon as she can, he needs to have a long chat with her. Wednesday Rebeca had lunch with the President, not even Ronald was there, just the two, he wanted in a nice way an explanation on how she had obtained the facts about what he had planned to do about the storm damaged island. There is no way she would ever tell another soul about Them, it was yet another story she was going to invent for the President, she had expected that very question and she was ready with an answer, which for now will do, but eventually she will take a bit more time thinking of what to say, to be certain that she always has a way out. 'You must think of me as an atheist, yes is it just convenient to have a God, which of course could easily be a man-made person, he is there just to explain the big question (WHY), I tell you that so that when I tell how I know so many things that come to my head all day long, especially at night. It is so simple I must have heard someone somewhere talking about the money, which is required to rebuild that country, I also knew that you are a caring man wanting to help those poor people, your problem, is always the same, it will be the opposition party who will paint you as cheapskate if you do not part with money for them: you lose! The other side is if you give them money you are wasting tax that people have paid through hard work: you Lose again. Well, I thought that this way the opposition did not have time to react, they were all too concerned trying to find out who the hell I am.' He now understood, but he still had no idea how she really knew, why did she mention Religion, yes there must be something else, can she hear voices telling her? Again, why did she mention God? He asked about the Vice President's rescue, why was she on the Lifeboat? Does she enjoy messing with people's brain?

Why did you never had to pass exams at school? There were so many questions, she gave them all a proper answer which he always accepted. It was time to finish the lunch which had all gone cold in any case, he had things to do but wanted to spend more time with Rebeca so they will arrange another suitable time, she will hear shortly from Alison, and for now she will be driven back to the Vice President's house in the same limousine that had carried her to the White House. When she arrived, she needed to go straight to her room and for ten minutes or so sit in a chair by the window looking at the trees bending in the wind and completely unwind herself, on her right was the desk which had the computer sitting on it, she noticed something which to her was a little strange, she brought with her an active loudspeaker, only one not the usual two, she remembers that she had plugged in the sole loudspeaker into what the socket at the back said, left not right as it is now. Dear oh Dear I hope they have not messed up my programs. Whilst she had spent all that time with the President, they took my computer apart, speaking to herself: 'I bet it does not work now' she was right of course, she waited for Jim to come home, and then collared him to help her with it. As soon as someone attempted to start it up, all it did was to reformat the hard drive, it did leave her normal emails live but there was absolutely nothing about Them, so that anyone looking into the computer would think that it was completely inoffensive, it only contained files about letters which could for them help to obtain other people email addresses. When she goes back down, she will go straight to the point, she will inform them that it appears that her computer has broken down, if perhaps Jim could take a look at it, maybe he could fix it, if not it does not really matter, it was mostly to keep in touch with her mother, but of course she can also use her telephone to send a text from time to time. She really made out that she was not at all concerned about it. When Jim arrived back from work, she asked him if he could look at it, and he did, he ended up being perplexed and gave up, of course he had the knowledge that experts had attempted to find out if Rebeca obtained her information via her computer, and so far, it seems as if the computer has nothing to do with her knowledge. That had been the only possibility which had been thought off, and now people were beginning to think in the supernatural, although that obviously went much against the grain!

It is now her second Saturday in America, the first lecture was going to take place in approximately two weeks' time, she was excited at the thought of teaching some Professors something they did not know, so far, she had not worked out in her head, what it was they were not supposed to know! The weather suddenly turned hot, and she was going on a long flight with Jim on Saturday afternoon. The Friday before, Rebeca, Alison and Rose had almost a whole day out doing the shops. They were always alright in the department stores, as their escorts were not obvious, it was always in the small establishments that the two secret agents where noticed, then it was the same repeatedly, people in the shops wanted to know who they were. It's not long before Rebeca will be recognised by everyone. That happened on Saturday afternoon, that day the weather was not the best for flying even though it was a hot day. Jim and Rebeca arrived at the flying club earlier than usual so that Rebeca had a chance of showing off her memory skills with the two-pack card trick. The idea had been to make it a competition with a winner, two things wrong with that scenario, first they never managed to have a competition, the other thing was that Jim and Rebeca wanted to go flying, she did the trick and all watching thought that it must be a trick, it cannot possibly be her memory, they all had a good look at the two packs of cards, which by the way, they had given to Rebeca a few minutes before. One of the guys there was adamant that she could read the back of each card, he would not stop so he followed them to the plane, stood there for almost a whole half hour hoping Rebeca agreed with him, which of course she never did, eventually he left them to get on with the matter at hand, flying his aeroplane, when he climbed into the plane, he mentioned that he was feeling light headed, or something strange at least, when the noise of the engine filled the cabin he seemed to improve dramatically. He called out everything he was doing at the time, then called air traffic, they allowed him to taxi and then take-off five minutes later, it was just like last time for Rebeca who then witnessed the ground disappearing below her, they must have passed one thousand and five hundred feet when something awful happened, the plane started to do a sharp right turn, Rebeca stopped looking at the ground below her, to see what Jim was doing; good job she looked, he had, it appeared to her, passed out hanging on to one side of the control which was the cause of the sharp turn, her reaction was absolutely instant, she disconnected his hand from the control column,. Brought it back to the centre, and pushed it forward so as to stop climbing, then she pushed the throttle forward a tad to slow the aircraft, and now she had it more or less under control, she called Jim as loud as she could, but there was no reaction, now it was a matter of surviving, she remembered which was the pushbutton Jim pressed to be talking with air traffic, she noticed the identical push button on her side, she had seen many movies where a call for help was made and she did push that button and called out "Mayday" at first she did not hear any response then she realised that she is supposed to release the button to listen.

Eventually she got it right, and then got into a conversation about her predicament, it was not so simple, the air traffic man wanted to know the registration of the aircraft, which of course she did not know even though there was a placard as big as could be right in front of her, so she gave the man the Pilot's name and the fact that they had only just left his airfield. That was enough information for the air traffic man in the tower. Rebeca heard air traffic close the airfield because they have an emergency, it felt strange, she knew that she was in trouble and that message she had just listen to confirmed it, it was not the best thing for her to have heard, but she must keep calm and what-ever fly the aircraft without going up or down.

The man asked her if she was managing to fly, she answered yes, then he asked her to make a right turn, that is by moving the control in her hand right about one inch then tell him what is happening; 'the right wing has gone down just a bit, and it appears that I am turning' she heard the reply 'I can see you on my radar and the turn is absolutely fine, keep it going until I tell you to go back to normal, by the way I have an instructor coming up to the tower who will coach you down to a nice landing, how is Jim?' she gave him an instant quick reply 'the same' Rebeca was relieved that the turn she was undertaking was working out. She had time to survey all the instruments, she knew the airspeed indicator, and she was flying at 110 Miles per hour, she remembered Jim telling her that below 75 miles per hour the aircraft would no longer fly and stall which she does not want to do, so now she takes a look at the instrument as often as she can, then she found another which was going to be useful, apparently it tells the pilot how fast the aircraft is descending or climbing, she is also going to keep looking at that one. 'Halo Rebeca, you are doing well, my name is Roy, and I am going to talk you down, let this be your first lesson, can you hear alright and is there any change with Jim?' Roy had a smooth way of talking, it was just what she wanted to hear, he obviously was not in a panic and conveyed that to her with the tone of his voice, she looked out on her right and in the distance she could see the airfield, that was reassuring for her, just then Roy asked her to go back to flying straight, she did that manoeuvre almost without thinking, that really surprised her. She was now flying parallel to the runway and that also pleased her, and she also worked out that she will fly past the runway then in time make the same turn again until she is facing the start of the runway, then she will be on the home stretch! Roy told her to look on the instrument panel for a lever marked up above it and down below if she could not remember it also had the word Flaps. she will have to use that lever whilst landing. He asked and she told him that she knew the control for the speed already, he asked her if Jim had moved at all, the answer was no, they did not tell her but there was now an ambulance waiting for her. The start of the runway was now at her three o'clock, after one minute not more it appeared at her four o'clock, then she heard Roy telling her to make a right turn just a bit sharper than last time, say one and a half inch or so. it did not take three minutes and now the fun was going to begin, Roy told her not to reply just listen and follow my instruction, the first one was to push the speed lever a bit at a time until the aircraft has slowed to ninety miles per hour, the aircraft will start to descend and that is what we want so to start now.

, she looked at the instrument that showed the descent and it was showing three hundred feet per minute, then she had a look at the altimeter which now showed just over one thousand feet. 'You're doing fine Rebeca, as you get closer be prepared to increase the speed do that right now for ten seconds, and you will see yourself climbing, he asked her how it felt. 'It did what I expected it would do, I see now how important that is thank you, by the way it is a lovely day isn't?' Poor guy he did not know how to respond to her so he said nothing, but he was glad that she felt confident, then he asked her to pull the lever down all the way to get the flaps down, she was now almost at the start of the runway and about twenty feet up, he asked her to slow the engine right down and just keep the aircraft in line with the runway until the wheels touch the ground, it was a good thing that it was a long runway, as the aircraft seemed to not want to get on the ground, well of course before the end of the runway the machine settled onto the ground with not a single bounce, she managed to cut the engine, never finding the breaks it just run on until it had lost all of its momentum. She was pleased with herself, now for the first time it was the worry about Jim, why on earth would the ambulance have its sirens going full blast in the middle of a runway? No, he was not dead he seemed to move when they transferred him to the ambulance, Roy, a man she had never met in her life was there, he was so pleased with her that he gave her a big hug, somebody had called the press because of Jim and her landing was filmed including the voice recordings, his parents had been called and they were there as well, they both went into the ambulance with their son. Luckily Rose had also arrived and witnessed Rebeca handle the media; 'Alright, we are going to have a press conference, but my friends it will not happen until I hear that Jim is alright, for the arrangements please contact the Vice Presidents communication people, and I will be only too pleased to oblige thank you all.' The pilots who happened to hear the whole thing were just amazed on how cool she was in the air, they all knew that she had never flown before, the guy who did not believe her earlier left after having apologised to her, of course the media stayed and had a word with nearly all pilots who knew her, some were surprised of course but the majority of them said that they were not at all surprised, not so much that she was an intelligent person but that there was something about her that no one can explain, and that eventually was what got the media going about her!

Home again, at last, Rebeca and Rose were waiting for good news at least, not a half hour had passed when Laurie called her daughter to tell her that Jim was beginning to wake up, so far nobody at the hospital could give them any information, a lot of tests still must be performed before the medics can start thinking of the cause. He is a fit young man which will help his recovery no doubt, usually on a Saturday he flies on his own, which today would have been a total disaster. Two hours went by, and his father called Rebeca, he is now sitting up on the bed just as if nothing had happened, he is asking for Rebeca to come and visit him as soon as possible, she offered to come right now. That is what she did with the usual escort, she well realised that he did not ask for his sister to come a well , she did not worry about it, but made out that he wanted to see Rose as well, his father should have realised not to leave her out of it, when he set eyes on the two coming along a corridor he was pleased to see his daughter coming along with Rebeca, who later told him that she had decided for Rose to visit her brother. Laurie was emotional when she saw Rebeca, she just had to give her a big hug, at the same time thanking that the good lord had placed Rebeca in the plane, Rebeca was not too happy about that, having the good lord in the same sentence as Rebeca, for her it was simply good luck, nothing else. Rose went in first to talk to her brother who confided in her, whilst he was unconscious, he can now remember seeing Rebeca outside the aircraft, holding it up with a gold rope, he could tell that he was totally disabled and that had it not been for Rebeca holding it up they would have crashed from a great height.

When Rose came out, she told Rebeca what her brother had just told her, Rebeca was shocked and made Rose promise that she will never repeat that story. When Jim set eyes on Rebeca he was so happy or one could even say that he was Joyeuse to see her walking towards him, when she was close he just had to touch her all over to make certain that it was her, he stopped for a long time looking at her right hand, he had a slight disappointment not finding traces of gold on the palm of her hand, after all that, she sat on the edge of the bed and gave him an ever so long hug, the first one to speak was Rebeca asking him the way he felt right now, perhaps she should not have asked him, his response was definitely not what she wanted to hear: ' Rebeca I have had the best trip ever, I have been all the way to Heaven and I watched you up there getting ready to bring me back with that golden Rope you were holding in your right hand, the trip back was so gentle.' She was trying her very best to bring him back to reality, it was not easy, and it was going to take a few days. Sunday, Jim was still in hospital, all he was allowed to do is rest, Monday they were going to start all the important tests, the first one was a scan on his brain to see if he happens to have any abnormality there, it turned out that he was totally clear of that, then they looked for a malfunction of his heart, they found nothing, alright everybody were glad so far, but the reason for his problem which was real has now eluded them, for a moment they were thinking of bringing in a psychologist, the problem there was that it would most definitely upset the parents, the question of a Sun Stroke came up a few times but an episode of very high blood pressure, high enough to cause a stroke would always leave a trace which in this case they never found. The medical team looking after him decided not to discharge him, they could not trust themselves to give Jim an all clear, they had all heard him telling about his connection with Rebeca when he was out of it, and they needed at least one chance of going down that route, they had no idea what they should be looking for, they asked his parents if they could bring Rebeca and leave her with Jim for two or three hours, of course they said yes, so now they had the difficult job of asking Rebeca if she would agree with the medics, she did not feel that she had any choice in the matter, she quickly thought that to say no, would not be very nice, in any case maybe she herself could solve the mystery, so Tuesday was going to be a hospital day for Rebeca.

When she arrived Rebeca discovered that they had moved Jim into another room, which she found out had cameras and microphones installed, they wanted to record the conversations between Jim and Rebeca to see what his reactions were, they would get a hint at least of what to look for. Jim was a little fed up still being in hospital, he wanted to be home so that he could talk with the person who had saved his life, then he found out that instead of going home she was coming to him, now he was ever so pleased, especially that she will be on her own with him. The visit started with a big hug again, the first question from Rebeca was no more than expected 'how are you Jim?' he was somewhat positive but at the same time he wished that he could go home, 'you know Rebeca they had given me many tests, one for my brain another for my heart, and they keep finding nothing, the FAA are going to withdraw my medical so at the moment I am not allowed to fly, maybe after they declare me fit here, I can get my medical back, but I guess it is not going to be easy,' then it was her turn, 'perhaps they will allow you to fly with a safety pilot, and in time they will realise that this episode was strictly a one off, in any case Jim, surely in your mind you will always want to survive, so you will never gamble on your own life, I think I am right on that point.' He agreed with her and that relieved some tension from him.

Rebeca now had the difficult job of convincing Jim, that nothing whatsoever that had happened to him when he was unconscious, had anything to do with the supernatural. 'Look Jim, when you were out of it with the fairies, I was doing everything to get us both back down on the ground safely,' it gave him a reason to reflect, he felt obliged to agree with her, that was his first step towards recovery. 'I think part of your brain was still functioning in the knowledge that I was the one flying the dam thing, another part wanted to paint a picture as a way of helping you think about what was happening.' He did not answer her, but it was obvious that he was beginning to sort of wake up from his personal nightmare, she was pleased so far, and she was almost enjoying her role. 'Jim, when you have recovered and you are back home, we all have to have a serious talk about my role in life so that you can begin to understand me, I am not the person you think I am, the only thing different about me is that I remember everything I read or hear, as well as that I have an unusual way of making deductions which sometimes gets me into trouble, you know Jim, they are all saying that I saved your life, not once have I heard somebody say that on top of that I saved my own life. Of course, I understood that if I managed to save my life, I would have also saved yours, can you start to understand me?' This time he answered her, 'Rebeca I think I am beginning to understand, yes your absolutely right, so far I have never heard that you saved yourself first, yes I can see how I was secondary to you,' he for the first time had a smile on his face, then she gave him another thing to think about: ' do you remember last week you showed me how to keep the plane level at the same height, well you know, that knowledge was crucial for me, and is the reason why we made it back, well Jim we could almost say that it was you that saved our lives, maybe you should have dreamt that it was you directing me, now honestly I think that together we have released you from some supernatural happening which really was no more than a figment of your imagination!' With a big smile he jumped out of his bed, stood in front of the window, he raised both his arms and screamed on top of his voice, Alleluia! 'I am free at last! She went over to him and gave him another big hug, they stood there for ages it seemed not saying anything but both in tears of joy, he was feeling so proud of her, now he did not even care to be flying again, he had been through an experience that has changed his life. Rebeca wanted to take him home that day, but the medics who had heard the whole thing wanted a chance of going through it all with him at least once more, she fought for him and convinced them that to interview him tomorrow would be too soon, they needed a lot more time to prepare questions, in any case they need to have the time for a psychologist to review before they even speak to him, they felt that they were confronted by a higher power and gave in, she did ask them to call his mother at least and let her know that it was my decision that you agreed to.

His mother and father were ever so pleased that he was coming home, one of the doctors in passing told them that Rebeca ought to be on their team! They all went back into his room, and he could tell by the smile on their face that he was going home with Rebeca. That is what happened, he was going back to the hospital in a weeks' time for a short check-up. When they arrived home nobody asked him how he was, they just wanted to know what had happened, he looked so happy, his mother had not seen him looking like that for a long time, when he told her that he had given up flying for good, his father took Rebeca to one side and asked her what had happened, she said that they had a talk that's all, but if he wants to know more, he should ask the hospital team to give him a copy of the recording, it will be very informative, one of the doctors told her that her talking to him is going to be released to the medical fraternity as a training tool, now he could not wait to find out what she had done. Rebeca then repeated what she had told Jim about them two in the plane.

The media was now looking for the press conference Rebeca had promised, that was a little bit awkward, but it had to go on sooner than later, if what Jim had dreamed started to appear, it would not gp well, Rebeca wanted to put a quick end to it, that came first, so, it was arranged for Thursday morning at the White House Press room, Ronald was going to attend as well. That morning was like a family reunion, they had breakfast in the White House, present were, the President, Alison, Ronald, Jim and Rebeca. There was a feeling that today was going to be a great day, outside it was a clear blue sky, with a light breeze, the press conference was organised for right after breakfast, only Rebeca will be in the room with the media, however if she thinks' it would help at any time to answer a question which is serious enough, she can call on Ronald or Jim or even the President himself, who will all be in the neighbouring room. Rebeca was much happier that way, and at nine sharp they were at least twenty-five reporters and television people assembled waiting for Rebeca. They were no introductions, or fanfare for her, she just walked in, with nothing in her hands, not even a single sheet of paper.

The paint in that great room must have aged for at least ten years having been exposed to all the nonstop high intensity lights emanating from all the reporters, it was their first chance of having closeup photographs of Rebeca. The first question was from a New York Times reporter, a serious newspaper, 'how is Jim? Is he home yet? The answer was as expected by all. 'He is home now and has almost completely recovered, the hospital after a multitude of tests found no physical problems, but they were not happy with the way he felt, and luckily yesterday he had a breakthrough, they could do no more for him, and they let me take him back home.' Same reporter asking a second question, 'will he be able to fly again?'

Rebeca answered by saying yes, then went on to the next reporter, he asked Rebeca how she felt when she discovered Jim had passed out, 'at the same time I discovered Jim out of it, I also discovered that it was now up to me to save myself, I now had an awful lot to learn in the shortest time, my first concern with Jim was that he should not fall on the controls again, I had no idea whether he was still alive.' Some of the reporters gave out a gasp at what she had just told them, others appreciated her honesty, that press room over the years has not often witnessed honesty, it made a change. She stopped the questions for a moment to make a statement; 'I have an announcement to make.

In the room behind me are three very special people, at the end of my turn here I will choose three of you, the three who have asked me the most intelligent questions, each one will be allowed to ask one question to each of the three people.' What a reaction, they all looked at each other, first they all attempted to guess who the three were and realised that it would be better not to ask awkward questions, then they all wondered if this is a new idea they are going to have to put up with. The next question was how she managed to fly the aircraft. 'Glad you asked, the Saturday before was the first time I had been up in a small aircraft, we were airborne for no more than one half hour, and I asked Jim if he could explain to me how it is that he can keep the machine going in a straight line, without going up or down, he did well to explain as within ten minutes I was flying the aircraft by myself, there is no doubt in my mind that we were both saved by him, I was not worried all the time I was in charge, I had help from the air traffic guy who got me an instructor to see me down to the ground, you see, when you find yourself in a situation you don't start thinking oh I am going to die, no your thinking is more like how will I land this machine? The only time I thought about Jim is when they kept asking me on the radio how he was, my answer was each time "the same" if they had told me to give him a drink of water, I would have told them to get lost, the last thing I wanted to do is not to lose control of the aircraft because I knew for certain that I did not have the skill to recover and I would not be here today telling you a happy story.' Halfway through they started asking her about her life, she did not mind too much, and she skipped a lot of it. It was unusual in the press room, but at the end she did get a big applause, no stupid questions had been asked, then four special secret service men came into the room, they preceded the President who was the first one so to speak, he just waited for the question from the first reporter Rebeca had picked. 'Sir, how well do you know Rebeca?' it was short but well thought out as a question, he had no problem telling them all that the first time he had met her was on Airforce one, at that time he had been warned about her capabilities by their Ambassador in London, he has met her a couple of times in the White House and he thinks of her as a very bright person who always seems to have the right answer to any problem, she happens to speak fluently in five languages and at the moment is learning Russian, she is a guest in our country and I will always wish her well, thank you all.

He left, the next guest was the Vice President, he was asked how it came about that she was staying with his family. He told them about the rescue ten years ago at that time they had made up their mind to wait until she had finished her education, to bring her over for an extended vacation, in the UK they nearly all look at the television Sunday mornings to see Rebeca give her point of view, then he left and now they all wondered who was coming, a young man smartly dressed came in, he introduced himself as the son of the Vice President, yes him that was rescued by her! There was an immediate applause, and the last question was asked: 'Is it true that you had seen Rebeca holding up the aircraft by a golden rope? 'It is not too easy to explain, but when I was unconscious I was aware of being in mortal danger, somewhere in the back of my mind I must have been aware that my saviour would have to be Rebeca, so I must have put her onto a pedestal, just like Rebeca it did not enter my mind even once that she also was in the same danger, its one hell of a thing to have happened, but I have learned about near death, thank you all for coming. That was a wonderful press conference, and absolutely everybody there had learnt something.

It was now time for Rebeca to record her ten-minute television for the UK, she had also prepared one for America, Rose, and Alison both were going with her and of course two secret service escorts went with them, after the recordings they had planned of showing Rebeca some of the sites, one is called VISARTS. It is a modern Museum which includes many unusual modern exhibits. The management surprised Rebeca, they got on right of way with recording her talk for home, they could not understand how she was so up to date with the news in the UK, but they could not detect any controversial subjects, when it came to America, they more or less gave her a script for her to read, she did not even look at it, they have a real problem because as a television company they support one of the two political parties, and it goes against the grain for them to say anything good about the other party. Rebeca is not politically minded, but sometimes she reflexes badly on something a government has done. They came to a compromise, Rebeca let them read what she was going to talk about, if they disapprove of it, forget the broadcast. As it happened the talk was all about her recent experience, she told everything, including some of the questions asked at the press conference, she wanted people to realise that she is no angel and has no special powers, of course it was broadcast

When it was reviewed, it was much appreciated for its honesty. Touring a museum did make a change for Rebeca, one good thing, she was not recognised which pleased her, she hopes that it stays that way, That night she asked Ronald if it was possible for her to spend a day working with a police team, her being a qualified policewoman should make her demand possible, it took just one telephone call for Ronald to arrange a full day in Washington's number one police station, it was going to take place the day before her first lecture which was going to be at the Catholic University of America, Ronald's wife chose that particular one to give the students some food for thought, her possibly being an atheist, and they were looking forward to her appearance! It was nice, Alison returned with them to the house and that evening she had a meal with them, the three girls had a lovely evening, there was not a single moment when one of them was not talking, two or three time Ronald asked Rebeca what she was going to talk about the next day at her lectures, of course she knew already but made out that when she has felt the audience she will decide as she goes along, she never ever brings notes with her, she might talk about Jim passing out, or, she might not. She did tell him that she is going to be dressed seriously in a grey suit with a white blouse. She will speak in Arabic, French and German, she will tell a couple of jokes, and demonstrate her memory, she is certain that the students will leave the lecture having been enriched. That evening right after Alison had left, it was early bed time for everybody, Rebeca was pleased about that, when she opened up her emails, there were not many, but one stuck out, it was from the Prime Minister, who first wanted to find out how she was getting along in America, at the same time he was inviting her to spend some time with the English delegation at the UN, she can stay with the Ambassador whilst in New York, and perhaps address all the UN representatives, she can also bring a friend with her such as the Vice President's daughter if she likes. It is just a matter of her saying Yes, which is what she did right of way, and Rose, she hopes will agree to go with her. The next morning at breakfast Rebeca told them all about the UN, at the same time asking Rose to go with her, that part was going to be somewhat difficult, as the secret service do not usually enter the UN building, let alone the British Embassy, but if they try hard enough, they will no doubt find a way.

The lecture was to start at three in the afternoon, the place was packed, and because the Vice President and his family were attending, there were many more secret service personnel there, the President also wanted to be there, but then he did not want to spoil it for Rebeca, however he will see it all on television soon enough, the other thing was that there was a large group of reporters attending, they were not allowed to ask any questions which was most unusual. The Dean of the faculty gave the introduction, oh boy had he ever done his research, he seemed to know an awful lot about Rebeca, she was surprised, and then it was her turn. It was not really a joke, no, just a bit of a wake up for the audience, much in the knowledge that her audience could all possibly be Catholics, she started her lecture speaking in Arabic, only one sentence which she translated right of way (are they any Muslims here?). The reaction was delayed but when they caught on it was pure laughter, then she started by explaining how her having learned to speak Urdu and Arabic saved the whole British government.

Of course, she exaggerated here and there to make it a little more exciting, she was good at that. She had asked Ronald if they minded her telling about their rescue, he said that it was alright to talk about it, she first mentioned about the crew on the life boats who sometimes have to risk their own lives to rescue mariners, after a quick explanation of why she happened to be on the life boat that day, it was a brilliant rescue almost by the book, even though I was only fourteen years old at the time, I could see the way they were looking that they were somewhat traumatised, and when they were taken below where they are no windows, I decided to go with them and find out what had happened. That was a problem as none of them wanted to talk, so I decided to keep talking, mostly about myself, and I noticed that all four after a while started to listen to me, two hours later when we arrived in the harbour, they had brightened up, when they left they all in turn thanked me and gave me a hug, I must tell you for me it was a beautiful feeling that helped guide my life. 'Now if you remember I started this lecture by talking in Arabic, I should imagine that almost all students in this University are Catholics, and what interests me is this, you have not become Catholics, no you were born Catholics, I think that I am right. There must be a Patrick and a Mary in the audience I am sure, well I am addressing them both and telling them that had their place of birth happened to be in let's say Persia, both their parents would have been either Muslims or Jews, your names would have been different, and you would not have followed the Catholic religion. For me the strange thing is that there are over four thousand religions in the world, and all are certain that the other three thousand ninety-nine do not matter and are all miss guided, I will say no more except to tell you about the flying problem I had, you might all have seen the press conference in the White House the other day, no matter. My lovely pilot Jim is sitting in the audience somewhere, and he won't mind me talking about him. When he first came to, well after I had landed the plane, talking to his sister, he had just come out of a dream which was about me, he thought that I was an angel who had a golden rope holding the plane up in the sky, part of his brain knew that he was in real trouble and another part of his brain was telling him that it was all under control, when he had finally realised that, his recovery in the hospital was almost instant, had he not have showed me how to fly in a straight line, at the same time keeping level, we might now both be in the long sleep.

I will tell you something about me which is not easy to understand, when I was sixteen years old, the University at Oxford had already given me a place and instructed my head master never to have me sit for an exam, instead of studying for exams I managed to learn four languages which were Urdu, Arabic, German and French, I am fluent in all four including the ability of writing in Arabic, when I arrived at Oxford, the University had me stay in one of the lecturers apartments and I was the only student with a car park, I messed up a bit and only got an A not an A+ still it did not matter, I joined the police force for the training, then did a law degree, I ended being a sort of a star in a famous Court Case, Now I am absorbing your lovely country, and by the time I go home I will have made up my mind on my future, which I guess will be working in the Government. It might just have already started, I have just found out that shortly I will be addressing the United Nation, it is a real honour. I thank you all for having had the patience of my little storytelling, in the meanwhile I am quite happy to answer any of your questions only if they are one at a time, but first for your well-deserved entertainment. I have given your Dean here my bible which I have had since I was a little girl, your Dean is going to ask me questions about it' she looked at him to indicate for him to go ahead and start: 'on page 175, first is it on the left or right side of the book' she replied (left), 'on the same page, what is the first word on the fourth line, she replied with the word (was), 'on page 280 the tenth line the second word' she replied with the word (not). He eventually asked her twenty questions, all similar, she correctly answered each time. Then he changed and read a sentence somewhere, asking her its precise location, after 20 more questions without hesitating she named the page and the line each time.

The Dean could not make up his mind about her, how did she manage to learn the Bible to such a degree, if she were a priest, she would find it easy to plan a sermon, is that skill given to her by God? Now I cannot understand what she is about, I cannot believe that she is an atheist, the whole audience seemed to be in shock, what they did not know yet was that she could do the same with the Koran, when they found out they were all even more confused. It was time for questions, but so far nobody had a free enough mind to think about anything else. The religious people could not make up their mind whether that gift Rebeca has, was given to her by God or by the Devil! The not so religious students had their faith tested, all the time thinking that they do not know enough about their religion. Eventually one of the students asked Rebeca a single question, as it happened her name was Mary, the question was: why are you an Atheist? 'Unlike you Mary I was not born an Atheist, my mother used to be a Catholic, but apart from giving me a beautiful Bible, she let me make up my own mind, when I decided that it is now time to study religion, I did it with no bias what so ever, I studied all the available religions to me, and using my intelligence I came to the educated conclusion that all 4200 religions are manmade for the benefit of a few, I will admit that in some cases religion can be a good thing for some uneducated people, but when you balance the good, the bad hits the floor, it is so much worse. Just think of looking at the history of a Cathedral building over the Ages, it was always the poor that either worked for nothing or gave money to the Church, some of those peasants actually died of poverty, they made do without nourishing food and died at an early age, oh I forgot, at the time they were told that dying was just another way of arriving at heaven, just like these days young Muslim man will also be making their way to heaven with sixty odd virgins waiting to greet them, again just like on earth they will be there just to serve them, when that tale was worked out somebody forgot that on earth there is only one woman for every one man, so where did the other fifty nine women come from? The answer to your question Mary is that when I properly examined the role of religion in society, I discovered that was all in men's imagination, alright, some very good people are religious, but unfortunately, they do not realise what they are doing, and they look at religion through rose-coloured glasses, because it suits them. I have no problems with people who want to believe, it is very much their own business, but as time goes on and we are all better educated, it will slowly disappear.' Dear oh Dear, suddenly, the hall exploded with the loudest applause they had ever heard. No more questions were asked.

All the students wanted to shake her hand, they all lined up and at the end her right hand was beginning to ache, but for Rebeca that did not matter. The Dean was smiling, he told Rebeca that it had been the best lecture they ever had, all wanting to shake hands with her was a first. The whole lecture was posted on YOUTUBE and as they say it went Viral, there is a large society of atheists in America, they were quick on the mark inviting her to give them a lecture, she turned them down immediately, she had not come to America to preach against religion, she also made sure that everybody knew that, it was appreciated by the religious groups, it was so strange for them, because they should really be hating her, but no, they all thought that she had added to their thinking. Rebeca had learned a long time ago that if you want to influence people, it's best if you get on with them. On the way home Ronald could not get over it, he kept telling her what a good job she had done, 'Rebeca you have given them all some food for thoughts, I was surprised at the Dean's reaction, you know I spoke to him, and he told me that the Pope would have enjoyed being there, you have a simplicity in your thinking, and you are able to be direct with your subject, I find it refreshing.' She was pleased to hear that, Jim did not say a single word in the car, he was contemplating his role in life, like most of the students who shook Rebeca's hand. An unusual happening happened Sunday morning, Ronald developed a serious headache, Rose was not feeling well, her mother suggested that they should forgo the Church this morning, they all had a feeling of guilt about it.

However, it did not stop Rose and Rebeca having a couple of games of tennis, Rebeca did not have a chance against Rose, she was an accomplished player, Jim would never play with her, she used to beat him every time. Rebeca was learning, she was hoping to become a good player one day. That night Rebeca decided to never speak religion again in America, she got away with it once, and now it was best left alone. That was going to be a problem, the Media had got hold of the story, they were not about to leave it alone, so that night just before falling asleep, Rebeca formulated an approach to dissuade any further discussion on the subject. This week the two recordings were organised for Tuesday, apart from that, she had no other meeting planned, she was free for the rest of the week. The three girls on Monday morning were in Rebeca's bedroom attempting to do some planning, she opened her computer and showed them some of her writing, for the broadcasts. They kept asking her where do you get your ideas? Just then her own telephone rang, she could see who was calling, it was the television producer who had some good news for her, the management had agreed to make her position permanent, she will be the one deciding the contents, when she returns to England the BBC have already agreed to have the same arrangement as they have now, she will have to sign a contract of course, the money has to be discussed, but their starting figure is in the thousands for each broadcast, they want to set up a meeting after the recordings tomorrow. Well, that did bring excitement in the bedroom, it was now just time for a pot of tea and some lovely cakes, on the way down they decided that for this afternoon they are planning to do absolutely nothing. All this left Rebeca thinking how lucky she has been, now she does not need to work to keep herself, and back in England the first thing she wants to do is to buy a house with the Thames River at the back of her garden. The next day was a good one for Rebeca, accompanied by the two girls, she spent the best part of the day in the studio, they had the chance of meeting some famous people, which bought some excitement in their lives, The two girls watched Rebeca in front of the camera, she was completely at ease, again the Director wanted to know where on earth did she get all that information, that question was almost asked at every recording, it was one thing she had got used to, but sometimes she just wished that they never asked. Rebeca was on her own, discussing a contract with some important man from the management. The money they were offering was more then she could make sense of, so she did not attempt to make it even more, eventually she left the office with the second copy of her contract, there was one thing in the contract, which was interesting for her, she had to visit them in person for a period of two weeks four times a year, she was already looking forward to the visits.

Chapter Sixteen - The Holiday

Time had flown for Rebeca, she now is in her second month, the talk in the house is all about the summer holidays, A very rich friend of Ronald's, is letting the family have a vacation on his private yacht, which includes a crew of eight. When they start their vacation, the yacht will be in Quebec City for the first two days, at which time they can take part in an amazing festival which they will all enjoy, then they motor on to St Pierre et Miquelon the totally French Island where they will spend a whole day. The next port of call will be Halifax in Nova Scotia, it is not going to be a swimming holiday, it's too cold up there, but there is so much to see and learn, if they run out of time they will end the trip in Boston, but they can, they will attempt to make New York to a small harbour up the Hudson River which is close to the owner's house. Ronald had studied that part of the world, and for him it is going to be a special holiday, they are going to be surprised learning even more about Rebeca, which is starting in three weeks' time.

 For Rose and her mother, it is the perfect excuse for a totally new wardrobe, Rebeca could not be bothered, as far as she is concerned, she has enough clothes. The week before she managed three talks for England and America each, she was not taking her computer with her. They had asked Alison to come with them, but she was not allowed, however there are still two secret service men coming along as well. Rebeca was pleased thinking that perhaps Rose's mother will not have much to do, and she will get the chance to know her. The day before the holiday, they left for Quebec City. They would have preferred to drive there, but it would have taken too long, instead they flew in a private Jet, and before they knew it, they were being greeted by the happy looking crew. Rebeca was ever so pleased to find herself on board a boat, it did not matter the size of it, there were only two conditions for her, one it had to be floating on the water, second it had to have a marine engine on board, it was like being in heaven, that was difficult for her, after all she does not believe in Heaven! There was a light lunch laid out in the dining salon, and the whole family assembled there after their visit to each of their cabins, the crew all arrived to introduce themselves, they even had already heard about Rebeca, they were proud to be looking after her. The ship's Captain was on the young side, he seemed to be a pleasant type of person, interestingly he spoke four languages, he did get a surprise when eventually he discovered that Rebeca spoke five languages. One could not call the boat a yacht, it was too big, no, it was a ship, the ship is going to move, the morning after next, if they don't stop, they will arrive in St Pierre and Miquelon two Days later, the second night in Quebec Ronald wants them all to have a meal in a famous restaurant, he had already booked it. Today because they are still ashore, it was up to Laurie, Ronald's wife to plan the menu, just like the posh people in the old days! The three young ones decided to go ashore right after lunch, they managed to go before anybody else found out when they were going, it was one plus for them and one loss for the secret service, they had a wonderful time mixing in with the crowds, nobody knew who they were, and for a change they felt free, a lovely feeling. They had one problem for sure none of them had any Canadian Dollars.

Luckily Rebeca had her credit card with her, so eventually it all worked out. Jim and Rose wanted to explore more fully, which would have taken them away from the crowds and Rebeca put her foot down, they argued for a short while, at the end they stayed with their guest, eventually the parents found out and when on their own with Rebeca, they both thanked her in turn. The sky that night was illuminated by a never-ending display of fireworks, it was warm on the upper deck, the time passed without anybody realising that it was gone past midnight, one person in particular, had felt the call of the sheets, and took the decision to retire, after all Rebeca was feeling very tired, five minutes later they had all turned in. The next morning, again another lovely day, a slight cool breeze coupled with hot sunshine, just what the doctor ordered! There was one thing for certain, tonight is a special meal arranged by Ronald. This morning Rebeca had made up her mind to get to know the two secret service chaps, and as well as that, get to know the captain and all of his crew, she is interested why they had chosen that role in life, she can understand that it gives them a chance of seeing the world at a leisurely pace, but surely it cannot be a full time job, that is what she would like to find out. After the morning breakfast the family went out for a stroll, a sort of exploration of the city and the great harbour, there are many monuments celebrating both British and French Generals, Ronald was in his elements telling them how a battle in this city affected the United States. In the meanwhile, Rebeca sort of grabbed members of the crew one at a time, they would sit in the lounge, and they would discuss their lives so far, then what they had planned. Only the captain was aware of Rebeca's position in the family, she left him until last.

The first one was the cook, she was around late thirties and enjoyed her work, to her, if she was cooking, she was happy. Her number one ambition was to own a restaurant and cook all day, Rebeca asked her if one day she might get married, the answer was frank: if it helps get my restaurant, why not! As it happened, she is a dam good cook, the next person she managed to grab was the first mate, he was not at all young, almost in his sixties. He had always been a sailor he even has what they call a ticket which allows him to be in command of a ship. She asked him how come he is working here as a mate, all his life he had a problem with drinking, so he would get himself in trouble and lose his job, no he never got married or even close to it, the last ten years he has managed to control his drinking, he does not want to take on any responsibility, just in case he starts again, when he can he really enjoys visiting his sister with her family, he gets on well with her husband and he loves all his nephews and nieces. The third man of interest for Rebeca was George, he had been with the ship the longest, he is a decent sort of person, well-educated who has spent his life messing around boats, his attributes are that he is always there, he can put his hand to doing almost anything that has broken on the boat, he is the one who looks after the engines, the generator, the water maker, the blocked toilets and anything else that comes up, he has a workshop with a bench, a vice and a cupboard full of tools, he is a friendly person who loves talking to people, he was surprised when Rebeca told him about her first trip on a warship, how she diagnosed a shaft seal problem, thereafter got on ever so well with the chief engineer, who at first did not want to be even talking to a woman, who had no business looking around his engine room! Then she told him that she has studied marine engines which of course surprised him, Gorge was a bit of a slippery character, she knew that there was a lot more to find out about him. But he just needs to know her.

He did tell her that apart from the captain, the other four in the crew are only on the ship for eight weeks this summer, so she is not going to bother about them, now she has to interrupt the captain in his duties to have a serious chat with him, of course he has his own cabin but as well he has a proper office, she went to it and the door was shut, so she knocked on it and he said a single word, enter, now he was the one to be surprised, she asked him if perhaps she could sit with him for a half hour or so, he replied that right now would be a good time, he pointed to the only other chair, and they started the conversation; first she asked him about his life so far, what gave him the interest to do this work; that was quite a long answer about him having been in the American navy, qualified as a captain, but after eight years, got totally disillusioned with the system that had kept him all that time from having a ship of his own, it was so interesting for her, she told him about the man who was going to be her husband, she met him on board a frigate which she had stayed on whilst they were following a sail boat coming to England loaded with drugs, they managed to catch them completely by surprise and recovered all of the drugs, he was the one who had been made in charge of looking after her, eventually he had a serious accident, he ended up with a shore desk job, I told him to train and become one of the intelligence people, that is what he did, we got engaged then we decided to buy our first house together, the wedding was in the planning stage, unfortunately because of my notoriety in England he got cold feet and called it all off. 'Looking at you here, you are not thinking of making this your life for ever?' He was afraid of giving her an answer, she was right of course to ask, but now it is a question he has not been able to resolve. 'Are you still able to re-join the navy?' He was certain that it would not be a problem.

They talked for over an hour, he was fascinated by her story of the time she spent on a frigate, he told her that he had followed her exploits including saving her life in the light aircraft, she noticed that he said her life, not his life, she was pleased her message had got to him, that was good. She eventually told him to re-join the navy, train for a more important job, 'just think you are now, say in intelligence, none of the others working with you would not wish to be in your shoes. Your extra qualification will get you right up to the top, you will have more time to yourself, you can even have your own ship, you would have time to be married and time to go sailing! What else do you want?' It was the first time in his life that somebody cared enough to give him what he had just realised was good advice, he could not get over it, in the back of his mind he had a quiet thought, he did not want to lose touch with Rebeca. Later that day he was in conversation with Ronald, he could not help mentioning her, he told Ronald that she had given him some real advice. 'What an extraordinary person she is' Ronald answered by telling him about the rescue all those years back when she was a guest on the Lifeboat. The captain joined them for the special meal in what was an amazing establishment, the waiters all wore white gloves, they gave every person their special attention, the food will be remembered by all for the rest of their lives, it was so delicious. High tide was at seven thirty in the morning and to catch the outgoing tide that is the time they will be leaving, that will give them six hours with the tide running with them, that will be a good start. In the St Laurence

River, it is not their intention to be sailing at night, unfortunately there are not many harbours to shelter in. Their first stop will be on the south bank, a little town called Riviere du Loup (wolf river), gently motoring with the tide they should have no problem making it in ten hours or so. They had a wonderful first day underway, the scenery was as advertised, one could not take their eyes from both coasts, it was a good thing the ship was equipped with sat nav, it would have been so easy to miss the little harbour which had been built in the sea itself in the entrance of a river, there was only just enough room for them, but the captain had some skill! It had been a Bikini Day, as the sun started to disappear, it was a quick rush to the cabins to get properly dressed for the evening. There was a small electronic piano in the lounge and the nice thing was that Rose was an accomplished player, of course she learnt the classics, but she was not half good at boogie woodie, feet started tapping, they all had a good time. Whilst Rose was playing, Laurie was sat on a small settee, Rebeca went out of her way to go sit next to her, 'Laurie, can you still remember sailing across the Atlantic, all those years back?' she was surprised to hear that question, she was almost pleased to answer it, because she remembers it every day that goes by, it had been the worst experience ever in her life, at the time it seemed that all that she could do on the boat was to worry about the two children, in her mind it was a constant what if.

Sometimes Ronald would be having a sleep, she was then in charge and the intensity of her worry at least doubled, when that scenario was at night in total darkness, she was literally scared to death, a rogue wave would hit the side of the boat, it would shake it, something below would fall, sometimes she would just scream at the top of her voice, she could not be heard below for the constant crashing noise, the longest ever Ronald would sleep was two hours, yes two hours of pure agony for Laurie. After that six weeks of hell there was hope at last, they had actually seen the coast of England, she was beginning to have hope again and for the first time in the trip she had started to relax, however she was not going to forgive him that easily, then it happened! They hit something, the boat developed a serious leak which could not be stopped and the next thing she knew was to abandon ship. Her number one worry now was the two children which they managed to place in the life raft, then it was her, for a few minutes she started getting in a panic when Ronald had gone below to fetch the passports and other documents, it was a relief when she saw his face again. Laurie was almost in tears, she turned to her side and gave Rebeca a hug at the same time telling her that she thinks of her every day of her life, she always has the same picture of Rebeca in her mind, standing on the deck of the rescue boat! Rebeca had not realised what she had gone through all those years back, she was glad that they had a talk that evening, and now perhaps they can become friends. In the night the wind came up, George got up and inspected the ropes and the fenders, they were exposed, and he thought that the sooner they get out of this tiny dock the better for the boat, but they were all sleeping, he decided to stay awake to keep an eye on the situation, he did have a smile to himself looking forward to a rough trip which he was going to enjoy.

By morning the wind had shifted a bit and the situation had deteriorated, so now that the captain was up, there was only one thing to do, get out of this location. George started both engines, he helped with freeing the boat from the dock, and with the captain at the helm they made for the open sea, they had reached a part of the river which the locals call the sea, it is no longer possible to see both banks at the same time. Breakfast was simply scrambled eggs and toast, all eaten in a hurry before the eggs met the deck! The captain and the mate where both at the helm, it became difficult for them to be standing, the boat itself was in its element, it was a real sea boat with a deep keel, although sixty five feet long with two powerful engines, its cruising speed was no more than twelve knots with a range of six thousand miles, it could easily make Vancouver from Nova Scotia using the north west passage in the summer when the ice has disappeared, the only change for a long transit was to have a proper qualified mechanic on board with many spare parts for the engines. The next port of call was another little harbour in a famous town called Gaspe, the name is spelt with an accent, the town is situated in the furthest north and east part of New Brunswick, the town is famous because they have a monument that sits on the spot where Canada was founded, Ronald wanted to take a photograph, it is one of his interests, the wind was blowing from the west, which will make for an easy docking, once they have turned right past the headland they will be protected from the west wind, then normal life will resume on board! Rebeca was enjoying herself, remembering her long trip in Robert's boat, they came across fishing boats on their way to the famous Grand Banks, they did not let the rough sea slow them down, to them time is money. Rebeca noticed that Laurie was very quiet, no doubt remembering her sailing those years back, she thought it better not to interfere with her thoughts, it seemed that Rose also was keeping quiet, both Ronald and Jim were reading, so Rebeca did a complete tour of the boat including the galley and the engine room, she did come across George a couple of times, they exchanged words, eventually she ended her walk around the bridge where the captain and his mate where almost enjoying themselves, They were both pleased when she walked in, the mate did not waste any time, he offered her his seat and left the bridge to get himself a coffee, the captain was sure that he would not be back without having been asked, but for the moment it did not matter there were two on the bridge and that was alright.

They started talking where they had left off, it was unexpected, but he asked her if he could keep in contact with her, of course she did not mind, she had given him some good ideas about his life, he had already made up his mind to research the possibility, and he wanted to be able to tell her about his future. Nobody had lunch that day, when they eventually turned right, that is now heading South instead of East and the sea decided to have a rest, it was now six in the afternoon and their next destination soon became within their sight, the cook was now excited, she could get on with her work. No housework had been achieved that day, the beds had not been made the bathrooms had not been cleaned, the decks had not been washed, all that now was for tomorrow. The cook now had a helper, and she was planning one hell of a meal for all, she would not tell what it was, to keep the excitement going and have everybody sitting at the table with an appetite. Docking was easy against the wind, by the time the boat was all tied up and secure, was the same time that the supper was ready, one does not always recover the moment calm waters are reached, that feeling of going from side to side can persist for at least a quarter of an hour. The captain did not have the opportunity of joining the guests for supper, he had to waste over a half hour talking to the harbour master, who wanted to know where they had come from, and then where they were going to, he also wanted to see the ships documents and he wanted to look at all the passports! The captain had a hard time telling him that he does not have to look at all the passports as we have just arrived from Canada, 'Yes sir you are right, but tomorrow you tell me that you are going to St Pierre et Miquelon, that is a foreign country, you might just leave before this office is opened, so please go and get all the passports, crew and guests' the captain had no choice, he went back to the boat, disturbed all onboard and he went back to the office where the harbour master did his duty and copied every one of them, for what purpose nobody knew, maybe he had a secret ambition of becoming a customs man! At least now they can leave at any time they want.

They cannot leave too early in the morning because Ronald is intent on taking photographs of the famous statue, so they will leave at around midday for a day and a half journey to (France). If the weather remains the same, it is going to be a difficult trip, the waves will be catching up with the boat from aft (the back) which will tend to push either to the right or the left, so, the autopilot will have to work overtime, the other problem is going to be that both engines will have to run at a higher speed to attempt to keep up with the never-ending waves. From time to time the boat will be surfing, not at all pleasant, especially when the propellers are temporally out of the water and the engines start screaming, it sounds like being at the entrance of an inferno, most guests tend to attach themselves to their beds, and show their face when entering harbour! The captain and his mate loved that weather, they will spend most of the time looking out for fishing boats, for them the time will fly, of course they will have some help from Rebeca, she loves it too. That day the beds were made, bathrooms cleaned and best of all the cook prepared a lovely healthy lunch, which they had in the comfort of the dock. The family were all hoping that the ship was not going to leave until the sea had become a veritable mirror, that was not the plan, French baguettes and croissants were calling. The boat left at one in the afternoon, the crossing should have taken almost thirty-six hours, both the captain and Rebeca independently worked out that because of the following wind and the higher speed they were going to make, they should arrive within thirty- two hours, that is just as it is getting dark the next day, the forecast was for a slight improvement, so they left as planned. Now there were four on the bridge, they organised a rota for who was making the coffee at any time in the crossing, who would be paired when two of them went for a sleep, and as far as they were concerned it was all sorted, so they thought!

Rose was the last one up, she had a very good attempt at staying awake, including walking around the whole boat, she lasted two hours, no more. George was enjoying himself on the bridge telling some of his many tales about the sea. They had been on the go for the last three hours and they all agreed it was time for coffee, they voted for Rebeca to go below to the galley and come back with four coffees, the captain made a point of telling Rebeca to make sure that the mugs were full to the brim, it did not make sense to her, she was going to spill most of the coffee, she had to have one hand for the drinks and the other for holding to the boat, she was not going to complain, she started to make her way to some stairs to go below, very apprehensive about the return trip. Just as she reached the top step, she heard her name being called; it was the mate who was telling her to come back. Now she was confused, then she discovered that her making coffee in the galley was just a joke the other three were playing a joke on her. During rough weather crossings they make the coffee on the bridge, it is all there in a small cupboard, they had a laugh at her expense, she did not mind at all, no she was pleased, they had accepted her as one of them, it made her feel good, and yes, she made four coffees, there was also a small barrel of digestive biscuits, she offered them around and had a couple herself. They had lost site of the land they had left, there was nothing to see ahead, but the white horses formed by the breaking waves, as difficult as it was they were making good time, every half hour, Rebeca would look at their position on the satnav and mark a cross on the chart at that very spot writing the time in pencil of course, so far they had managed to keep to a straight line. From time to time, they listened to the shipping forecast hoping that the state of the sea is going to improve.

At seven in the evening all four felt hungry, coffee and biscuits were not enough, so George went down to the galley and made some ham salad sandwiches, he came back holding a sort of shopping bag which contained the snacks plus glasses and a bottle of red wine, that was just right! The state of the sea had not changed. It was the same wind blowing from the west, now they had entered a strong current which was taking them towards their destination. With the satellite navigation they could see the speed of the boat over the ground, and it was ever so fast, if it continued at that pace, they would reach the island just after lunch tomorrow. It started to get dark, which is always exiting when out at sea, they had a visitor, it was Rose who could not sleep, at the same time feeling hungry, so George offered to go below again and make another sandwich. When he came back up, he again had a bag with another bottle and glass for Rose to help her with the huge sandwich he had made for her. Rebeca did not have any more wine, the mate did not touch it, instead he had made himself another coffee, it was almost as if they were having a party on the bridge. The mate was the first one to turn in for a sleep of two hours, an hour later it was the captain himself taking his turn for two hours, Rose decided to stay with them which was nice, she was good company. The first two hours had passed, they had kept up the same speed, no change in the weather, not a single ship had been sited. The mate came back as planned and just as George was getting ready for his turn the left engine sounded an alarm, something was wrong. The revs had gone down, George pushed the throttle all the way for top speed on the left engine, not much happened, the revs only went up a fraction. George could not help but to feel in charge for the moment, he sort of recited out loud all the conditions with the engine that could cause that problem, was it an Injector problem? Or was it a piston ring? He could fix neither. Rebeca had thought about it and told him that marine engines do not die whilst running, it is either a shortage of fuel due to a blocked filter, or it could possibly be a shortage of air due to the turbine not operating as it should, it could be due to a seal that had collapse. She told George that she is going aft on the deck, but she needs a flashlight first, now armed with the light she went down to observe the smoke coming out of the left engine. In the meanwhile, the captain had woken up when the engine sound had changed, he met Rebeca on the stairs, she was going down and he was going up, she explained what they knew so far and why she was going to the deck at the back, he told her that it was a dangerous place to go to in this weather, so he turned around and went with her.

They did not have to spend anytime whatsoever, before he had opened one of the doors by sliding it fully it was obvious that the fuel was not being burnt, one could smell it and with the flashlight the smoke appeared black. That was enough information for Rebeca to go to the engine room and decide what it was causing the problem. She asked the captain to tell George to come and join her in the engine room. By the time he arrived she had determined that it was lack of air causing the problem, she pointed to a couple of nuts she wanted him to partially undo, after a few turns a gap began to appear and the rush of air started to get loud and the engine came back to its normal speed, he was mesmerised, 'how the bloody hell did she know that?' he asked himself. She spent another ten minutes making certain that there was nothing around that joint that could be sucked into the engine through the gap they had made, on the way out she managed to close the door but leave a sensible gap for outside air to enter the engine room. In the meanwhile, because the left engine had not run at the same speed as the other engine the boat had been fighting the autopilot that was working overtime to stop making a left turn. Rebeca had got a little bit dirty so she wanted to go back to her cabin to clean up, she will be back a couple of hours later, no, she was not going to have a sleep, she just needed some time on her own listening to the engines. Eventually night turned into day.

The sunrise was magnificent, they were headed almost straight for it, Rebeca had not slept at all since the night before, now she was beginning to feel the tiredness, it was just a matter of time until she made her way to the sleeping room, she was no longer making comments, she also had difficulty in hearing anybody attempting to speak to her, she eventually made her way to her cabin, it turned out to be a pure luxury when she laid down on her bed before changing her clothes, she fell sound asleep the moment her head touched the pillow. The captain followed her example and had his second two hours fast asleep in his cabin. Both Ronald and Laurie got up with the idea of going on deck for some exercise, as they passed the entrance to the bridge, they stopped and went in to speak to the captain who was not in attendance, instead they spoke to George, who was ever so pleased to be telling them about the left engine packing up, of course he could not wait to tell them about Rebeca, they could not believe what they were hearing. George could not help himself and he built up Rebeca's role in the affair, especially Laurie could not understand how it was that Rebeca was able to repair the engine, if they made a movie which included Rebeca, she would have to be a man! There was good news, somebody thought they had seen the land way ahead, but better still the cook was in the kitchen, and breakfast was ready for those who were prepared to eat.

The sea had calmed down a tad, and a short while later everybody was up except for Rebeca. Jim was out on the forward deck peering into the distance, looking for the land, once when a huge wave lifted the boat so high, he was sure he had seen it, he did not know why but he was ever so excited about visiting that French island, he could not wait to get there. Not one person onboard ever became seasick, when the sea was at its worse almost all were asleep. At breakfast most of the talk was about Rebeca and her exploits, just as well she was in the arms of Morpheus. However, she did eventually wake up, it was gone ten in the morning, and the land was definitely there to be seen, the captain reckoned that they should be arriving between one thirty and two o'clock a good four hours ahead of their original ETA, they had made extremely good time due to the weather.

Ronald had a discussion with the captain and although they had originally planned a one day stay, they were now going to stay for at least three days, waiting for the weather to calm down. Cook was happy about that; it was going to give her a chance of cooking real French food. Jim still had that excitement that he could not explain. It was one thing to see the land, but it was another thing actually arriving there, it seems that they were going to arrive in the harbour at the lowest state of the tide, the captain was not happy about that, so he slowed the boat so that it would take at least one hour longer, which gave him more chance of not hitting the bottom, he certainly did not want another problem! He called up the harbour to make certain that they have space for him, they did, so now he had less to worry about, his mind kept on repeating the same thought: what would he have done if Rebeca had not been on board? Rose and her mother more or less cornered Rebeca to find out about this new skill she happens to have; Rebeca did not mind telling her that it was part of a test to see if she was a suitable candidate for Oxford, she did not know at the time, but what happened; her and her mother were visiting an Uncle who lives close to Oxford, he had a wonderful library, she would usually borrow a couple of books, one day he slipped another book in her bag, it was all about marine engines, she read it all to the point of becoming an expert, she even one day warned the chief engineer in a navy Frigate that one of the seals on the propeller shaft was about to blow, she reminded them both that she has a photographic memory, and she can refer to any subject which is in the book itself. They were so proud of her. Rebeca did have a big breakfast which she much enjoyed, then she made her way to the engine room to have a look to see where the air intake comes from. It comes from the top deck where the radar scanner is situated, it's just a six-inch pipe, she was thinking at that moment that something must have fallen into the pipe itself, she planned to be looking at it once they have securely docked. The girl whose job it is to make the beds and clean the cabins was a university student on vacation, interestingly she recognised Rebeca, but she had no idea who Ronald was, so Rebeca told her, oh boy! Was she ever pleased to know that. For a while they both sat on the edge of the bed, and she told Rebeca about her own life story. She told her about the boy she loved, who one day decided he liked her own friend better, so she lost a boyfriend and a girlfriend on the same day, it reminded Rebeca about Norman

Afterwards Rebeca looked for a warm jacket to wear, she knew that she had bought one with her, eventually she found it and felt somewhat comforted to wear it. No one in the family had remembered the two secret service men on board, they kept to themselves, they had their meals with the crew and the rest of the time they stayed in a cabin, they were two discreet patient men, not much was liable to happen on the boat, so they did not need to be close to anyone, but after the boat had docked, they were going to resume their surveillance. It was almost a shock when Rebeca came across one of them on the aft deck, they exchanged a few words. Just before leaving the close space between them, the man asked Rebeca if it was her in the engine room in the night, she had no problem telling him what had happened with the left engine, he was ever so pleased to hear the story because the different sound from the engine woke him up, he heard voices and a short while later, it was all back to normal. Rebeca decided to have a chat with the man and find out what the reason was for him to be employed in that job. He was honest with her, when he told his life story so far, he was bought up by his mother and always felt that he should be protecting her, especially as she was of a nervous disposition. These days that is the way he feels in the job, he is happy protecting nice people, then he added: 'It has been a pleasure to have met Rebeca!' They had to pass the harbour entrance and then turn back straight into the harbour, the captain had never been there before, he manoeuvred the boat just as if he did that every day, it was not difficult for him as there are many books published on the approaches of harbours giving every detail. They were now all faced with what looked like a little town, it looked so pretty and especially colourful, the mate had a bit earlier raised a yellow flag, which is called the Q flag, it tells the harbour people that they have come from abroad and they deem themselves to be in quarantine, so they will not leave the ship until they have been visited by the customs people at least and received the all clear. The harbour master who was also the customs man came on board, he asked the captain how many souls where on the ship, he was given the correct number, and he asked that they all present themselves at his office with their passport as soon as they disembark from the ship.

To the captain he appeared to be doing his job too well, they call people like him with some authority "Little Hitlers" one learns to put up with them. It took over a half hour for the guests to be ready to leave the boat, the five guests had their feet on the land first followed by two secret service men and the captain. It was more than obvious where they had to go first, it was the only official building in the dock with much signage on it, first it was the Customs, then the Harbour Master's office, then Immigration and last the Police. Each one followed by the man's full name; one could be surprised that he was not also the mayor! whom might just have been a relation. One would also find it hard to believe that he had a wife, not many residents had met her, she was a shy person, absolute opposite to him, but yes there was a but, he had a daughter who happened to live in Virginia and at that moment was home on holiday sitting in the office next to his with the doors open. The first one to dare cross his threshold was none other than Rebeca, was it the Avant guard who had been pushed ahead to soften the opposition? Well she sat on the other side of a huge desk which seemed to give him that little bit more authority: he asked her name, where she had come from and asked for her passport, which she happily gave to him all the time doing her very best not to laugh, then her problem started; 'Miss how did you come here from the UK?' she simply answered, 'flew to Washington then to Quebec City and here.' Now he was in his element 'Miss, your passport tells a different story, so please tell me the truth. She was beginning to realise that her passport had never been stamped, so now she had to start explaining what happened, it was not going to be easy for her.

When she told him that she had flown to America from England she was on Airforce1 with the President, he had concluded that she was taking him for an idiot, then he began to lose his temper. It was lucky for everyone that as he raised his voice his daughter next door could hear her father getting upset, so she came over to his office, as she walked past Ronald the Vice President, she recognised him, then entering the office she knew right of way that the woman sitting in front of her father was the now famous Rebeca. She spoke to her father in French of course, and gave him the facts, she was most surprised when Rebeca turned around to thank for her intervention, she did not only just speak in French, but she also spoke in Parisian French not what they speak on the island, which was more of what is called a "Patois" which these days is only spoken in Quebec. Her father made a complete turnaround, and suddenly became friendly and most accommodating, he left his desk and made his acquaintance with the Vice President, no, he did not apologise, of course he had not realised who Rebeca was. His daughter "Helene" could not wait to have a few words with Rebeca, she had heard her speech at the United Nation, she was going to tell her father about her. Her name is going to confuse people, in French it has an E at the end, which is the way she spells it, she is a beautiful and graceful person. Nobody had yet realised that Jim had not taken his eyes away from her, now he much wanted to be talking with her. Laurie Jim's mother was the first one to realise that her son for the first time ever could not take his eyes away from a woman, without telling anybody else she had already made up her mind to invite her on board tonight for dinner. Rebeca also had decided something, she wanted to have a one-to-one long talk with Helene's father, she wanted to get an idea of life in such a small, isolated island, what happened during the second world war? She had a long list of unanswered questions to put to him. Helene offered to be their guide, which they accepted, at the same time Laurie invited her for dinner on board the boat. There were three bars in town and most of the crew were going to try one every day, on the first day even the two secret service men were seen drinking with the crew at the first bar, drinks were cheap, they had to make certain that no one managed to drink too much, the mate never left the boat, especially to have a drink. Whilst they all went back to the boat with the addition of Helene, Rebeca did not go back with them, she stayed to talk to the boss of the docks! At first, he was a little surprised, but after a while he begun to understand Rebeca, and on various occasions he apologised to her about his coldness

She managed to convince him that she thought he was a great guy, he could not get over the fact that she was a most interesting person, and over two hours later she made her way back to the boat. The first person she wanted to talk to was none other than George, they had a mission to accomplish. There she was wearing a pair of man's overhaul which were too big for her, she had to find a ladder which George brought up, it reached the top roof of the boat, she pulled it up and leaned it against what she had worked out was the air intake for the left engine, or should we call it the Port engine! Then with the torch in one hand she was peering down the stainless steel pipe. 'It's a bird!' She shouted, then asked George to find a steel hook and some strong thin rope, a quarter of an hour later she came down from the roof with a dead seagull in her hand. George put the ladder away and joined her in the engine room, she told him to undo that connection completely, clean the joint, apply some sealant and make it good by tightening the nuts again, some while later George run the left engine and it run the way it is supposed to run. It was now no more than an hour for dinner, all the guests were assembled in the salon and finally Rebeca joined them, not dressed in overhauls, no, she was in her best attire, looking as if nothing much had happened, the captain was there, and he congratulated her on her knowledge and her resourcefulness. One could see that he liked looking at her, that talk they had at the beginning of the trip about his future, he had not forgotten. Helene wanted to ask Rebeca so many questions, never really got the chance, she wanted first and foremost to find out how she had accumulated so much knowledge, and how did she manage to learn so many languages? Rebeca told her that to answer her interesting questions properly was not a five-minute stint, they would need to spend a lot of time together, maybe they might just be able to organise a day together, then she asked her if she happen to have a friend who is fluent in Russian, because she needs help with the pronunciation, unfortunately Helene could not help, but the two enjoyed their company. Whilst Rebeca is still in America they are planning to meet as often as possible, now on the boat it was going to be Jim's turn to get to know Helene, it was so strange how that happened, their first half hour of conversation was all about Rebeca! He did not mind, as long as they were together is all that mattered to Jim, the more he found out about Helene the more he was attracted to her. Helene finished her education in an American University, she has an Art degree, at present she works in a museum of fine art in Richmond Virginia which is almost eighty miles from Washington, a two-hour drive. Her interest in art well compliments his interest in design, they forgot about Rebeca and three hours later they were discussing the relation of art and design. Laurie was ever so pleased; she had never seen her son having any interesting discussion with a young lady. By the end of the evening everybody on board knew about Helene, they knew where she lived, what she did for a living and that in two days' time she must return to work. That was so sad, but Laurie was not about to give up and she had formulated a plan, oh boy! Some plan! It was not often that she requested anything from Ronald, but when she did, he always gave in, he was a normal human being who always wanted a quiet life, and he learnt over the years that when his wife asked him for a favour, he had no choice. The next morning, he telephoned Estelle, she was the President's private secretary, who after his instructions telephoned the Museum in Richmond asking for the director of the Museum to call her back in the White House. When she received her call, she told a trivial lie telling her that the President wanted Helene to advise him on some paintings for a couple of weeks at least. The President himself enjoyed being part of the deception, he knew and understood Laurie, the other thing was that the director of the Museum was herself a bit of a tyrant which made it all that bit more exciting. Of course, she agreed. It was going to be part of the museum advertising, she thought.

The next morning it was arranged for Helene to visit the boat again, was she ever so surprised when she was told about the plan; another day and she was going to join the boat for the trip back to the Hudson River, it was going to take at least another week and perhaps more, in Washington she is going to spend some time in the White house, even meet the President. She could not wait to tell her grumpy father, and now she will have the chance of getting to know Rebeca. Her last day on the island, Helene had to visit friends, and buy at least one new outfit, she was already thinking what she was going to tell the director of the museum. She had a choice, mostly because she was not going to tell the truth, that would not do, what she did not know was that the President was planning to have a photo shoot with her in the White House to show that he is interested in the arts, for good measure he is going to mention the Museum in Richmond. In the meanwhile, the day of leaving has arrived, she found herself in a nice cabin with all facilities, she was not too far from Rebeca, their next port of call was Halifax in Nova Scotia, at least a two day trip, the wind had all gone, the sea was as calm as it ever gets, the boat made a constant V in the water, it never seemed to end, for a change it was pleasant to be sitting out on the deck. The left engine had completely recovered, then lunch was called, Helene managed to get lost attempting to find the dining room, she was lucky because Jim had realised that she had not been shewn around the boat, he met her going the wrong way, it was perfect for him, he held her hand and they both arrived for lunch, she was sitting next to him, that had been arranged by Laurie of course, during the conversation between them, Jim found out that she was interested in Rebeca's exploits, he suggested that after lunch they should have a drink at the bar, and he will tell everything he knows first-hand about Rebeca, then she will be able to ask her interesting questions, Helene agreed, she was looking forward to the chat.

By three in the afternoon, they had lost sight of land. All they could see was just water all around them, so far Rebeca had spent the time on the bridge, she was looking forward to the mysterious nighttime, her thoughts where often about England, sometimes she was a little upset with herself not having been able to find a Russian speaker to learn with. She also was interested about Helene, she already had questions for her mostly about all year-round life on a small island, the winters must be the worst times, how did she as a French person manage to work in the USA? That was one of the first question she is going to ask. That afternoon Rebeca and Laurie got together, and they had a most interesting discussion: Laurie was worried about Rose, she did not seem to want to do anything, she was quite happy seeing the world go by. Laurie found out that Rebeca had a plan, she had already noticed the same about Rose, and all along she was thinking of what was needed to be done. First, she had to be taken out of that environment, then she must be given some responsibility, would Laurie agree with her, this was the time to ask her; 'You know Laurie what would be good for Rose? I think she should come back to England with me and help live my life, she will learn so much, I will make sure every single day, she has to come to term making decisions, I'll get her to do half of the cooking and be with me almost all the time, she can write my letters almost every day, she can come with me to the Courts, my life in England does not seem to stop, She can visit Scotland Yard and talk with my friends there, she will have to plan a ten minute talk for the BBC, she will never have the time to look in a shop window'. Just as they were shaking hands on the deal, Rose walked in; 'what have you two concocted?' Of course, she was no told. Later, Ronald realised that something had gone on between his wife and Rebeca, Laurie appeared so happy, in her mind both her children were well on the way of being sorted, it was a great relief for her, the other thing was that she has now made a good friend. By dinner time, Jim and Helene had not moved from the bar, they were both so happy getting to know each other, it turns out that they both believe in destiny. A couple of times Ronald had attempted to go to the bar for a drink, but each time his wife stopped him.

The sunset on a calm sea is never forgotten, it is a wonderful sight, and it is also the time for diner, they all arrived at the same time, there was a little salad to start with and the main course that followed was a delicious roast beef, complete with Yorkshire pudding, roast potatoes and parsnips and a lovely gravy laced with brandy, there is no desert, just a good selection of cheeses followed by coffee. Helene asked Rebeca what the best time was for to have a talk together. as much as Rebeca wanted to talk with Helene, the bridge was a powerful magnet at the start of the night, she suggested tomorrow morning right after breakfast, say ten in the morning in her cabin, she will be there waiting for her, Jim heard all that and he was pleased to have the opportunity of being with Helene a bit longer, he has to work out how he was going to make it look like an accident. He need not have worried about that, Helene went over to him as soon as Rebeca had left for the bridge, she wanted to ask him something; she had been wondering who the men in suits were, are they part of the crew? Jim had a smile telling her that they were secret service agents from the government to make sure the Vice President was always protected, then they talked about the President's role in her extending her holiday, they had a good laugh, strangely laughing together became normal for both. Rebeca was on the bridge until eleven, she asked to be called at four in the morning to do at least two hours or even three hours on the bridge. The night passed with no incidents, George went below to look at the engines which were both doing well, Rebeca and the captain spent at least a whole hour on their own on the bridge, he told her some interesting stories about navigation around the world, he also explained how navigation used to work with a sextant, it was a matter of measuring the angle of a heavenly body, such as a star at night and the sun in the daytime. Apart from the sextant itself, what was most important was to have the precise time, when the first steam trains started to go from one city to another, they had not devised a way of telling the time in each city, they eventually relied on both; the sailors and clockmakers who eventually decided to use Greenwich as the starting point. Rebeca was ever so pleased to have learnt what the captain had taught her, she kept thinking how it is we take things for granted, when she turned in again, she fell asleep happy.

She managed to get up early and she was the first one down for breakfast, she was back in her cabin before ten in time to rearrange her bed and make the cabin look presentable. A while later, Helene did not knock on the door because it was already open, so she called to Rebeca who was there waiting for her, and an exchange of information and views started between two curious people. Rebeca had planned not to be the first one to ask, she was quite happy to answer Helene's questions. The first one was 'Rebeca, have you ever had a serious disappointment?' Of course it was an easy one to answer, she recalled almost every day with Norman, with the exception of the sighting in the MI6 building, she explained what happened when he was recovering in hospital and she woke to him whispering in his ear, it was a lovely moment for him and for her of course, she enjoyed sharing those times with another person, she realised how lucky she had been to have loved another person. The last day with Norman of course was a sad time for her. Helene was mesmerised, it took her a long time to ask the next question which was about her time at the University. Again, she found it hard to believe that she did not have to pass an entrance exam, and why did they give her the special treatment? That was also an easy one to answer, 'at the age of fourteen I could speak fluently five languages, I could tell anything about the St James Bible, just mention a page and I can recite the whole page, I can tell you each letter and their position, I am now in my mind looking at page 354, it's on the right the first word is "they" the fourth letter in the 34th word is "V", they tell me that I have a photographic memory, it was something I was born with.' Then before being asked Rebeca over an hour at least told her most of the interesting happenings in her life, she also told that she thinks of the Prime Minister as being a friend, it is the same with the top man at Scotland Yard, the head of the Royal Navy, one of the Royals and so many other people.

Now she told her that she is having a hard time finding a Russian speaker that she can spend time with, to polish up her pronunciation. They had to have a rest Helene could not digest anymore, so they left the cabin made their way to the bar for a nice hot milky coffee which they took with them on deck. Rebeca did not ask a question, no she asked her to describe a day in the middle of winter, when the wind is so strong that one feels safe being on land, what happens with school, shopping, visiting the Doctor or waiting for the ferry to be able to dock? Helene had no problem telling Rebeca how awful those winter days were, all she wanted to do is curl up under a warm soft blanket, sometimes it was the screaming wind that was the most disturbing, other times when there was no rain it could become fun trying to press oneself into the wind and then be blown back. Families tended in the winter months to cook a never-ending stew, which was nourishing to eat, but after a while it became dead boring, but the kitchen fire tended to keep the whole house warm, and that became the central part of the house, to sit in the lounge would mean having to light another fire which nobody wanted to do, especially as it meant a trip outside where it was so cold. There was always a shortage of teachers, which meant that often one teacher would teach all the subjects. The saving grace was access to the internet and the television, where most of the real learning came from, that is the main reason for all the islanders being able to speak English these days. One of Helene's uncles became an American citizen. He lives in Main, and Helene would stay with him and his family every summer holiday, that is where she almost became American, her last two years of school were in Main, which was followed by the University, now she has the right to live and work in America, she is very interested in the arts, herself being a good painter, she has the job that was made for her! Jim came over to them because lunch was on the table, it was perfect timing as they had almost reached the end each recounting their previous lives. Listening to Helene, Rebeca was wishing to spend a winter in her home, she had felt that cold wind and the warm fire in the kitchen as Helene was talking. Just at that moment whilst still on the deck, at last they could see a ship on the horizon, Rebeca exclaimed 'It's a warship!'

For Rebeca, lunch was in her way, she wanted to be on the bridge to use the powerful binoculars to work out what type of warship it was, but she waited until lunch was finished. The talk at the lunch today was mostly about the good weather they were in, and that tomorrow morning they should be docking in Halifax, a port with a lot of history, Ronald was beginning to get excited about it, there is so much he wants to see there. What nobody knew at this time; is that Jim and Helene had planned to eat out by themselves the first evening there, after lunch those two took off on their own, they found a sort of corner which was in the sun but shaded from the wind, they stayed there for hours. Laurie was a happy mother. Rebeca had identified the warship; it was big and when they came closer Rebeca was able to tell them that it was a destroyer. The sea was still as calm as it could be, that V the boat made in the water was still there, the odd seagull would rest on the deck for a couple of hours, the captain would go out of his way to stay a long way from any fishing boat that would have come close. Rebeca started to think about England, she was beginning to miss her friends, it was the first time she had felt a little homesick. At around four Rebeca went below to have a cup of tea and a delicious cake. Rose was there at the same time, so they had a chat, after which Rebeca took Rose by the hand, to her surprise, and took her straight to the bridge.

The captain was there, they greeted each other, and Rebeca sat Rose in front of a chart, she asked her to have a good look at it and at the same time see if she can understand anything she is looking at. Rose was really taken by surprise; she had no idea whatsoever as to what she was looking at. Rebeca showed her the coast of Nova Scotia which happened to be the present destination, next she pointed out all the figures which are all over the sea, she explained that each one of the numbers represent the depth of the sea at that particulate place, it is usually measured in fathoms which is six feet, sometimes closer to shore it is measured in feet. It was so strange it seemed to appear that Rose was pleased to have learnt something, the captain had realised what Rebeca was up to, he approved. There was a pencil mark with the precise day and time written next to it, she explained that the navigator made that mark, as it happened four hours earlier to indicate the location of the boat, then with a divider: which is no more than a compass with two points, was able to "walk" it to a place with the name Halifax, and that would have told him when the boat was going to arrive there unless a strong head wind started to blow, then of course it would take a bit longer, Rose had never realised how interesting navigating was. She grabbed her hand again and took Rose to the source of the constant noise, it was the engines of course; when she unlocked the engine room door the noise became extreme, poor Rose had to place her hands on both her ears, but not for long because Rebeca handed her a pair of ear defenders. They both walked in and stood next to two huge engines, they were painted white, on top of that they were absolutely clean, there was not a single drop of oil anywhere, now shouting to the top of her voice, Rebeca explained what it was had slowed the left engine, she pointed to the air intake pipe which had become partially blocked, she showed her the coupling she had opened up to let the air from the engine room feed the motor, she showed her the huge fuel tanks with the multitude of filters, then the generator that is always on making all the electricity for the boat, good news! Rose asked her what those huge pipes all wrapped up in white fabric were, she told her that they were part of the exhaust system, they were extremely hot, the wrapping was to protect any engineer who might have to work in that area. On a wall there was something which had a lot of pipes that seemed to go nowhere, Rose asked what they were all about, Rebeca said 'OK I will explain when we get out of here'. After the door was closed and locked Rose discovered that it was the water maker, it never stopped making water from the sea to the dining table, it was modern science working using what they call reverse osmosis. To explain, one would have to understand what osmosis was, that is a science problem which would take a long time to learn.

Next naturally was dinner time, Jim and Helene being the last one to arrive at the table, for a change Rose was looking interested and happy, for the first time in her life somebody took the time to teach her something, now she wanted to do it again! Her mother had noticed the change, and she was pleased about it, there is still some hope, Rebeca also had noticed the two who had become inseparable. Ronald made an announcement: he wanted Rose when they get back home to have a tour of the White House with Alison for Helene, and if at all possible have a picture taken with the President under one of the paintings, to make it possible Helene will have to stay with them for at least a couple of days, it was a lovely gesture from the Vice President which they were all pleased with. The plan for tomorrow was to arrive at Halifax by about nine in the morning, thereafter he did not mind what anybody else wanted to do, but him and Laurie where going to visit one museum and many sites of interest, years back there had been an infamous explosion in the harbour that killed many people and demolished half of the buildings in the town he wanted to learn more about it, another thing he wanted more information on, was the fact that most of the coloured people who lived in Canada, the majority lived in Halifax, the first black Canadian was called Mathieu da Costa he arrived from France in 1604, a long time before Canada had become a country, he worked as an interpreter. There was a lot more Ronald wanted to see and learn about. The forecast for tomorrow was good, no wind and warm sunshine. The diner was excellent, the chef now had a steady kitchen so that she can concentrate on the food, not the rolling motion

Tonight's diner was beef wellington for the guests, she had made the pate herself the day before, the desert Rebeca was looking forward to it, was a huge apple pie served with a generous slice of Canadian cheddar on top. Nobody had ever seen a couple so close after having met less than 48 hours before. It was as if they had known each other a long time ago, and met by accident years later, strangely it was a pleasure to see them talking to each other. Sunset was again a lovely site, everybody was out on deck to observe the sun which appeared larger and larger until only the very top of it was visible, there were a few photographs taken, it would make for a lovely memory of that moment. Rebeca was puzzled, she heard a slightly different sound coming from the engine room, so she quietly made her way there, she listened carefully to each engine and yes, one was going a little faster than the other one, this time it was the right engine which had slowed down slightly. Before taking any action, she thought it better to check on the bridge first. The captain was there, he was pleased to see her, she told him why she had come up, they both looked at the two throttle levers, and right enough, the left engine one was slightly ahead of the other one. How that had happened, nobody knew, she decided to pull the left one back, and then for a change both engines were in unison with each other, the sound then became easier to listen to, he was surprised that she had detected the anomaly, he thought to himself that she must also be a musician, and he was wrong, it was not the difference between musical notes, it was the difference between two mechanical objects! That night Rebeca did not spend any time on the bridge, but she was the first one there in the morning, she wanted to see the entrance to the harbour. From the time they had seen the entrance to actually be there was almost a whole hour, it was difficult to see the sky for the constant flight of Seagulls overhead, it was a good job the yacht club was well displayed on the chart of the harbour, even first thing in the morning there was so much traffic, big ships making their way out to sea, fishing boats coming in with their catch and a hundred or so Seagulls circling the boat, there were ferries with passengers crossing the harbour, the captain had to slow right down, so that he could read the name of the next buoy he was about to pass. They arrived at the yacht club, what a friendly club, they were there to help and made everybody most welcome, no one asked to see the passports, they just seemed to be happy that they had arrived, one good thing is that they accepted the US dollar, the first thing Ronald wanted to do is to rent a car, oh no! he had to rent two cars, he had forgotten the secret service men, they also needed a car. Jim and Helene went off on their own, Rebeca and Rose went with Ronald and Laurie, he was driving, not before telling the two secret service agents what his plan for the day was.

They were going to have lunch out and possibly dinner as well. The car rental company supplied him with a map, and he made his first destination the tourist office, so did the two behind! First, they found out where the best restaurants were situated, then it was a matter of finding where everything of interest was. That was not difficult to achieve, and after all Halifax is not a big town, it has grown, yes but although it is an important harbour on the Atlantic coast, it has not got a big population, there is an awful lot of emigration for a city which is known for its lack of employment opportunities. That first day in Halifax, Rebeca was the first one who discovered that the inhabitants of Halifax are called Haligonians, and the other people in Nova Scotia are known as "Blue Nose" Ronald drove around the whole town, they visited the Citadel, the old town clock, and the maritime museum. He had arranged to visit the art gallery of Nova Scotian tomorrow with Jim and Helene. All this time Rebeca wanted to stay on her own, she wanted to send some cards, she wished she had sent some much earlier, but there was always something going on, but now apart from Rose who had been left behind, Rebeca had some time for herself, but first the cards had to be done! It took her the first part of the afternoon, that's all. That first evening in Halifax there was only Rose and Rebeca who eventually got together and found a restaurant not too far from the boat which had been recommended, their speciality was fish which they both enjoyed, it was a busy place, before they left, Rebeca asked the owner if they could visit the kitchen, Rose was surprised but happy to go along with her, the request was granted, and for the very first time in her life Rose realised how hard people have to work to make a living, that was a lesson and a half for Rose to learn, No! it did not change her life, but, her life was changing, Rebeca had noticed, she was going to keep at it and on top of that, she had a plan.

When they were both back on the boat, Rose told Rebeca that she was puzzled, it did not make sense, 'what did not make sense Rose', she answered right of way; 'people in that kitchen have to work so hard in that hot place, yet, they all looked happy, can you explain?' Rebeca was extremely pleased to explain. 'There is more than one reason for their happiness Rose, one reason for sure is that they enjoy the work they are doing, they also enjoy the fact that most customers in the restaurant actually enjoy their cooking, they also look forward to tasting it, you can be sure Rose that if the cooks did not like their job, the food would not be as good, then at the end of the day, around ten in the evening, they are all so pleased to be going home for a well-deserved rest, just think, you go to the hairdresser, can you not see at the time, that person loves that job of making you look as best as you can, they are always friendly towards you, all they ask for is for you to be happy with their work , that is how the world round us keeps going. Just think, why do I do the Sunday morning broadcasts? Because I want people, I have never ever met to appreciate my work, now about you, what do you do to make one person happy every day? Rose did not say another word for now, they had just reached the boat, they were the first one's back, Rose was about to go straight to her cabin, she had an awful lot to think about, but Rebeca did not want to let her go, so they both ended up at the bar for a night cap. Rebeca started to explain to Rose what she does every day, all the people she is friends with, some she visits others it is a matter of communication either with the mobile telephone or it is sending emails to their computers, she spends a whole day every week planning her next broadcast.

She attempts to keep up with the latest news, she visits all her relatives and most of her friends, right now it is not going to plan, she still has not found a Russian speaker, she will do her absolute best when she gets back home. 'By the way Rose, you did see your mother and I do some planning, as it happens it involves you, I thought that it would be a damn good idea, if when I go back to the UK, you were to come with me, meet all of the people I know including my two sets of grandparents, my father, of course my mother the person responsible for my education, she loves playing jokes on people, oh yes of course, there is also somebody you know, her name is Debra, you most likely not remember her, but surely she will remember you, I might be asked to prosecute in a trial, that would definitely be very exciting.' The more Rebeca talked the more Rose wanted to go with her, that was one particularly good result for everybody concerned. Laurie eventually told Ronald, she was a little worried about his reaction, but it was positive, he also thought that it would be good for Rose. The new couple were the last ones back, it was so strange now thinking that the two were now officially a couple, they were making plans on how they were going to meet in the future, they would take it in turn to drive, she sometimes has to work on Saturday and Sunday, then she gets three days off in the week, at that time she will spend the three days at their house. Sometimes they might visit Alison in the White House or go out with Rose, normally he would have taken her flying, but he had promised his mother and Rebeca that he will never fly again. The next morning the four "young ones" went to the beach, which was not far away, but it was a taxi ride. When they got there, they discovered that it was already busy and they made a B-line for the water, was it ever cold! Somebody thought that is why it is called the North Atlantic! They were going to spend yet another day, they all loved the friendly people of Halifax, they eventually left the fourth day in the morning.

They arrived in Boston a day and a half later in the late afternoon, the cars were waiting for them to take them home, the owner of the boat was there with his wife, she could not wait to have a chat with Rebeca which went well, the Captain was the last to leave, he wanted to have another chat with Rebeca, they had exchanged addresses and he was going to keep in touch with her, she reminded him to have that air intake permanently repaired as soon as possible, the owner heard that, and he wanted to know what it was all about, then he discovered Rebeca's role in the affair, he now wanted to also have a chat with her.

A convoy of cars had arrived, and they were all back home before dark, two special agents disappeared never to be seen again, did they enjoy the trip? Nobody had the slightest idea, on top of that they did not seem to have a name! Rebeca was ever so pleased to get back to her computer, had somebody attempted to investigate it? yes, did somebody copy the hard disc? Yes, whoever it was, they learned absolutely nothing, the real work it is used for, went into hiding, it cannot be discovered, it appears to be a person's machine who uses it mostly for writing and sending next Sunday's ten minute broadcast, However she was a bit upset that they were still at it, one day she will confront Ronald and tell him that she has been aware that somebody had copied the hard drive more than once, she will explain that there is a file which records the day and time when the hard drive is copied, she did that because she has the same problem in England, people all want to know, she cannot blame them too much, but sometimes it's annoying. Helene is going to finish her holiday with Jim and Rose, the next day they are going to the White House, mostly to meet the President and have a photo shoot with him under a famous painting, Rebeca did not feel that it would be all right for her to go as well, that was a mistake, the President took it for granted that she would also be with them. He then organised a car to go and fetch her, he wanted to have a private talk with her, he was hoping to discover her secret! He had asked Alison his daughter to befriend Rebeca with a view of discovering her source of the fantastic knowledge. He listens to her every Sunday morning, and he still is amazed on her knowledge, sometimes it is so detailed that he is thinking about it all that day. That day he had made up his mind to call the Prime Minister in England and speak to him about Rebeca, that is exactly what he had done that morning and after a one to one talk he had learned a few things about her: she is always welcome by any of the military in the UK, they will do anything for her, it is the same with the Police force, whatever she asks for they will always oblige, the law is always on her side, she has a Law degree and she has appeared in Court to successfully manage an impossible cross examination. She reads all the time, she can tell the BBC what she is going to do, she also has the power to order any police officer in the land to do what she wants at the time.

The Prime Minister explained to the President that was most unusual but that is correct, and he cannot explain it, he just has to get along with it, 'Mr President we are talking about a most unusual person that has captured the nation here, we have tried over and over again to work out how she managed to get into that position, how does she know before anybody else what is about to happen? I must tell you, when I am with her I feel that I do not have to talk, because she has already read my thoughts, I can switch to another totally different subject and start talking about it without having prewarned her, she will then answer any question in the knowledge of the subject, it is so strange, but yes, there is a but, on top of all that she is a lovely sincere person who is most difficult to fault, I cannot wait for her to come back, I love being with her. In any case, did you know that she saved my life' Yes, he knew already about the attempt on the British Government. The President took the advice and just enjoyed her company, once or twice he thought that he had detected her answering a question before having heard all of it, for a moment he was wishing that she was not going back to England, he already knew that she must come back four times a year, and he will make certain to see her each time. He was looking forward to meeting Helene and pull a fast one on her boss, he had not done something like that since he was a teenager. The White House has its own photographer who will take the picture and arrange to distribute it to the media and send a quality print to the museum. Just before twelve they all met under a famous oil painting, he was kind to Helene telling her that she should consider herself a lucky girl, he knows Jim who is a real man, so to speak. Then he turned to one side and faced Rebeca, an idea came to his mind, tomorrow the White House will host his team, about twenty men and women who run the government for him, would she like to sit in and if need be, pass comments? She answered right of way with a simple yes.

Helene was well impressed, she felt as if she was dreaming it all, she could not believe any of it, surely, she must wakeup soon! After the photography was finished, the President had to return to the oval office, before doing so, he asked Rebeca if she could accompany him, and stay a while listening to a couple of meetings he is about to have, of course she was only too pleased to accept the invite, the others, led by Alison his daughter were going to hang around the Gym and play table tennis. One nice thing had happened, Jim had been able to extend his vacation for a few more days, tomorrow him and Helene had planned to spend the whole day completely on their own, they were both looking forward to the event. When Rebeca entered the Oval Office, it caused some surprise, his personal staff had not been forewarned and one of them his secretary had not recognised Rebeca, she looked much younger in the flesh. As soon as she had worked out who she was, the secretary rushed over to Rebeca to shake her hand and welcome her to the office, when she discovered that Rebeca was going to sit in a couple of meetings, she volunteered to stay with her and quietly tell her what the meeting was all about. Rebeca and the President were both pleased about that idea. Nice fresh coffee was bought in with a barrel of various biscuits and then the first visitor walked in, she was shown a chair for her to sit on in front of the desk, strange, there was some classical background music playing, what it did was to hide any soft speaking behind the visitor, the secretary now speaking softly could explain to Rebeca what the meeting was about. The woman sitting there in front of the President, had lost her husband a year ago, due to him following the advice of a "Quack" Doctor on the internet. It was a tragic case where the advice given is what had killed him, the doctor himself could not be prosecuted because her husband signed a form which protected the doctor. She was asking the President for funds to take the case to the Supreme Court. The President himself did not want to be seen as a soft touch, so to speak, although he wanted to help, it would not leave a good impression for him to have spent the people's money on what is likely to be a lost cause.

Especially for Rebeca it was painful to listen to the woman's pleading. Rebeca nudged the secretary and quietly told her what he should do: he should arrange for her to sell tickets; the winner will have a quarter of an hour uninterrupted with the President in the Oval Office to discuss any subject of their choice (within reason of course) he will publicly start the sale of the tickets and help organise the whole thing! The secretary typed it all on her telephone and immediately sent it to him as a text, his own telephone was already face up on his desk, and he was able to read her message without causing any attention, he was then happy to tell the woman and in turn she was most happy about his solution, they shook hands, she left with the understanding that he was going to start the ball rolling! 'Hey Rebeca, you should be here all the time, thank you indeed for getting me out of trouble, what a good solution that was, thank you again'. They just had time for a coffee, but they need not have rushed it; the person arriving next, was no longer coming, they had been involved in an accident, so now they had a bit of free time. Rebeca was able to tell him about Helene and Jim who seem to have got together, she also told him that Rose was going to go back to England with her, and she is going to attempt to educate her into the habit of working, for a while she hopes, he had a laugh when she told him the episode about her passport with Helene's father.

She also told him that next Friday she is going to be in the television studio all day, she does not yet know why? But she hopes it is not going to be anything political, 'By the way Mr President I understand some so-called experts, have attempted to record the hard disc in my computer, I say attempted because I know that it is not at all possible, I developed the software myself years ago when I discovered that my mother would attempt to look at my stuff! The other thing of course it always leaves a marker so that I know, you are the only other person who knows that, and of course I do not blame you, I realise that sometimes I get ahead of myself and it is difficult for people who do not know me to accept the truth, sometimes it surprizes me and I have no idea why it happens, I have been told that I should use that skill for gambling and get rich, I want only to be useful in my life, one day I guess I will get married and have children, then I might just attempt to relax. I have already found out that the man I marry will have to be a special man who can put up being second to me, especially in knowledge. His secretary had been there all the time, she loved listening to Rebeca telling part of her life to the President, it was inspiring for her, then it was time to re-join the others and go back to the house for lunch.

Chapter Seventeen- The Return to England

Friday arrived too soon for Rebeca, she was not enthusiastic about the long meeting in the Studio, she still had no idea whatsoever what it was to be about. But now she is going to find out within a couple of hours, she had asked Rose to go with her, this time not wait for her in the lounge, but be with her all the time, she is starting her training! The same day Helene and Jim were sorting out their lives, because they were both going back to work on Monday and this Friday they were making their way to her little apartment, to sort out her clothes for Monday morning, do some food shopping for the week, she was looking forward to cooking lunch for both of them, she had been thinking about it for at least a couple of days, the two of them when in her little lounge unwound the huge photograph the White House photographer had given her, she looked just as if she was his daughter or at least a very good friend, in the museum people will be struck by the picture, and best still, it will always remind her boss who Helene is, Jim said he was hoping to get half of the picture to put on his wall, he did mention to Helene that he was in love with the picture, that statement bought them a little closer, it was the first time the word "Love" had been mentioned. And they had both noticed it!

At that same moment, there were two young ladies standing in front of the receptionist's desk waiting for the two badges they will have to ware whilst in the Studio, Rebeca already knew the way and the two arrived in a reception area to be greeted by a happy looking gentleman, Rebeca had never met him before, she had no idea as to what his role was in the organisation, he has a serious job, even though he is still on the young side, he is the head of programming for the network. Today he is interested in meeting up with Rebeca to see if there is anything else she could add to her existing work. He told her that now she has their best program, with the most viewers. Rebeca turned to Rose and whilst reminding her that she knows her well, she asked her if she had any idea of what else she could do on the television. Even Rose surprized herself; 'Well you could teach a few languages, you could demonstrate how to find and repair a fault on a marine diesel engine, there was a pause for a moment, the executive chap was still trying to recover from imagining Rebeca in greasy overhauls, then Rose had a brilliant idea, for Rebeca to teach wives and girlfriends of general pilots how to survive when the same pilot cannot operate the plane anymore. 'Oh yes we could make that into a ten-week course, that would work'. No, Rebeca was having none of that, she preferred just having a discussion with an interesting person. Sitting on a stage with a live audience, say once every two months when she is over from England, that was agreed apart from the boring contract which will allow her to earn even more money, the house with the Thames at the end of the garden, was beginning to look like an old house on the beach!

So far the President had not forgotten his talk with Rebeca about her computer, he called in a team of experts to tell them what she had told him, they heard, they went away, then they came back two days later, after having agreed amongst themselves that what she had described to him was not possible, he then played them the recording that had been made when she was telling him, now that they were realising that she had reconstructed the software, that was a different thing altogether, and to make matters worse there is no way they could possibly work out what she had done, they would never have enough information to break into her thinking. Now the President knows that she was telling him the truth, that is what she wanted to leave him thinking, of course it was all a lie! When they arrived back home, only Rose's mother Laurie was in, Jim was coming back on Sunday afternoon, Ronald had gone abroad for almost a week with a team of manufacturers, so the three women in the house were going to a show Saturday evening, in the meanwhile Rebeca had to do some work for her programs, and best of all Rose picked up an exercise book and started writing about the life story of someone who she is close to! That really pleased her mother, especially when she found out who it was, she started to write about?

Laurie made a plan for the three of them, for the whole day and evening Saturday, in the morning they went to a flower show, Rebeca was not too excited about going, but when she arrived there, she just could not believe all the flowers which are grown by amateurs, it seemed that there had been no expense spared towards making the flower show a real success , Laurie knew many people there, and the three enjoyed themselves, even drinking rose petal tea which was very different to the normal tea, they got back in time to have a light lunch, in the afternoon they were at the tennis club, Rose did some more teaching, so that when Rebeca returns to England she will be able to play. The late afternoon it was a matter of deciding on the dress code for that night. First, they are going to eat out with Alison and her mother, Rebeca had never met her yet, she was looking forward to it, she had heard that she was a kind and caring person, who as it happens did not like the limelight, she avoided appearing with her husband if she could, but having heard the President praise Rebeca so often she really wanted to meet up with her.

After the meal they were all booked in a box at the theatre. The show was great, the conversation before and after was all about things that Rebeca loved to talk about, at the meal table she told them about her mother dressing up as a clown, and then fooling the whole school. Rose was beginning to have her book in her mind, she thought at the time that Rebeca must take after her mother. Alison's mother was so pleased to have met Rebeca, now she will have something to discuss with the President, she is planning to ask her if she could come and give a talk to one of her women's clubs, she seems to be more than intelligent, she is also happy to do comedy, it just seems to flow from her. Sunday was going to be a quiet day at home. Rebeca was pleased about that, she needed some time on her own, to review the last four months in America. It had definitely been an eye-opening time, she has learnt a lot, she was amazed on how nice all the people she had met were towards her, then she remembered Helene's father, that made her laugh, she wished that she had got to know the secret service men, but then they would not even be allowed to talk about their thoughts, yes, she did like the Captain with the problems. He was a decent sort of person who would be a good father, that is if he got himself a job that did not keep him away from home! Then she started thinking that perhaps she should not have offered to look after Rose, she might just become a handful! She then worried a bit about having lied to the President, it was not like her to do that, but then! Yes, but then young lady, those thoughts were like a merry go round in her head, they kept coming back, how is she going to manage to bury that episode? First, has she hurt anybody. 'No' Would she ever do it again. 'Yes' Well: she willingly joined into the deception, and that is one of the prices she must pay, 'Remember Norman' That is all the time she is allotting to that subject, what's next? It was meeting the first lady yesterday, what a nice person she is, she really cares for people, yes, it will be a pleasure to be talking to some of her friends, when he is no longer in the White House, the President will miss the loss of power, but it will not change his wife at all, she will still be the same person, and she will be there for him, that's nice she thought.

Her thinking stopped abruptly when the screeching of tyres in the drive shook up the household, it could not have been anyone else but the son of the house Jim. At the same time her computer alerted her that a new email had just arrived, it was from Debra who wanted Rebeca to know two things, the first one is that she is the very first person to know that she has just found out less than an hour ago that she is with child! The second bit of news surprised Rebeca, she has accepted a nomination to run at the next election, she might just become a Member of Parliament! With the same party as the Prime

Minister. She answered that email by return, telling her how please she was for her, and hoping it all goes all right, on the political side, of course she was pleased for Debra, if she gets in, she will introduce her to the PM her friend. They say that sometimes news keeps on coming, well that is what happened, within a half hour another email arrived on her computer. It was from Robert, he was thinking of selling his boat, but, if she wanted it he would be only too pleased to give it to her, that was a shock for her, then she had an idea, if she was to accept his gift, what she would do when she is back in England, is to make the trip back to Oxford in the boat and surprise him, then he can have it back and enjoy it on the river for many more years, and that is what was going to happen, possibly in the middle of the winter when he would be the most surprised. She wondered if she was going to get an escort again, supplied by the Royal Navy.

With both the replies she was pleased to mention that she would soon be back, and she was looking forward to it! As it happens the next General Election is soon enough' she is going to need some help looking for a house for herself, she does not want to live in London, and if possible, the dream of being within site of the sea should come true, hopefully. When she went to bed that night, she fell into a deep sleep, and then it happened again; in the early hours of the morning she woke up screaming, again it was Norman, she was conscious of perhaps having woken the whole house, and she felt bad about that, at breakfast nobody mentioned hearing anything, she wondered how many more times is she going to have a nightmare, and it worried her, she did not think that she had been under any pressure lately.

The museum where Helene works has almost fifty employees, Monday morning when she arrived for work, they all had arrived a half hour early, then they formed themselves in two lines for Helene to walk through, was she ever surprised, especially when they all sung "She's a jolly good fellow", she did blush, they all wanted to thank her for what she had done with the President, they had all seen the picture which she is about to unravel. Her boss much to Helene's surprise, was in tears when she saw the huge glossy picture. For a moment Helene had a fleeting thought of going back out for another day, but that would not have been her. The museum has the means of making perfect picture frames, the problem was that they could not make up their minds which type of frame would be best. By the afternoon the framing problem was solved, it was wood finished in Japan black, the second problem is where to place it? Some thought that somewhere near the entrance so that it is seen by everybody who walks into the museum, that was going to be too brash, so they decided a place, soon after one has left the entrance. That was not enough for the decision makers: what are they going to write at the bottom of the picture? At one time they even asked Helene what she would like to see, just before going home time, the picture was framed and hung, the writing will come later. Helene that day was asked over and over again what had happened that she was in the White House, she explained that she had been invited by the Vice President, to finish the cruise with them and this famous but very smart lady who has been in the news a lot lately, she is English they call her Rebeca, as it happened the President himself wanted a fresh look at some of the paintings in the White House, 'by the way I am getting an official invite there soon to a garden party,' she was not going to tell them about Jim, that's private!

That whole day Rebeca spent in the house, sometimes on her computer, other times chatting with Rose and with Laurie, Rose wanted to know more about England, she was now beginning to think about being away, is she going to like England? Is she going to be homesick? What was happening in her life, she was waking up. Her mother had noticed it. Rebeca also had realised that she had changed, now she has become inquisitive about anything, maybe it had been the episode about her brother who could have died, Rebeca had something to do with her change. At work people were asking Jim about his relationship with Rebeca, they had noticed that he had changed his aspect in life, one of the girls even suggested that he was in love! Well, that was a correct assumption, that morning he had a telephone conversation where not much was being said, he was aware that a couple of people could hear him, just before putting the telephone handset down, his last words were heard 'me to'. In the afternoon Laurie had finished organising everything for the lecture which is going to be in two weeks' time. Rebeca received a telephone call from the Presidents' secretary, to tell her to be at the White House Wednesday morning before nine to attend his cabinet meeting which had been put back, she will be picked up in good time. Laurie was surprised, he had never done anything like that before, she was pleased for Rebeca, and she was hoping that it turns out right for all. Then Rose sat with Rebeca for the rest of the afternoon, they talked about England; Rebeca explained the role of the Queen in the government, she told her how a Prime Minister is chosen, how the education system works, how the national health service also operates, and because it was on her mind, she told Rose how complicated buying a house was. Regarding houses, which is the first thing they are going to do when they both arrive in England, she must buy herself a new house, she does not want to live in London. Of that she is certain.

Wednesday morning arrived, Rebeca was ready when the chauffer arrived, Rose came with her, she was going to spend some time with Alison, the President's daughter, they were both happy to spend time in the White House, there is always something going on, it is an exciting place to be in. There was a man at the entrance who accompanied her straight to the cabinet office next to the oval office. She went in not knowing what to expect, his secretary was already there sitting at a big desk in the corner of the room, that was nice for Rebeca because they already knew each other. Now they were sitting together at the same desk, the first thing the secretary did was to explain what looked like a large calculator, it was her way of communicating with the President, if she realised that he needed some more information, about the subject he was talking about, she would use her computer on her desk and usually manage to find the information he needed, she would type into the special unit, he would then read it and now be in a good place, others in the room would not have noticed what had just happened. At least twenty people arrived and sat at their designated place around the huge table, on another corner the press would sometimes attend, and they would operate from that corner, today there was nobody in attendance from the press, then the President walked in with the Vice President by his side, he explained that he had invited a friend of his, at the time pointing towards Rebeca, to see how the American democracy operates at the White House. Today there was a problem with one of the Arab States, it was only a small country which had been ruled by the same family for the last one hundred years at least. The man in charge was the eldest Prince, the King had not long passed away, the problem was that this Prince wanted to make war even with his neighbours, the situation was upsetting at least four countries in that area. He was making very anti-American speeches, and back in the USA they could not decide how to deal with the problem. The Secretary of Defence with the backing of most of the Generals in the Pentagon wanted to go and invade the country, however thinking people were all against that plan, the discussion went on for over an hour. Alright they could occupy the country, for how long? At what cost? Not just a monetary problem but then some other states in the area might just take a dim view and give America a problem they had never anticipated.

That is when Rebeca had already heard too much on the subject, she whispered to the secretary to send him a message that says that I have the answer! Within seconds the President interrupted the meeting by telling all assembled there that Rebeca was going to speak, so could they please keep quite whilst she got up to the big table and said what was on her mind. Although there were five women there she addressed the assembly by just saying 'gentlemen; you all have just spent over an hour attempting to resolve a problem which you definitely have no answer for,' to be fair nearly all were pleased to listen to her, only the Secretary of defence with two others who were absolutely certain that they wanted to invade the country made it known that they did not care to listen to a girl telling them anything. The President was not happy with them, he did want to listen to Rebeca's idea, it was going to make a change for the moment at least. Then she went on telling them; that the thing to do was to fly in what looked like a full battle-ready army on their border, that will give the prince a shock, and he will realise his stupid mistake and join humanity. 'The King of the neighbouring country will never allow us to place an army on his land, you must be dreaming young lady, thank you for your input, but I think we will give it a pass today,' that was the defence secretary speaking thinking that it was a good put down.

Of course he did not know Rebeca, she stood her ground not by responding to the Defence man, no, she turned to one side, asked the secretary sat in the corner to find out what time it was in that area it took three minutes to find out that they were twelve hours ahead, so she asked the secretary to dial a long number, which was a direct private line to the King, she did not even need to look up the number it was already in her mind. Some sat around that huge table, did not know what to think, was she making it all up, they will soon find out because the telephone was on speaker. The telephone was now ringing, it took a long time to be answered, eventually the ringing stopped and a man's voice speaking in Arabic was heard, right of way they all heard Rebeca also speaking in Arabic, although they could not understand what was being said, they could tell by the intonation that the man at the other end was ever so pleased to hear from Rebeca, she told him where she was at the moment, she also told him what they were trying not to plan, then she asked him if they could send a small army disguised as a bigger one on your land to give that Prince a bit of shock, he answered by telling her that they will have to come by air and we will incamp them within the perimeter of our military air base which is right close to the border, then knowing that she was speaking to him using a speaker telephone he broke into English, 'Rebeca my dear I am so glad you called, I have never forgotten our meetings and I guess you have never forgotten my telephone number, please can you give your President my well wishes, this operation should be done as soon as possible, say in three days' time', he then gave Rebeca the telephone number for their secretary of defence to call as soon as possible, this number is the direct line which he uses and is direct to the commander of the forces, he will already know that he had approved the plan. They both signed off in Arabic.

Rebeca was a little upset, it was never her intention to show the secretary of defence in a bad place, perhaps he could not be that bad, it is just the idea of a young girl having better knowledge than he had, she need not have been too bothered about it, because there he was thinking that it was all a prank, the first part in Arabic could have been to tell the other person what she wanted him to say, The President on the other hand knew that it was all legitimate, he ordered the man to get on with it, he called the top man at the Pentagon and gave him the number to call, within a half hour the planning on both sides had started. One of the women sat at the table asked Rebeca how it was that she knew the King of that country; ' maybe you might remember that I gave a speech at the United Nation, I was there for almost a whole week and one day by accident I collided with the King, of course I apologised in Arabic, he was so surprise that I could speak his language, that was that, but after I had given my speech on behalf of my country, I received a hand delivered message from him, inviting me for a coffee which I accepted, we talked for three hours over one cup of coffee, he was so interesting, we got on so well, he invited me to visit him at home, he also gave me his personal telephone number for me to use if ever I needed his help, today was the right day to call him, he is ever so nice. I ask of one thing from you all, as tempting as it is going to be to repeat this story, please can you refrain now from telling anybody else! I must think of my security, and if it all turns out all right then that will be a different scenario.'

Everything went to plan, what looked like an invasion force gave the prince a bit of a scare, it stopped him in his track, he discovered that running a country is a most serious business, plus his friends in the government all had a go at him at the same time advising him to change as otherwise he was not going to last long in the job. It took him no more than two days to take the advice he was given, he personally contacted the King, they had a long talk which led to a meeting, and he discovered that it was much easier to have a friend as a neighbour. When he discovered that it was a young woman who had sorted what had just happen, he wanted to meet with Rebeca to thank her.

Eventually the troops came back, what had just happened made Rebeca's effort to being talked about in the media, the President was ever so pleased, then it was all back to normal. Rebeca and Rose were beginning to get ready for the return to England. Rebeca had only two more talks to give, one to a group of influential women and the other talk was in a university, it was not exactly a talk, it was a discussion with a well know aggressive Evangelist man. The women all enjoyed listening to Rebeca telling some of her latest stories, including the latest one, all went home feeling that bit better having listened to Rebeca for over an hour. The next day, Rose discovered that Rebeca had her own Old Testament: the two spent two full days in Rebeca's room counting how many times God had asked someone to eradicate complete cities including all inhabitants, then how often God had asked a man to murder a family, even including torture before the death to make them suffer, that was not enough sometimes he even asked for their bodies to be mutilated after death. So, in those times, the murderers always used the excuse that the crime they had committed had been ordered by God, King David was one of the worst followed by Goliath and many others, it was a violent time for our civilisation. That is how Rebeca is getting ready for the next big discussion, Rose was completely taken aback from what she had just learnt, but for the moment kept it to herself, the evening at the University was coming soon, it was already reported, as the man himself did his best to publicise it, he dropped a few hints from time to time that he was going to give Rebeca a headache, that made her more determined to be absolutely ready for him, she is going to have a real go at him. Well, the evening was there, and the hall was packed, the media were there giving a live broadcast which was unusual, yes, he had arranged it. The first time the two had met was on the very stage, they did shake hands both with a smile, she had a good idea what he wanted to talk about, there had been some rumours that it had been confirmed that she was an atheist, the problem he had is that he had no idea what she was going to say. The University was backed and promoted by a religion, so they organised for him to speak first. They were both introduced by the Dean of the University who gave the floor to the man. He did not waste any time, 'Rebeca, I have one question for you; do you believe in God?' One might call that a direct attack, he did not beat about the bush, she was not surprised, oh no, she was well ready, looking at him she thought that he fancied himself, he thought that he was good! She had come on the stage holding what looked like a large handbag from which she removed two books, she had to get up and walk a couple of steps, she then handed both the books to him, one was the Old Testament and other the King James bible. One thing for certain he had not expected that at all.

Then she started by asking him to be ready to read the Old Testament: 'You have asked me an interesting question, before I give my answer, I want to show you about my knowledge of the bible, which you are holding in your hands, please, turn to any page you want and tell me the page number you have chosen, this is from the Old Testament. He was not happy about taking orders from Rebeca, but he had no choice. 'How about page 312.' She then asked him to select a word and tell her which line it was on and which number it was in that line, he did that, within a micro second she told him that first it was a page on the right and the word he had chosen was "donkey", he nearly dropped the book, that really shook him up, then he started remembering that he also had the King James bible, now he was a little unnerved. 'Well I just wanted to show you that my knowledge of the Bible is much greater than yours, If we had the time, I could recite all of it just from memory, you can if you wish give me a sentence and I will tell you its whereabouts, I believe that I am regarded as one of the most knowledgeable person in the world on the subject of the Bible, and the Koran. She stopped for a short while to let him digest the position he has got himself into. He did not reply, there was complete silence in the hall, as they say, one could hear a pin drop, for the man himself, he was beginning to think that it was a mistake.

Because of his silence it was now her turn to ask questions: 'would you admit that the new bible is based on the Old Testament?' He now had an idea of where she was going but he had no choice but to agree with her. What happened next shook him and the audience for sure: 'I guess hardly anybody in this audience has studied the Old Testament, I could if required speak every word in the book but we would all be here all night, so instead of giving you example after example I will instead give you the result of my research which I did over two working days last month, I found that God had ordered the death of over a million people, whoever it was in the story killed a single person, a family, a town, an army it was always as a result of a command by God, one of the biggest killers was King David, another you all now was Goliath, there were many, sometimes God ordered that the victim or victims must be tortured to death, and some other times they were to mutilate their bodies after death. Well now, that particular God if one was to believe the Old Testament, was not a kind protecting and loving God who looks after his flock, on the other hand thinking people will tell you that all those commands from God were not true, the killers cheated and they did not hear anything from God, well, if that was the case then the Old Testament has repeated those lies, and it is no longer a valid record of our early history.' She paused for two very long minutes before continuing, again it was complete silence from the audience, the man on the stage with her now definitely regretted the moment, now he is going to be asked many questions to which he has no real answer. 'Now sir, you have asked me whether I believe in God, I think the question is impertinent, it is my personal business about my beliefs which I do not need to advertise, it could be that the answer is yes, or perhaps the answer is no, I will however tell you my thinking on the subject, I think that all religions are manmade, if one wants to believe in a supreme being, one should be free to do so without always trying to convince others to do the same, I think that there are more than four thousand religions doing the rounds, people are killed about how they believe in a God. Some leaders of some religions might be good men, but they have no problem interpreting the past to reinforce their thinking, religion should always be about doing good, the story telling should be abandoned, that is my belief!' On that note she stopped and sat down.

Oh, what a reaction she did get, every member of that audience clapped and cheered, all without exception standing. The man who had dared ask her that direct question, said not a single word, the Dean had to get involved and asked Rebeca if she could give the audience the actual details on how she managed to bring peace in the Arab world. Obviously it was the end of the religion discussion, Rebeca then went on giving the identical talk she had given the other day to the women's group, that also got a standing ovation, it was all shown live, most of the reports in the media the next morning were all about her own beliefs and about her being an Atheist, others said she was more religious than the average person, none of the Church people came out with a comment about her, one thing that was well reported and recorded was the religious leader who was on the stage with her, he never clapped, that got him a lot of negative press. The next day she was absolutely exhausted, she did not appear downstairs until about eleven, they were all waiting for her to congratulate her, that surprised her, and she was pleased, she was also pleased about her effort last night, Rose had now told her mother what they had been doing a couple of days before, she also told her that she was on the verge of becoming an atheist, no, she really had no idea about Rebeca.

Only three weeks left in America for Rebeca, arrangements had already been made for the trip back, her and Rose are going to be picked up by the Airforce, taken to Andrews Field, then unto a luxury 747 that the Airforce use to move high ranking officers around the world, they will be flown to an American base in England, and driven to her apartment, and again she will not have to show her passport! On the Thursday of the last week Rebeca received a telephone call from the Defence Secretary, to witness a special meeting of all the force's leaders, there were at least forty of them. The other thing about that meeting was it is taking place on Saturday, Ronald had no idea what it was all about, but then he did not bother to find out as he was much too busy, she did not ask Rose to go with her, instead she asked her mother Laurie, the main reason was she wanted to have a chat with just her, mostly about Rose. One thing she wanted to do is to reassure her that she will take great care of her daughter whilst she is with her in England, she will never leave her alone. Rose wondered why she was not going with her, but soon forgot about it. It is always the same, a car with a chauffeur arrives at the entrance, they drive in almost complete silence to the venue, and all the time you worry about the driver outside who is waiting for you, it might all sound glamorous, but once you are used to it, he is always on your mind.

Laurie was the first one to realise that the driver was there waiting for the both of them, she called out to Rebeca, who rushed down the stairs, then they were both gone. Rose called Alison and arranged the rest of the day with her, that might just be the last time she sees her until she comes back from England. It is not a five-minute drive to the Pentagon, not anymore now it is almost a half hour, there is so much traffic, so the two had a chance of having a private conversation, which they both were pleased with. The Defence Secretary himself, greeted them bearing no grudge with

Rebeca, she had taught him a little lesson and now that he had witnessed the result of her thinking, he had become an admirer. They were led to a large office which had two doors one opposite the other, they were both offered a place where to securely leave coats and handbags, they left the coats only. The other door opened; it was just like in the movies. A gigantic room, with two walls covered in television screens, all active, a single table half the size of the room, over forty high ranking officers all in their Sunday best uniforms all decorated with what must have been at least a total of eight hundred medals, as soon as she stepped into the room, they all stood up started singing: 'she's a jolly good fellow' then there was one hell of a fanfare, there must have been at least twenty soldiers blowing as hard as they could into their trumpets, at the other end of this gigantic room there was a dozen drummers beating their drums. After it all quietened down the top Admiral of the navy gave a speech, he congratulated Rebeca for having avoided a war and made enemies become friends, which now has made all of them happy in the region.

Then a drum roll started, there was now expectation amongst the assembly, a small door a long way from where the honoured guest was standing, a fresh recruit in the Navy started to walk towards Rebeca with his two lower arms he was holding a decorated small casquet, it was about the size of a modern office printer, made of a dark wood, almost black. The sailor was walking in step with the drums, He then arrived in front of Rebeca. She had not realised but right in front of her was a small table, the sailor deposited the box and opened the lid most carefully; he only said a few words 'miss this is a gift from a king for you' he then backed away, the Defence Secretary whispered for her to investigate the box. It was full of documents, again he whispered 'Rebeca it's your friend the King who has given you a beautiful house, her legs started to tremble, she managed to fight the tears, she wanted to run and have a good cry, but she managed to appear happy and appreciative, she could not wait until she was in the car, she was offered to make a tour but she excused herself for now, Rebeca thanked everyone there, she told them that soon she is going to visit the King to thank him personally, they both made their way back, in the car it seemed for no reason she burst into tears, Laurie tried to comfort her, it was as if she enjoyed having a good cry, by the time they arrived back, she had recovered. The next day she was all over the news again, it was a good job, she had managed to keep the tears away! Of course, both the President and the Vice President knew about it, the King had asked the President for advice, he was told that she is going to buy a house as soon as she gets back, possibly a house close to the Thames River. They did not tell her, they wanted her to be surprised, and it was!

Now, only a week and a half left in America for Rebeca, it was easy for her to pack, she left it to just a couple of days before leaving, her computer will be packed by professionals, but she has a simple easy way of packing, she just throws everything into a large suitcase for her cloths and then sits on the lid to compress it well, she will have to spend a day ironing, that is alright for her, she finds it somewhat relaxing. Every day now was visiting friends to say goodbye, she did go to the White House where she had a talk with the President, he did ask her to make sure that the USA was always well presented in England, almost to act as an Ambassador, he also wanted her to visit the embassy at least once a month, and have a discussion with the Ambassador, she will now be invited to all the functions there. She found that to be most interesting. She spent two long days at the studio, there were a lot to sort out before she left, then it was the last meal, and after tea the limousine came for them both, there was a lot of excitement in the house that day; Laurie was going to miss her daughter, at the same time she was so pleased about her being looked after by Rebeca, Rose should be coming back a more mature person, complete with ambition and more knowledge about life, Jim was realising that he was going to miss his sister, Ronald was just pleased, but now the house is going to be on the quiet side, especially with Jim spending all possible time he could with Helene. It is now just before five, and they are going to arrive in

London in the middle of the night, not too good for those who will be waiting for her, but as they say: 'that's the way it is!' They both looked back, they saw almost nothing, only the car with the two secret service men which was blocking the view, Rose was a little upset, so she grabbed Rebeca's hand, she did not let go until they arrived at the base, it was the very first time, she had left home for such a long time. But now with the smell of jet fuel and the view of the jet fighters, she was beginning to forget about her worries. Their luggage had been picked up earlier, the car drove them straight to the aircraft, which they boarded, they felt strange, the two so far seemed to be the only passengers, there was nobody around to ask if anybody else were going to board the plane, so they started to walk around and explore, it was exciting for the both of them, they opened one door and it was an office complete with two computers on two desks, which each had two telephones, then they found a bathroom with a shower, after that they visited four cabins with one large bed a toilet and sink in each one.

Towards the front of the plane they found a door which Rebeca opened, Rose had become a bit nervous about that door, quite rightly because there was a man working on some instrument, it was the cockpit where the two pilots will be flying the aircraft, they both excused themselves, the man was not at all worried but surprised, he was quick telling them what he was doing and they stayed there a while having a chat with the friendly engineer, that helped to pass some time whilst they were waiting, the man eventually packed his tools and walk past them in the lounge, saying 'have a good flight girls!'. Now things were happening, two big fuel trucks turned up, one under each wing, then the pilot arrived, he left the door to the cockpit open, sat in his seat and started looking at a bunch of forms and mess about with some switches, they were both mesmerised, Rebeca was reminded of her own survival flight with Jim. They were wondering if anybody else was going to England with them, the answer was no, but they did not know is that they will be stopping in Germany to pick up the Ambassador with an entourage to go back to

England. That was interesting Rebeca thought, it is the very man she is supposed to meet at the London Embassy, well, that is going to save her a trip, that's good. A young man in uniform walked in, he was in charge of looking after the two friends, he will cook at least two meals, snacks and of course supply whatever drink they wish for, during the trip. He is the one who told them about the German detour, the co-pilot arrived, he also left the door open, that was nice for the girls, both the pilots had been briefed about their two passengers. There were some metal-to-metal sounds which was the doors being closed from outside, then the first engine started, two minutes later it was the turn of the second engine, another five minutes and all four were roaring away. Now they both had their heads glued to a window, they started to move forward, picking up some speed, another minute and they stopped, the engines revved up then down and it started rolling again, there was a sharp turn and the speed increased, one could feel the back of the seat pushing them forward, then it was a lovely silence: they were now airborne. The young man approached them to find out if they needed a drink, the answer was not, then he asked them again, this time for their preference for a meal, he gave them a good choice, they asked for the Salmon with a glass of white wine as dry as they have on board.

After an hour their food arrived, it all looked good and it was also very nice food, after they had a coffee, then after that the young man came and told them that the pilot would be happy for them to visit the cockpit, Rose was not sure, but Rebeca just loved the idea, so she went on her own, as she walked through the doorway the pilot on the left side who was the main pilot greeted her, he said that she could sit on the jump seat and strap herself in. He knew very well who she was, and they started to have a long conversation, he might be an Airforce pilot, but he was also a bit of a politician, he was well aware of her exploits, especially the talk with the religious man, he thought that she had done a great job sorting him out, 'did you know what the subject was going to be?' It did not take long for her to tell him that the University could not tell her in advance, because they kept changing their minds from day to day, which had made her suspicious, so she planned for the worse and she caught them out. He was pleased for her, then he reminded her about her first landing, was it also the last? 'Rebeca, do you think you could land this aircraft?' After a bit of thought and having looked at all the controls, she answered with a big "Yes" that is as long as somebody tells her what to do over the radio. He was a little surprised, the Co-pilot had heard it all and started to worry, he knew him too well, he looked at him and said 'I know you John, and the answer is absolutely "NO" at that moment Rebeca decided to leave the cockpit, she had guessed what John was thinking, in a way it was tempting, but she did not want the responsibility. It's one thing when you do not have a choice, there is much too much at stake here, then he could get himself in all kinds of trouble with the authorities.

When she got back to Rose, she was fast asleep, then Rebeca removed her laptop from a bag and started writing in it, she did not stop for over an hour, she put it back in the bag, Rose was still sleeping, so Rebeca made herself comfortable in the jump seat behind the two pilots, they talked for the next three hours, about politics, religion, she told them that her father was a fighter pilot in the RAF, she told them about Rose who happens to be the Vice President's daughter, also how she was on the rescue boat when theirs had sunk. She could have been with them for the whole flight, but then she did not want to worry Rose, in any case supper was now being served. Rose was not eating too much, but Rebeca was famished, she was only halfway through her meal, when the co-pilot came towards them, he could hardly stand and his face was as white as a sheet, something was happening to him, the two girls took him to one of the bedrooms and he collapsed on the bed, he was trying to talk but could not make any sense. Rebeca called their attendant, he had had a first aid course, all he could think off was that he had just had a heart attack, he had a look on a computer and decided that is exactly what had happened to him, he now knew what to do, Rose stayed with him, Rebeca went straight to the cockpit she explained to the pilot what had just happened, he could not leave his seat, so he asked Rebeca to sit in the now vacant seat, they were almost four hours before reaching Frankfurt in Germany. He asked Rebeca to look at all the dials and switches, if any of them change, she is to press a switch on the yoke and just say there is a problem, he will come straight back. There she was for the second time in her life, left in charge on her own. She soon stopped thinking that way, she spent all the time whilst she was on her own, learning what every switch and display were all about, the pilot soon came back, the first thing he did was to send a message about the position he was in. The first reply he received was within a couple of minutes, it was an acknowledgement of them having received his message, things had begun to roll, his closest airport was in Ireland, they will get there almost a whole hour sooner than Frankfurt, so now they have to change direction, first he will plot a new course to Shannon airport on the west coast of Ireland, then he will have to reprogram the navigation computer.

All this time Rebeca will oversee looking for possible problems, the co-pilot was not getting any worse, the pilot told Rebeca that within the next half hour they will be able to talk to Shannon, they spent that time with him teaching her how to land the aircraft at night, as serious as the situation was, Rebeca could not help herself enjoying the trip. She did not want anybody else knowing what she was up to now, she had had enough publicity in her life, people seem to always go overboard with her so-called achievements, she is just happy doing her two ten-minute talks every Sunday. Rose now was on her own looking after the co-pilot, she just wished that she had known more so to be a real help to him, she kept thinking how good it could have been if she had been a nurse or even a doctor, she also thought that Rebeca must be enjoying herself up in the cockpit, all those dials and switches by now feeling at least a little in control, it will be good comparing notes after they had landed.

One more hour had past, the slow descent had started, the pilot showed Rebeca how to slow the four engines at the same time, then asked her to do it, her hand was only big enough to hold the levers, she pulled them back about an inch, she did get a surprise when she heard the sound of the engines change, all that power was under her control for a moment, oh if she had pulled them all the way back the plane would just drop out of the sky, that was an amazing feeling for her, Shannon was waiting for them with an ambulance ready to take the patient to the hospital, they will touchdown in less than a quarter of an hour, The pilot now was concentrating on his flying, he pointed out to Rebeca the white lights on the left of the runway, they look to be twenty feet apart, one on top of another, if the aircraft is too high the two lights will stay white, if the aircraft is too low, both lights will be red light, the whole idea is to have the lower light red and the upper light white, if you can see two white lights you are too high, if you see two red lights, you are two low, it's that simple. A couple of moments later, and they were on the ground, Rebeca thanked the pilot, he told her that they now cannot leave until a replacement co-pilot had arrived, so they might just as well have a good sleep on board, unless of course the Irish authorities will not allow that, in which case they will be driven to a hotel for the night.

Strange, Rose was asking if she could accompany the co-pilot to the hospital, that surprised everybody on board, it was looking as if they were not going to depart until at the earliest at about eleven in the morning, The American Ambassador in Ireland had been flown in from Dublin because of Rose being the daughter of the Vice President to help with the authorities at Shannon, he also had been made well aware of Rebeca. They could not stay on board for the night, there were four crew and two passengers, it was agreed that Rose could stay with the patient in the hospital, and a car will be waiting there to take her to the hotel whenever she is ready to go. Rebeca thought of going with her, but on reflection she thought that it was Rose's turn to shine, in any case she was tired. It was not until she sat on the edge of the bed in the hotel, when exclaimed out loud:

'I've done it again, there is not a single entry on my passport.' The telephone by the side of the bed was ringing, it was a kind lady asking her if she wanted any food or drink, 'oh yes please, just a pot of tea thank you'. That call reminded her that she should call her mother to tell her what has happened so far and that she should arrive in London late tomorrow afternoon, she will call her before they leave Germany, that is as long as there are no more changes, her mother of course was ever so pleased to hear from her, and hoped also that they were no more problems for her daughter. The medics were all nice people, they told Rose that they had been right with the diagnosis, the patient did have a stroke, she did well keeping him from falling asleep, he was now wide awake, they suggested that she spend a bit of time with him, but in about an hour when they have finished all the test, they are going to put him asleep, so she can stay until that time. When she walked into his room, he recognised her right away, he tried his best to smile at her, it was a smile she will never forget for the rest of her life, later in her life she will often tell people that it was the smile that changed everything for her, she was so happy about that.

Now she had real ambition, no more window-shopping trips, no more night clubs, no more lazy days, she is going to ask Rebeca for all the help she can give her. The morning was strange, first it was raining, on top of that the two girls were both tired, they did not seem to have the energy to do anything, one thing however they were both hungry, to make it to the dining room, they both had to take control to overcome Jet lag, when they arrived where the food was, they discovered the crew had already finishing their breakfast. They in turn were pleased to see the girls arrive, they all had a good chat, Rose told them that the last time she saw the co-pilot he was doing his best to smile at her, she also told them that the doctor told her that he will recover in time. There is going to be a small problem, because the Airforce will want to be taking care of him as soon as he can be moved. The pilot had heard that the new co-pilot will not be with them before lunch time, 'which one of you can play the piano?' there was one in the corner of the room and he thought that it would be a good way of passing the time, one thing they cannot do for certain is have a drink. The two ordered egg and bacon toast and coffee, the marmalade was already on the table. No one played the piano and Rose was too tired, but there were some playing cards in the lounge. After having eaten their breakfast the girls joined the crew, first they played cards, yes the cards reminded Rebeca about herself, she did not tell them that she had a photographic memory, she had everybody try their best to remember many cards that had just been face down on the card table, the best one was the pilot he correctly identified twenty one cards, Rose of course knew what she was up to, but for the fun of it she said nothing. Rebeca now told them that she was certain to better the pilot, she got him to shuffle the cards and place them all face down as she was looking at them, she got up to twenty six cards, the pilot now wanted to have another go, they now were all watching hoping he does not win over Rebeca, he took a long time studying each card and he only reached twenty five, Rebeca said that really it is not fair because he uses his memory, and for her it is just a trick, she obtained a second pack, gave it to the pilot to shuffle with the first pack, now he held one hundred and four cards, she asked him to place them all face down giving her enough time to see the face of each card, there were some other guests in the lounge who now wanted to see what was going to happen, after all the cards were down, she asked for total silence, then without stopping even once, she named each card just before turning it over, when she passed fifty two cards, people started to look at each other, then when she was in the seventies, it was complete silence, and she eventually had turned all of the cards without a single mistake, one of the guests an older gentleman asked her how on earth did she do that, she told him that she will tell him if he gets her a coffee, he ordered it right of way, the coffee arrived and she just told him that he has now met a person who happens to have a photographic memory that's all, she was born with it, at the age of fourteen she had already learned five languages, she once read the old testament and if there was one here she could recite the whole bible or tell anyone, say, what is the fourth word on page 201 on the 15th line down. 'Sir, have you a pen and paper at hand' she waited for his answer, then he pulled out his pen and picked up a brochure which had no print on the back. 'Now ask me at least four questions about pages lines and number, write down your details and my word for each one,' he asked, she told, he wrote the answers, 'unless you can find a bible here check it out when you get home, you will be surprised!' Rose butted in telling all that Rebeca is absolutely correct, nobody there could get over it, the pilot's telephone started ringing, the message is that the new co-pilot will arrive within the next half hour, so now there was no time to lose, and who cares about the rain, they all moved fast and they were out of the door within twenty minutes, in two taxis they arrived at the airport, again no immigration or customs for them, the taxis drove them straight to the aircraft, for a moment it felt like home. The new co-pilot was already on board, he had started to verify the controls.

They were off for an almost two-hour trip to Germany, Rebeca did not disappear in the cockpit this time, Rose wanted to have a serious talk with her, she had something on her mind, she still had the picture of that man, whose face had been disfigured by having had a stroke, doing his very best to smile at her, that smile had come from her heart, she could feel it. She told Rebeca about it, she also told her that now she knows what it is she wants to do for the rest of her life, I don't know exactly what, but it is in medicine, I want to help people! Rebeca was pleased to hear that. At that moment they were over England, they could see nothing for the grey clouds below them, soon they will be landing in Germany to pick up the Ambassador, again they were landing in an American base, so no passports to get ready. They did not get out of the aircraft, six people joined them, it was obvious which person was the Ambassador, he came and sat next to the girls, of course, he was well aware who they both were, after all he had lunch with Rebeca six months ago, he addressed them both, saying that them being there was going to make the trip a bit more pleasant, first he asked Rose about her father, is he a happy man? Is he home often enough? There were a few more similar types of questions, then he turned to Rebeca, first thing he said was, 'Rebeca, it appears that we are to meet a few times, I am looking forward to it, would it be a good idea to always make it at lunch time like last time?' She had no problem whatsoever about that and answered in the affirmative. Then he asked her how did she manage to call that King and talk him into having an invasion force from America on his soil, 'it was not difficult first because he happens to be an intelligent person, and then him and I had a three-hour meeting at the United Nations and we got on well, did you know that he has given me a gift? His answer to that question was no, 'well, it's a most beautiful huge house with five acres of land on the bank of the Thames at Henley, I can't wait to go and look at it, I already have a motor yacht, now with my own dock, isn't it great!' of course he was pleased for her, after all she must have saved many lives with her action, then he wondered if the President had done something similar for her, it was a good thing he did not ask her as at that moment the answer would have been "nothing", yes, she had called her mother just before they got airborne, so they should be home in her apartment in about two hours' time, just another half hour and they were landing at the base, as soon as they had stopped, Rebeca visited the pilot, she asked him the details for the co-pilot they left in Ireland, it was for Rose so that she can find out how he is recovering, he was not really authorised to give her the info, but he did anyway, now Rose can keep in touch with his wife, Rose will be pleased for sure.

Now it was time to disembark, first the hand luggage, then they waited for the cargo hold to be opened, the cars arrived, there were six of them, the two pilots walked by, one of them stopped, walked over to Rebeca, he thanked her for her help flying the plane, then gave her a quick hug and then goodbye. The Ambassador was within earshot, he turned towards Rebeca and asked her a question: 'What did he mean Rebeca?' Well, when Rose was looking after the co-pilot,' I was sitting in his place to learn as much as I could about flying and landing that aircraft, the pilot and I both thought that it would be a good idea just in case, plus of course it was most interesting, time disappeared for me during the training' He did not know what to think, the only though he came up with a little later, this girl will stop at nothing! There was a driver of course, and a security man sitting in the front of the limousine, the two girls and a mountain of luggage were all in the back, making their way to north London, they arrived at three in the afternoon. Rebeca was very pleased to be back home, she could see her old car, it was exactly where she left it, she knew all the tenants in the block and she was wondering which one had that wonderful car next to hers, it was a pure white Rover SUV, it must be bran new, the two men in the car brought up all the luggage, they were saying goodbye at the same time Rebeca was turning the key in the lock, what a surprise there were people in the apartment, her mother, Robert and his wife, her uncle and his wife and her father with his girlfriend.

There were tears and big hugs, Rebeca introduced Rose, then there was a knock at the door, it was Debra, more hugs, her mother made a huge pot of tea, half of the people there had no choice they had to stand. Robert made a comment about the Rover car parked below, 'Rebeca, I must tell you that The President of the United States has given you a gift, it is that very car parked next to your old one.' He then gave her the keys, her hand trembled as she gripped them, she really was speechless. Debra started to speak to Rose who of course did not remember her, but they both had something in common, Rebeca's mother Sarah had already seen her new house, from the outside, they did drive to the other side of the river to get a better look at it, apparently, it's almost a mansion with two other buildings, 'well mum I have the keys to it and the sooner we take a look the better for all, how abouts if we all go tomorrow? I don't think that I should be driving the Rover just yet, I bet it's an automatic, Uncle Robert can you teach me?' Of course, he was extremely willing, and the plan was for all assembled here today to go and visit the new house tomorrow afternoon, Debra lives not too far from it, and she will meet them there.

What a building! when they arrived outside, all they could see was a ten-foot wall, beautifully made with red bricks and concrete, it had a design to it and looked to be strong. The gate they were all standing by was made of solid steel painted black, there was an intercom outside, which included a digital keypad and a place for a wireless fob. Robert had worked out that the fob was for the residents, (there were nine of them in the fancy box) and the code was for visitors, it could easily be changed from time to time. They all stood by the intercom and let Rebeca present the fob to the reader: it was like pure magic, without a sound the huge gate started to slide towards the left, it was just like turning a page, the house slowly became visible. Was it ever lovely? The drive to the house was straight, it was covered in pure white gravel, there were trees on both sides, they were still young trees, then there also were bushes, lawns and six flower beds, all that was missing was a fountain! The entrance was between two tall pillars, the door itself was huge and it appeared to be very thick made up of various panels.

There was an actual lock for the door which will open with one of the many keys in the box, this time Peter took charge and turned the largest key in the box, the door was now unlocked, and again it was left for Rebeca to actually open the door: Of course she was excited, first she discovered that the door opens outwards, she closed both her eyes and pulled the door towards her. She could not miss the gasp behind her, now with her eyes wide open she admired the scene. First it looks as if the house is furnished, that was a good thing, because she could have never afforded the quality of furniture that house needed. There seemed to be a lot of marble, on the floor and especially on some of the walls, there were mirrors, large oil paintings and beautiful furniture to match. One could not miss looking at the impressive spiral staircase. There were four doors on the left, so they all walked through the first one: it was a lounge, no not just a lounge, but a beautiful lounge! The floor was covered with a two-inch-thick pure white wall to wall carpet, again more oil paintings, the furniture looked expensive the two settees and the armchairs looked to be covered in a thick well decorated blue silk material, there were some occasional expensive looking tables, the ceiling had not only a beautiful chandelier, but it was a huge oil painting of many types of beautiful birds in full flight. The expression "my God!" was heard may times, the windows were looking towards the front garden, at the back of the living room was a set of glass double doors which opened to the dining room. There was one very long heavy dining room table which was set for dinner, there were fine plates set for twelve people with what looked like gold-plated cutlery, they also had two glasses for each place. The furniture in the dining room was also of good quality, there were two doors, one to the reception area, and the other to a long hallway that led to the kitchen. That was another story, first there were two kitchens within the same room, it appeared as if there was one for the residents and one for the guests, perhaps not, but Rebeca will find out one of these days. One could say that it was very well equipped with all one might ever need in a professional kitchen. Debra had to sit down for a couple of minutes.

Rose was admiring it all, she wondered, then she turned the cold water tap on and the water came out with a fair amount of pressure, then she wondered again and turned the hot water tap on, of course water came out, but was it hot? Everyone in the room were all surprised when they could see the steam coming out of the sink. From the kitchen there were two more doors, one led to the garden and the other to the basement, it is where some of the visitors went. The basement was a cross between a small supermarket and a proper workshop, there were a multitude of shelf units, all with food resting on the shelves, it was all dry food. They also found in one of the corners a cold room for storing vegetables and fruit, Peter and Robert loved looking at all the tools and machines that were there.

They were getting tired, Rebeca wanted to have a quick look upstairs, first to see how many bedrooms there were, and then did she need to buy sheets if the beds were there. Of course there were six bedrooms, each one fully furnished including the sheets and Duve's, each bedroom had its own ensuite and a big walk in wardrobe, the same white carpet on the floors, two of the rooms had a connected office room complete with a computer and printer, just right for Rebeca, she at first could not imagine herself in that house on her own in the middle of winter, it was at that moment that she had a good idea, 'Peter, I have a new idea, you and Juliet are saving up to buy a house, well if you were to move here with me, and make this house your home you could save that much faster, I will keep the apartment in London to use if I am there late at night, if you want to invite your friends for the weekend, I'll move to London, and the same if I want to give a party, what do you think?' He liked the idea, but he must discuss it with Juliet first. Robert thought that it would be a good idea, he would be happier knowing that she was not on her own. At the back it was a busy place, first there was a heated swimming pool, which was covered by a roof that could slide out of the way in nice weather, then a normal size tennis court with an extreme high fence, Both Rebeca and Robert could not wait to have a good look at the dock and the boat house. They were both surprised, the dock would have no problem accommodating two motor yachts, the boat house was complete with a speed boat, it was made of mahogany which was highly varnished, Rebeca whispered into Rose's ear 'we better get my boat back from Cornwall before the weather turns too cold.

There were many things to attend to, Robert elected himself to do everything, he had to settle the rates, the house insurance, the electricity company, find out about the rules for keeping a boat on a private dock, organise a company to look after the swimming pool, also organise a land line for a telephone and the internet, he also wants to speak to both neighbours to find out if the house had ever been occupied, and of course explain who the new resident happens to be. If he has time he will visit the local police station, just to have a chat with them.

Rebeca had decided to visit her old headmaster, no he was not old, it just seem to be so far back, that will be in the morning. Then she hopes to make it to Oxford for lunch with the Dean. The next morning the two girls left early to be at the school before nine thirty, they both walked into the secretary's office, the lady who used to have that job must have left, it was a new person, she asked how she could help, Rebeca replied by telling her that the head needs to see her, the secretary asked her why, then became confused when Rebeca told her that he was her friend. That did not work, no he was busy with a teacher now and in any case one must have an appointment. Rebeca did not want to waste any time, she excused herself, grabbed Rose's arm, left the office, with Rose she went to the Language department, found her mother, knocked on the door and in Arabic asked her to call the head and tell him that she is outside his door, oh better wait until I get there, say four minutes, of course no one in the class understood a single word, Rose loved it all.

It was even more interesting because just as the secretary had got up from her chair when she had seen Rebeca walk past her door, she could not help hearing the head screaming at the top of his voice 'Rebeca come in' he sounded so enthusiastic, now she was ever more confused, then she realised that he had got up to open the door and greet Rebeca with a long hug, the teacher knew who she was and he stayed in the room, they had a lot to talk about, the first thing was that now the school is one of the best schools in London, all because he is able to send one pupil a year to Oxford, so far it has worked out very well, and they are going to keep it going for ever. Rebeca was pleased to hear all that. Because they now teach Arabic and they have become the only school in north London that go that far in their teaching. After the girls had left, he had a word with the secretary, he told her even if he was interviewing the Queen he would still want to be interrupted by Rebeca, the secretary eventually found out what it was all about. The drive to Oxford was not at all easy, there was so much traffic on the road, she had worried about the parking, when she turned into the private car park, there was only one space available, but it must belong to somebody, if they come back when she has taken the place they will be very upset, she also realised that was her parking place all the time she was there, it's a matter of "needs must" so that's what she reluctantly did, next it was up some funny old stairs with a thick rope against the wall to hang on to instead of a banister, eventually they made it to a door, she knocked, a voice said 'enter', they walked in, the Dean was there reading, it seemed that he had no intention to look up, then he heard the voice of an angel saying 'good morning Sam', that really woke him up, without looking, he shouted 'it's Rebeca'. He stood up, they were both the same height, he placed his arms around her, gave her a kiss on her left cheek and took his time letting her go. He looked at Rose and promptly told her that he knew who she was, and he welcomed her to England.

Of course all the people who are involved with Rebeca, know that she has Rose staying with her for six months, They all three sat on armchairs and had a good chat, especially about the school sending them very well educated students who have all done extremely well, Rebeca just remembered about the parking, she apologised, the Dean had a laugh when she told him that she had parked in her old place, the man who now parks there is the very first student that came from your school, when the head of science retires in two years' time he will take his place and become the head of science himself, if you remember his name is Michael. Of course, she remembered him. Suddenly Sam was looking at his watch and decided that it was lunch time, so the three of them made their way to the big hall, where those who wanted to, had a good lunch. The staff there always make a fuss of the Dean, and this time he had two lovely girls with him, when they sat Rebeca happened to not be facing the entrance, that turned out rather well, as Michael was making his way to the Dean, most likely to complain that somebody had parked in his place, that is exactly what he did. It was amazing for Rebeca, she recognised his voice, she had her head down and he never recognised her, the Dean told him that the person who parked in his place used to park themselves there, it is somebody you must know he said; Michael realised right of way who the person was, 'come on Rebeca look at me'. She had no choice but to look up, she was working hard in attempting not to laugh, but she was so happy to see him, it bought back so many memories, he grabbed her and lifted her right out of the chair, then it was a big hug, both the Dean and Rose enjoyed the moment, other people were looking on wondering what it was all about, especially as the Dean was with them. Rebeca was speechless, something had come over her, she wanted to tell him that she had missed him, but that was not true, why did she feel like that, it was so strange for her, she did eventually apologise for parking her car, he gave her a very strange reply; 'Rebeca for you I would happily walk to the North Pole' she liked that, the subject changed when he remarked about her car, 'it must have cost a fortune'. She then told him that it was a present from the President, then she mentioned the house on the Thames at Henley, which reminded her about having a party or a reunion with the four students who were at her school, at the same time she asked the Dean, would him and his wife like to come as well, then there was the Headmaster and his wife, she wondered if any of the students had married, in which case they should bring their wives, or maybe their husband. The answer was in the negative, Rebeca caught herself thinking that she was pleased that Michael was not married! Rose also had read her mind; she was going to tease her tonight.

The next day was almost boring, it was spent all day at the BBC, the morning was all about Rebeca answering questions to everybody there, the Producer wanted to know how come she got on so well with the Arab King, so she had to explain about the United nation, then she showed him a photograph of her new home, she then told him that the house was a gift for having been responsible for saving many lives. The Producer was very impressed, but that was not enough, he now "had" to know where she gets her information, this time she had no problem telling fibs! She told him that it was for his ears only, she made him promise that he would not tell anyone, all the international comments were her listening on the net to local radio stations, she could understand most languages, for home news, she would sometimes ask the Prime Minister's secretary who did not mind telling her in advance of the article or happening is published, there were also a couple of people who she cannot mention who from time to time would suggest something newsworthy for her to talk about, he was ever so happy and no doubt he could not wait to repeat what he had just heard, he was no doubt not a trust worthy person, she thought that now he will never ask her again, there will be times when he will not be able to get his head around something which did not make sense.

The afternoon was spent in the wardrobe area, testing a new makeup for her, she had to be filmed a few times, so that they could judge the results, then they were now going to have her wear a business suit instead of a dress, then, to her surprise, she had to try many pairs of shoes, that was strange as the viewer had never seen her feet. Debra never came, these days she was spending a lot of time at home because of the new arrival, due in about four months. Even Rose was feeling as if they should be home, she was getting a little bored with the media, the first thing when they arrived home, she called the co-pilot's wife to find out if he has left the hospital in Ireland, she thought about him often, she also hopes that when she arrives back in the States, she will still feel the same. There was a message on her telephone from Juliet to tell Rebeca that she is looking forward to living in her house for the time being, Rebeca was pleased especially that it was Juliet who sent the message. Both had an appointment tomorrow at eleven thirty, it is at Scotland Yard with the Chief Constable, her friend. This time the parking is well organise and they have kept a place for her. After having tried the business suits at the BBC, Rebeca fancied herself in one of them, so that means half a day at least trying some on, maybe next week, or the week after, no that would not do, Wednesday next week they are visiting the Law firm she qualified in, they cannot wait to have a meeting with her. This Sunday they are spending the whole day in the new house, Peter and Juliet will be there also, they all intend to fill up the kitchen with food, the two fridges are much too big to fill, they are going to have a go. They are now approaching Scotland Yard, Rebeca kept her fingers crossed, she is going to find it hard parking that big car, she was now remembering that the parking slots were quite narrow, this time was totally different, the attendant recognised her and had been well briefed, to her surprised she had no problem what so ever, by the time they were approaching the entrance, there was a young man who greeted them, and escorted them straight into the Chief Constable's office, he got up to shake both their hands, just like all the others he was so pleased to see her. It now seemed to always be the same questions; how did you manage to get involved stopping a war? Of course, it was always the same answer, he also wanted to know what her plans were for the future, she told him that the Prime Minister is after her for something or rather, she has been invited to another garden party at Chequers, his country residence.

He could not ask her too much more whilst there was another person in the room, in any case it was lunch time. They made their way to the dining room, which is reserved for the eight top ranking officers, they can discuss any subject. Today there were ten sitting at that table, Rose was properly introduced to all, before the meal was served, it was question time again, one of the topmen asked her if one day she is going to join them. 'At this very moment I do not have any idea as to my future, I enjoy sorting out difficult situations, and I believe that I do a good job, I love the broadcasting of my personal ideas, I always try to talk about something which is up to date'. She stopped for a couple of moments, it was obvious that she was about to say more, what it was, she decided to tell them something, they would have no idea how it was possible for her to have that knowledge, 'Please do not bother to ask how I have come across this little titbit of knowledge, I am going to tell you by just asking a question of you all; you have just arrested a policeman, his first name is Raymond, he is a sergeant, you all no doubt think it a good idea for now to keep quiet about it. That is a big mistake, when the public find out that you have played for time you will be in more trouble than this Raymond fellow, there is a time when honesty is the winner, what, you were going to wait until the trial? Unless there is a third party involved, that could be a possible excuse, but my recommendation is to face the problem with a clean sheet.' That made an impression and a half, they had just been lectured by a young lady who they all admire, they spend quite some time just looking at each other, they all were remembering how she helped them in Court, they had to agree with her, facing the music, when they are in charge is much better then attempting to get away with it

The first one to speak was the Chief, he simply agreed with her, he had a good idea how she found out, of course he could not tell, he knew now that it will most likely leak out, and they would not look good, the meal was being served, Rebeca got up and suggested that after lunch when the coffee is steaming on the table, she will call for a vote at which time a simple majority will prevail, they all agreed. Not one person asked her how she found out. Her and Rose enjoyed the meal, the conversation was subdued, now the coffee was on the table, she got up told them it was a show of hands, she asked one question; if you agree to make it public now, raise your hand: eight hands went up, so that was it. Later speaking with the Chief he was pleased with her approach, the problem was that no one wanted to make the decision, as if it went wrong, they would end up having to take the blame, it needed an outsider to make it work, she suggested that it might be good to tell that it could be her handling the prosecution just like last time, it will give people something positive to think about. They did not leave Scotland Yard until four, now they were struggling in the London rush hour it took them a couple of hours to get home, they were both exhausted, instead of cooking they made it to Rebeca's favourite Indian restaurant and had a great meal, a first for Rose. The next day they visited her old law firm, of course they were pleased for her to visit, they had lots to talk about, she did mention the next case for them, it was the first time they had heard about it, yes if she wants to be involved it is no problem, 'I understand that you have a friend who is one of our most regarded Justice on your side Rebeca' she agreed and then they made their way to Regents Street to visit a well-known tailor who will be making her a suit, even Rose was excited for her.

Rebeca sometimes would wonder what happened to her ex-fiancé, he was no longer listed in the telephone directory which means that he is now in the secret service, but his parents are not, so she is going to look them up and have a pleasant conversation with them. Tonight, they are cooking, on top of that they managed to leave the Law Courts in good time, they were home before four in the afternoon. Tomorrow was free for them just to hang around, between the two of them, they decided to visit the house after dark, Rebeca wanted to get the feel for it at night, is it too quiet, are they some odd noises, well they will see later, now the television was on, Rose was the only one watching it, Rebeca spent an hour on her computer, then they both met in the kitchen, they started their supper, after having finished the washing up they made their way to the big house in the car, when they arrived it was already dark. Good job they had a flashlight with them as it was truly dark, she presented the fob to the reader at the entrance and it was lovely to see that heavy steel gate slide towards the left, she did not bother to shut the gate, just a couple of minutes and there they were, in that beautiful marbled entrance, the lights came on automatically, they closed the front door and made their way upstairs, Rebeca wanted to lie on a bed and listen to all the sounds. She heard sounds alright, it was a car coming up the drive, that worried her a bit, now she wished that she had taken the time to close the gate behind them, at that moment for the first time in her life she felt scared, next, someone was knocking at the door, they delayed going down, if only there was an intercom at the front door. Rose had a good idea, why not look out of the window? They did just that and discovered a police car parked next to her car, they now both walked down the stairs, and opened the front door, now they had a policeman and a policewoman looking at them, the man looked to be in an aggressive mood, it seems that he had been kept waiting too long, that immediately put Rebeca in a defence mode, which he did not appreciate, he had just asked who she was, she then replied that it was none of his business, that was too much for him.

The policewoman stepped back, she could see an argument about to develop, he told Rebeca that if she does not answer his questions, he will have to arrest her, she replied asking him what crime she has committed, then added that all she was doing was looking around her house. Now that really was too much for him, as far as he was concerned she was pulling his leg because he knew that the house belonged to an Arab Prince, at the same time Rose was beginning to worry, but all of a sudden his attitude completely changed, neither the policewoman or Rose had noticed Rebeca showing him the gold bar, now they were both invited in, straight to the kitchen where Rebeca boiled a kettle and made four cups of coffee. Now in the light, the policewoman recognised Rebeca, was she ever pleased, they had a great chat, he is going to tell the top man at the station, who most likely will come and visit her. Before they left the two girls, Rebeca explained about the house and the car, he suggested that they always keep the gate closed, and that is what is now going to happen. Rebeca and Rose stayed another two hours, Rebeca especially wanted to make sure that the heating was working, that there were sufficient sheets and duvets, that the washing machine was hooked up and working. Whilst listening to the silence Rebeca decided to move into the house as soon as possible, it looked as if the only thing missing so far was a telephone line which was needed for her computer. This Saturday coming was when the Prime Minister was having his garden party at Chequers,

Rebeca was wondering if the Royal fellow was going to attend, if so, she was going to introduce Rose, it would please her, especially when she tells people back in the States. When they arrived home at the apartment, Rose telephoned the co-pilot's wife, they had an ever so long talk, her husband had told her how caring Rose had been, he was soon going to be discharged, of course he can no longer fly aeroplanes, but that did not seem to bother him, it had become just a job, there was no longer any excitement for him. When he leaves the hospital, he is going to call her.

When they arrived at Chequers, the first person they met was the Prime Minister's wife, she sort of took charge of them both, they went into one of the small lounges and sat there talking for over a half hour, Rebeca was dying to find out if the Royal was coming, she however did not want to look as if she cared, so she never asked, still she found out a few things, one of them was that the Prime Minister was going to ask her to join the Ambassador Corp, she already had a good idea that her husband had that in mind, especially as he wants her to stay behind when the others have left. There was no fanfare when the Royal entered, he made a B line straight to Rebeca, the first words he uttered were: 'it's so nice to see you Rebeca', it was obvious that Rose was with her, so the next words were: 'will you not introduce me to your friend', Rebeca did just that and he made a point of spending some time talking to Rose, for a while Rose was blushing, but eventually recovered.

The three ended up in the same little lounge so that he could ask Rebeca all the questions he had on his mind, the very last one was would they like to visit the Palace where he will introduce them to members of his family. Although Rebeca could have turned down the invitation, now she had no choice but to accept because of Rose. Some refreshments were served and the two had never eaten so many cakes in one go, no, they did not touch any of the amazing sandwiches, just the cakes, Rebeca kept thinking what she will serve at the first gathering in her new house`. Rebeca and Rose found themselves to be the last of all the guests, it turns out that Rose is a good piano player, so his wife took her away to the piano room, and they started to play some Chopin. During this time Rebeca was in deep conversation with the Prime Minister, it did not surprise her at all when he asked her to join the Foreign Office with the view of becoming an ambassador.

She surprised herself when she answered him, 'Thank you so much for asking me, I have done a lot of thinking these days, almost everything that has happen to me, has never really been under my control, I sometimes feel that I have become a carrier for common sense and justice, alright I have achieved a lot in that respect, and of course I feel that I am at my best when sorting out people's minds, and you are absolutely right I would have no problem as an Ambassador, the question I would have would be, what type of Country would be the one where I would be the most effective, since I am now looking to finish my Russian, I guess that would be the place.' She had to stop for a moment, she just realised that she had already said too much, then she went on again: 'however there is a problem for me that I have to sort out, you must know by now that the King I helped has made me a gift of a house at Henley on Thames, it's on the river with five acres of land and a most beautiful house, all complete with all the extras you could possibly have. To be able to stay in that house I must keep those two jobs with the two broadcasting Companies, I have no idea what an ambassador earns, but I suspect it will not be enough, would it be possible for me to have another income whilst working as an ambassador? The Prime Minister was pleased having heard her response, he did mention that it would be within his power to increase what she earns from "Them", she will need at least a whole year to wind down the television work and become a total Russian, for now it has to become a secret to be revealed at the right time, she then asked him if she should go to the Palace to meet the family, he thought that it could only do her some good. She decided at that moment that she will not tell Rose about this conversation, there are only three men in her life that she would tell, it was Robert, the Dean, and the old Judge. She felt so much better now that she has a goal, for the first time in her life, she feels that she is in control. Even Rose on the way back home realised that Rebeca was happy. In the following months Rebeca spent time in various Embassies in Europe, although Rebeca had promised to never leave Rose on her own, things are different now she is concentrating on medicine, she never went with her, instead she studied as much as she could, she wanted to return home to enrol for a seven-year course in medicine. The first three months had passed and Rebeca had a week's work in the States, she stayed an extra week so as to be able to visit some friends including the President of course, Rose went with her, she found time to visit the co-pilot who now was recuperating at home, it made his day, he was so pleased, they talked a lot about flying and about medicine, his wife was there and she was really surprised to have the daughter of the vice president in her house, after having met Rose, his wife now understood why her husband though so much of her.

Rose's mother could not believe the change in her daughter, she has become serious, she now reads an awful lot, she cares for people and best of all she knows what she wants to do, her mother now is looking forward to having a doctor in the family. Rose's brother Jim is now engaged to be married, it is causing a little bother because she is a foreigner, however anyone who has the pleasure of meeting her, always says how lovely she is, even the President would vouch for her, Ronald the Vice President is happy that it appears that his children have both come up trump! And it appears that they have almost adopted another winner. Again, her passport still has not been stamped in the USA, she was hoping that it would be the same pilot, but it was not to be. Before leaving she managed to tell one of the producers what her plans for the future are, he was pleased for her, and when she is ready to appear on the small screen, she will be most welcome, she will definitely take part as an ambassador in discussions from time to time, and of course it is to be kept a secret. The flight back was with not a single problem, she did not visit the cockpit, the Chauffer dropped them home, no, not in the Apartment, in the house, now the scene looked proper! Rebeca wanted to speak to Debra the next day, but she had just given birth to a healthy baby boy seven pound eight ounces, she spoke to her husband, yes, she can go visit her in a couple of days, that is what happened, so she was able to tell her about her plans for the future, Debra was pleased for her and in turn Rebeca was also pleased that Debra approved.

Chapter Eighteen - She Is Now in Charge of Herself

It was good news for Rebeca, the Dean at last had found a young Russian man who lives in London, who will be only too pleased to teach her how to speak like a Russian, he works for the British government and his department is giving him every Monday off so that he can teach her, his name is Dmitri, he is going to come to her house every Monday afternoon, for as long as it takes. They are now living permanently in the house, Peter and Juliet are enjoying every minute of it, Juliet's mother came with Robert, she had one hell of a surprise, she had heard that it was a lovely house, but she never imagined that it was that lovely. Some while back, Rebeca's school friends, the head and his wife and the Dean with his wife had a good party, first the house itself was a great surprised for them all, then a real intellectual discussion about education. It was decided at that first meeting, for them all to meet once every six months and at the time invite, serious educators in all walks of life. After ten years had passed it was the meeting of the year in education circles to be asked to attend, always taking place in the house!

They did not move the boat from Cornwall until the next Spring, Rose had returned home, she had been enrolled on a course which started in a few months to become a Doctor, her brother is now a married man, Rebeca and Michael always seem to find a reason for them to meet up, they like being with each other, when they meet they both feel happy, however they both have a complicated career that takes up a lot of time, she is about to become the ambassador in Russia, she speaks Russian as if she had been bought up in Moscow, to the surprise of all Russians she meets.

Rebeca at one time was leaving the MI6 building just as Norman was coming through the main door, he had some spare time, so they decided to go into the building, and spend some time in the cafeteria having a coffee. He had eventually discovered that she was one of "Them" and now he knows where they are located. The security man at the barrier gave him the third degree, he examined his card, it seems by reading every single word, looking him up and down many times, and then not even speak to him to let him through, he just pointed in the direction he has to go, after him it was Rebeca's turn, she flashed the gold bar, he smiled, then with a friendly wave directed her through.

Norman was already a little annoyed, he felt as an unwanted idiot, then she had the nerve to remark about the incident, they did have a coffee and a couple of cakes with icing sugar on top, she let him do most of the talking, he did appreciate that it was because of her that he has a good job, he thinks of her almost every day, he has not been able to go out with anybody else, one thing is that he cannot tell anybody about his job and does not like telling lies. Although she felt that she should feel sorry for him, but no, that is not how she felt. There was no point in telling him what she had been up to, because he has read every bit of news about her, sitting there having that coffee, she was beginning to feel a little responsible, out of nowhere she had the idea of asking him to the house one day when Michael is there, maybe the two of them can make him feel better about himself, it had to be on a Saturday or Sunday soon, she was going to take a risk on Michael being free, but hopefully she hopes that it works out, he wrote down her details and they made a date, telephone numbers were exchanged, then she left him in the building and drove home, it took her almost two hours, but that was normal.

The telephone was ringing when she opened the front door, she managed to pick up the handset before it stopped, now she really had a surprise, it was the King; 'Oh Rebeca, it's so nice to hear your voice, how is life treating you these days? She was so pleased to be talking to her friend, she told him about her trip back to England, and of course thanked him again for his lovely gift. Rebeca was aware that there had been a fire in the King's embassy only the day before, she now wondered if it was the reason for his call. Or was it to talk about the rumour that he wanted to retire soon.

'Rebeca, I need your help, there is a problem at my embassy which I hope you can help solve for me,' Rebeca was only too pleased to be of some help. 'What can I do for you?' 'It turns out that the fire was caused by the wife of the ambassador, she had attempted to burn him alive, it all went wrong for her, he did not die, he is now in a bad way in hospital, they say that he will recover.' That had not been reported in the media so far, Rebeca was now beginning to understand the reason for his call.

'The London fire people of course were allowed access to the embassy, but nobody else, if I give you complete control with the situation, could you please take charge, if you think it would be beneficial for you to deal with the wife, I will leave it up to you, what do you think?' Of course, Rebeca wanted to help, and she was quick in telling him. She started right of way, 'you will have to first instruct your staff here and I think also you should tell the foreign office in London of my position.' The King gave her the name and telephone number of the man who is temporarily in charge at the embassy, he told her to wait at least one-half hour to call him, then go to the embassy and take charge.

Rebeca now had two calls to make as soon as possible, the first was to Scotland Yard, she managed to speak with the chief constable who will organise a team to investigate at the embassy when she is ready, the other call was to the Prime Minister, he was so please to hear from her, especially with the news she was giving him; for him that was her first job as an ambassador!

The man who answered her telephone call at the embassy, was not surprised, to hear from her, no, what surprised him was her knowledge of his language, she arranged to visit within the next hour or so. First, she needed a bite to eat, then the drive back into London, this time against the rush hour, she made it within the hour. Amir opened the front door to Rebeca, and she could not help noticing that he looked relieved to see her.

Her first question to Amir, 'where is she? He told her that she was in the "lock-up" she was not surprised about that but at that moment she thought it unnecessary, for now she wanted to be shown around, the fire was in one of the bedrooms, Rebeca when looking at what was left of the bed really had a shock, she was imagining what he must look like now. She made herself comfortable in the ambassador's office and interviewed six people, they all knew who she was, as she is well liked in their country. The man who deals with communications had a good idea what had happened, the wife of the ambassador had just found out that he was having an affair with an English non-Muslim woman, that was too much for her, so she gave him a night drink laced with sleeping tablets, then she must have poured petrol over him and set him alight. Her problem was she had not realised that the building was equipped with fire control equipment which flooded the bedroom. The London fire brigade had no problem putting the fire out, and an ambulance took him straight to hospital.

A while later talking to Amir, Rebeca discovered that the wife was a gentle and very kind person. Amir told Rebeca that back in their country, what she had done will result in a death sentence, the next thing was for Rebeca to have a talk with the wife, so Amir brought her back to the office. Was she ever surprised! There she was sat at her husband's desk being interviewed by this well-known clever young woman; on top of that she had her fate in her hands, it took Rebeca hardly any time to tell the ambassador's wife that she is going to be prosecuted in England and never made to return home.

Rebeca called Scotland Yard and asked for two police people to visit the embassy, it should be one man and one woman if possible.

They both arrived within a quarter of an hour. Rebeca put them in the picture, she gave them the authority to arrest her and take her back with them. It is only much later that the ambassador's wife discovered how lucky she had been, first she was not returned home, then she was prosecuted by Rebeca's own legal team who had taken advice from her, nothing ever appeared in the media, she did serve three years in prison, but under an assumed name, eventually her husband more or less recovered and apologised many times to her, officially he caused the fire because he was smoking in bed! Rebeca added two new friends!

Rebeca had a wonderful time for the best part of a week at the embassy, she had to answer many calls from well-wishers and of course the foreign office people, she organised a company to renovate the bedroom, and then when the new ambassador arrived, she put him in the picture, the staff could not have done more to help her, the King fully approved what she had done, he wanted to have another coffee with her!

One day when Michael was at the house, him and Peter lowered the speed boat into the water, it had two powerful motors, they gave the battery a charge for a couple of hours, they checked the fuel, pressed the starter button, good job it was tied down as it would have shot down the river, now she had yet another toy to play with, almost every night she went to sleep thinking what the best thing she could do to give Norman a feeling of achievement, it seems that he had descended into a dangerous negative frame of life, she discussed it with Michael who unfortunately was too serious about science to be much help. She really wanted to help him as she felt just a little guilt, he had spent a day at the house, of course he was well impressed, especially thinking he could have lived his life in comfort with her. The Russian fellow thought that he did not need to teach her anymore because she could speak just as well as himself, so he stopped coming, she now had more time to herself, so she prepared her two talks every week with even more research. Every so often one of the Sunday papers would concoct a long article about her, always ending with attempting to find out how she is able to discover the news (almost before it happened). Sometimes, she would have a visit from some elevated cleric, who had come across the recording of her famous debate just before she had left America to return home, they would usually want to have a discussion with her, it bothered them that they could not be sure if she was an atheist or not!

One year she did a tour of many Arab countries with the King's two sons who were beginning to learn about running their country, they always made a fuss about her, but when she arrived back home, she was happy, her passport had been stamped more than twenty times, it took Rose a full eight years to became a good doctor, eventually her brother became a politician like his father, he was always pleased to be seen with Rebeca when she came to the States for a visit. It took her until the late spring to convince Norman to take charge of moving the yacht from Cornwall to the Thames, Rebeca's father and now his fiancé came on the trip, the boat is tied at the dock, it completed the picture. She keeps going back and forth to Moscow where she is a well-liked ambassador, it's not so much the Russian politicians who are fond of her, it's the people. The house now has a beautiful grand piano, Rebeca loves entertaining, she invites the people she likes, one of them is the skipper of the lifeboat, he usually comes for the whole weekend with his wife, they really have a great time.

Rebeca no longer is regularly seen on television, she has learnt to keep a low profile, she has a great circle of friends who all want to be with her, no she has not yet found 'her' boyfriend, the difference is now at last she is looking!

THE END

Printed in Great Britain
by Amazon